Heathen's Hurricane

A Stormy Encounters Series Novel
(Book 2)

TANYA BENOIT

Heathen's Hurricane

(Book #2 Stormy Encounters Series)

Copyright © 2015 Tanya Benoit

Reprinted: August 2018

ISBN: 978-0-9947668-4-7

www.tanyabenoitbooks.com

For Jess

You Amaze Me

ACKNOWLEDGEMENTS

Special thanks to the people in my life who are forced to listen to my "grasshopper story-lines" until they're set in stone. XOX

Ashley-I'll keep you stocked in pretty pink sticky notes as long as you need them. XOX

Mister Al- I can't thank you enough for paying attention to even the littlest details and of course, for being such a grown-up! XOX

ONE

Jack Manning straddled his great steed and waved a fond goodbye to the lady of house Ryan. He knew that no matter what, this journey home would prove to test his patience and force him to look deeper into his own inner demons.

'I'll have too much time to think on that damned road,' he quietly sighed, gazing over his shoulder at the beautiful Lady Beth disappearing from view.

His mind raced. So much had happened in the past few months. It had become hard to fathom just how he found himself there, once again on the road between Clare and Galway, alone, weary and mentally drained.

When he'd arrived on the banks of the River Shannon on this particular trip, he'd been accompanied by his best friend's brother, Liam Kelly. They weren't there for pleasure, but the black business of death.

Jack's efforts to clear Robert Ryan of a murder he hadn't committed had been successful. But regretfully, Jack had been forced to slaughter the man who'd been responsible, Gregory Pearce – a scholarly fellow, with his sights set upon marrying Robert's daughter, Violet. At the time, it had been an easy decision. With Gregory having already fired one bullet into Brady's shoulder, and his gun trained on his best friend's head, Jack hadn't thought twice about thrusting his dagger into the bastard's chest, ending his string of lies and sins.

Unable to control his chaotic thoughts, Jack replayed the entire scene in his mind, coming to the conclusion that there had been no other solution. It was either wield the blade, or let Gregory open fire for the second time, finishing Brady off.

It had been a split-second decision, one he'd make again if he had to. He could live with ending the man's life, but there was no way he could live with losing Brady.

The soldier in him reminded his conscience that it hadn't been his first kill, and more likely than not, it wouldn't be his last.

Delivering Gregory's gray corpse back to Clare had left Jack with conflicting emotions. On one hand, a sense of relief that Gregory would cause no further harm to the Ryan's, spiked in his bloodstream. But on the other, having to explain what had transpired, and witness the horror in Beth Ryan's eyes when she realized she'd been deceived in such a way, caused a spasm of sympathy to form in his belly. Their daughter's tutor – a man they'd employed and trusted – had been a falsifier of truths and a manipulator of situations.

Gregory's dreadful plot to rid Violet's world of Brady had backfired. Instead of killing Brady – eliminating his competition – he'd killed Brady's father,

Sean, instead. When he'd realized his mistake, one would think he'd flee. But no, not Gregory. He'd decided to become the girl's saviour.

Plotting a plan to rescue her from Brady's clutches, asserting himself as a hero, had uncovered the truth, but had consequently led to his demise. Jack couldn't find guilt or regret within himself for having played a role in it.

How could he explain it all to the Ryan's? They'd demand more than a watered-down explanation. They'd demand to know where their daughter was and why Jack hadn't brought her home, as he'd promised.

When first he'd set out to help them, he'd assured them the safe return of their daughter – vowed to save her from Brady's hold. Through no fault of his own, he hadn't done right by them. Violet had chosen to remain with Brady…they'd fallen in love.

He would never forget the look on Beth Ryan's face when he and Liam rode through the courtyard with Violet's carriage in tow. As she moved to fetch

Violet from its confines, Jack halted her with one curt, "Stop!" Her expression would haunt him. Her soft eyes appeared utterly stricken.

"She's not in there, Beth." Jack leapt from his mount, moving to block her from seeing the gruesome sight of Gregory's body, or catching a whiff of the decaying flesh.

"Well, where is she, Jack? Ye said ye'd bring her back here, but all ye bring us is an empty carriage?" Beth's eyes were filled with rage. No doubt, she would have pummelled Jack with the bulk of her agony, but he sensed she hadn't the strength. Violet's abduction it would seem, had had a lasting deteriorating effect on everyone.

"I would've brought her back. I would've saved her from Brady, but the lass didn't need savin'." Jack walked around the horses and unhitched the carriage. "Robert, ye can take care of this, I presume?"

"What do ye mean, she didn't need savin'?" Beth asked as Robert opened the carriage door and viewed Gregory's corpse, a disgusted scowl taking residence upon his face. Jack knew the body would have been a ghastly sight by now, and thanked his gods for not having to bear witness to it, or the stench any longer.

"Just that. She didn't want to come back with me. Violet *chose* to stay with Brady. She flat-out refused to leave him with a bullet in his shoulder," Jack told her, and then turned his attention to Robert, who was still holding a kerchief against his nose. "'Tis exactly as I first predicted. He loves her, and she returns his affections," Jack explained carefully. But no amount of caution could save him from Lady Ryan's fury.

Beth's face reddened, her fists balled at her sides. "I don't understand. How could my beautiful, free-spirited and educated daughter conduct herself so foolishly? After bein' kidnapped and dragged off to some God-forsaken cottage in the middle of no-where, Violet should be eager to come home!" Beth boomed, throwing her hands up, pleading with her own gods, to be sure. Praying for strength perhaps?

Jack understood where Beth's feelings of be-trayal stemmed from. He too, believed that Violet's actions had been impulsive. Brady deserved to be punished. He deserved to lose her. He'd done unfathomable things to earn everyone's mistrust and loathing. Violet had rewarded his misdoings by staying.

"How could she just fall in love with that monster?" Beth sobbed.

Jack drew in a deep breath. "'Tis exactly what happened. While her captivity had started out tough, I assure ye, they are happy now. She seems content to remain there, workin' the farm alongside him. He is good to her, I promise ye," Jack replied, trying his hardest to keep Beth calm. However, the matter of Brady and Violet's approaching nuptials was yet to be discussed.

For the first time, Jack locked gazes with the tight-lipped Liam. It was time to introduce him to his new in-laws, and hopefully, the Kelly's and the Ryan's could salvage what remained of their business relationship – merge their two shipbuilding companies, once and for all.

But before Jack had had the opportunity, Beth narrowed her gaze on the young Kelly. "And who are you, lad? Haven't ye got a tongue?" she spat. Liam remained mute, shifting from foot to foot, shooting nervous glances toward Robert and Jack.

"Well?"

"My lady, I am…" he started.

'*No time like the present*,' Jack thought, and then robbed the tongue from Liam's mouth.

"Beth, may I present Liam Kelly, or should I say, your soon-to-be son in law's brother?"

"Son-in-la…?" Beth muttered, her hand flying to her lips, as if she couldn't quite grasp the words. Her husband hurried to her side, draping his arm about her shoulder for support and then called the stable hands to fetch the mobile crypt.

"Let us all go into the house, for we have much to discuss. I want nothin' left out," Robert sighed, as they fell into a silent shuffle into the manor.

Once Robert, Beth, Liam and Jack were all settled in the study, Beth finally caught her breath after

Jack's none too subtle announcement that Violet planned to marry Brady. Jack braced himself for an attack when Beth's gaze pinned him to the spot.

"*Mr. Manning*!" she barked. "Please tell me what ye're talkin' about! Are ye sayin' that my dear, sweet Violet intends to marry this Brady fellow? That awful excuse for a man who stole her away from us? I want her back, Jack! And 'cause ye let this happen, and ye knew what his motives were, ye're *goin'* to go and get 'er!"

Jack winced, but no contradictory arguments would come. The lady of this house had earned her anger and Jack let her have it.

Robert rushed to her side, engulfing her into his arms, as if his very touch could melt her icy frantic state.

"Shh, Beth, me love. It will be alright, ye'll see. We didn't rear a lack-wit. I don't like it any more than ye do, but if our sweet Vy says she loves 'im, then we have to let her be," Robert whispered, caressing her, holding her until her shaking and sobbing began to subside. "Ye know what she's like. If we forbid it, she'll come home and be forever miserable and at twenty-two, she's too old to be bossin' around anyway. Don't ye think? Perhaps she sees good in 'im," he added, as if he, himself believed there could actually be good in Brady Kelly.

"Oh, Robert. I hope so," Beth sighed, choking back another sob. "I have to go lie down, my nerves can't take much more." She reached for the knob on the study door and turned back to her audience with tear-filled, blue eyes. "'Tis nice to meet ye, Liam, despite the circumstance," she murmured exhaustedly, "And Jack, I do apologise for my outburst. Ye know where your room is. Stay as long as ye need to." Defeated, Beth disappeared through the door, out into the large expanse of the family home…now an empty home.

Jack turned, facing Robert who was sitting silently with Liam at the large wooden desk. Robert had been proven innocent, so now what? Someone had to break the ice.

"So, Robert, have ye any ill judgment toward Kelly and Son's? 'Twill be big of ye to go ahead with the merger," Jack stated, as it seemed Liam had once again forgotten how to speak.

"Nay, lad, I've no hard feelin's. At least, not with *this* Kelly. I knew ye were a savvy businessman when first we met. And I know losin' yer father was a great loss for yer company and yer clan. But I hope that we can still carry on as planned," Robert replied, not even looking up from his paper stacked desk, "Aye?"

Jack sensed that Robert was reaching down within the depths of his entire being to extend the courtesy. It must've been quite taxing to despise Liam's brother and still have to conduct business with him. Jack blew out a grateful breath when Liam finally spoke.

"Yes, sir. As do I. I apologise for the hardship that Brady has caused you and yours, but I can see no reason not to carry on with the merge. I hope we can put this entire mess behind us," Liam politely replied.

Jack breathed a sigh of relief. When he felt it was safe to do so, he took his leave and went to his chambers.

'Will the she-devil *be about this evenin'?'* he wondered mischievously.

Even though he'd been anxious to return to Galway and his duties at Kelly's keep, he just couldn't leave until he looked upon the golden-haired devil, Kylee, one last time. She'd haunted his dreams with a fiery tongue, and yet he'd been drawn to her like a moth to flame.

When Jack opened the door to the bedchamber, he'd expected the ill-tempered girl to meet him there, going about her duties, cursing him out for making her job difficult, as she'd done in the past. She would make him want to spank her until her arse was as red as the sun. But Kylee wasn't there. Instead, he'd found an elderly lady humming a tune, while she'd put the finishing touches on his bedclothes. She regarded him with a warm, inviting smile.

"Mr. Manning, my name is Nora. If ye need any-thin', love, just let me know an' I'll try me best," she winked.

"Thank ye," Jack said, surprised. "Umm, where's Kylee? She tended me last time I was here."

"Kylee? The sweetling," Nora began, confusing Jack. '*Sweetling*' was not a word he would use to de-scribe Kylee. "She had an emergency. 'Tis a good thing we work for Lady Beth. A chamber maid wouldn't get a week off like that workin' anywhere else," she huffed.

Jack's gut twisted into a knot. "What kind of emergency? Is she all right?" he asked with growing concern.

"Aye, she will be. Her fiancée found her the other mornin' at the bottom of the stairs at his father's pub. What she was doin' there, I'll never know. The girl never takes part in the drink. Her betrothed does enough of that for the both of them," Nora grumbled. "Perhaps she'd been cleanin' one of the rooms up-stairs or somethin'. No one knows anythin' yet, only that she was dealt a nasty blow to the head. The poor dear," Nora explained, rambling on and on almost absentmindedly.

Jacks heart sank. He pictured Kylee's tiny body laying nearly lifeless at the foot of a staircase, immobilised in stale beer and whiskey. Then, curiosity got the better of him.

"Who is her betrothed. Do ye know 'im?" Jack asked, trying not to sound too interested. His fantasy of having Kylee would have to remain secret, for it was just that – a fantasy.

"His name's Garvan O'Shea and everyone knows that scoundrel," Nora blew, and then immediately dropped the subject, continued her tune and promptly left the room, leaving Jack to ponder and worry over a woman he barely knew.

Jack scanned the chamber. It looked strange now, since he had no purpose in being there. He'd found Sean Kelly's killer and delivered death to the Ryan's doorstep. It was time to go home.

Kylee's absence was too much to bear.

Jack ached inside, unable to go to her and see if she was all right. He couldn't shake this girl from his mind. As much as he wanted to forget her, he couldn't. At least, not until he returned home and put all of this behind him.

'Nothin' but a distraction! That's what she is!' Jack growled inwardly.

When Jack bid his farewell to Lady Beth and Lord Robert, he'd put the River Shannon and the grand estate behind him. Liam would remain there for a time to finalize the merge, and talk strategy plans with Robert.

With the winds of autumn blistering his face and numbing his hands, he pushed his mighty steed onward with one goal in mind – home.

With Brady and Violet's wedding taking place in a few weeks, and getting back to his regular duties at the keep, he hoped he could forget he had ever met *'Kylee the Wicked'*.

When finally, he'd stopped to make camp for the night, the loneliness and solitude forced his memories, both fond and malevolent, to taunt him.

He wondered how Emma had been doing in his absence. He hadn't seen her since before Sean Kelly's murder, and he missed her terribly. Despite being merely close friends, she'd been the one person in Jack's life who knew his inner-most secrets. She'd been the constant tide in his raging storm. Emma had known things even Brady couldn't understand, and she'd never judged him.

In fact, she had helped him face his demons a long time ago. When he'd been only a lad, he'd been apprehended by authorities and thrown into jail for taking his fantasy-play too far with a pubescent lover.

While Brady had paid Jack's debt, releasing him from prison, Emma had been his real saviour.

He'd had his entire life ahead of him at that time – been enlisted with the Anglo-Irish Regiment like his father and grandfather before him. But when the recruitment office got wind that Jack had been prosecuted for such heinous crimes against an innocent young girl, he'd been dishonorably discharged.

Rape and battery, they'd called it. But that simply hadn't been the case, for at first, it had been consensual. It wasn't until he'd tied her to the support beam in her father's barn and whipped her until she was bloody, when she'd began to scream and cry uncontrollably. Begging him to stop.

It was like some force, deep within him had completely taken over, orchestrating every blow he'd delivered. Then, as fast as it had taken hold, he was released, and shook himself back to reality. Her pretty features had distorted from passionate and lusty, to terrified; reflecting real pain. He'd stopped dead, dropping the belt to his side, but it was too late.

With his arousal waned, he'd untied her and apologized relentlessly at her feet, with no effect. The horrified girl – Maggie – told her father, who then nearly killed Jack with the blade of a shovel. The girl's mother had saved Jack's life that day, hauling her enraged husband off. They'd tied Jack to the same blood-spattered beam, until authorities arrived to take him away.

At the time, Jack wished he had been killed. He felt utterly dejected – abnormal – and it nearly sent him over the edge. Until, that is, he found Emma, or at least, until Emma found him.

He could still see her silky black hair shimmering in the torch-lit cell when she'd first come to see him.

As she pulled the green satin hood down from her face, she revealed the iciest green eyes he had ever seen. The glacial reflection of the torches in them were angelic, taking him by surprise.

He had no idea why this breathtaking and flaw-less creature had come to visit the scum of the earth, and his first instinct had been to order her away. But, he couldn't bring himself to do it. He had to know exactly what she wanted with the likes of him.

"Jack Manning, I presume?" she whispered in the softest old English, the tone as satiny as flower pet-als.

"Aye," was all he managed to choke out.

"I've heard a very interesting story about you, love. Is it true you were brought in for crimes against a lover?" When Jack didn't respond, she continued, "What exactly are the details? Why did you have the girl bound and gagged, then tied to a whipping post? Is my information correct?" Emma had asked quietly, searching his features for the tell-tale sign of remorse. Jack was oozing with it, accompanied by self-loathing.

"I'd rather not speak of it. Not now, not ever. Could ye please leave?" he growled, crawling away to the back of the cell, out of sight and that inquisitive stare of hers. Never had he ever, come across someone so bold. *How dare she ask such questions?*

"Oh now, come back into the light. Do not shy away from me. I have a sense about you. Please, tell me what happened."

For some reason, Jack had been compelled to do as he was told, as if a greater force had clawed its way into his brain, completely taking over, causing him to mechanically obey. He shifted closer and met her enchanting glare, the cell bars he held anchoring him. Something about this woman commanded his obedience. Something familiar swept over him.

"What is your name, woman?" he asked, gripping the iron life-line so tightly his knuckles whitened. He stared her down curiously.

"Emma. Just, Emma."

"Well, Emma, I was involved with the girl for some time. I was not the first lover she'd taken, but I'm almost certain, she will no longer carry on with the other lads in the village like she used to." Jack stopped and thought for a moment, and then, "We'd been a little more than curious when it came to love makin', and I admit, I'd pushed her sometimes to do things that were creations of my wildest imagination. She'd always consented; always let me lead the game," Jack explained, holding nothing back. The fact that he'd been so inclined to divulge all his inner monstrosities to this strange beauty, still niggled at him.

'I've nothin' to lose at this point. I'll be dead soon. If this woman wants to know how sick I am, well, by Jesus, 'tis just as well to tell 'er,' he thought, self-pity eating him alive.

"What kind of games did you play?" she asked casually, like this was a conversation she'd had every day.

"Listen, I don't know what ye want from me! And I don't care. I'm a monster. I know it, and now ye know it, too. Who craves pain in others? I crave control, and I'm losing everythin' 'cause of it. Now, please if ye don't mind, I'd like to stay here and rot, so I can't hurt anyone else," Jack shouted, sinking back into the darkness.

Without a word, Emma pulled the velvety hood back up over her head, and slipped an envelope between the bars, letting it fall to the floor.

"When you've had enough of your self-contempt, come and find me. But never, and I mean never, speak of me. I don't exist," she smiled kindly, and sauntered back into the darkness from which she came.

Jack retrieved the note and held it to the tiny candle which barely still burned on the little oaken table next to his cot. With quivering cold fingers, he pulled the card from its confines.

'*Heathen's Haven*,' Jack thought, swirling the name over his tongue again and again, until it piqued an interest he could not abandon.

A safe haven for heathen's just like him. Little did he know, it would become a safe place for him to learn and harness his particular tastes for the despicable.

Like it had been yesterday, Jack remembered his first visit to the grand manor which stood regally on Merchant's Road, it's three-storey elegance putting all that stood around it to shame. He recalled having to crane his neck backward just to count the fourteen windows wrapped in smooth, grey stone. Only hours after his release from prison, Jack found himself standing on the threshold, a single wooden door begging to be knocked. He clenched a nervous fist, and made the first connection which would forever change the path of his very existence.

"Jack, I've been expecting you," Emma sweetly said, opening the door, welcoming him inside.

"I had a hard time findin' this place. Its appearance doesn't mirror its name," Jack chuckled uncomfortably. He'd expected a place called Heathen's *anything,* to resemble a gaudy site of ill-repute.

"Appearances can be deceiving. Remember that. It is only select few who know this place by its true name. Most folks just call it The Haven. A lovely name for an inn, isn't it?"

She's an inn-keeper?

Jack nodded and followed her all the way into the large sitting room, where she poured him a cup of English tea, and urged him to relax.

He could feel her distinctive, exotic gaze seeping into his psyche, like she could read his mind. What might she find beneath his layers of curiosity?

"Why do you think you are here?" she hummed after an intolerable silence.

"I'm here, 'cause ye invited me," he began, "And, 'cause I'm curious. Ye seem to think ye know what's wrong with me," he said, hanging his head in shame, refusing to meet her gaze. Would it have served as an effective distraction for the remainder of his first visit, he would've stared at that same splatter of color on the rug beneath his feet.

"Is that what you think, Jack? You think there is something *wrong* with you? You couldn't be more mistaken. Come with me," she said. Emma rose from the chaise and took him by the hand. She led him downstairs to a large, well-lit hallway beneath the manor. On each side, three colorful doors stood there, imploring to be breached.

Jack took notice that while none were open, he could hear faint noises coming from within.

Emma knocked on the yellow door, and a charming girl dressed in a costume resembling a fairy, answered pleasantly. When her gaze met Emma's, she immediately dropped to her knees in front of the raven-haired wonder and bowed her head.

"Yes, Emma. How may I be of service?" the girl asked, emitting obedience and respect.

"Will it be all right if my guest observes, but for a moment? Will it be all right with Mr. G?" Emma asked kindly.

The girl quickly rushed to the other side of the room, where a man was strapped to a large pale pink table, so entirely covered in feathers that not one trace of his flesh was left exposed. The girl whispered low in his ear, he nodded his approval, and then she motioned for them to enter. Had the man not been wearing a blindfold, would Jack's presence have embarrassed him? *Bloody fool!*

"You see, Jack, everyone has fantasies. Heathen's Haven is a safe place where the most extreme desires can come true. Safely, and without judgement," Emma explained, as they strolled the perimeter of a room decorated beautifully in bright, merry colors.

This was a themed room where pixies, cherubs and angels were painted on the walls and high ceiling, giving it an almost heavenly appearance.

"This is a brothel?" Jack asked, quite shocked. Emma didn't look like a madam from a regular whore house. She had an air about her. She reeked of high-class and exuded an unmistakable professionalism that Jack noted from the first time they'd met.

"No, love, not a brothel," Emma purred. "Both men and women come here to have their needs met – their most primal needs. Sometimes, a soul merely desires human contact.

"However, we stay in operation due to the '*donations*' from our satisfied, wealthy clientele. And of course, confidentiality is of the utmost importance, as you can understand.

"We play games here, based on power shifting and control. Everyone wants power and domination. Here, you will learn how to attain it, but more importantly, how to let it go."

That first taste of the life Emma would help him discover, seemed like an eternity ago. Jack thanked the heavens that Emma had found him when she had.

With Kylee O'Roarke eating away at his mind and tearing at the fabric of his heart, he yearned to unleash his penchant for debauchery upon her. No longer the quivering and over-zealous adolescent, he longed to show her a world of pleasure, consisting of her worst nightmares and most delicious fantasies.

Cursing the possession of his mind, Jack turned over onto his side, facing the flames licking the circlet of boulders. He shut his eyes tightly against the hunger and chanted, *'Emma. She'll help release me from this purgatory.'*

Yearning to have Kylee in his bed was one thing, but now, he'd add worry to the mix.

A tumble down a staircase.

Betrothed to the town drunk.

Nothing about her situation sat well in his brain. He cursed himself for leaving.

'*I should've seen to 'er myself,*' he reflected wretchedly, shutting his eyes, praying for sleep, but sleep wouldn't find him this night. '*I should have never left without checkin' on 'er!*'

Aye, a training session at Heathen's Haven was just the necessary distraction Jack needed for a reprieve from *Kylee the Wicked.*

TWO

When Galway finally came into view, the few, but long nights of sleepless torment Jack had suffered while on the road, left him feeling lethargic and beaten. It was good to be home.

Brady's wedding to Lady Violet was fast approaching, and it was clear to see that everyone employed within the walls of Kelly's keep were in the thick of it.

Mary, the cook and do-it-all was buzzing around in preparation for the upcoming nuptials so frantically that she'd barely noticed Jack as he wearily sauntered through the front door.

"Mary, m'love!" Jack bellowed to get the portly lady's attention. When she caught sight of him in the corner of her eye, she immediately ceased her bustling and waddled to greet him with a mighty squeeze, sending him staggering back to catch himself from toppling over.

"Jack Manning, ye devil! I've been expectin' ye. Where's the little lord? Hasn't Liam returned with ye?" Mary asked, her eyes searching the busy foyer.

"He's fine, Mary, no worries. He's decided to stay with the Ryan's and finalize some minor details of the merge. He'll be home soon, I promise," Jack smiled.

"Oh! I do hope so. He'll not want to miss the weddin'," she paused, and it seemed her mind wandered as a gigantic smile dimpled her cheeks. "A weddin'! Such a blessed event, don't ye think?" Mary sighed happily as if *she* were the one preparing to wed, and then wiped her brow with the dish towel sloppily hanging over her shoulder.

"He's still angry with Brady, but as stubborn as Liam is, he'll need to witness it for himself. He'll never believe Violet will walk down the aisle on her own accord. So, he wouldn't miss it for anythin'," Jack laughed, linking his arm in hers, and then led her to the kitchen, where he knew she would whip something up to satisfy his empty belly.

Jack devoured the leftover stew Mary had placed in front of him like it might be the last meal he'd ever eat again.

"Thank ye so much, m'love. I'll be headin' down to my quarters now. Would ye mind sending down some water? I'm sure I smell like a sty by now. And then I have to get some sleep." Jack gave her a small kiss on her cheek as she nodded. She beamed with pride over this handsome young fellow who adored her so, and paid her so much attention.

Jack languorously forced himself down the steps to the floor below the keep, finding his quarters just as he had left them.

This windowless cavity lacked style of the times, but it had the basic necessities Jack needed to function.

In one corner was a large soft bed, covered with a coarse bear skin blanket for the long nights of chilly solitude. Next to that was a small round wooden table. He picked up a candle holder and struck a match to illuminate his stony sanctuary, so he could better see how dank and dreary this place truly was.

It was times like this, when he dearly missed his modest little cottage on the outskirts of Galway. But he vowed to never go back there until he found someone to share that family home with.

'I'd give anything to have what Brady's got,' Jack sighed thinking about his friend, and how truly lucky Brady was to have found someone like Violet Ryan, who complimented every aspect of his being.

Jack stripped the heavy, dirty clothes from his tired body, exposing his sinewy, thick physique to the cool damp air. As expected, Mary had sent two of the prettiest young maids down with steaming hot water to add to his tub of cold.

Mary must've understood that an unattached man like Jack would appreciate the company of two pretty colleens, but tonight, Jack sent them away. He sank into the tub of soapy water, trying to wash away his unease, for his thoughts were back in Ennis with Kylee.

He recalled what Nora had told him and thought it strange that Kylee would promise to marry such a drunkard, as the girl seemed very assertive, overly confident, and even brazen at times. Jack couldn't imagine her loving a man who was no match for her battle of wits.

When he'd dried off, Jack bore himself into his soft mattress, struggling to shake Kylee from his mind. But it was no use. He was utterly vexed.

Despite his weary bones commanding rest, Jack found that his mental focus was wrapped in a vision of Kylee, helpless, ill, and unable to perform her duties at the Ryan's. He was thankful that Lady Beth was her employer and that her position would remain open for her when she was well enough to return.

Suddenly, a chuckle bubbled up from within with the remembrance of the first time he'd met the *she-devil*.

He had arrived at the Ryan's and insisted he stay in Clare to conduct the investigation. After briefing the Ryan's on Violet's situation, he had been led to his chambers by the most curvaceous and svelte beauty he had ever laid eyes upon.

It was only when she spoke that Jack relaxed, and the throbbing in his trousers began to subside.

"M'names Kylee O'Roarke, an' don't be callin' me sweetie, honey, or anythin' else of that nature. Ye'll do fine to remember that," the golden-haired lovely scolded. Jack thought it better to call her Ms. O'Roarke and leave it at that, but when she returned the next morning with his wash water and to freshen up his room, her sharp tongue and spiteful temperament reared its ugly head, yet again.

Upset that Jack had fallen asleep at the desk instead of the bed she'd made up for him, Kylee let loose, almost making him swallow his tongue.

"Well don't ye be thinkin' that I don't have enough to do 'round here. I don't need ye makin' unnecessary work for me ye know," she'd spat cruelly.

Jack pictured the way her nose wrinkled when she was upset and scolding him. Her demeanour was almost charming, until she used her betrothal to a *'handsome brute who'll have some wicked and naughty things in store for me on my weddin' night'* to make him savage.

She must have felt the attraction between them, for he felt it stronger than anything he'd ever felt his entire life. It was a thick and oozing kind of lust that left him longing to restrain and spank the little imp until she begged for deliverance.

Jack rolled over onto his side and watched the candle casting shadows upon the far wall, until he stopped thinking of the mysterious girl he left behind in County Clare. He prayed his guts would stop quivering with concern for her so he could finally get some much-needed sleep.

The very next morning, Jack awoke but felt like he'd never slept at all. The entire night, his dreams were filled with visions of Kylee.

He dreamt she was knelt at his feet, looking up at him with love and true adoration, waiting for instructions from her master. Her hands clasped in front of her, her bright eyes beaming at the mere sound of his voice. Then all of a sudden, she was gone.

Jack ran for what seemed a life time in slumber, but he could find her nowhere. Panic set in and he was startled awake.

'Augh! I gotta get out of this bed. I'll go see Emma and forget I ever knew Kylee, the spiteful wench,' Jack thought as he quickly washed and dressed.

After he had broken his fast and briefed his men, he set out for town. A thin blanket of snow had fallen throughout the night, leaving Galway beautifully refreshed. Even a place called *Heathen's Haven* could be masked by the tranquillity of the morning; for only select individuals really knew what went on inside its confines.

"Emma? Are ye awake yet?" Jack bellowed in search of his friend. When Emma appeared in the entrance of the sitting room, she quietly held out her hand and Jack moved quickly to retrieve it.

"I am so happy you have returned. It has been very dull here without your visits," Emma said, her lips curling into a light smile. There was never any doubt that this woman adored Jack Manning. She'd always said their friendship had been the making of destiny, and Jack supposed she'd been right.

In his youth however, their relationship was based upon a student/teacher bond that had never to this day been fully broken.

"Emma, ye are as lovely as ever, but ye do perjure yourself. We both know there's never a dull moment within these walls," Jack laughed as he raised her hand to his lips and placed a chaste kiss in her palm. "Now, I have an itch to scratch and some pent-up frustration to get out. Ye think ye can help?"

Emma sheepishly grinned, for she knew exactly how to scratch Jack in every possible place to ensure his satisfaction.

"Lead the way, Master J. Your desires are my desires," she hummed. Emma called him *Master J* only when they were in role, as it was a way of stepping out of one's self. He would never tolerate being addressed as Jack or Mr. Manning once he entered one of the six rooms below. Even though sometimes, he wasn't *Master* either. When this world had first been introduced – when Emma had saved him from his ignorance regarding his own beastly nature – he'd mostly been referred to as *Slave*.

It took Jack many years and hard lessons to graduate to Master, and now, he was a professional. He could take a woman to the brink of ecstasy and almost to the edge of insanity with need for release. When it was all over and he'd permitted her to let go, she would love him for it. But love wasn't what

Master J craved. He possessed a pure hunger for satisfying a woman through sensual domination.

Jack led Emma to the room with the black door at the end of the long hallway beneath the estate. Her face showed little surprise. This room was reserved for dark play only, equipped with a St. Andrew's cross, and a spanking table. Various whips and belts used for pleasurable pain were hanging on the walls. This was Jack's favorite playground.

"Undress behind the curtain. I want all skin exposed," he instructed, quickly falling into his authoritarian character. "Then, return to me, eyes fixed at the floor. Do not look me in the eye today."

"Yes, Master J," Emma replied, retreating behind the black curtain to remove her satin morning robe. Would she know something was amiss with him today? Jack always wanted eye contact, and most times he even demanded it. His gut told him she'd see straight through him but he couldn't stomach the thought of making such an intimate connection with her, while obsessing over Kylee.

Either way, the session would bring his troubles to light, whether he wanted them to or not. Emma naturally had that way about her.

Now kneeling before him, her shiny black hair cascading down her back in one straight line, Jack resisted the urge for intensity. Today, more than ever, he'd have to keep a level head, for he couldn't stomach the thought of hurting her. And the possibility of that was very real. The obedient lust radiating in her shimmering gaze nearly made him dizzy, and the knowledge that she was always a willing submissive for him to play with, filled him with a special appreciation for her. *God's teeth, this woman amazes me.*

Jack peered down adoringly and took a deep breath. He knew this would be a long day; he needed it to be the longest day.

"Stand, turn, and lay on the board, face down," he commanded, his voice low and gravelly. This was certainly a different Master J than she was used to, and he wondered if she'd still trust him.

He'd oft-times commanded things of her with force and fervor, but today he was gentle and soft, despite his anticipation for brutal debauchery.

Emma complied and sprawled onto the hard, cold wooden board with her legs held firmly together. She had to know this would displease him, as Master J always wanted her to be at her most vulnerable with thighs spread wide, exposing her bare bottom for spanking, and her most intimate parts for driving her to madness. *Ye play a dangerous game, Emma.*

Jack arched a crooked brow at her disobedience. He sensed things were going to be different today. Everything about the scene caused him conflicted feelings as he struggled to get into the character that Emma was used to.

He went to her side and slid his rough calloused hands down her body. From her shoulders to her ankles, he prepared her with his touch.

"Have ye been a good girl while I was away, Emma?"

"Yes, Master J. I have been as good as ever," she snickered devilishly. She pushed her bottom upward against his touch – an intolerable act of desire. She knew he wouldn't stand for it.

"Stay still, Emma, or I will spank yer arse 'til its blisterin' red," he whispered.

Emma arched upward again in defiance, peeking over her shoulder, gauging his reaction. When he firmly planted a slap to the left cheek, she yelped, but continued her mischief.

When she rolled over onto her back, her eyes filled with surprise. Jack didn't stop her. He didn't punish her. In fact, he hardly even noticed her change in position. Despite his gaze being still trained on her nude body, she sensed that he was staring straight through her, failing to be in the moment.

It didn't matter that they were in his favorite room, nor did it matter that he'd requested playtime. The game was over. She pinned him to the spot with a quizzical gaze, and his head fell.

"I'm sorry, love. I can't," Jack whispered.

Emma rose from the table and retreated back behind the curtain, slipping back into her robe. When she emerged, Jack was slouched by the wall, legs pulled up to his body, resting his arms upon his knees. She crouched down, her sweet breath tickling his senses, and then his gaze found hers. Concern etched creases into her brow.

"Jack, you must tell me what is going on. This is so unlike you," she said, sliding down onto the stone floor next to him.

"Her name is Kylee O'Roarke. She's a girl I met when I was away conductin' the investigation," Jack began, "I don't know what to tell ye, Emma. She's set a curse upon me. I can't get 'er out of my mind." He shook his head.

"Oh, I see. Well then, tell me what vexes you so." The worry in Emma's voice was unmistakable, and Jack poured his heart out to her in effort to make sense of the feelings he had never felt before.

"The first time I laid eyes upon 'er, I was instantly addicted. With hair spun from gold, and the most brilliant blue eyes I have ever seen, she's taken my heart and soul.

"Even the way she moved, Emma, nearly sent me to madness. She's a slender lass but has curves which most women lack. Utterly enchantin' to look at." Jack watched Emma, as she nodded in understanding. "But, when she spoke, I wanted to take 'er over my knee and spank 'er so hard she wouldn't sit for a week. The girl is outspoken and brazen. She lacks respect, composure and the sensibilities of any lady," Jack said, exasperatedly.

"So, what do you want from this little imp?" Emma cocked her head, delicate strands of obsidian falling into her eyes.

"I don't know what I want from 'er!" Jack rose and began to pace back and forth, agitation radiating from him in thrashing waves. He could see Emma's concern and feared if he didn't temper his passion soon, he'd frighten her. This too, was a side of Jack Emma had never been privy to. "How could the lass be so exquisite that she makes my blood boil, and then strip me to the core with her tongue.

"She spoke of her fiancée and compared me to 'im, leavin' me in envy of the bastard. I can't get 'er out of my mind."

"Have you realized that you're in love, my darling?" Emma asked, catching his arm, halting him instantly. "And perhaps a little jealous."

"I don't know anythin' about 'er! How could I love 'er? This is fool's talk," Jack rolled his eyes, but the torment remained etched into his expression. "And jealous? Apparently, she's betrothed to a complete arse! I've nothin' to be jealous about."

"Alright, so you say you're not in love with this girl," Emma began.

"She-Devil," Jack corrected.

"Fine, dear, I'll call her the she-devil if it suits you. But, if you're not in love with her, could it be that she possesses the power to make you second guess yourself? Or, could it be that you know she can't be tamed and you want nothing more than to do just that?"

Jack's feet itched to run, for he knew she was right. His urge to dominate and claim ownership of Kylee from the very first moment he'd laid eyes upon her, swirled around in his mind. And although he couldn't admit it to Emma, he knew he'd fallen for the brazen wench. Hard.

"Coming here to try to forget about her was unwise. You should be in Ennis, trying to win her from her fiancée," Emma chuckled as she rubbed Jack's arm in comfort.

"Aye, I know. I had to return for the weddin'. Brady would never forgive me if I weren't here. And, as for that man Kylee is betrothed to, I hear he's a piece of work. Won't take much for me to win 'er from him," Jack started to relax a little and so they took their conversation back upstairs to the sitting room.

"Jack, I'll always be here, anytime you need me, but right now, if this is your chance at finding love, go and get it," Emma said, laying a steaming cup of tea in front of him.

'*Why does this woman think she can fix everythin' with tea?*' Jack thought drolly but daren't point out the fact.

"Perhaps, after the weddin' I'll find a reason to go back there. Hopefully, her betrothed would've drank himself to death by then," Jack laughed and sipped his tea. "For now, I think I'll take a run out to Brady's cottage, spend some time with the couple to see how they're makin' out.

"I was wonderin' how his shoulder was healin', or if Violet had had enough of his temper and killed him 'erself."

Emma finally laughed then. "Sending you on your way will not weigh too heavily on my conscience, for I know Brady will help with your needed distraction. Visiting them is a splendid idea," she replied. Emma passed him his tunic and bade him farewell with a friendly kiss on the cheek.

Jack spent a few days at the keep, finalizing some last-minute details regarding his men and their duties for when Brady and his bride returned.

Security had to be as tight as possible, for one could never know who was out to harm the heir of the largest shipbuilding company in Galway, or his soon-to-be bride. Jack took no chances with their safety.

After he'd dished out orders to his men, he packed a bag and headed out to the cottage with the hope that he would be welcome to stay for a few days. Perhaps he could help Brady and Violet close up the cottage for the winter, as they were going to remain at the keep until spring. No doubt, Brady would give him a list as long as his arm.

When he arrived, there wasn't a soul to be seen. The livestock had already been sent back to the keep, as well as the bounty of their first harvest.

"Hello? Is anyone here? Brady! Where are ye?" Jack hollered. A sigh of relief rushed from his lungs when Violet stormed through the door, her emerald green eyes filled with delight at the sight of her new-found friend.

"Brady! Brady! Jack's here! Oh, come inside, Jack! It is freezin' out here," Violet smiled, taking Jack's arm, linking it with her own all but dragging him inside.

When he entered the cottage, there was a new air about the place. Where once it was filled with despair and anger, it now felt comfortable and full of love.

Jack sighed with a pang of envy for the lovers and rested in the chair by the window, as Brady wearily made his way from the bedroom cradling his injured shoulder.

"Jack, what are ye doin' back here so soon? How did everything go in Clare?" Brady asked, gingerly inching into a chair at the kitchen table. Violet brazenly placed herself upon his knee.

"All went well. Liam's stayed to settle the merge with Lord Robert, but you, I fear, are in a whole mess of trouble with yer father," Jack said stabbing his finger at Violet, who blushed, wearing her crimson shame.

"Aye, I did receive a letter from Ma. What did ye tell them?" she asked disgracefully. It was unheard of for a girl to be living alone with a man out of wedlock. And the circumstances surrounding *why* she was there in the first place was surely making everyone uneasy. Violet had to know folks would talk, but she'd chosen Brady over her reputation. Jack suspected she'd not regretted her decision, as her arm wrapped about Brady's neck. They appeared so at ease. So in love.

"No worries, Miss Violet. I believe I've smoothed things over with yer folks. I've explained to them that ye just couldn't leave Brady here alone and injured. Yer ma seemed to understand after some convincin', but yer father is not happy. Regardless, they'll be at the keep in time for the weddin'," Jack grinned; covering up his own silent misery was becoming a challenge.

"Brady! Did ye hear that? They're comin'. I didn't think they actually would, ye know," Violet exclaimed as if she'd won a battle between her and her folks.

"It will be a perfect day for ye, sweet Vy, and ye deserve it. I still can't believe ye agreed to be my wife," Brady laughed and tenderly squeezed his bride-to-be with his good arm.

The two were enthralled by one another. Jack cleared his throat to remind them of his presence.

"Aye, it will be a perfect day for ye both. I've assigned extra security detail for the entire week of the celebrations, and Mary has been frantically workin' day and night makin' sure she gets it just right.

"Ye'll need to get back to town a few days before the big day to wrap it all up. Do ye think ye can pull yourselves away from yer piece of paradise?" Jack teased.

Violet looked down into Brady's freshly shaven chiselled face. "I'm unprepared to give him up, just yet, but aye, we do what we must. I'm not ready to brave a cold winter on this farm. I love it here, but we're still ill-equipped. At least if we stay in Galway through the winter, we'll be better prepared to come back in the spring and live out the rest of our days. Here, in our own perfect heaven," Violet smiled.

Jack held in a chuckle. Brady must have had a tough time convincing her, for her words were laced with lingering uncertainty.

"Well, with Brady crippled for the time being, you my darlin' will need help packin' things up and loadin' 'em onto the wagon. Can ye agree to let me help her?" Jack asked, turning his attention back to Brady.

"Aye, I do need ye here. To be honest, I'm glad ye came back so soon," Brady scowled, his injury causing a wince. "I thought I'd have been fully recovered by now, but I've not been listenin' to my woman when she tells me to take it easy.

"As ye know, I've already sent the livestock home, along with everythin' we harvested. And if that wasn't hard enough, chasin' after this little brat every time she gets my blood boilin', has slowed my progress some," Brady laughed. Violet's cheeks turned bright red, as if she really thought no one knew what was really going on at the cottage, all alone, in the middle of nowhere.

She huffed and dug her elbow into Brady's stomach, making him flinch. Jack could see their relationship had really come a long way and that they were completely right for one another.

"Alright then, 'tis settled. I'll stay and help ye and Violet close up the place. Then, we'll get back to the keep and get ye two married, instead of livin' here in sin," Jack said, seething with utter jealousy. He wanted nothing more than to share this kind of life and love with Kylee, but that would never happen as long as she was marrying Garvan O'Shea.

After Violet had gone to bed, the two friends sat up listening to the crackle of burning wood, as they'd done since they'd been boys. Only now, the silence between them was nearly maddening. It was only a matter of time before Brady would have enough and force Jack to speak.

"What's the matter with ye, Jack?" Brady sighed, his gazed fixed on the flames licking the stove's glass door.

Here it comes. Jack had been wondering how long Brady's patience would hold up. "Why does everyone seem to think there's somethin' *wrong* with me?" Jack huffed, his arms crossed across his chest.

"Probably 'cause yer not yer usual arrogant and demandin' self. 'Tis like yer mind ain't here at all. Did somethin' happen in Clare, somethin' yer not tellin' me?" Brady turned then, searching Jack's eyes for the answers.

"Aye, Brady. Somethin's happened, all right. No use hidin' it," Jack blew out an exasperated breath and rubbed the back of his neck. "I think I've found the woman of me dreams. She's an unruly spitfire with a nasty disposition," Jack explained, realizing how ridiculous it sounded. "But she's also beautiful and mysterious, and I know she's hiding somethin'.

I've a feelin' there's somethin' deeper, somethin' lurkin' beneath that hard surface of hers."

Brady tipped his head back and let loose a loud chuckle, even though the movement caused him noticeable discomfort.

"'Tis no laughin' matter! She's to be married to someone else." Jack shouted, holding on to his anger by a mere thread. *What was I thinkin' comin' here?*

Brady wiped the smirk off his face and pinned Jack with a serious gaze. "Well then, ye know what ye have to do. Ye have to go to 'er and figure it out. If not for her sake, then for yer own. Put it to bed…not the girl, the issue," Brady laughed again.

"Stop carryin' on! The lass has me bewitched. And I would 'ave stayed on in Clare for a while and made an utter fool of m'self, but she'd mysteriously fallen down a set of stairs and was at home restin'. Ye see, she works for Lord and Lady Ryan. I'm sure Violet is acquainted with 'er," Jack said, then turned again to his oldest friend, a familiar foreboding threatening to smother him. "Brady, I think her accident stinks, and the circumstance surroundin' her betrothal to a drunkard reeks as well."

Brady nodded. "Jack, ye have a way of findin' out the truth. Go and see for yerself. At least yer questions will get the answers they need. But can ye wait 'til after the weddin'?" Brady chuckled.

"Aye, perhaps ye're right," Jack paused. "But to be honest, I just want to forget 'er. 'Twould be easier than learnin' truths I can't handle. Either way, I'm bloody-well shagged. And don't mention this to Violet. I don't need or want the opinion of a love-struck girl," Jack rose, then ambled outside to steal a breath of the late autumn air.

He had a decision to make. Either go back to County Clare to win her over, or stay in Galway to spend his days and nights alone. What if he learned that Kylee actually loves Garvan? *The lucky bastard.* He couldn't stomach the thought of it. But, it could force him to forget he'd ever met *Kylee the Wicked* in the first place. *Forget 'er.*

The next morning Brady was ordered to remain in bed, while Violet and Jack began packing up the cottage. As they loaded the wagons, Violet's excitement was contagious, as she sang pretty songs in her ancestors' native Gaelic. Jack found himself humming right along with her.

"Oh, Jack! I wish I never had to leave this place," she sighed.

"I never thought I'd hear ye say that," he chuckled, wiping a bead of perspiration from her brow with his kerchief.

Violet's gaze darted to his. "He's changed so much. When he finally let go of his suspicions regardin' his father's death, he was instantly transformed into the lovin', carin' man I first met. It seems so long ago," Violet said wistfully, lost in reflection. "I always knew there was good in 'im. Now, he shows it every day, and in everythin' he does."

"Aye, Brady is a good man, and he's plenty lucky to have ye," Jack nodded, and then planted a friendly kiss on her rosy cheek. Elation that his best friend had finally found what he'd been looking for, made a smile creep up his cheeks. But as fast as it had appeared, his own loneliness and the longing to find the same lot in life, reared its ugly head, leaving him feeling completely beaten.

Jack decided then and there, to push his feelings down into the depths of his soul, for no good ever came from wanting what couldn't be attained, anyway.

THREE

Upon arrival to Brady's childhood home, the three were welcomed by everyone who'd had the pleasure of employment within the walls of Kelly's keep. Mary was the first to run and greet them, with massive displays of affection toward both Brady, and his new bride-to-be, folding Violet into an inescapable embrace.

"I just knew it all along, ye know!" Mary beamed, and then regarded Brady scornfully. "Although I've never agreed with his methods, I'm certainly glad ye've found love in one another. 'Tis a blessed thing ye know, to find love," she added.

Jack turned away from the lot of them, unhitching the team of work horses which he'd only a few months before, brought from their stable here in Galway and delivered to the farm. He chanced a glance back at Violet, whose beaming expression had everyone about her feeling the weight of her enthusiasm. Their eyes met but for a moment, a knowing shimmer emanating between them. The last thing he intended to do was to rip the happiness from the pretty bride. Right now, he craved solitude more than air.

"Mary, I'm very happy to be back," Violet sweetly said, turning her attention back to the red-faced frazzled woman before her. "Have ye any word from my folks? I do hope they arrive soon."

"No fear, child, they're s'posed to be arrivin' on the morrow. Now, come, let's get ye unpacked and settled," Mary patted Violet's hand, linked her arm with Brady's and then led them into the great hall. "Now, I s'pose ye don't think ye'll be sharin' Brady's room 'til yer lawfully wed!" Color rose in Violet's cheeks. Jack's gaze shot between the mortified blushing bride and Brady. *Certainly, they haven't lain together before the weddin'! She best hide it better than that before her kin arrives!*

"Nay, Mary! Of course not. Lady Violet can stay in the East wing. Ye can ready the guest apartments as well. That way, she'll be close to her family before the big day," Brady smartly stated, then smirked at Violet in a way that said *'our secrets safe'*. Jack knew that look – all too well. His and Brady's friendship was based upon secrets kept tightly beneath a smirk or a nod.

Jack retreated back outside and then finally appeared again, winded and dripping with sweat, carrying a large brown trunk.

"Where to, Violet?" he blew.

"Come with me, dear. Her things will go to the East wing for now. Ye can help move them again after the weddin'," Mary giggled.

~

Jack did as he was told with a grunt, yet without uttering a word. Brady stood back and watched his tormented friend trying to do anything and every-thing just to stay busy. He would have offered to help, but his injury was on its last days of healing, and he didn't want to risk hurting himself, hence jeopardising the wedding night. Brady nodded to one of the stable hands who were making his way back outside to retrieve more of their belongings. The boy caught the signal and rushed to Jack's aid.

"I can do it m'self alright!" he barked, sending the lad running for his life.

When Jack was out of sight, and Violet could no longer hear his grumbling, she turned to her groom-to-be and held his hands up close to her chest, kissing each knuckle affectionately.

"What's gotten in to him?" she whispered, searching Brady's face for an answer.

"No worries, sweet Vy, yer friend and saviour is in love, that's all. But with a woman he can't have," Brady smiled, disregarding Jack's wishes to keep it a secret. "'Tis not a love like this though, for no man could ever love a woman like I love ye. But, he's in love just the same," he explained. Brady leaned in, breathing his words into her ear, "I'm a lucky man. I'm finally able to claim ye for me own. For good." Violet's breaths quickened, her cheeks flushing once again. Brady placed a finger under her chin and tilting her head up, he brushed his lips over hers.

"Poor, poor Jack," Violet whispered into his mouth, then pulled away. "I remember how heartsick I'd been when I first realised how much I really loved ye. 'Twas awful bein' so close to ye and unable to have ye. 'Twas like bein' lost in some sort of purgatory."

"Those days are just a fadin' memory now, love. Let us not ever think of 'em again, aye?" Brady replied softly. He held her gaze, lost in her mesmerizing emerald pools, and sighed with satisfaction. He'd been the first man who'd tasted her sweet kiss. He'd be the last man she'd ever touch and make love to.

She would now and forever belong to him, heart and soul.

Brady walked her to her room in the East wing of the estate, her amazement painted across her pretty cheeks. Because he'd stayed away from this wing since his mother died last year, he too appreciated how it had been kept up. It was as if it hadn't been touched by time and vacancy at all. Sensing Violet's wonder, he began to explain some of the home's history.

"Ma decorated this entire side of the house to represent and honour her family and heritage. Ye see up there at the end of the hall? That's her family's coat of arms," Brady pointed. "It was important that her kin-folk felt as at-home as possible when they visited."

"'Tis beautiful. So colourful. Did yer grandparents come to visit often?" Violet asked, paused to examine another wall of art work his mother had painted. It was a vibrant and unique mural of her Spanish homeland.

"Nay, they never did. That always broke her heart. I think that's why we spent so much time at the cottage when I was young. I assume any other lady with a household as grand as ours, would've stayed here to run things. Receive company, should some arrive. But not Ma. I s'pose she knew they wouldn't come." Sadness swept over him just speaking of his mother. How he wished Caitlyn were here to meet his bride. Violet seemed to notice his pain and changed the subject.

"In which room shall I stay?" she asked cheerfully, shifting focus.

Brady smiled and then opened a large, carved wooden door, stepping aside for her to enter. Her gasp was audible, her mouth agape in awe of the grandeur awaiting her. It was as if the entire room had been dipped in gold and ivory. Just as Brady remembered it.

"Brady," she breathed. "'Tis my favourite room in the whole house, I'm sure," she said, half-covering her gaping lips. "Ma and Da will be so pleased. Ye're gonna spoil 'em. They'll feel like royalty." Even though Violet's family were as close to royalty as commoners could get, they would have never seen anything quite like this. Brady beamed with pride.

"I'm glad ye like it, love. But don't get too comfy. Yer movin' back up to my end of the house in three nights' time," Brady kissed her thoroughly yet quickly for fear that someone might catch them. "I'll let ye settle in. I have some work to do in the study, so that's where I'll be if ye need me."

Left to her own devices in the vast chambers, Violet unpacked her things into a large alabaster armoire. Regretfully, her once lovely dresses were rent with holes, bore mud and soot stains or had become threadbare. A smile crept onto her cheeks. Despite the toll it had taken on her wardrobe and the once delicate skin on her fingers, she wouldn't choose to change a single moment.

Missing the cottage already, Violet blew out a small huff. ' *'Tis one winter...just one season,*' she thought bravely, laying out a pretty, blue frock, scrutinizing it carefully to find and temporarily repair the damaged spots. It would cause an uproar were she to greet her kin looking a fright. *I'll have Mary send for the seamstress first thing.*

~

Brady rested behind his father's old mahogany desk in the study, sorrow consuming him in a torrent of grief. The physical pain of it would've crushed him, had Jack not appeared in the doorway.

"Anythin' else b'fore I retire for the night?" Jack asked quietly. Brady peered up from the piles of paperwork scattered across the desk and wiped his face in his calloused hands.

"Can ye believe Liam? Jesus! He can't even keep this place in order. Da would roll over in 'is grave if he could see this," Brady cursed.

"Aye, he would. But cut the boy some slack. He's not been right since he came home from school in England. And might I remind ye, ye were off playin' house while he was left here to sort yer father's affairs! Yer damn lucky that Kelly and Son's didn't go belly up," Jack snapped.

"Get out, Jack," Brady growled through clenched teeth. Jack's contrary manner was due to his own heartache, but right now, Brady refused to be his friend's punching bag.

"Ye've got everythin', Brady. Snap out of it," Jack slammed the door behind him, leaving Brady to curse and organize his father's study alone.

~

The next morning, Violet awoke in her fine linen sheets, sprawled in the middle of the most spacious canopied bed she'd ever had the privilege to sleep on, and stretched her arms wide.

Just as she sighed with contentment, her belly began to somersault and she had to make a run for the privy. With the contents of her stomach in the bottom of the wash basin, she wiped her face and took in her reflection in the mirror. Her sun-kissed skin appeared ashen, her fiery locks, now a dull reddish orange.

Where was the sparkle which once danced in her eyes?

What if they hate him for all he's done? Violet began to cry into her hands, sobbing uncontrollably.

Just then, she felt a presence behind her. Her gaze snapped back to the reflection and standing behind her, was Brady. She turned into his open arms and let loose her fears upon him, holding on to his shirt for dear life.

"Shh, love. Don't cry. Can ye tell me what's gotten ye so troubled on such a beautiful mornin'?" Brady whispered. "Yer Ma will be here any minute. Ain't that enough to lift your spirits?" Brady crouched, meeting her gaze. His sapphire eyes flickered with unyielding understanding, causing her heart to swell with love and appreciation for the beast before her.

"That's the reason I'm upset. They'll be here soon and I'm so worried. I haven't seen them in months! What if I look different to them? What if they hate ye? What if…" she trailed off.

"Well, sweet Vy, if they hate me, 'tis 'cause I gave 'em good reason. And ye're more beautiful than ever, so that won't be an issue. I think ye're worried for nothin'," he smiled and kissed her feverishly, a low growl resonating from his throat. "I've missed ye. Last night was the longest night of m'life. I've grown used to havin' ye beside me. I don't know if I can do it for two more nights. I am hungry, Vy," he snarled playfully.

His attentions always seemed to distract her in the most perfect way, as her heart filled with joy, and her mind flooded with memories of their lovemaking. "I missed ye too, love," she hiccupped. "Let me get dressed and then we'll head down stairs. I'm famished," Violet sniffed, wiped her flushed face and then tried a smile.

"I'll be waitin' on the bench outside yer door. If ye need help with that corset of yers, just sing out," Brady added with a crooked playful grin.

Oh, but he is exasperating!

"I'm sure," she replied with a wry smirk, "And don't get caught leavin'. If Mary sees ye, she'll chew ye out good!"

"Yes, Ma'am!" Brady winked, and with a mischievous glint in his eyes, bolted from the room.

Violet smoothed her gown, conscious of its many flaws and opened the door. Brady, as promised was waiting. "See? Ye look stunning, as always," he said at first sight of her. He took her hand in his and led her down to the dining room. Mary was bustling about, getting breakfast ready and setting places at the large table, but stopped dead when her gaze fell upon them.

"Did ye sleep well, Lord Brady? Lady Violet?" she asked, sweetly.

"Aye, but 'twill be better in a few nights time, when we can sleep in the same bed – or not sleep," Brady murmured that last part under his breath so only Violet could hear. She squeezed his hand and shot him a disapproving look. *Behave yerself, Lord Kelly.*

"What was that, dear?" Mary asked, cocking her head as if she'd heard his remark, but misplaced it as something else.

"Aye, Mary! 'Tis great for a man to be restin' in his own bed!" Brady laughed as Violet nodded sheepishly and blushed. But just then, the sight and scent of poached eggs and bacon sent her running from the dining room to heave the remainder of her stomach into a defenceless rose bush in the adjacent garden.

"She's nervous about her folks' arrival. She said she's been ill all mornin'…." Violet heard Brady explain. Thankfully, he trailed off when he must've realized his near admission of being in her room.

"The poor dear," Mary replied with worry cascading her rosy cheeks. "I'll go see to her."

With Mary at her side, cradling her arm, Violet returned to the dining hall and took her seat across from Brady. As if her tongue had fallen to ashes in her mouth, she suffered down a slice of warm freshly baked bread and a cup of tea. Just as she began to feel better, her stomach flipped again at the sound of the door in the foyer swinging open and Liam bellowing his arrival.

"Mary! I'm home and I'm starved!" Liam laughed heartily, appearing in his impeccably starched duds. He stopped in his tracks as he spotted Brady and Violet quietly sitting alone at the table. "And I've brought something for you, Lady Violet," he smiled.

When Beth and Robert appeared in the archway, Violet jumped up and ran to her parents, clutching them with brutal intensity.

"Oh! Vy! I'm so happy to see ye. Robert, doesn't she look well?" Beth stood back, holding Violet's hands, looking her daughter up and down, and then smoothed an unruly curl.

"Ma, Da, I've missed ye so," Violet sobbed, holding on to them both.

"Now, now, no time for tears. This is a time to celebrate. Yer gettin' married! We've so much to do!" her mother exclaimed, but Violet could feel the rigidity in her father's caress and knew the reason for it was standing beside her.

"Da, ye remember Brady? Ma, Brady Kelly," Violet introduced the love of her life with unease, waiting for her father to beat Brady senseless.

Instead, Robert extended his hand quickly – harshly – but Brady accepted it. The men stood for a long moment, staring into each other's gazes. It was as if they were making a silent agreement in which only they could understand.

"Aye, Lord Ryan. I will take care of 'er. Ye have no worries 'bout that," Brady smiled kindly. "And now that I have ye here in person, I'd like to once more apologise for all I have done.

"Takin' Violet into hidin', and keepin' her against her will, was no act of a gentleman. But yer daughter has transformed this boy into a man. A man who'll forever cherish this woman, that is, if you'll let me have 'er," Brady avowed.

Knots grew tighter around Violet's heart and in her stomach with each penetrating second. Could

Brady feel it too? Perhaps he could now understand Violet's anxious condition, for Robert Ryan was an intimidating man.

"Aye, I believe ye. Ye can relax, boy. Liam! Lead us to the study. Brady needs an update with regards to Kelly and Ryan Shipwrights." Robert boasted the new company name with pride. "We'll leave the ladies to their plannin'." Robert kissed both his girls and waited for Liam to lead the way.

After the men had taken their leave, Violet's mother seized her attention with a worrisome frown. "Oh, Violet! Ye look so weary all of a sudden. What's on yer mind, darlin'?" Beth asked, urging Violet to sit.

"I'm fine, Ma. I was just so worried about ye comin' here and havin' ye meet Brady for the first time," Violet replied, seeking reassurance that all would be forgiven.

"I have to admit, I was upset that ye stayed with him, even after he'd learned that Gregory was responsible for killin' Lord Kelly. And ye know 'tis not proper for a young lady to live with a man 'til they're wed, Violet," Beth scolded.

"Ma, what would ye have done, if it were Da who'd been wounded? Would ye've left 'im alone?" Violet searched her mother's face for the approval she'd been longing for.

"Yer right, love. I'd never 'ave left yer da's side if he'd been injured while tryin' to protect me." Beth gave Violet a pat on her knee and blew a defeated huff. "I'm sure Brady's not a beast, like he'd first had us believe. I just pray he makes ye happy."

"He is wonderful, Ma, and he makes me *very* happy," Violet replied, sincerely.

The two ladies walked about the grounds until late in the afternoon, going over details of the big day, talking to the staff about the feast, listing details for the decorators, and then she showed her mother up to their apartments in the East wing of the keep. Beth was just as astounded as Violet had been only the day before when she'd been shown there.

When Mary rang the supper bell, everyone arrived dressed in their best. The portly housemaid had been a saviour, sending one of the other girls into the village early in the day to procure the perfect gown. Violet deemed it as utter perfection, with velvety gold material, trimmed with emerald appliqué matching her eyes. The mere sight of her left everyone, especially Brady, captivated.

As Brady was now the master of the household, he took his place at the head of the table and placed his beauty to his immediate right. Sitting across from Violet, Liam gave up his place at the head with no argument, no doubt relieved that Brady was finally home to take over the responsibilities involved as lord and protector of Kelly's keep.

Robert and Beth placed themselves on either side of the table, next to Violet and Liam, undoubtedly to obtain the best vantage point while they scrutinized the new couple.

The great dining hall, where oft-times was a bustling frenzy of soldiers and house-staff, appeared sadly desolate, as everyone else had been instructed to sup earlier to give the party privacy.

"Where's Jack?" Violet asked, quietly whispering in Brady's direction.

"I haven't seen 'im all day. He's probably holed up at Emma's place, tryin' to avoid all the happiness floatin' in the air here," Brady smiled charmingly. "Besides, he would've taken his supper with the rest of the help," he added, dismissively.

Violet became instantly furious.

"Would someone go and find him? After everythin' he's done for us, I'll not have him treated like *'the help'*. Mary!" Violet's outburst gathered the attention of everyone sitting at the table. All eyes were on her, but she didn't care. Jack was her friend, not just an employee of the keep.

When Mary appeared in the doorway, Violet had regained her composure, but just a little. "Mary, could someone please find Mr. Manning and let 'im know that his attendance would be greatly appreciated?"

~

Brady thought for sure he had swallowed his tongue, for words were lost to him. He knew Violet was spiteful and vicious when she needed to be, but this behaviour was so out of character, even for her. He would speak to her about it later, when, and if they were permitted some time alone. Until then, he was left speechless by her uncanny behaviour, and prayed her folks wouldn't assign blame to him for her altered personality.

The second course had been placed in front of them when Jack graced them with his presence. He positioned himself at the other end of the long table – straight across from Brady – and their gazes locked. The tension in the room was so thick that one could surely taste it over the savoury-flavoured pea soup, which everyone was politely sipping.

"Alright, so I'm here. What could ye possibly want with the likes of me?" Jack snarled, scornfully.

"Jack, I'm so glad ye could join us," Violet pleasantly said. Brady loved her even more at that moment, for she seemed to have an astute ability to sense painful emotion in others and express her empathy. And she'd been right to invite Jack back; he was not just a member of the staff. Jack Manning was family. *Bollocks! I am a fool!*

"Aye, thank ye for the invite," he said directly to Violet. "'Tis *your* company I am grateful for." Jack winked at her, which didn't go unnoticed by Brady, who was finding it difficult to be on his best behaviour in front of their guests.

"So, Liam," Jack began. "How did Kylee treat ye when she returned after her accident? Did ye get the *royal* treatment?" he asked through snarled teeth, as jealousy visibly twisted within him.

Watching Jack closely, Brady understood it all now. His friend was in sheer agony over this Kylee girl and the result had altered his very being into a contemptible, petulant, shell of the man he'd once been. Brady hadn't seen him this tormented in years.

"Kylee? I never had the pleasure of meeting a Kylee. However, a sweet lady named Nora took very good care of me during my stay," Liam replied through slurping his soup. Beth merely nodded and smiled, obviously taking his statement as a direct compliment toward her home and hospitality.

Minutes passed. Brady could feel the tick of his timepiece in his pocket, as silence enveloped. His attention turned to Jack, who's gaping expression fell between Beth and Robert with mounting intensity.

"Hasn't Kylee returned to work? Don't tell me that ye terminated her employment!" Jack finally shouted, red-faced, his fork and knife tightly fisted in his grasp. Brady prayed he wouldn't have to diffuse a situation, were one to arise. These people were to become his in-laws after all, and he'd already done enough to displease them. *Calm. The. Fuck. Down. Jack.*

"Nay, we'd never let her go! Kylee is precious to us. She just never returned. She's been missin' for over a week now," Beth began to explain sadly.

"Robert went to her mother's house to check on 'er. We feared that her injury was more serious than we'd first heard, and we wanted to make sure she had enough money in case she was strugglin' with doctor fees. But her mother said she hadn't seen the girl since two days after the dreadful tumble."

"That mother of hers didn't mind snatchin' the money from my hands though," Robert added disdainfully.

~

Jack's heart began to race, his mind conjuring up so many scenarios where each dire circumstance seemed to gel into the next. One thing was for certain, Jack had a sinking feeling that her betrothed was involved somehow. He just couldn't shake the dreadful suspicion.

"What do ye know of this Garvan fella?" Jack asked the Ryan's, searching their eyes one at a time. "Nora told me Kylee is engaged to marry the damned belly-gut."

Robert wiped his mouth with a linen napkin. "Just that he's the town drunk. His father is wealthy however, and owns a brewery back home, but he could never get any use out of the boy. He's been a nuisance for years, that lad. Garvan O'Shea is unruly and mean. I honestly don't know what the lass sees in 'im," Robert replied. "What's your interest in Kylee, anyway?"

Without answering, Jack rose from the table, quickly kissed the ladies' hands, and excused himself before his urge to explode could no longer be suppressed.

An uncomfortable silence fell upon the dining hall, until Violet whispered to her betrothed, "Please go to him. Find out what's going on."

Jack rushed down to his sombre sanctuary and packed the bag that he'd only gotten around to unpacking that morning.

"Where are ye goin'?" asked Brady, who was leaning in the shadows of the door frame.

"Back to Clare, is where. I have to find her. She's in trouble. I can feel it," Jack growled. "Now go back to yer supper, 'tis gettin' cold."

"Jack, ye can't leave! I'm to be married the day after next. Yer my best friend and I want ye there. Can't ye wait 'til after Violet and I are wed?" Brady reasoned, using guilt and duty as ineffective weapons against him. It wouldn't work this time.

"Brady! For Christ's sake, stop thinkin' 'bout yerself. I have to find Kylee. I *will* find 'er. Get out of the way," Jack shoved past Brady, knocking him into the wall. A strained expression and a hiss fell from Brady's lips, a reminder that his friend wasn't quite ready for combat yet. Jack nearly apologised until Brady's temper surfaced.

"Fine!" Brady roared, grabbing Jack's shirt collar with enough force to cause him to drop his duffel filled with weapons and clothing. "If ye find 'er, and if ye make it out alive, ye keep her. Ye can't treat 'er like all the others, Jack, that's not love.

"If ye yank her away from whatever's holdin' her, make sure she doesn't live to regret it," Brady growled, throwing Jack's past back into his face.

"Ye know nothing, ye bastard!" Jack shouted, yanking himself away from Brady's grip. He took the steps two at a time, back out into the cold, Galway air.

The following days while everyone back at the keep were enjoying the festivities, Jack would be alone again on that same road between Ennis and Galway in search of a woman who had shown nothing but distain for him. Sometimes he thought it most laughable, but he never once considered turning heel and heading home.

'*I must be off me hooks,*' he thought comically on more than one occasion. Fear of never looking upon Kylee's pretty face again drove him onward, and at times, in a worry-fuelled frenzy. He just had to find out what had happened to his spear-tongued wench.

~

Brady and Violet stood facing one another in the great hall, as Father O'Malley blessed their marriage. They stared into each other's eyes, as they repeated every word spoken by the old priest.

Brady tried his best not to dwell on the fact that his boyhood friend, his best friend, wasn't there to share it with them.

'*Today is about her, for she is my saviour,*' he thought lovingly, watching one lone tear trickle down Violet's rosy cheek. These were tears of joy and he was proud that he had finally caused them to track happy stains down her face.

Beth was visibly overcome with joy and sobbing fiercely, while Robert had almost hesitated when asked '*who gives this woman to this man?*' His first instinct might've been to burst out, "*No one, I'll never give her away!*" But Brady predicted Robert could finally see how exultant Violet was to be standing there with her man, and so, he reluctantly placed her hand in Brady's instead.

Later on that night, as her family slept far away in the East wing, Violet was finally shown to her husband's room. He could barely contain his excitement with sharing his bed with her again. It mattered naught that they were at the keep, instead of the little piece of Heaven they'd carved out for themselves. They could've been in a different galaxy for all it mattered, but in each other's arms, they were *home*.

"Ye looked beautiful today, my sweet Vy. And ye've made me the happiest man alive," Brady whispered as he pulled the crown of flowers from her hair. Standing behind her, he tenderly folded her into his arms and helped her untangle the corset strings of her lace wedding gown.

"These have been the longest days of my life and I've missed ye so. Show me no mercy tonight. Love me with everythin' ye have," she breathlessly whispered.

Brady's manhood throbbed in his trousers. Having her in front of him, finally as his wife and willingly exposing her beautiful body and soul to him, it would be his undoing. He slid his hands down to her navel, in awe of the silkiness of her glistening skin. *How did I ever get so lucky?*

~

Violet turned, facing her husband, gazing amorously into his once stony irises. The cruel, thorny man whom she once feared, no longer returned her gaze. He was beautiful and seemed finally at peace.

She carefully and seductively removed his shirt, baring his chiselled upper body so she could plant tiny kisses there. He held her tightly. Skin to skin. The heat between them ready to detonate as she moved her hands up his back and then through his wild, raven hair.

She tasted his mouth, delving her tongue inside to explore him, savouring his heat, as his hands wandered to places that she'd only recently become aware of. Places that were only for him.

Her dress fell to the floor, and she looked up at him with innocent, yet needy eyes. Brady took her hands and brought them to the string of his breeches, and without hesitation, she slid them down his muscular legs. They stood face to face for what seemed an eternity, exploring, tasting, and driving each other close to madness.

Brady held her tightly, moving her radiant body to the bed, laying her down gently.

"Brady, come to me," she implored softly, nodding her approval. This was a stubborn habit he'd picked up in the time since their first lovemaking. No matter how much they craved their joining, Brady refused to proceed without permission. *A habit I'll gladly break!*

He moved his body over hers and entered her, watching her expression intently, as if he could read her greedy mind. A firestorm sizzled within her as he sank further inside, his arms bracing on each side of her head, his thumbs dancing across her temples.

"Sweet Vy, ye do amaze me. I love ye. I never knew love 'til I found ye," he whispered and then kissed her violently.

She returned his kiss with a thirst she'd never known existed and then stopped abruptly, "But darlin' you *will* love someone more than this, I swear it."

Brady stopped his slow and tender thrusts to look down into her eyes with confusion and mounting panic.

"Only ye, Vy. I swear, only ye," he promised.

"Do ye think ye could love a little bit of me *and* ye?" she giggled.

Brady's lips turned into crooked little grin. "A baby?" he breathed.

"Aye. A little bit of Brady, and a wee bit of Vy."

He perched himself up on his hands and gazed down at her fully exposed belly and then placed a hand there.

"There's a baby?" he questioned again with excitement glistening in his eyes.

"I wasn't sure 'til a few days ago, and we can't say anythin' for a while, but aye, a baby." Violet nodded, and he cradled her tenderly and wept with tears of pure joy.

FOUR

Jack's first stop when he'd finally reached Ennis two long and weary nights later, would not be to the Ryan's stronghold near Ardnacrusha, as he'd done in the past. He couldn't bring himself to go there knowing that the Ryan's were still in Galway and that his wicked little temptress would not be there either.

This time he decided to find an inn within the village and find out as much as he could about Kylee O'Roarke and Garvan O'Shea.

The first dwelling he came across resembling an inn, bore a massive wooden carved sign that displayed the words *The Nest*. It wasn't much to look at from the outside, but he was tired and needed to rest his head.

Tonight, he required a warm bed, some hot food in his belly and shelter from the brewing pre-winter storm that had been chopping at his heels since he'd left Galway.

The Nest was pleasant enough and possessed a comfy air. This wasn't just an inn, but a tavern and restaurant as well.

'*Ahh, 'twill suit just fine,*' Jack thought, dragging his aching bones to the bar to check-in and seek out the tastiest tankard of ale he could find.

"Barkeep, a room and a pint," Jack demanded, slapping a coin on top of the long sturdy bar.

"Aye, stranger, comin' up," smiled the old man, retrieving a key from the hook behind the bar, and then placed a frothy tankard in front of Jack. "Room number two, just at the top of the stairs. There'll be no housekeepin', so yer free to sleep as long as ye like. And ye'll have no interruptions if ye want to avail of one of me daughters."

"Yer daughters?" Jack choked, his mouth falling open in disbelief. Was this man seriously offering up his own children to the highest bidder? All instincts told Jack to get as far from there as he could, but his body groaned in protest.

"Aye, lad. They're the cleanest whores ye'll find this side of the island." The old man winked and clicked his fingers, signalling for one of his girls to come forth.

A pretty young lady appeared from the other side of the room, scantily clad, yet wearing a greasy smile. Jack knew it then. *Here's the catch.* This place was too good to be true. He hadn't been looking to stay at a punch-house, but this was indeed the home of many women, whose tricks were for hire. Jack wanted nothing to do with any of them. None of them were Kylee.

"Nay, just passing through, friend. I'll need no companion for the night but I offer ye my thanks," Jack turned to the waiting lass, and felt a little sorry for her station. "Ye're a lovely thing I'm sure, but

I've no need for yer company tonight," he said, politely kissing her hand.

The girl turned up her nose and looked to her *father* behind the bar. The old man nodded his head, directing her back to the other guests sitting on the far side of the tavern.

"So, what brings ye here?" the man asked as he cleaned the dirty cups and tankards with the tail of his stained apron, causing Jack to seriously rethink his decision stop there.

"I'm lookin' for someone. A girl," Jack replied.

"A girl? I told ye, ye could have any one of my daughters. She's not the only one ye know, there's eleven more..." he replied, quickly scanning the room, taking inventory of his property.

"Nay sir, not just any girl, although I'm sure all twelve of yers are special in their own way. There's one specific girl I seek. Do ye know a Kylee O'Roarke?" Jack asked with wide, speculative eyes.

"Aye, I do. Her mother used to work at the inn down the street when the girl was still in swaddlin' clothes. What do ye want with 'er?" The barkeep stopped the disgusting cleaning ritual he'd started, and was scrutinizing Jack with furrowed, bushy grey brows.

"I just need to find 'er, that's all." Jack didn't have any other explanation than that. He thought regretfully that perhaps he should have had some believable tale conjured up before he started asking after Kylee. These were her people, and therefore would probably keep her whereabouts hidden from strangers.

"Well, if I knew where ye could find her, I wouldn't tell ye. But, it seems no one knows where the girl has gone."

Jacks heart twisted in his chest, restricting his breathing with a mean sense of panic. "What do ye mean? She's just disappeared? *Someone* must know where's she gone?" Jack shouted, resulting in all eyes in the tavern to become fixed on him.

"Calm yerself, lad." The old man hushed Jack as if he was an errant child. "Rumor mill says Miss

O'Roarke never returned to work. She was supposedly workin' for some wealthy folks up near Ardnacrusha. Some of the townsfolk believe her '*betrothed*', and I say that loosely, knows where she is. And some say he's hidden 'er. But if I were the poor dear, I'd run as far away from this place, puttin' as much distance between 'erself and that drunken fool, as I could."

"Garvan O'Shea? Is that right? I'm told his kin owns and operates a brewery here in Ennis. Can ye tell me how to get there?" Jack asked through a clenched jaw and grinding teeth.

"Now, now, b'y. Don't go runnin' off half-cocked. The O'Shea family are very powerful and wealthy. If he's got 'er stashed some place, he'll never tell. And if ye go looking fer trouble, I assure ye'll find it. But no one will ever find *ye* again." The man's receding, shiny forehead had started to sweat a little, despite the frigidity in the air. Jack noticed the change immediately.

"Tell me, old man," Jack snarled, grabbing the man's shirt collar from across the bar top.

"I'll be sorry fer even havin' this talk with ye if the wrong fella overhears. Let go of me, stranger," the barkeep whispered, frightfully. "I'll be talkin' to ye in the morn'. I'll wake ye at first light. I have an order to fill in the market, so ye can come with me then and I'll show ye his place."

Jack relaxed his grip on the clammy, fearful old man, whose *daughter* had rushed to his aid.

"It's alright, Allaine. Me and Mr…"

"Manning," Jack stated.

"Right. Me and Mr. Manning are done talkin' fer the night. He'll be headin' on up to his room, and 'tis where he'll stay. No more trouble?" Jack nodded in agreement and flicked an extra gold coin onto the bar for the disturbance he'd caused thus far.

"Send me up some grub, then. Leave it next to the door. Meat and cheese, if ye have it," Jack ordered angrily, and started up the staircase with bubbling annoyance.

He couldn't help but picture beautiful Kylee in a place just like this, lying at the foot of steps just like these. His head began to throb just thinking about it, and without answers, he felt utterly helpless.

Jack had eaten his platter of meats and cheese, and as quickly as they'd hit his belly, the nervousness and exhaustion had sent the meal back up. He decided to go back down to the bar, buy a bottle of whiskey, return quietly to his room and empty the amber contents until sleep claimed him.

The next morning, he had hoped to feel refreshed and have a restored state of mind, but it had been just the opposite.

When the barkeep quietly rapped on his door at dawn, a repulsive thump echoed in Jack's head as soon as he opened his eyes. *Hangover.*

"Come on, lad. If ye wanna know about O'Shea, ye better hurry up and get dressed. And don't be wakin' the rest of the house," he whispered through the door.

Jack groaned and quickly rose to dress.

The portly fellow led Jack up a long street in the centre of town and then pointed out the largest building on the block.

"There's O'Shea's brewery. It's a tavern and hotel too ye know, so ye might be able to blend in for a while. But don't go askin' after Garvan or the O'Roarke lass, that'll land ye in a mess of trouble," instructed the barkeep.

"Aye, thank ye. Keep my room, for I will return this evenin'," Jack said, patting the man on the back.

Jack couldn't help but wonder why this man, who clearly feared the O'Shea family, was helping him at all. That was a question he would find the answers to later. As for now, he found himself huddled in a concealed alley across from O'Shea's, where he could watch and wait until the place opened for the day.

The storm had finally caught up with him, and he trembled from the icy, winter wind blowing through his thick over-coat. *Christ! I'm gonna freeze to death!*

When he thought his feet might turn to chunks of bitter rime, there was sudden movement at the front door of the brewery.

Disregarding his plight but for a moment, he watched a red-haired slob stagger out through a wooden-framed wrought iron set of double doors, their shiny hinges and fixtures reflecting the sun barely yet risen above the morning fog. But Jack could clearly see the man pull his member from the confines of his breeches and take a piss right there in the street.

A moment later, the degenerate wobbled back inside.

Time seemed to yawn into oblivion when Jack finally noticed the sign in the front window changing from *closed* to *open. The hour must be close to ten by now.* Blowing warm breaths into his bundled fists, he wasted no time dodging across the street. Like any customer would, Jack heaved open the door, seeking refuge from the tortuous, frosty bite.

His first impression of the tavern was that the O'Shea family were in fact, wealthy. This wasn't just another hovel, where drunks and idlers wasted away their lonely days and nights. This was a place of high-class repute, with soaring beam-work ceilings, and expensive brass furnishings. While the walls were mostly carved wooden masterpieces, they had been delicately trimmed with a glossy emerald finish.

Identical to the colossal entryway out front, there were large double doors leading to the back of the building. An inside entrance to the brewery out back, perhaps. Scanning the empty room, he spied the staircase, his line of vision following it up to a balcony over head, where lodging rooms lined the corridor beyond. His gaze then trailed back down to the foot of the stairs, where Kylee must have been found. Envisioning her there, broken and helpless, caused an ache so great it threatened to knock the wind from his lungs.

"Can I help ye? 'Tisss a tad earrrly for a dri…nk ain't it?" a voice interrupted. When Jack turned, he came face to face with the same sodden slob he'd witnessed only a while ago emerging from the pub to relieve himself in public.

"A…Aye," Jack stuttered for a moment, shaking himself back to the present. "But I'd like one just the same. Been a rough night. Hair of the dog… ye know."

"Aye, I do," the redhead hiccupped. "Well, pull up a bar stool. Surry, t'ings ain't quite ready…" *hiccup*, "Wha'd ye wann'?"

'Jesus, this fella's drunk outta 'is mind!' Jack thought but made no comment on the matter.

"A pint 'ill do," Jack replied.

"Fine…A pin'." The sloshed brute slammed the tankard of ale down upon the bar with such force, the pale liquid went splashing all over the place. "I got wooork leff to git done. S'cuse me." And off he stumbled again, vanishing from sight.

Jack decided to take advantage of his solitude. He strolled around the room, looking for any clue within the many portraits scattered about, of who Garvan O'Shea might be.

He climbed the staircase and plodded through the hallway at the top, fighting the urge to beat down each and every door in search of Kylee.

Instead, he returned to the bottom floor again, taking one step at a time, slowly, and calculatedly, as if he could step back in time and feel her pain as she fell from the great height.

Retrieving his cup from the bar where he'd left it, he found a cozy booth in the corner of the room to sit and observe. Here, he would have an excellent viewpoint of the entire tavern if the O'Shea's ever showed their faces.

Jack's tumbler had long been empty when an angry thunder boomed. "Garvan! Garvan! Where are ye, ye good for nothin' little bastard?" Jack's eyes quickly shot to the owner of the voice, descending from the top of the stairs. "Oh! I'm so very sorry, sir.

I didn't know anyone was in at this hour," the irritated man explained apologetically, noticing Jack at the far corner of the tavern.

"'Tis alright. I'm just tryin' to warm m' bitter bones," Jack replied casually, making his way to the bar to refill his cup.

The old fella poured Jack another and said, "Fine, fine. 'Tis a bitter bite to the wind t'day, aye?" he asked rhetorically and then flummoxed Jack with an odd question, "Do ye have children?" Jack laughed and shook his head. "Well then, if yer ever foolish enough to have 'em, make sure ye bring 'em up with a whip, not a silver spoon."

"Aye, I'll remember that," Jack chuckled, nodded, and then went back to his secluded little corner to stare at the table in front of him. The barman seemed completely bewildered, and Jack was dying to see how this might all unravel.

And then it struck him.

'This must be Garvan O'Shea's father,' Jack thought. The man shouting after Garvan had the

same fiery red hair, the same blood-blotched face, and identical beady, brown eyes as the drunkard who'd served him a while ago. *'Twas Garvan O'Shea himself. I'd bet my life on it.* The revelation made his blood boil, but he managed to keep his temper masked. Perhaps the louse would lead him straight to Kylee.

When the man who Jack assumed was Garvan appeared again from the back room, he was sloshing around his own tankard of ochre liquid.

Jack silently fell back into the shadows of his corner booth once more, watching the family dispute fall apart before his eyes.

"I told ye, Garvan, time an' time again, the drinkin' has to stop," the older man shouted. "I'll not have ye runnin' the place into the ground and drinkin' all our profits. Not after everythin' I've worked for!"

"Mind yer business, ol' man. I'll drink when I want, eat when I want and I'll even rut when I want. Stay out of my life!" the slob barked in retaliation.

"Is this what I get for providin' ye with the life I never had growin' up? Disrespected by my own flesh an' blood? Ye should be ashamed of yerself, Gar." This was the confirmation Jack had been looking for. Without a doubt, the elder of the two had indeed sired the drunken buffoon. Garvan's father dragged sausage-like fingers through his tangled hair with mounting frustration.

Before he could say another word, Garvan ran his thick arm along the length of the bar, sending everything in its path crashing to the floor. "I never asked for any of this! But mark my words, I'll be dancin' on yer grave when ye knock off. I'm sick o' listenin' to this bullshite. I'll live as I damn-well please when yer gone," Garvan shouted, seemingly sobering a little. A winning, shit-eating grin took its place beneath his thick beard, until his father's next words suffocated the air around them.

"You'll not receive one taste of the family fortune when I *knock off* – so you call it. I'll see to it that yer wee little sister gets it all. Straighten up, Gar, or lose everything. 'Tis your choice. Now, clean up this mess!" he said, a finger digging into his son's shoulder amid each syllable. His father had turned the tables on the spoiled youngster and tempers were high. Jack thoroughly enjoyed the show.

"Ye can't leave it all to Fiona! I already promised to marry that little O'Roarke wench 'cause ye threatened to cut me out. Now yer givin' me more demands?

"I would've never consented to marryin' that peasant bitch if it hadn't been for ye. I would've at least, chosen a lady with a bit of class!" Garvan was screaming now, and Jack could see his father beginning to shrink before him.

But at the mere mention of her name, Jack's ear was cocked and hanging on to every word thrown between them. It took his maximum control to force his boiling blood back down for the manner in which this unworthy bastard was speaking of Kylee.

"Marry another? You're out of yer mind, Gar! I set ye up with the pretty thing 'cause no lass of higher breedin' would have anythin' to do with ye. Rachel would be disgusted with ye! God rest, 'er.

"Now, I'll not tell ye again, clean up the mess ye've made." Mr. O'Shea disappeared momentarily up the grand staircase and then returned with a sleepy-eyed young lady. "Fiona, ye'll take over here for the day. Yer brother needs to sleep it off again and think about the choices he's makin'"

The tiny red-headed girl yawned and curtsied, and said, "Aye, Da."

"Oh, that's right! Gar's been a bad, bad boy again, and is banished to 'is room," Garvan laughed sarcastically, making an obnoxious snorting sound. "But seeins' ye got 'er here, and she's so capable, she can clean up the mess too. And ye both can go to hell!"

Fiona jutted out her chin in defiance, stomped back behind the bar, and began sweeping up the broken glass and the remains of the decorative dishes that only moments ago, occupied space atop the solid slab.

"You," his father growled, pointing his finger toward the stairs, "get yer arse up the steps. Git to bed and don't come back down here 'til yer sober. 'Tis a wonder Kylee, even in her station, ever agreed to marry ye. The possibility of wealth does make people do strange things," the man said, shaking his head.

"Kylee O'Roarke can join ye in hell, for all I care. Haven't seen the little bitch in weeks. But when I find 'er, she'll be sorry she ever ran from Gar O'Shea.

"I'll be payin' a visit to her dear mother in the mornin'. If she knows where the wee wretch is hidin' I know she'll tell me. The price is always right for that one," Garvan said, pounding his chest and making a spectacle of his thick build.

Jack bit back his anger. Acting on the need to pound on the heartless beast himself, pulverizing the man with his fists, surely wouldn't help him find Kylee. But Jack was certain Gar knew more than he was letting on. *I 'ave to keep a clear head.*

As if just remembering Jack's presence, Garvan turned and began to stagger toward the lone man sitting peacefully enthralled in his tankard of ale. Jack reached for his knife beneath the table and was blade-ready if the drunkard chose to lunge at him.

"Fiona! Get this fella (*hiccup*) another. I'm sure he's thirsty after the show," Gar shouted and then stumbled toward the steps, not giving Jack another thought.

'*She's run off?*' Jack thought suspiciously. His patience was wearing thin, for someone had to know *something*.

He decided to leave the tavern then and return to The Nest. There, he hoped to learn as much as he could about his vanished waif, starting with why she was even betrothed to Gar O'Shea in the first place. Now that Jack had seen for himself the kind of drunk bastard she was really tangled up with, he was more determined than ever to have his questions answered.

The entire mess had left him baffled. If she had run off, and was missing, Jack had to find her before O'Shea did.

When Jack returned to the little hovel, the smell of fresh bread and fish filled the air, igniting all his senses. His idiotic booze-binge the night before and his encounter at O'Shea's had left him spent, hungry and cranky.

"Barkeep!" he shouted from the door, "Send out a plate of whatever your *daughter* got cookin'."

The man rushed to the table Jack had chosen. "Mr. Manning, I hadn't expected ye back 'til this eve'n…err, I mean, might ye want to get cleaned up first?" Jack met his gaze, shooting him an irritated glare. Clearing his throat, the barkeep acquiesced, "I'll fetch yer supper for ye right away."

"Well, I *am* back. And I'm hungry, and in no mood for yer shifty disposition," Jack grumbled.

"Aye. Right. The special is fried fish, with pork and potatoes. I'll have Allaine bring ye some bread while ye wait," the pudgy man fidgeted, wringing his hands over and over in that dirty rag of an apron. Jack eyed him suspiciously.

The barkeep then retreated behind the bar and leaned into a young woman's ear. Enthralled in conversation it would seem, for her fingertips danced across her lips and she nodded intently, following instruction from her employer. With a slight nod, her eyes darted to Jack's, and then she disappeared through a swinging door behind the bar.

What *in God's name is goin' on 'round here?* Jack wiped his face in his hands as frustration welled up inside him.

When the girl he assumed to be Allaine reappeared with Jack's plate of eats, he patted the seat next to him.

"Sit, Allaine. That is yer name, aye?" he asked. The girl nodded sheepishly. "Now that I'm bein' fed, I promise I won't bite ye," he smoothly said. Jack's new plan was to get as much information out of these people as he could, for the O'Shea's had been of no use yet.

The girl's gaze scanned the tavern, Jack supposed, looking for her *father*. Apparently satisfied with her search, she smiled sweetly and placed herself on the bench next to him, letting out a dainty breath.

"So, ye changed yer mind about wantin' a companion, did ye?" she purred.

"Yer not really that old man's daughter are ye? Ye look nothin' alike," Jack casually inferred and then without waiting for her reply, wolfed down some of the best fried fish he'd ever tasted.

"Ahh, yer a smart gentleman," Allaine giggled. "That's the way of it here at The Nest. He calls us his daughters 'cause men covet what they're not supposed to have. 'Tis a brilliant sales gimmick, don't ye think?

"Since Joe's been callin' us his daughters, we get enough business to earn a decent livin'," she explained, her eyes shifting from table to table.

"Why are ye so nervous to be sittin' here talkin' with a potential customer then? Relax." Jack laid his hand on her knee, for the more comfortable she became, the more she was likely to divulge. As he hoped, she relaxed instantly.

"I'm not nervous, Mr. Manning. Joe already informed us yer not interested. He wouldn't like it too much if I paid too much attention to ye, and none to the real customers," she lied, but Jack could see the fabrication written all over her pale, yet pretty face. He decided to get right to it, throw it all out there and hope that she'd fear him enough to be honest.

"Well then, as long as I have ye here, let's talk about Kylee O'Roarke," he said, his focus shifting from eye to eye, gauging her reaction. He had thrown down the pewter cutlery just in time to catch her arm as she attempted to flee, and pulled her back down beside him. Her response to his request was proof enough that these people were either protecting Kylee or were responsible for her disappearance.

"I don't know 'er. Let me go," she quietly seethed through grinding teeth, a full burning flush turning her pale flesh crimson.

"I think ye know more than yer lettin' on," he replied. Then, an idea struck. He could try a more delicate and subtle tactic to get the truth from this little liar. He began, "If I became a paying customer, I'd bet I could get ye to tell me whatever I need to know," he grinned, running his finger down the side of her hot cheek. Allaine turned away from the onslaught of Jack's advances, but the pinch of his thumb and forefinger against her chin promptly brought her back to him.

"I can refuse a client ye know," she said, biting her bottom lip. She attempted to make her escape once again, but Jack's unforgiving grip on her thigh proved too much for her slight build.

"But I'm sure ye won't. And I assure ye, ye won't be sorry for it in the mornin'," he whispered in her ear causing her breath to quicken. *How very responsive, ye little minx!* "Ye will stay with me tonight, won't ye?" Allaine nodded with down-turned eyes and a slight grin. This wasn't a question, it was a demand.

'*This one knows my game,*' he thought triumphantly. Jack would free his inner beast tonight, and the girl would turn to honey in his hands, telling him everything he needed to know. He was sure of it.

"I'll see ye at seven. If ye don't show, I'll come for ye," he said, his voice all gravel. He rose and left her still seated on the bench, speechless and heated. It appeared she was trying to find her tongue when Jack fished a shiny gold coin from his trouser pocket and slapped it on the table. "Seven," he confirmed and then swaggered toward the staircase.

Looking back over his shoulder a few beats later, Allaine was still anchored there, staring at the coin. Her lithe fingers quickly darted from her lap and retrieved it. Jack couldn't help but smile. This little lass would serve as a perfect instrument in his search for Kylee. Oh, Allaine knew Kylee by name, alright, and just because no one was willing to give up information, didn't mean Jack couldn't go about his own way of forcing the truth to the surface.

When Jack returned to his room, he took out his note book and documented all that he'd observed thus far. He jotted down details regarding Gar O'Shea, his father, and the tiny fire-haired sister, Fiona. He couldn't understand how two siblings, sired by the same man could be so different.

While Fiona was happy to obey her father and honour what he'd spent his life working for, Gar was completely oblivious to the sacrifices that had been made to provide the luxuries he possessed. It was almost unfathomable how or why Gar had turned out to be such a good for nothing miscreant, but Jack refused to waste any more time thinking about it. He had other things to prepare for this evening.

At a quarter to seven, a quiet knock upon the door shook him from his contemplations.

'*Anxious and brazen. I'll like this,*' he thought devilishly. Yet, ever since he'd propositioned the woman, he'd regretted it.

He'd promised himself he'd end this contest as soon as he secured the information he required, and he wouldn't let his male need cloud his judgement. Emma had taught him that. *"Practice restraint and patience to get what you want,"* she'd instructed. Then, what he'd wanted was complete trust and to bring a woman to pure bliss. Now, those words were ringing in his ears. This wasn't about Allaine's needs or gaining her trust. This was about Kylee. He desperately needed to pull this off without a hitch.

Jack took a deep breath and swung the door wide. Allaine was seductively leaning against the door frame, her soft auburn locks bouncing down in front of her lush breasts. She had changed out of her uniform and had donned a sinfully provocative low-cut black and rose number. The slit in the side went all the way to the top of her thigh. She obviously thought she was going to seduce Jack and have the upper hand, but as always, he knew better.

"'Tis not seven yet," he pleasantly stated, and then shut the door in her face, leaving her standing in the corridor flabbergasted. She knocked again and when he opened the door, her words were abruptly and severely cut off. "When I tell ye a specific time, I mean a specific time. Ye'll not have me displeased, would ye?" And then he slammed the door again.

He knew she'd be shocked with his display of bad manners but he also knew women. Her compulsion to please him would have her waiting just outside until the grandfather clock at the end of the hall finished chiming seven times. Then, she would try again.

This time, Jack swung the door open, stepped aside and greeted her with a kind smile. "When ye enter my room, Allaine, ye'll disrobe, and kneel quietly 'til I tell ye otherwise. Do ye understand?" Jack's dominating alter ego was in full swing, and he could tell that this silent wench had already had a taste of this before. She brilliantly done as was instructed with no objection.

He would have remember to be tender this time. This wasn't *The Haven*, and this young lass who was now kneeling at his feet, refusing to meet his gaze, wasn't one of Emma's girls. Allaine had no idea what was in store for her.

Jack remained clothed from the waist down only, baring his sinewy, bulging chest. "Ye've had a taste of this before, aye?" he asked, the air around him thickening with regret already.

Allaine raised her head ever-so-slightly, and then lowered it again. Her hushed reply sent chills down Jack's spine. "Aye. A client once. I'd never felt so free. I've craved this ever since."

Calming himself, Jack replied, "Lay belly down, Allaine, upon the bed. Turn yer face toward me," he quietly directed. "Stretch yer arms as far as ye can above yer head." The quivering bar-wench stretched her arms, grabbing onto the wrought-iron headboard. Then, he slid his warm, tender, hands up and down her exposed goose-fleshed body. Her silent gaze burned into him as he took two lengths of rope from his bag and gently fixed her wrists to the posts. When she still didn't object, Jack felt a little admiration for the brave little one.

Sitting beside her, he stroked her hair, whispering sweetly into her ear, never once treating her like the piper's wife that she was.

"Do ye like whips, Allaine? Ye can tell me what ye like. I won't judge," he urged.

"I…I like to be spanked, Mr. Manning," she breathed.

The girls at The Haven only referred to him as Master J.

Allaine had just called him by name – his real name. A heady sensation crept up inside him.

"Then, ask me to spank ye and I will. But ye have to ask nicely," Jack challenged, setting the small wispy, whip aside and rubbed both his palms together.

"Please, Mr. Manning, spank my bottom," she whispered, brazenly.

Jack rubbed the right cheek of her plush arse in circular motion until she tried pushing her flesh up off the bed to meet the heat of his hand. When he knew she could wait no more, he laid a quick thwack across her needy skin, and then rubbed the assaulted cheek, easing the sting.

He repeated this until the cheeks of her arse were glowing and her eyes were glossy, begging for more. Then he suddenly stopped, rose from the bed, and went to the hearth mantle and poured himself a small glass of whiskey. He downed it in one gulp and continued playing his devious game.

He watched her closely, gauging her need with a snarky smirk. *"Give her a taste, make her beg for more,"* Emma would've told him. When he returned to her side, the poor waif was all but panting under his scrutiny.

"Why did ye stop?" Allaine whined.

Without even touching her most intimate places, she was quickly falling over the edge. Now was the time for ultimatums.

"I'll continue, but what are ye gonna do for me, Allaine?" Jack teased, as he took the whip in hand, sliding it up and down her legs, thighs, and back, taking his ever-living sweet time with her torture. When

Allaine began to fight against the restraints, he sensed her desperation.

"Anything! I'll do anything. Touch me, please, do somethin'," she said in a whispered plea.

Jack raised the whip, its soft leather hot in his hand. Its vicious tendrils crashed down upon the back of her legs first. Placing his other hand under her belly, Jack lifted her slightly onto her knees, exposing the slick folds of her womanhood. "Stay right there…just like that," he instructed. Then, the satiny rawhide struck again. Her minuscule whimpers were like a symphony to his ears. He'd often heard appreciation for this type of bliss referred to as millions of tiny stars bursting behind one's eyes, and there was no doubt, Allaine was feeling it too. She was panting now, her red-streaked bare bottom arching for more. For one split second, Jack thought he would go mad, for he was a man after-all, with male responses.

Shaking his concupiscent tendencies from his mind, Jack shifted his tight trousers, putting his head back into the game, *'Information about Kylee.'* His purpose here had to remain clear, and so he pushed away the visions of sinking his throbbing member into Allaine's wanting bliss. His reward today would be that information, not the joining of two twisted bodies.

Tenderly pushing two fingers into her paradise, he then recoiled, leaving her panting, moaning, begging for more. Every time he rubbed, tickled and played, and then retreated, the growing intensity of her responses told him she was ready.

When he sensed her exhaustion and frustration, Jack knew she could take no more. Finally, he ceased his madness, and rose to take another swig of whiskey. One more offer to release her from purgatory, that's all it would take, and so Jack bent at her side, gazing into her half-masted eyes. Her deep brown eyes shimmering with unshed tears, her breaths coming in hurried huffs, her flesh, pink all over with arousal.

His fingertips drew circles on the small of her back. "I can make ye feel better, Allaine," Jack offered with an affectionate murmur. The heated lass nodded furiously, pinning Jack with a smouldering gaze. He stood then, breaking all contact with her hot flesh. "Kylee O'Roarke? Tell me what ye know."

Allaine turned her face into the pillow, raised her needy flesh to him and struggled with her restraints once more. When she looked back at him, he was seated in a chair across the room. She seemed to ponder his words for a moment, torment etching creases into her sweaty brow.

Then, as if the waves of realization had finally hit her, she cried, "Room nine. She's in room nine!". Jack rushed to her side and untied her restraints.

Taking her into his arms, he petted and massaged, tickled and prodded, until pleasure engulfed her, finally allowing her to find release.

Curling her body into his strong arms, spent from passion, her shoulders shook and he could feel her hot tears sliding over his forearms. "I've betrayed them," she cried.

"'Tis all right, Allaine," Jack comforted. "I'm not here to harm 'er. But ye're not to tell her I'm here, for I fear she'll run again."

Jack helped her sit up on an arse that was no doubt feeling the sting of his whip and passed her a kerchief from his pocket.

Allaine wiped her tears and blew out an exhausted huff. "We'd hoped ye wouldn't return so early today. Joe was tryin' to get her out of here," she whimpered, searching his eyes for the forgiveness which wasn't his to give.

Jack reached into his satchel, retrieved a small coin purse and placed it in her hand. "Shh, Allaine. Go back to yer room. Ye've done a good thing here," Jack reassured affectionately. But in truth, he couldn't wait to get rid of the girl. Get to Kylee. He prayed that while he'd been attaining the information he needed, Kylee wasn't being quietly ushered out the door and into the night, where she might be lost forever.

FIVE

Kylee paced her tiny room, waiting for her uncle to return with a directive to relocate. Since Jack had arrived at The Nest, her nerves were frayed, leaving her unsure of her decision to remain there and wait him out.

What could he possibly want with me?

Earlier that day, her uncle had suggested she be moved to a safer location, but Jack had returned too early for her to make a run for it.

She had no idea where her uncle Joe was planning to send her, but she trusted his judgement and had agreed. Now, she was waiting for the patrons of

The Nest to settle down for the night, so she could slip out unnoticed.

She'd hoped and prayed that Joe would be able to convince Jack that the O'Shea's were responsible for her disappearance. That would take the heat and scrutiny off The Nest, where she'd been hiding while recovering from the fall at the brewery.

Kylee bit her fingernails fretfully as she remembered every small detail about that day. It had been the worst day of her life to date, and she was grateful that Fiona had been quick to rush to her aid. The girl's cries still echoed in her mind.

"Oh, dear Lord! Kylee! Kylee, can ye hear me?" Fiona wailed as she shook Kylee's lifeless body. Kylee couldn't make out the owner of the voice, as the blood trickling into her ear seemed to muffle all sound. "Da, come quick!"

Kylee struggled to open her eyes. She didn't know for how long her world had gone dark, but when she forced them open, Fiona and Paddy O'Shea were knelt beside her, wrapping her head in rags to control the bleeding.

"What have ye done to yourself, lass?" asked Paddy.

"Oh, I don't know. I...I don't..." Kylee mumbled with confusion.

"'Tis a good thing that Gar found ye and fetched me right away. He'll be back soon with the doctor, so just lay still," Fiona pleaded as Kylee tried to raise herself up onto her elbows. At the mere mention of his name, the scene came flooding back and all of a sudden, she knew how she'd come to be at the bottom of the stairs with blood curdling in her ears.

She thought for a moment about telling Mr. O'Shea that Gar had pushed her in a heated drunken rage, but decided against it for fear of Gar finishing her off.

'*I have to get away from here*,' she'd thought, closing her eyes again, falling back into unconsciousness. The next time she awoke, she was in her own bed at her family home. Her mother was sitting in a chair next to her bed, rinsing a washcloth with warm water and cleaning Kylee's blood-stained cheeks.

"Oh, my girl. Yer finally awake. Just look at the state ye're in," her mother scolded. "No fear, I'll get ye all cleaned up, for Garvan is eager to see ye."

"No! I don't want to see anyone right now, especially…" Kylee coughed and winced at the sudden sharp pain in her head. "I especially don't want to see *him*."

"Come now, dear. The boy's sick to death worried about ye. The least ye can do is let him see that yer alright."

"Aye, mother. He's so concerned for my safety and well–being, that he's the reason I'm layin' here right now," Kylee sneered sarcastically.

"He told me that ye had an argument and that he may have gone too far this time, but ye'll see. He's wretched with regret, and I just know this won't happen again," her mother smiled, attempting to soak the sticky mess from Kylee's golden mane with a warm water compress.

As if the sting of open lacerations being prodded weren't enough, hearing those words coming from her mother's lips had nearly sent Kylee into shock. She would have hoped that after everything Garvan had done in the past to humiliate them, that this would be the last straw. Kylee had hoped her mother would finally consent to voiding the betrothal. This conversation was definitely not going in the desired direction.

"Ye can't be thinkin' straight, Mama. What will it take for ye to let me out of this contract? He's treated me like a common whore in public, he's beaten me, turned me into his slave at that God-forsaken brewery. And now this! He could 'ave killed me this mornin'. I can't imagine why ye'd have this continue," Kylee sobbed hysterically, waiting for her mother to come to her senses and agree.

In the back of her mind, Kylee knew that it would never happen as long as her mother was accustomed to living in the style that she was, a style in which the O'Shea's provided.

"Can't ye stop thinkin' about yourself for once, Kylee? Ye know we need this union to solidify our survival. When ye become Mrs. O'Shea, we'll never have to worry about money again," her mother exclaimed, walking the floor and throwing her arms up in frustration. Still, Kylee couldn't understand what kind of mother would rather see her only child in danger, than safe and happy. Kylee would rather work her fingers to the bone for the rest of her life than to marry into the O'Shea's.

"Never mind, Mama," Kylee gave in, but only momentarily. "I am being selfish, I know," she lied, appeasing the furious matriarch.

"There now, ye'll see. Everythin' will work itself out in the end. When ye two are married, we'll move into the manor and rarely even have to see them." Her mother patted her hand, but the false concern was making Kylee want to vomit. She knew the only person who *wouldn't* have to consort with the O'Shea's after the wedding, was in fact, her mother.

Right then and there, Kylee laid out her plan to leave the lot of them behind, but she would have to wait until she got just a little better.

The Ryan's, who had employed her when she was just barely old enough to work, had saved her from being sent to a brutal workhouse. And for that, she would be forever indebted to them. If only she could get back there and explain the whole mess to Lady Beth, perhaps they could help somehow.

"Aye, Mama," Kylee blew out in defeat. "What did the doctor say, then? Am I to miss work for a while? Or can I return to the Ryan's in the mornin'?" she asked, optimistically.

"Nay, child. The doc said you'll live, but yer to give the healin' at least a few more days. Can I let Garvan in now? I'm sure he's goin' out of his mind with worry."

"Aye, I'm *sure* he is. Let 'im in," Kylee replied quietly. Her heart was up in her throat. She knew how this was going to go. His apology would be short lived if he offered one at all, and she'd live to regret letting him in.

Siobhan washed away most of the stuck-on blood, and tied her daughter's hair back into a perfect bow. When she'd been made presentable enough for company, Garvan was permitted to enter.

Kylee watched in horror as her mother and Gar exchanged a whisper as he let himself into the room, inducing an immediate pain of betrayal. This woman was supposed to guide and protect her, not feed her to the wolves. It was then that Kylee decided she had no choice but to get as far away from them as soon as possible.

Gar sauntered into the tiny room, his build taking up much of the space around them. He might've been standing on her chest with the stifling panic, attacking her nervous system. He remained silent, his gaze fixed to hers, until her mother closed the door, affording him the privacy he needed to strike. Kylee had been expecting it.

"So, I s'pose ye've told Fiona and Da that I've done this to ye? Well, we both know I'm not the only one to blame here. If ye weren't such a stupid an' foolish little girl about everything, none of this would've happened," Gar growled through grinding teeth with fists clenched. "Ye're to be my wife, so 'tis my right to have ye in my bed whenever I want. Ye had no right in refusin' me! I've had enough of it. So, if ye won't spread yer legs 'til we're wed, I'll push up the weddin' date. Done!"

Kylee's heart filled with revulsion. The smirk and terrifying glint in his eyes told her he loved every minute of this. It was abundantly clear that Garvan O'Shea would make it his life's work to see her miserable and living in terror.

"I'll not be yer wife, Gar! Not now, not ever," she snapped back, burying her fear. "If Ma won't break this contract, I will!" she shouted in retaliation.

Without a second thought, his arm raised up and came crashing down with a slap across her face so hard that it opened a gash in her lip. Stars fluttered behind her eye lids. He leaned in close, pinning her arms to the bed with such a grip that caused tingling in her hands, his hot stagnant breath, an assault to her senses. And then he said the most wickedly evil words she'd ever heard.

"I just need to marry ye to collect my share of the business. After that, whether ye're dead or alive… I don't give a fuck," he released her arms, and violently dried her tears with his shirt sleeve. The rank stench of stale beer lingered in her nostrils until she nearly gagged.

While Kylee had always suspected that his intentions were sinister, hearing him say the words aloud triggered severe chaos within her. Their union would serve one purpose: to get Paddy O'Shea to finally sign over half of the brewery's profits to an ill-entitled off-spring. If Gar was speeding up that process, now was the time to run.

Garvan left right after that, leaving her with visions of what would surely be the end of her if she didn't escape him.

Soon after her mother had fallen asleep that very night, Kylee made her move. Not weakness, exhaustion nor injury would keep her there another unnecessary moment. She packed everything she held precious into a small carpetbag and tip-toed down the hall, past her mother's door, and then out into the freezing night air.

When first she arrived at The Nest, she had entered through the rear entrance as quietly as she could. The patrons of the pub, and clients of her uncle's *daughters* would still be in full swing of whatever hedonistic acts they had come there to perform. She would have to be invisible.

The hour was late, and her uncle would undoubtedly be asleep in his room by now, letting one of his night barkeeps take over. As expected, she spied Deke washing tumblers behind the bar. As quiet as a mouse, she slipped by him and up the stairs.

Kylee drew in a long deep breath as she reached her uncle's room, and then knocked on the door.

From within, she could hear him groan, unmistakably cranky that he'd been disturbed.

"What is it, Deke? Can't ye handle things and let me get some rest?" Joe grunted, but when he opened the door, and seen his brother's only child standing there in her night shift, long over coat, with bloody bandages wrapped around her head, he looked up and down the corridor to make sure no one had seen her, and frantically ushered her inside.

"Kylee! What are ye doin' here, child? And what's happened to yer head?" Joe asked, guiding her to the hearth, sitting her in the chair there.

"I need a place to hide, Uncle. I can't go back home. I can't go back to the Ryan's to work. I have nowhere else to go," Kylee spat through wracking sobs.

"Aye, love. Stay for as long as ye like. But ye have to explain what's goin' on first." Joe sat on the end of his bed, facing his only real relative, his expression becoming more and more enflamed as Kylee went into her story. She told him about her mother's plans to marry her to Gar, and the *wealthy* reasoning behind it.

"So, you see, Uncle? Mama knows if I marry Garvan, we will be well-off for the rest of our lives. She's lookin' forward to movin' into their manor and thinks she can even win over ol' Paddy. Lay claim to the man and his wealth." Kylee looked up at her uncle through glossy tears. "Uncle, if I marry Gar O'Shea, he will kill me. He only needs to marry so his father will sign his trust over to 'im."

"Kylee, why is it that the boy doesn't seek someone more…ummm…oh, I don't know…," Joe fidgeted.

"Someone of higher station than I, Uncle? Ye can say it, I know *who* and *what* I am," Kylee cut, bitterly.

"Well, aye. I don't mean to be cruel, love. Ye're beautiful, and a kind, gentle lass, but ye weren't born into a high-class, wealthy family. I would think Garvan O'Shea could have his pick of the young girls, if he wanted."

"That's where yer wrong," Kylee blew her nose, and went to the basin to wash her face. "He's such a revoltin', rowdy, and mean-tempered drunk, that not one family, in all of Ennis would consent to a betrothal with him. Not for all the money in the world! Except for Ma, she seems unconcerned for my welfare," she added, sadly.

"I have heard some tales about the lad, and when I learned that ye two were to be wed, I have to admit, I was concerned," Joe replied, and then hung his head. "But what was I s'posed to do?" Kylee sensed her uncle's guilt and felt as horrible about it as he did.

"There was nothin' ye could do. It was Mama's duty to protect me from the likes of him, but she's only thinkin' of herself these days." Kylee began to cry again and Joe came to her side, resting a hand upon her shoulder in comfort. And it did comfort her; this gentle man was the only person she could depend on now.

"Ye know, after yer father disappeared, I went to yer mother and pleaded with her to move in here. I wanted to provide ye with a life that ye were accustomed to. The rightful life that yer dear daddy had set up for ye. But she refused to let me have anythin' to do with ye," Joe smiled, reflecting on those first days after his only brother, Rolan, vanished into thin air. Kylee was just a girl back then, but there was nothing that Joe would have denied her or her mother. And then he added shamefully, "This wasn't always a brothel, ye know. A long time ago, this was an upper-class establishment, where business men would take their wives after a long work week.

"That all changed after the famine set in. No one had any money, but most seemed to find a few coppers for a drink and loose women. So, I did the only thing I could do. Offer them both. I stayed afloat."

"Ye don't have to explain that to me, Uncle. I've never judged ye, not since the day I found ye," Kylee comforted Joe in the only way she knew how, turning and taking his weathered old hand in hers. "I am so very glad I found ye. If I hadn't, just think of where I'd be tonight."

Joe seemed to shudder at the thought. Her mother would certainly force her back into the arms of the dangerous Garvan O'Shea, if it meant a life of lavish extravagance.

"Everyday, child, I wished I hadn't been forced to watch ye grow up from a distance. There were times when yer mother would bring ye into town, holdin' yer tiny little hand. I wanted nothin' more than to run out to ye and take ye in my arms. But she refused to let me know ye, especially after I hired me *daughters*," Joe explained with teary eyes. "Now then," he said, coughing back his gloom, "what are we going to do with ye?"

"Well, as ye can see, I need to rest. The doctor says I am not to return to work for a while. Not that I could anyway, for Gar would surely find me there and put the Ryan's in danger. So, if it is alright with ye, I'll stay here for a while. I can help out around the place, but only where I won't be seen. And yer girls aren't to know who I am. I can't risk Gar findin' me. I fear if he does, he'll never let me go."

Joe nibbled on his bottom lip and then said, "Aye, child. I think I can come up with a lie or two to cover ye. But I'll have to tell Allaine. She's my best girl, very trustworthy. Ye need a friend right now, and I need to know that someone's lookin' out to ye. Deal?"

Kylee considered this for a moment. If this Allaine was trusted by her uncle, she would have to trust her as well.

Everything was going as planned for the most part. She had been in hiding at The Nest for almost a week when the stranger arrived, and then alarm bells went off again.

Kylee had been in the kitchen, lost in her thoughts as she washed and re-washed the same dish, until she heard a familiar voice coming from the tavern. Her stomach lurched as she recognized that distinct Galway drawl.

'*Jack Manning*,' she thought, fear and anxiety welling up inside her like flames over a mountain of parched tinder.

"Barkeep, I'd like a room and a pint," she'd heard Jack say. Kylee couldn't believe her ears. '*Of all the lodgin's in Ennis, he had to choose mine.*' She poked her head out from the kitchen door just enough to see that it was in fact, Jack standing there at the bar, demanding a room and something to quench his thirst. Her heart fluttered and thumped so hard, she was sure it would break free from her rib cage. She couldn't decide whether she was afraid or elated to see him.

When she first met Jack Manning, he'd been working for Robert Ryan, trying to recover the man's daughter from the grips of a tyrant named Brady Kelly.

She recalled how smitten she had been with Jack, even the first time she laid eyes upon him. He was beautiful that day, wearing some form of soldier's attire, and had an air of authority about him that was unmistakable. His blue eyes pierced straight through her upon introduction, his gaze gauging her every move as she led him to his room in the Ryan home.

Regretfully, she also remembered the callous manner in which she'd treated him. Shame bubbled within her, recalling each and every evil syllable she'd thrown his way.

She had berated him, and cut him down to the bone, despite her undeniable attraction. It was so thick, that in his presence, she found it difficult to breathe.

The evening in which she barged into Jack's room unannounced, stuck out in her mind the most. He'd been so angry with her uncouth and unprofessional behaviour, he'd given her a good dressing down.

"Jesus woman! Have ye lost yer mind? Ye can't just go bargin' into a man's room unannounced!" Jack had hollered. *"What if I were indecent?"*

"Oh? And what if I'd seen yer little peter? Is that what yer afraid of? Does it possess some magical powers that if I look at it, I'll burst into flames?" Kylee was embarrassed for her taunting words, even now. But if she hadn't been so awful, she could have

let herself get lost in him. *"Well, no matter 'bout it. I've no interest in yers! I'll be married soon to a handsome brute, who I'm sure has some wicked and naughty things in store for me on my weddin' night,"* she'd lied.

Jack had been livid with her for her outlandish behaviour, and even ordered her away. Kylee felt at the time that she'd won, that Jack would leave and she would never have to see him again. Then, she'd accidentally said what was on her mind. She hadn't meant to, but the words came spilling out just the same.

"Aye, I'll leave. But we both know I won't be gone. I'll be lingerin' in yer memory, Mr. Manning" she'd spat.

If only she'd known those words would haunt *her* instead, she'd never have dreamed of saying them.

When Jack had left the Ryan home, she'd been plagued with thoughts of him. How would it feel to be loved by a man like him? Protected? Cherished? He was very much with her in every chore, every minute of every day. Righting his room at the Ryan's when he'd departed had been pure torture, as his virile male scent lingered everywhere.

But now he was here, and at her uncle's inn. She had nowhere to run, no place to hide.

Kylee stood motionless in the kitchen, hanging on to every word exchanged between Jack and her uncle. The notion that his mission was to find her nearly sent her to her knees.

'Why in Jesus' name does he want to find me?' she had thought, causing her body to take to trembling uncontrollably, waiting for Joe's response.

When Joe didn't give her up, Kylee had scrambled up to her room and waited for her uncle to come, as she knew he would.

She'd been waiting by the door when Joe knocked. She swung it open and frantically hauled him inside by his arm with one quick tug.

"Kylee? Who is that man downstairs? I know ye heard 'im. Why does he want to find ye?" Joe asked irritably.

Kylee's face turned bright red, and she didn't want to tell him how terribly she'd treated Jack, but she had been left with no other choice. Shame burning in her cheeks, Kylee's gaze met her uncle's soft questioning orbs with fear and trepidation, regret for ever having met Jack Manning threatening to burn her where she stood.

"He mustn't know I'm here, Uncle. I don't know why he's lookin' for me, but I do know that if he finds me, he'll be in danger too. He's a good man, Uncle. I don't want anything to happen to him. Please don't tell," she'd pleaded.

"Ye can't stay under the same roof undetected, child! He seems to be a smart lad and I'm sure he'll figure out that yer here, soon enough. Not to mention Gar. 'Tis only a matter of time before yer Mama tells O'Shea of our relation. Then, that bastard will be here lookin' for ye as well," Joe replied, rubbing his head, worry permeating the space between them. "I have no other options for ye. No other place to hide ye. Perhaps this Jack fella can help."

"Nay! I can't let 'im risk his life for me! We need to put him off as long as we can. I'll get word to Lady Ryan, and perhaps she can find some place where I can hide for a while," Kylee said, trying to assure Joe that everything would be all right. They just needed to steer Jack in another direction for a while until she heard back from Lady Ryan. Simple, right?

"We'll get ye moved tomorrow. I'll show Mr. Manning to O'Shea's place in the morn' and hopefully that'll occupy him a while, buying us time to get ye packed and gone. I only pray Lady Ryan welcomes ye right now, for they're better equipped to protect ye than I," Joe insisted, gripping her shoulders with shaky hands. He kissed her forehead as if to say '*It will be all right*'. But Kylee wasn't so sure. "I'll draft a letter to take with ye to explain everythin' and implore their assistance for sanctuary," Joe added. "Get packin', girl. I'll make arrangements for yer transportation while Manning's out for the day."

The next day, as they'd planned, Kylee was ready with her carpetbag in hand, anxiously waiting for Deke to arrive back at The Nest with a rented coach.

Time ticked by like a river of frozen molasses. Kylee quietly lingered in her room, anticipating her salvation, waiting for her uncle to arrive with word that Deke was ready. As the afternoon sun had begun to fall behind the hills, Kylee's resolve too, had begun to wear.

A quiet knock fell upon her door and she hastily opened it. She was about to rush out past her uncle and down the back steps to her awaiting chariot, but Joe caught her arm and softly moved her back inside the room.

"Ye have to wait, lass. Manning's returned early, and Deke still hasn't shown up with the wagon. I am sorry. Do ye think ye can wait another day? I'll take ye there m'self if I have to," Joe offered sincerely.

Kylee sighed. The longer Jack was there, the odds of him finding her were increasing. She could not let that happen! He was too good a man to get caught up in this. Kylee nodded, but disappointment engulfed her.

"He's not asked after ye today, so that's a good thing. I think he's suspicious of Gar now and that'll help if we're to get ye out of here unnoticed," Joe assured her naively.

'*Perhaps Jack's focus is on Gar now. Perhaps, he believes Gar to be responsible for my disappearance,*" she thought, crawling into the warm comfortable bed for the night. She only wished her nerves weren't so frayed. Sleep wouldn't come easy as long as Jack Manning was under the same roof as she. *'Tis only one more night.*

Just as a pleasant dream took hold of her consciousness, the unthinkable happened. Her door rattled and shook as a fist thumped and hammered against it.

Kylee jumped from her bed and held fast next to the closed door. She recognized the unrefined brogue booming from the other side. *Jack.*

"Kylee, I know ye're in there!" he roared. "Dammit, Kylee, let me in."

She trembled but kept silent. Even the sound of her own breathing jeopardized her stealth.

What sounded like a battering ram, echoed throughout the room, so she instinctively backed away from the door and covered her ears.

When the wood came crashing down and the frame was reduced to splinters, her petrified gaze met Jack's determined one. Kylee fell to her knees like a little child, distraught with fear. The last thing she needed was another beating from a man, or to be chastised by this handsome brute standing breathless in her doorway.

Jack rushed to her side and knelt down beside her. He took her tremulous body into his arms and cradled her, wiping away her tears, shoving an errant tendril of blonde hair from her face.

"Shh, Kylee. 'Tis all right, now. I'll not hurt ye. Ye'll fear nothin' ever again, I swear to it," he whispered tenderly.

SIX

Jack met Kylee's troubled gaze and then she instantly melted into him. He peered past to find Joe standing in the crumbled doorway, assessing the damage that he'd had inflicted.

"Kylee? Do ye need me to fetch Deke? Mr. Manning, I think ye should leave," Joe asserted.

"Nay, ol' man. I'll not be leavin' without her," Jack growled, and then wiped another tear from Kylee's pink cheek. Jack's stormy gaze penetrated her with ease, her body relaxing in his arms as he stroked her cheek, whispering, "That's why I'm here, love, to take ye away from this place and from that bastard to whom ye're betrothed."

Kylee nodded her reply, her trembling bottom lip caught between her teeth. Despite everything she'd said and how terribly she'd treated him, Jack knew a lass who needed saving when he seen one.

"Uncle, please leave us," Kylee quietly said, never taking her eyes from Jack's soft stare. "Jack, how did ye know I was here?"

Joe cursed under his breath and left them.

A small shameful grin formed on Jack's chiselled face, thinking of *how* he'd learned of her whereabouts. Allaine had been an eager participant in his game initially, but she couldn't have known Jack would force her secret to the surface. A small pang of guilt for manipulating her in such a manner rushed at him, but after-all, Allaine was accustomed to being used. It was the norm within her profession and he had, in fact, paid her for her secrets.

"Never mind that, Kylee. Let's just say I can be very creative and persuasive when I need information. Now let's get ye ready. We're leavin' immediately," Jack said, lifting her from the floor and dusting off her night gown.

"Why are ye doin' this? Why are ye even here after all I've said and done to make ye hate me?" Kylee asked as she moved about the room, to behind a curtain to dress and then to the bag lying on the floor amongst the splinters.

Jack thought for a long moment, for he himself didn't understand why he was so drawn to this spit-fire imp. Explaining it would be torture.

Unable to find the right words, he studied her as she picked up a sketch of an unknown man and kissed it, and then placed it in the bag. He suspected it was a routine of hers, as it appeared second nature for her to do so. He couldn't help but wonder who the man was, who had captured her adoration.

"I…umm, I was out by Ardnacrusha just a few weeks ago, tying up loose ends for the Ryan investigation. I was, for lack of better words, surprised when ye weren't there to cut me to the bone with your spiteful tongue," he winked. "An elderly chambermaid, named Nora, I think, explained to me that ye had an unfortunate accident." Jack waited for Kylee to pick up on the cue to explain what had happened, but she didn't. She continued getting ready, almost oblivious to Jack's hidden question.

Jack moved toward her, his colossal frame shadowing her. He drew her close, her sweet rose scent unfurling his senses.

~

Kylee thought back to the first time she'd been that close to him. The effect he'd had on her resulted in panic, and thus, resulted in her treating him as awfully as she had. Falling for this rogue was a great possibility, for she'd felt the heated attraction surging between them. Regretfully, the only way to save him was to drive him away.

She feared that if she was to be noticed swooning over Jack, Garvan would seek revenge and surely make an attempt on her life, or worse, Jack's.

The entire time Jack spent at the Ryan's, Kylee had been secretly eager to tend to his every need, yet her mind was plagued with possible horrors of what Garvan might do if he sensed her betrayal.

The only thing she could do, was make Jack hate her. Although, his presence now proved that her approach hadn't worked.

"When Liam Kelly returned from the Ryan's and said that ye haven't been seen in weeks, and then Lord and Lady Ryan said that no one knew where ye were, I just had to come. I was worried somethin' might've happened to ye, despite yer not so warm welcome when last we met," Jack began. Kylee broke free from his embrace, turning to face the small window. "But if you're not gonna tell me what he's done to ye and why you're hidin' out here in this little hovel, I may have to force it out of ye," Jack chuckled, but then she turned again, fear flashing beneath watery lashes.

As if he'd sensed her need for comfort, Jack plucked her coat from a chair and hurried toward her, wrapping it around her trembling shoulders.

"'Tis a frosty night and we have a far distance to travel, lass," Jack said, affectionately wiping her tears with the pads of his thumbs. "All will be alright, ye have to trust me."

"We need to get as far from here as we can, before Mama sends Garvan after me," Kylee sniffled, straightening herself, and rushed past him out the door.

"What do ye mean? Yer own mother would give ye up to that loathsome bastard?" he asked, gently catching her arm. "Ye have a lot to tell me, Kylee, but it can wait. We'll have plenty of time to talk on our journey," Jack smiled warmly. Whatever it was about this man, she did trust him. He could lead her straight into battle with an open heart, putting all her faith in his hands. But that damned smile of his, that was another story. She most definitely did not trust herself when he smiled at her like that.

Downstairs, Kylee kissed her uncle's cheek. The finality of the farewell distressed her immensely, but she tried her best not to cry. "Thank ye, Uncle. I'll send word as soon as I get wherever I'm goin'," she said, then gazed at Jack with questions looming between them. When he said nothing, she turned back to Joe. "If Gar learns of our relation, he'll hound ye for my whereabouts. 'Tis best ye don't know where I'm headed. Please stay safe and watch after the girls. I'm very sorry I put ye in danger."

"Oh, m'little darlin', don't ye worry 'bout such things. Just get out of here and don't ever look back," Joe said, kissing Kylee's forehead. He released his grip on her shoulders, and turned to Jack with conviction and warning. "Mr. Manning, I'm neither a young man, nor a rich one with muscle behind me dollar, but I assure ye, I *can* use a revolver. If one hair is hurt on her head, I'll hunt ye down and put an end to ye. She's had enough hurt for one lifetime."

"Aye, I understand," Jack replied. Only having been reacquainted with Joe a short time ago, Kylee believed his warning, but only mildly intimidated, Jack added, "I'll take care of 'er, I can promise ye that much."

"Tell me where ye're takin' 'er. I have to know," Joe begged quietly. "She's me only remainin' kin."

"Oh, now ol' man, ye can't expect me to tell ye that. I can't have Garvan O'Shea comin' in here some night and screwin' Kylee's whereabouts out of one of yer *daughters,* now can I?" Jack drawled. He turned his attention to the top of the staircase where Allaine was standing red-faced and with arms folded across her chest. Jack kindly smiled up at her, tipped his cap, and then ushered Kylee out the door into the frigid moonlit night. Her first instinct was to ask what the little exchange had been about, an unfamiliar knot of jealousy wrapping around her heart, but better sense protested, and she held her tongue. Perhaps when they were better acquainted she'd find the brass to ask such things. Right now, they were strangers – he, her saviour – and nothing could come between herself and the freedom from Garvan's rein of terror.

Outside, when he'd fastened her bag to the saddle, Jack leapt up onto his strong steed, and then held out his hand, pulling her up behind him. His warmth instantly seeped into her, as she wrapped her arms around his waist and pushed her face into his back, shielding herself from the bitter wind.

"No fear, Kylee the wicked, we'll stop at an inn before it gets too cold for ye," Jack assured her. "Ride, Conan!" he roared. Kylee's grip on his overcoat tightened as she fought to hang on.

With his mighty steed at full speed, and without fully grasping how perilous her situation really was, she trusted he wouldn't take any chances with her safety. She admired the soldier in him.

Cautious not to take the main roads through town, they were sure to avoid any establishments the O'Shea's owned. The last thing they needed was an irate, drunken Gar O'Shea to rush to pursuit.

Kylee rested her cheek on Jack's solid back and let her mind wander. Wander from the cold, and the throbbing which still plagued her head from

Garvan's last attempt to demonstrate his authority over her. With every mile she put between herself and Ennis, her angst and worry lessened, and she began to day dream.

She pictured herself living in a modest little home somewhere between heaven and hell with a babe bouncing upon her knee. And a man – who looked a lot like this one – at her side. He'd be a strong and loving man who'd inspire feelings of calm and contentment with as little as a smile, a man just like Jack.

~

Kylee sighed deeply and a small moan escaped her. Not gone unnoticed by Jack, he arched around to gaze down upon his little imp and was quite pleased with himself for his rescue. She finally looked at peace.

'*What have I gotten myself into?*' he chuckled to himself, '*Nora was right, she really is a sweetling.*'

Jack decided that this would be a perfect chance to start over. 'Twas plain to see that the Kylee he'd met at the Ryan's was merely playing a role, and he was eager to find out why.

When the moon had climbed high in the night sky, and Jack was sure they hadn't been followed, he thought to find a warm bed for the night, and something hot to fill their bellies.

"There's an inn not far from here. I say we stop for the night," Jack suggested.

"Aye, I am cold and I'm famished," Kylee replied with a smile. And by God, he loved that smile of hers.

"Love, ye should've told me ye were hungry. We could've rested earlier."

"The need to get away from there was more important," she replied appreciatively. "Yer my hero, Jack Manning! Ye'll not hear a complaint out of me. Not my grumblin' stomach, the frost in my bones nor the aching in my backside could force an objection from me." Kylee batt her eyelashes, the humor in her voice, now something else Jack would crave.

He tossed his head back and laughed. "Aye. I hear ye. Loud an' clear, my sweet."

Jack ushered her inside a quaint little inn and asked the keeper for a room on the bottom floor, to ensure a quick escape if necessary. The man nodded his head, and silently passed the key to Jack and then winked at Kylee, making her blush with embarrassment.

Jack pinned the innkeeper with a stony glare. Kylee was not a girl for hire and she'd not be regarded as one either, dammit. "Get a fire in the hearth and some supper sent over to us, sir. 'Tis our weddin' night," he lied, foiling the man's implication. Jack turned to his faux bride. Her eyes were wide, her jaw slack, those perfect lips begging to be kissed. *She's either embarrassed or pissed as ol' hell.*

"Down the hall. To the right."

Jack merely smiled a dirty grin at the innkeeper, took Kylee's hand in his, and led her to their room. Once inside and the door had been firmly shut, Kylee stood in front of him, hands on her hips and a furrowed blonde brow.

"Why in Jesus' name did ye tell him that?" she asked, stomping her foot in annoyance. This was the side of Kylee that Jack had come to know, all too well. Her quick temper and heated expression made his blood boil with desire, yet, triggered an unquenchable thirst to tame her.

"Would ye rather him thinkin' that ye're some kind of common whore? Ye know how things are. Ye know what's proper and what ain't," Jack laughed. "Besides, can't a man dream?"

With a wink, Jack dismissed her, rummaging into his leather bag and drew from it, his note book. It would seem, the scrappy wench had lost her tongue. Jack took a seat at the writing desk while Kylee stood nervously and motionlessly in front of the hearth which had not yet been brought to life, staring into nothingness.

Just then, a knock fell upon the door. Jack lunged from the chair, his dagger fisted tightly in his grip. "Who is it?" he thundered.

"Ye needs yer fire lit, sir. And I got ye some supper from the kitchen," a young voice answered.

Jack slowly opened the door, allowing the young fellow to enter. He laid the tray of covered supper plates upon the writing desk, right on top of the note book, making Jack curse in exasperation. The boy quickly and apologetically put in the fire and then rushed out the door.

~

Kylee couldn't help but notice how Jack's discontent had made the lad nervous and edgy. She wondered if Jack imposed this kind of fear onto everyone he came into contact with. He certainly had a way of getting what he wanted and letting people know when he was displeased without having to say or do anything rash or ill-mannered. She admired that in him, as well.

"Come over here and eat yer supper, love," Jack kindly told her as he poured over the notes in the book. She done as instructed, placing herself at the corner of the desk and voraciously started in on her meal.

"What are ye readin'?" she asked, attempting to break the deafening silence.

"Notes that I made after I visited O'Shea's brewery," he replied, dismissively.

"What did ye find there?" she quietly asked, refusing to meet his gaze. Shame for ever having put up with all she'd endured seemed to bubble to the very edges of her being. "Did ye meet Gar? What happened?"

"Now, now, love. Don't fret. He didn't know who I was, but I learned so much about 'im. Would ye like to read my notes?" Jack asked, turning the book toward her and then started in on his own supper.

Kylee nodded, then craned her head to read the passages that he'd written.

'Garvan O'Shea: Drunkard, unkempt, ill-tempered. No respect for his father.

Fiona O'Shea: Polite hostess, mild mannered. How they're related is beyond me.' Kylee laughed at that part and looked up at Jack who was watching her intently.

"Read on," he quietly insisted. Her eyes darted back to the pages.

'Paddy O'Shea: Taken for granted, perhaps feels guilty for how the boy turned out. Will probably see an early grave.

Have to find Kylee. Witnessed an altercation between the father and son. Gar claims he doesn't know where she is but seems sure a meeting with her mother will resolve that.

He threatens to hurt her if he ever does find her. She'll be sorry she ever ran.'

Kylee felt the colour drain from her cheeks upon reading the last part, felt like the contents of her newly restored belly would come spewing out. She put her hand up to her mouth to keep the fear from escaping her lips, or to avoid vomiting. Garvan O'Shea would put an end to her if he could. Had she not realized his hate ran so deep before now?

When she regained some of her senses, and the fright within her started to subside, she looked up at Jack. Her eyes searched his for reassurance that Gar would never have the opportunity to follow through.

"Oh, now don't ye be worryin'. We're far enough from that bastard now, he won't be able to catch up this night." Jack stood, and then moved behind her trembling form and stroked her hair.

"What about tomorrow, Jack? And the day after that? I'll have to run forever, I just know it," she cried into her palms.

The warrior knelt at her side, taking her hand in his. "Nay. Seems to me, he's too wrapped up in himself to spend any more time than necessary lookin' for us. He'll move on to some other poor girl soon enough and torture her," Jack chuckled in attempt to make her feel better. But, Kylee knew Garvan better than most people. Leaving him would be considered a massive slight, a grand display of disrespect. He'd never stand for it. Aye, Garvan was coming for her. It was just a matter of when. When she neglected to offer her opposition on the matter, Jack added, "And besides, I'm gonna hide ye in the safest place I know of. I'm takin' ye to a place in Galway called The Haven. A friend of mine lives there. Her name is Emma. No one will ever suspect ye bein' there, for 'tis only Brady Kelly who knows of my affiliation with The Haven."

"*Her* name?" Kylee cocked her brow at that, almost entirely forgetting about Garvan O'Shea.

"Yes. A woman," Jack chuckled, but then became serious. "A very dear friend, Kylee. And I expect ye will show her yer gracious side, not yer wicked one," he stated with infinite authority.

"Wicked? That's the second time today ye've called me *wicked*." Kylee blew out, only slightly wounded.

"Well, isn't that how ye behaved at the Ryan's? Wicked?" he laughed watching her closely.

Kylee dropped her head, shame welling up inside her. It was time to explain herself, and she hoped he would understand.

She sighed. "Jack, the first time I laid eyes upon ye, I knew ye were different from anyone I had ever met. Ye took on that investigation with such confidence and authority, yet never lacked kindness and compassion." She rose from her chair and went to the hearth, staring down into the new flames and wondered how she was going to bring her feelings to light. This was the most humiliating admission she'd ever had to put into words. She continued after a short aching pause, "Somethin' stirred inside me when I felt yer eyes upon me, as if ye could see down into my soul. There was a severe and unruly attraction between us. Do ye deny it?" she asked, refusing to meet his gaze.

"Nay, I do not," he replied frankly, but with a roguish grin igniting his features. Kylee blushed and anxiously continued.

"And I, a chambermaid, betrothed to a violent, mean, horrible man, glimpsed for a tiny moment into the fantasy of havin' a man like ye at my side instead. But as soon as the impure thoughts entered my mind, they were pushed out by the realization of what Gar would do if he ever suspected betrayal or disloyalty. I feared for my safety, but what's more, the terror that filled my mind as I envisioned Gar harming ye, sent me straight over the edge.

"The only thing I could do, was to make ye hate me, make ye stop lookin' at me with those beautiful blue eyes." There, she'd said it, all of it. Regret and mortification overwhelmed her, and she reached out to brace herself on the mantle, as new tears surfaced.

Jack immediately rushed to her side, wrapping his strong arms around her. She could feel his hot breath on her neck, sending unfamiliar sensations through her.

"'Tis alright. I know ye're not really wicked. Shh…don't cry," he consoled.

"I'm so sorry for all the terrible things I said to ye, Jack. Ye have to know that I was tryin' to protect ye. But here ye are, puttin' yourself in danger. 'Tis like it was all for nothin'."

"Don't think like that. Why do ye think I'm here?" Jack whispered, pulling her head in close to rest upon his chest. "Foolish girl. I was drawn to ye from the first moment I cast m'gaze upon ye. Yer mean-tempered spirit caught my attention, but too, it haunted me.

"I know there's a spit-fire within ye, and I love that about ye. And when we learn all there is to know 'bout one another, I mean to take ye for my wife."

Kylee's heart thumped inside her chest so furiously, she found it hard to breathe. This man, who she'd dreamed of since the first time they met, was as infatuated with her as she was with him. But one problem still loomed between them.

"I'm still betrothed to Gar. He will search for me 'til the end of his days. Ye don't know him like I do. Ye say he'll move on to another, but 'tis simply not true," Kylee began to sob uncontrollably. She wrenched her body from Jack's affectionate embrace and slumped back into the chair. "Ye see, the only reason I was ever gonna marry him, is because my mother forced me to make such a union. We are very poor. We weren't always destitute, but since my father disappeared years ago, Mother worked her fingers to the bloody bone, just to keep us from starvin'. Then Garvan O'Shea came along."

Kylee took pause and watched intently as Jack went to his leather bag, retrieved a small decanter, opened it and downed a long swallow. When he passed it to her, she gulped down the potent liquid, causing her to cough and sputter, and then she wiped her lips with the back of her hand in a most un-lady-like manner.

"Continue, Kylee. I need to know everything," Jack urged.

"We'd heard stories of this Garvan O'Shea, and how much of a drunkard – and a mean one at that –

he truly was. Not one of the young ladies in his high society circle would even cast him a second glance.

"One night, while Ma was workin' as a chambermaid at an inn just down from O'Shea's, she caught sight of Garvan staggerin' down the street yellin' and screamin' in an intoxicated rage.

"Apparently, he was angry that his father would not agree to let him run the business, or in the event of his death, entrust it to him…not unless he married and settled down.

"That's when the idea struck 'er. I was about fifteen at the time; Gar was twenty-one. My mother thought she could trade me off. He needed a wife to get his inheritance. She needed a way out of the slums of Ireland," she sobbed.

"So, ye had to go along with the whole thing? Just a girl, ye couldn't very-well refuse, could ye?" Jack asked, sympathetically as he passed the liquor back to her again.

"Nay, I couldn't. Ye have no idea. The pressure of it all was nearly cripplin'. The only peace I could find was my work at Lady Ryan's. She gave me a room there, so I wouldn't have to live with my mother full time, and Gar couldn't get to me often."

"Why did ye go to the brewery the mornin' Gar pushed ye down the stairs, then? I mean, *'twas* Gar who pushed ye, wasn't it?" Jack asked.

"Aye, 'twas. Ye see, I received a message to return home immediately, that mother was distressed. So naturally, I did.

"When I got there, she was livid, screamin' at me. Gar had paid 'er a visit, threatened to cut us off and break off the engagement if I didn't show him the proper attention and respect he thought he deserved.

"He'd said the entire town was laughin' at him for bein' engaged for four, *long* years. And now that I was of a good age to bear children, we *should* be wed. I know he just wanted ol' Paddy to sign the papers givin' him control of the businesses."

Jack was appalled by her confession, by how the girl had been used and abused within her own family. What he wouldn't give to take her pain away, but unfortunately, all he could offer her was a strong shoulder and an attentive ear.

When *his own dirty little secret* came to light, he prayed she would be as understanding and accept him. He urged her on with a nod and placed his hand on her knee as a chaste sign of compassion.

Kylee fidgeted with a hem on her skirt pocket. "I hadn't realized it, but Gar was in the kitchen, waitin', and listenin' to the whole heated argument. He heard me when I told Mother I hated him and that he was a tyrant. That I knew he only wanted to marry me to get at his father's money, as no one else would have him.

"He became enraged, stormed into the sittin' room, and forced me to go with him. Mother did nothin' to stop him, as usual. She just kept sayin' it was for my own good and for the betterment of our survival," Kylee explained utterly tormented.

"And he took ye back to the brewery," Jack blandly concluded, trying to keep his own feelings and temper under control. If Garvan O'Shea was within one hundred miles of him, he'd put an end to his very existence.

"Aye, that's right. He kept me there the entire night, locked in his room, while he went downstairs and drank himself into oblivion. If anyone heard my pleas or me bangin' on the door, no one paid any mind. I was left to wait for his return, and I knew he'd be vicious when he did."

Kylee paced the room, holding her arms, rubbing as if she were still cold, despite the blistering heat roaring from the hearth.

"And when he did return? Please don't tell me he was inappropriate with ye," Jack said, horrified. The thought of another man having sullied her made his blood run hot, and anger smoulder within him.

Kylee laughed nervously.

"Nay, by the time he got back to the room, he could barely stand. He tried to tear my clothes away, he tried to be a *man*, but the ale had left him useless, thankfully. Then he passed out on the floor in front of the door.

"With my escape route blocked, I fell asleep in the chair by the hearth," she explained, with a small measure of vacancy and defeat in her eyes.

"I was startled awake by a savage Garvan who'd come-to with the memory of me refusin' him once again. When he was done shoutin' at me, shakin' me, he opened up the door and pushed me out to fetch 'im another tankard. Drawn to my freedom, I darted out. He must have sensed that I wouldn't return, and so he stalked after me like a savage beast after its prey. Thinkin' 'bout it still makes my skin crawl, Jack." Kylee stared out the window once again, unable to meet Jack's intense gaze. Were she able to look at him, no doubt, she'd detect the ticking of his jaw muscle, for he couldn't help but grind his teeth.

"I ran as fast as I ever had. But he caught me at the stairs, shoutin' that I wasn't to run from him. He called me a whore and accused me of spreadin' my thighs for other men. He said that I had been only punishin' him with my refusals."

When she turned again, Jack was shaking his head with clenched fists. "Continue, please," he said, lowly, his voice drenched with vehemence.

"I cursed him out…as ye know I can. I don't know what got into me, Jack. I'd just had enough. And the next thing I remember was Fiona screamin' in my face, tryin' to wake me," Kylee explained, now completely drained. "Then, they brought me to my mother's where Garvan had been waiting to pounce once again. He'd moved up the weddin' date. I fled the first chance I got, and ended up at Uncle Joe's place."

"He is a bastard, Kylee, and I swear ye will never have to lay eyes upon him again," Jack vowed. He went to her and placed an innocent kiss upon her cheek. "I know ye have suffered. It all stops now."

SEVEN

"Have ye heard from yer woman yet, Gar?" Paddy O'Shea asked his son, nonchalantly, while he studied the monthly figures. He hated broaching the subject, but Kylee hadn't been seen since the accident. Paddy had grown concerned for the girl's well-being and feared that Garvan had done the unthinkable.

Paddy wasn't oblivious to the fact that the engagement was for mere convenience for both Gar and the girl's mother, but what was he to do? All the old man ever wanted, was to see his boy settle down, and be fit to run things when he no longer could. When

Gar announced his betrothal to an impoverished and penniless girl, Paddy knew something was amiss.

He'd come to learn that the whole arrangement was made by the girl's mother, Siobhan, and that poor Kylee had wanted nothing to do with the brutish lad – like so many of the young ladies in the area. But Siobhan was more than willing to offer Kylee to Gar…for a price. Sometimes, the aching in Paddy's heart for this powerless girl was overwhelming.

He'd also noticed money missing lately, more than usual. He'd kept quiet about it, and like so many other misdeeds that Gar had committed, Paddy turned the other cheek. He first had suspected Gar of a gambling affliction, until Siobhan O'Roarke ceased working at the inn down the road and was seen on many occasions decked out in the finest women's fashion.

It was also common knowledge that when Siobhan's husband disappeared years before, the wealth he had achieved had vanished as well, leaving the woman destitute, forcing her to fend for herself and her babe.

There was no doubt that she had been accustomed to the finer things in life, but everyone knew she had sold everything of value, just to put food on her table. So, to now, all of a sudden, reappear in garb befitting a queen, was too suspicious.

Paddy had connected her new-found wealth to his son a long time ago, but still said nothing. The only thing that kept him from cutting Gar off entirely and leaving the whole works of it to his precious, yet meek daughter Fiona, was the prospect that Kylee could somehow change Garvan.

Paddy prayed that if Kylee could find the good in him, learn to love him, then Garvan might remember what it was like to be loved and learn how to return their love and respect.

He'd come to realize now, that it would never happen. Kylee was gone, and Gar hadn't sobered up long enough to even look for her. An irking feeling nagged in Paddy's mind. He wondered if Gar wasn't looking for his betrothed because he had done something unforgivable to her. It was time to sober the lad up.

"Well? I asked ye a question, boy. Have ye found Kylee? Or are ye even lookin' for 'er?" Paddy growled from behind his desk.

Garvan was lounging in a chair opposite his fathers, with his feet cocked up on the desk, causing mud flecks to pepper Paddy's ledgers.

"Nay, old man. The bitch can go to hell for all I care," Gar snarled through slurred speech.

"Ye know ye get nothin' if ye don't stop all this childishness. Ye have to settle down! Ye've seen twenty-five summers, yet still unmarried and a drunk. It's gotta stop!" Paddy roared, finding some semblance of the courage he once possessed.

Gar's father rarely confronted or chastised him, but the time had come for that to change. This was Gar's last chance. "What have ye done with the girl, Gar? I know ye had somethin' to do with her vanishin' into thin air! And I know her fallin' down them steps was no accident!"

"Ye know nothin', now shut the hell up! Perhaps she's got too much of her own father in 'er. Perhaps she'll never be seen again either!" Gar said, scratching at his five-day-old scruff in annoyance. Paddy rose from his chair, slamming his hands atop the desk.

"I swear to God in Heaven, Gar, if ye've done somethin' to harm her, I'm done with ye. Not only will ye never see any of the inheritance ye so desire, ye'll no longer be my son. I'll abandon all ties with ye. I'll go on with the rest of my life, forgettin' I ever had a son. Fiona deserves all of this anyway, and she'll get everything!"

That seemed to raise Gar's brow. Rising from his lounged position, he clapped his strong large hands over his father's ears, holding his head with a shaky fury-fueled grip. It was only a matter of whether or not Garvan chose to end him right then and there, and Paddy knew he was capable.

"Hear me now, ol' man! I don't know where she is, but if it's proof ye want, then 'tis proof ye'll get. When I find her and bring her back to ye, ye'll keep up your end of the bargain. I want what's mine by birth right. Ye'll retire and no longer keep me from runnin' things 'round here," Gar barked in his father's tense face, spittle splashing all over him. "If I bring the bitch back and marry 'er, do I have yer word that ye'll give in?"

Paddy nodded his head quickly but was speechless and very afraid.

"Very well. I'll find 'er. I'll bring her back here. Ye'll see. Ye'll be sorry, then," Gar shouted, releasing the quivering man, knocking him to the floor. "I'll rain hell down upon the lot of ye!"

'Jesus, why doesn't the boy just kill me?' Paddy thought, struggling to control his breathing, fixing his clothing before Fiona wandered by and witnessed the cowardly mess he'd been reduced to.

~

Infuriated that even his own father expected the worst, Garvan set his plan into motion the very next morning. If his own family suspected that he'd harmed Kylee, then the rest of Ennis probably did too. It wouldn't be long before the authorities were knocking on the tavern door in search of him. He'd have to find her, and he knew exactly where to start looking.

After he'd emptied the contents of the whiskey which usually took residence upon his night table, Gar washed and dressed for the day.

Siobhan would no doubt tell him anything she knew with regards to her daughter. She'd said in the past that the girl had been a burden for as long as she could remember. It seemed a good place to start.

Gar shaved and cleaned himself up, dressing in his finest for his visit with his O'Roarke wench. He always dressed his best when visiting his mistress.

As per usual, when he reached the meagre house, he didn't knock on the door. He walked on in like it was a place of his own.

Siobhan was still in her nightgown, as if she had only just risen from a long night's sleep. Her deep auburn hair hadn't been combed yet, but she looked well rested and fresh.

"Lover, 'tis been so long since I've seen ye. Where have ye been hidin'?" she drawled and then flung her long angelic arms around Gar's neck, kissing him deeply.

When Gar didn't return her affection, she withdrew and stared at him for a moment, bewildered.

"What's the matter?" she asked, taking him by the hand, leading him to her room.

"He's threatenin' to cut me off, Siobhan. To cut *ye* off, though he doesn't know it," Gar replied.

"Oh! Is that all? Gar, lover, that ol' goat's been sayin' that for years. All ye've ever heard is, "*Ye get nothing unless ye marry and settle down.*" 'Tis always the same. So, why are ye in such a foul mood over it now?" Siobhan asked, her eager fingers working the buttons on his trousers to free his manhood.

Gar's nerves were frayed. The confrontation with his father had left him wondering if maybe this time the old man would follow through.

"I think he's serious this time. And if that's not enough, he thinks I had somethin' to do with Kylee disappearin'," Gar replied, struggling against his craving for his lover of three years, now stroking his firm member.

Watching her please him caused an exhilarating wave of gratification. It was pure, ultimate satisfaction to know he could have the enchantingly striking mother while he lay claim over the sensual yet virginal daughter.

Siobhan laughed, and then took him into her mouth, leaving him breathless and gripping the edge of sanity.

Then, she looked up from below thick lashes. "Wonder what the ol' goat would do, were he to find out that the night she ran off, ye were snugly tucked into bed with me," she paused and then chuckled, "that would change his suspicions. Aye?"

"Well I can't tell 'im that, ye know I can't!" Gar shouted, lifting her off her knees and then tucked himself back inside his breeches. "Ye don't get it, do ye? I have to find 'er and bring her back to prove that she's alive. I'll lose everythin' if I don't. Do ye wanna go back to livin' in squalor?"

~

Gar paced the tiny bedroom, while Siobhan sat frozen on the bed, afraid to say or do anything that might provoke him to a violent tantrum. Her atrocious secret was that she didn't want the girl to return. Removing her competition meant that she could still keep her lover all to herself.

She loved Gar more than anything on this green Earth and for the most part, he was attentive and spoiled her ridiculously rotten.

It didn't matter that when he was drunk and in one of his moods, he often came to her to work out his frustrations, either with a good thrashing or tender love making. Despite his frame of mind, Siobhan took whatever he had to give.

Telling Garvan about her late husband's brother, Joe, who owned The Nest was a last resort. Her head was spinning.

'*What if Kylee knew about Joe, and was hiding there? Gar would bring 'er back and marry 'er. What if he fell in love with the little bitch? What if he chose her instead of me?*' Siobhan thought frantically, her top front tooth nearly drawing blood on her bottom lip. '*She should have met the same demise as her dear ol' daddy. Siobhan, yer such a fool!*'

Biting her evil tongue, she forced herself to remain quiet on that particular subject.

"Gar, if she returned, and ye married, would we keep our…*arrangement*?" she questioned quietly. Gar turned and faced her. Could he sense she wasn't telling him everything? His nostrils flared and the vein in his neck throbbed violently.

"Do ye know where she might be hidin'?" he asked, his body tense, hovering over her quivering form. Siobhan nodded with her head hung low, refusing to meet his thunderous gaze. Gar became instantly enraged. "Well, then tell me or I'll beat it out of ye, and ye know I will!"

Even though the fear of losing him was far greater than any punishment he could inflict upon her, she leapt from the bed, scurrying to put distance between them, but to no avail.

Gar caught her tousled locks and pushed her down onto the bed, straddling her tiny powerless body, encasing her with his meaty thighs. He held both her arms above her head with one thick fist, and she could feel his hot quick breaths on her face as he lingered for the answer. Using the only weapon she possessed, she strained her head upward to connect her lips with his, but was met with harsh rejection.

"No! Siobhan, ye'll tell me what I need to know, right now," he shouted, his voice thick with unspent wrath. Garvan possessed weapons of his own which weren't reserved for seduction, and planted a swift whack across her cheek. Another and another followed, until the lips that just moments ago were trying to kiss him were bloody and swollen. Tears trickled from the corners of her eyes, but she dared not look at him.

Then, the weight of his angry hands flew around her throat and squeezed, yet she kept her eyes firmly shut against the onslaught. '*He will not kill me. He loves me. He will not kill me,*' her tangled mind chanted, but when she chanced a glance at him, his face had taken a purple, violent hue, like storm clouds against a setting sun. Fear finally settled in and she knew what she had to do, even if it meant she'd lose him.

"She has an uncle," she sputtered, between tiny gasps of stale air. Garvan released his vicious hold, allowing her to continue. "He runs The Nest! I'm unsure if she even knows about him, for I kept their relation hidden all these years. But if she knows, she may have gone there," Siobhan trembled. "Please, Gar, don't do this. I told ye everything I know. Make love to me, but don't hurt me today," she cried, through a river of tears.

Her pleas fell upon deaf ears, for Gar's panic of losing his fortune turned to rage, and Siobhan took the brunt of every torrent.

"Make love to ye? After ye've been keepin' secrets from me? Ye'll be punished in a way ye've never dreamed of today, ye filthy whore," he growled, hauling her body from the bed as if she were weightless. She landed in the corner in a heap of terror and dread.

Siobhan shook her head, trying to regain her senses, but he was on her in an instant. Back-handed whacks landed wherever he could direct them. And then, the once beautiful night gown was torn from her body. The pure raw fury behind his eyes, was something she'd grown accustomed to, but today, she feared him like never before.

Evil radiated from every inch of him as his gaze trickled down her body – this deviant betrayer – with brooding intensity. To her horror, he licked his lips, and then shot her a crooked smile. She trembled uncontrollably, for she knew what came next. *Oh, dear God! He's enjoying this.*

Picking her up as if she were nothing more than a Fall leaf in the wind, he hurled her once again, back onto the bed. Garvan took from her, all she had left. He'd broken her body, he'd ravaged her mind, and this man who she'd adored so, had completely destroyed her soul.

Tasting his sweat mixed with her own blood on her lips as he rutted and manhandled her, her flesh seemed to turn to pulp beneath his fingers. She dared not cry out, even though her tears stung like hundreds of little bees attacking all at once.

When the weight of his huge form finally collapsed, pressing her into the mattress with brutal force, she couldn't help but to reach up and stroke his damp hair. This was how things were between them. Garvan, the hot-tempered dictator. Siobhan, his naughty little slave. But she realized now, trapped beneath his thumping heartbeat, that keeping information from him could've cost them everything. Her mind raced with culpability, regret and uncertainty tearing her apart. When her shaking hand slid from his hair to stroke the rigid planes of his back, Garvan rolled away.

Pulling the covers tightly to her chin, she stared into the flames licking the hearth stones, her mind reeling from the repercussions of what may happen, were she to lose him. Her gaze fell upon his cold profile as he rose and began to dress. She waited expectantly.

This was where he usually fell to his knees in her lap, professing his undying affection, swearing he would never let his temper inflict such punishment upon her again.

She patiently waited for her lover to come to her, only this time, the last thing she heard was coins clanging as they fell upon the dresser.

"For services rendered," Garvan growled icily, and then slammed the door behind him. Siobhan's attention turned to the closed door, the heavy thump of his every footfall causing her stomach to flip. She flinched when she heard the front door slam shut.

'*Someday he will love me. Whether he sees me as his whore or not, someday he will love me,*' she thought, curling up into a tight ball amongst the sweat and blood-sodden sheets.

And despite tonight's debauchery, she still refused to believe that Gar wouldn't someday marry her. Since the first time they'd made love, she dreamed of the day when he'd give up on Kylee and marry her instead.

The memory of it still burned fresh in her mind. Oft-times, it was the one thing she held on to.

As per Siobhan's invitation, Garvan had come to call on Kylee, but the girl's employment had whisked her away to Lady Ryan's estate. That morning, Siobhan had answered the door in her nightgown, as she so often did, but Gar was very drunk, and it seemed, noticeably aroused at the sight of her.

Siobhan was thirty-three at that time and still as beautiful as she'd been when she first married

Kylee's father at the tender age of sixteen. Not even giving birth to Kylee a year later had diminished her slender build. She had always been proud of that fact. And now, here she was in her prime, still exuding femininity, oozing with seduction. Like a forbidden fruit, Garvan craved the taste of her right from the start.

"Kylee's not at home, Mr. O'Shea," Siobhan had hummed.

"Oh, well, I could come in and wait for her, if ye don't mind," Gar replied, undressing her with a hungry gaze as if his mind's eye could see so clearly what lay beneath the near-to-sheer satin gown.

His eagerness, coupled with her own loneliness and longing to have a man in her bed, over-ruled her better judgement. She kept quiet about Kylee not returning until the end of the week and invited the brute in. And so began a most torrid affair, which always left her longing for more.

Siobhan blew out a long sigh as she reflected how tender he'd been that first night. And despite the fact that he was as drunk as she'd ever seen any man and reeked of cheap liquor and cigars, he'd taken her to the moon and back with pleasure.

'And now, after all this time, he treats me like some sleazy strumpet?' she thought, feeling used and dejected. Siobhan detested Kylee at this moment. Hers was a hatred that no mother should ever feel for their child. But it was there, thick, and tangible. She could taste it. And despite his callous departure, all she wanted was for Gar to return, without Kylee.

~

When Garvan entered The Nest, all eyes fell upon him. He knew immediately that Kylee had sought refuge in this hovel. It was written all over the faces which were now ogling him. He went wild inside. The need to exact his revenge on anything or anyone in his path took over the little measure of rational thought left in his brain.

'She'll rue the day she ever fucked with Gar O'Shea. Run from me, will she? When I get a hold of

'er she'll wish she was dead,' he thought furiously, examining the room, where the mostly male patrons had uncomfortably gone back to their womanising and drinking. He spied the bar, which doubled as the front counter for the inn, and watched as a thick-bellied man tried his best to scurry away unnoticed.

With a deep thunderous bark, Garvan commanded everyone's attention. "Where's the uncle of one Kylee O'Roarke?" he shouted, scrutinizing each and every man's expression. The uncle's identity was quickly given up when one poor lad's eyes shifted toward the swinging double door, the place where the portly man had been standing only moments ago.

Gar rushed toward it, without saying another word. The mood in The Nest shifted as all ears were listening, waiting for the outburst that the stranger would no doubt provide. Before disappearing through the door in search of the elusive uncle, Gar turned his attention back to the hushed room.

"Leave! All of ye…out!" he commanded, and then limbed the bar-top with his gigantic sweaty arm. The ladies hurried upstairs, while the men ran for the exit to protect themselves from the vicious animal who threatened their very existence.

Gar tramped through the door like a rabid wolf, seeking, searching for its new play-thing.

Just as the man's foot made first contact with the bottom step of the rear stair case, Garvan caught a thick fist of his shirt collar. "And where do ye think yer goin', old man? Ye have some talkin' to do," Gar snarled, pulling Joe backward, his hands flying to the back of his neck defensively.

"O'Shea, I've nuthin' to say to ye. What's this about?" Joe trembled.

"Ye're the uncle, aye? Ye know very well why I'm here. Now tell me what room she's in."

"I…I dunno what yer talkin' 'bout. If 'tis a woman ye seek, Garvan, I'm sure I can send for one of my best," Joe nervously sputtered. He might've been trying his best to feign ignorance, but Gar was on to him. It was almost as if the sorry bastard had been expecting this. If he was forced to beat the ever-living truth out of the pitiful lout, then by-Jesus, that's exactly what Gar intended to do.

The first of many blows came to the man's pudgy middle, knocking the wind from his lungs.

"Tell me where she is," Gar demanded through clenched teeth. "I swear I'll beat ye to death. Or I could just tear this place down plank by plank, yer choice. What room?"

"She's…she's not here. I swear to it. She ain't here no more," Joe fretfully replied, infuriating Gar-van senseless. He back-handed the poor old fellow, sending him flying, and then another and another, un-til Joe was backed into the corner.

"What do ye mean, she ain't here *no more*? Where has she gone? Ye better start explainin'!" Gar lay such a beating on Joe that his face began to swell and bleed. Just as Joe's world faded to black, his life-less body beginning to slack, Gar took pause to pull the man to his feet, staring him down, eye to grisly eye.

"Had enough yet?" Gar smirked.

"I'll never tell ye, ye bastard. Get the hell out," Joe groaned, spewing bloody spittle all over his opponent's boots. Gar saw red.

Reaching into his overcoat pocket, Garvan withdrew a pistol. He held the shiny weapon with a steady firm hand, and pressed the barrel against Joe's temple.

"How about now? Ye think ye can find the words now, old man?" Gar knew this was extreme, but he also knew he had nothing to lose. If he didn't make Joe talk, he'd never find Kylee. If he didn't find her, he'd never inherit, and he would be forever blamed for her disappearance anyway.

Gar pulled back the hammer.

"Stop! O'Shea! I'll tell ye what ye want to know!" shouted a female voice from the top of the stairs.

Gar looked up the narrow staircase to find a trembling and distraught woman frantically waving her arms. He lowered the gun, as his gaze fixed on her.

"No, Allaine, ye mustn't tell him anythin'. He's dangerous, he'll kill her!" pleaded Joe. The battered man attempted to get to his knees, but Gar held his shoulder, immobilizing him.

Garvan gestured with his hand for Allaine to emerge from her hiding place upstairs. When she reached the bottom landing, she rushed to Joe's side, and fretfully assessed his injuries.

"I'm so sorry I let him beat ye like this, Joe. I thought you'd cave before it got this bad," Allaine cried.

"'Tis alright, m'love. But please, don't tell 'im anything," Joe whispered. Gar pulled the girl from Joe's weary embrace and turned her to face him.

"What of Kylee O'Roarke?" Gar growled.

"Jesus Christ! Let me go," Allaine began, but twisting and fighting Gar was no use. He was too strong, towering over her like a stone pillar. Then, as the gun waved in front of her face, she opened her mouth and the words came tumbling out. "A few days ago, a man from Galway arrived in search of her. When he found her here, he took her away. That's it."

"Away? Where?" Gar's patience was at a breaking point.

"I said he was from Galway, didn't I? For all I know he could've taken 'er back there or to the moon," she spat, but her smart-ass remark didn't gain her Gar's favour, only a stinging whack across her cheek with the shiny revolver. She held her face in her hand, shooting him the most loathsome death-stare possible, but when he returned it, she hauled in her horns, and recoiled.

"A name. Gimme a name." Gar growled fiercely.

"Jack Manning," she whispered.

"Oh, Allaine! What have ye done?" Joe whimpered, and then collapsed onto a heap on the floor.

Allaine put her head down, and tended to Joe's beaten body, weeping over his bruises, leaving droplets of tears to sting the lacerations.

Outside The Nest, Gar drew in a breath of triumph. "I guess Galway it is!" he laughed aloud.

EIGHT

That first night Kylee spent with Jack, all alone in the little inn playing newlyweds, left her feeling a sense of trust and safety she hadn't ever felt before.

Despite the fact that her safety was always Lady Ryan's first priority, and Kylee sensed that her employers would move heaven and hell to protect her, this was the first time she *felt* safe and completely at peace.

When Jack vowed that no one would ever hurt her again, not her mother and certainly not Garvan O'Shea, she believed him.

She raptly watched as her mysterious saviour slept, curled up in an arm chair next to the hearth with his pistol lodged across his knee.

Kylee wanted so much to get out of bed, crouch next to him and study his handsome features, but she knew his eyes would spring open if she even stirred.

So, she forced herself to stay as still as she could and beheld him from afar. She fantasized about marrying him and what their children would look like, both of them being fair-skinned and golden-topped.

'*Silly, girlish thoughts. What if he doesn't want children?*' she scolded herself, but then giggled at the mere thought of *how* those children would be made.

Kylee licked her lips as the mere imaginings of his kiss watered her mouth. She'd never in her life experienced the sensation of lust, but here it was, creeping up inside her like a growing vine, uncontrolled and feral.

She watched as his blonde lashes flickered. A smile ignited her face when his brows furrowed, obviously dreaming of something very profound. She knew she would never tire of watching this brute of a man sleep.

The next morning, when Kylee awoke, the room was empty. Jack no longer occupied the chair, nor did flames lick the bricks within the hearth. She thought long and hard whether or not she should leap from the bed and make a dash to relieve herself, but when she realized she could see her own breath, she decided to cuddle back down beneath the covers and wait for him to return.

'Where could he be at this hour?' she wondered as she shivered in the middle of the saggy duck-down mattress.

Just as she found herself drifting back to sleep, the door swung open with a crash, startling her. Jack hollered his good morning with cheery conviction. Kylee relaxed with a sigh.

"Love, 'tis freezing in here. I'll put in a fire. Or would ye prefer if I come over there and warm ye myself?" he grinned devilishly, making Kylee blush and pull the covers back up over her cheeks to hide her embarrassed glow.

Jack chuckled and placed a plate of toast, fried pork-side and fresh fruit next to her on the table and handed her a mug of piping hot liquid. She raised it to her nose and let the coffee aroma fill her nostrils. She was delighted that he'd been so considerate.

"Ye must eat all your breakfast. 'Tis important for ye to keep up yer strength while we travel. We must be prepared if O'Shea is in pursuit, for we may have to go into hidin', and the old roads can be tough," Jack smiled, easing her worry, but added, "nice meals like this could be near impossible."

As she devoured her breakfast in silence, she couldn't help but consider how easy it was to be there with him. If he told her to eat her breakfast, then she'd do it. If Jack asked her to traverse the hot rocks of the sun, she'd burst into flames trying. And all because someone finally cared enough to tend to her for a change.

When she was done filling her belly, Jack took the plate from her lap, and sat beside her on the bed.

"How are ye feeling today, wicked Kylee? Did ye sleep well?" he asked, tucking a wayward strand of golden hair behind her ear.

"I slept well, thank ye. And I feel much better now, after eatin' and now that the fire is blazin' again. Where did ye go so early?" she asked, watching him absorbedly, studying the way his mouth moved when he spoke. This man mesmerized her.

"I went down to the kitchen to wait for breakfast is all," he replied, placing a kiss upon her free hand.

~

In reality, Jack had gone back into the forest, visiting a few hidden camps that Kylee hadn't noticed along their way. Friends, or more so, retired colleagues of his were living out their days all along the road from Ennis to Galway, in the peace and tranquillity that nature offered.

He could always count on these men to take note of each and every passer-by, so it made sense to pay them a visit to inquire if anyone had seen a man meeting Garvan O'Shea's description.

At the first camp, the frail old man hadn't seen anyone or anything out of the ordinary but was pleased to see Jack. And of course, make a merry tease regarding the *pretty passenger* he'd noticed tucked into the shelter of Jack's arms the day before.

After an hour of sipping black tea, laughing and listening to his old friend gripe about his declining health, Jack quickly shook the man's hand and bid him farewell.

Jack met with two more of his former brothers, but the stories were much the same as the first. No one had seen Gar or anyone else on the road since Jack and Kylee had passed them the day before.

'One more visit and I have to make it quick. I must return to her before she wakes,' Jack thought as he pushed Conan to a full gallop deep into the forest.

When Jack's friend answered the door of his tiny hidden log cabin, the whiskers of his long moustache turned upward with a smile and his grey eyes gleamed with joy.

"Jack Manning! Come on in, my boy!" Peter Dooley said, gruffly slapping Jack on the back, almost knocking him over.

"How've ye been, Peter?" Jack asked, secretly hoping that *this* friend hadn't become as cantankerous and ailing as the others had been.

"Ah, life's been great! The fishin' and huntin's been good to me. I'm lovin' my retirement. Although, a good dagger fight wouldn't go astray here lately," Peter laughed. "What brings ye back here? 'Twas you I spied yesterday mornin' with a wee lass atop yer steed, wasn't it?"

"Aye, and I have her tucked safely at an inn for now. We're makin' our way home," Jack said, rubbing the back of his neck, trying to rub away his anxiousness to get to the point, and get back to her.

"Have ye seen anyone on the road after us? Say, a rather large, slob of a fella' with bright red hair?"

"She's in danger, eh?"

"Aye, she is. I need to know if we've been followed."

"Nay, I can't say I've seen anyone. But if I do, I'll get a warnin' to ye. I'll send it on up the line," Peter replied. "Now go, get back to yer woman. Keep 'er safe."

"Thanks, Peter. I will. Yer brother, Marin, still occupies a camp just outside town, aye? So, if ye see anyone of interest headin' in my direction, get word to him. I'll check in with him when I get her settled in back home."

The two men shared a fleeting embrace, as comrades do, and then Jack left again, kicking Conan's haunches almost cruelly to set the expeditious pace.

Jack realized that he'd been gone half the night, and that when Kylee awoke, she would most likely be cold and hungry. He felt a pang of regret that he hadn't paid the blubbering young lad who'd ignited the fire the night before to creep in and make sure it hadn't gone out.

But could I trust him? Jack shook off the regret, for he would trust no one with Kylee, except for one. *I have to get her to Emma's. Then Brady and I can get a hold of this Gar bastard and put an end to 'im.*

When he returned to the inn, Jack was relieved to find her still nuzzled into bed. He'd ensure her safety, no matter what the cost, and if he could, he would achieve it without sending her into a frenzy of disquiet and nervousness. For that reason, he'd decided not to tell her where he'd been or that he'd been awake since he'd first heard her faint sounds of slumber.

"Didn't ye have any breakfast?" she sweetly asked. But the truth was, that Jack had grabbed the first plate that the cook had served up in the kitchen and rushed back to the room with it for her.

"Aye, I did. I picked a little when I was chattin' with the cook. Nice old fella' he is," Jack lied again.

He kept assuring himself that the little lies didn't matter if they kept her happy and feeling safe.

However, the truths he'd been hiding since adolescence caused the greatest angst and insecurity.

Once they arrived at Emma's, he would have to leave explicit instructions, lest Kylee ever learn of his sordid past and dominating tendencies.

He wanted to explore and introduce his lifestyle to her himself, not have her shocked and turned off by whatever she might witness at Emma's.

'It would have been so much simpler if I could just bring her to Brady and Violet's,' he sighed inwardly. But he could never put the responsibility on Brady and Violet or put their happy home in danger.

Bringing her to Emma's place was the best choice, for no one would ever think to look for Kylee there. Nonetheless, the practices performed at Heathen's Haven would have to be kept from Kylee. Jack shuttered at the thought of her finding out the truth.

"Will we be leavin' here soon?" Kylee asked sweetly.

"Aye, as soon as ye're ready, we can set out again, but dress warmly, for 'tis snowin' and the winds are up," he replied with a smile.

"Alright. Where will we be tonight?" she yawned and then stretched her arms high above her head.

"We'll be a day's ride from home. So, we'll need to stay at another inn and put on the pretence that we're husband and wife again," Jack grinned, pulling her gently from the bed. He wrapped his strong arms around her and engulfed her mouth with his. He'd been dying to taste her lips since the first time they met. "But I'm hopin' that it won't be just an act of fancy for very long."

"Jack Manning? Are ye proposin' to me proper? I mean, ye keep sayin' that ye mean to take me for yer wife, but not once, have I heard ye come out and ask me!" Kylee brazenly stated, coyly pushing him away and then made a circular motion with her finger for him to turn away from seeing her in her night-gown.

'*Brazen little imp*,' Jack thought with amusement. He turned his back to her, but for just a moment.

"Well, I can propose to ye all proper-like if ye need me to, but 'tis no matter, ye'll do as yer told anyway," Jack laughed and then spun around, landing a soft swat to her backside.

"Jack! Turn around for Christ sakes! I want to dress without ye lookin'," Kylee shouted light-heartedly. But, Jack *was* looking, and his loins tightened with appreciation of every exposed curve. She was truly magnificent, in every way.

Jack had had many women beneath him, on top of him, and in every situation imaginable. Yet, none were as beautiful and enchanting as Kylee was, standing there, holding a thick blanket up to her breasts in attempt to conceal her state of undress.

And there it was. Innocence. It was what made her so special. His mind drifted for a moment to what would happen when he robbed her of all that innocence. Would she come freely, or would she need a little *motivation*? The notion of using pleasure as well as discipline to mould her into a willing submissive made his trousers uncomfortably tight. He wanted nothing more than to taste, kiss and even spank every inch of that pretty flesh.

Exasperated, Jack went to the wash basin and splashed freezing cold water on his face, and let Kylee disappear behind the curtain.

When she emerged, dressed for the day in a thick tweed dress and matching overcoat, Jack gasped at her beauty. Enveloped in deep blue material, she appeared quite regal. With her long soft blonde curls framing her face and her natural air of elegance, she could easily pass for royalty.

"Well, then, let's get back on the road. I'd like to reach the inn before dark," Jack choked out, struggling to pack his things into his leather bag, but it was damn-near impossible to ignore the urges this beauty brought about. The little fox smiled sweetly and led him out of the room.

'Tis gonna be a long day.

~

If Jack had known Kylee had been fantasizing about him they would never have left the room, that was a certainty. She had noticed his licentious and shameful stares, but guarded her reaction to his un-yielding advances. The fact that his very presence caused an aching so very deep within her, was her secret to keep. For now.

Astride Conan's back once again, Kylee cuddled into her saviour, shielding her face from the burning wind, and to be as close to him as possible. Aside from knowing he was loyal, considerate and under-standing, she knew very little about who Jack Man-ning really was. She sensed he was passionate, and if driven, could impose fear into anyone deserving of it. He reminded her of some hero from a folk-tale she'd heard when she was a little girl. He exuded confidence and bravery.

'*Is this who he truly is? Everyone's hero?*' she swooned with a sense of pride that this courageous soldier was hers – if he ever got around to properly proposing.

Then, as if he'd read her mind, Jack stopped and dismounted, pulling her down after him. He held her closely and pressed his cold lips to hers, warming them instantly. His brawny arms were wrapped so tightly around her, heat began to bubble within, making her forget that winter was nipping at her bones. He pulled away, stroking her cheek with his thumbs, his gaze clouded with uncertainty and a need for acceptance.

"Kylee, I've never met anyone like ye. You're as beautiful as a mornin' sunrise and as mysterious as the stars in the sky at night," he started, his tongue darting out to wet his bottom lip, and continued, "Bein' a perfect gentleman hasn't always been my strong suit, love, but 'tis time I ask ye the question that's been burnin' b'tween us.

"I wish to witness all marvels of this earth and life thereafter with ye by my side, as my wife, if ye'll have me," Jack whispered, his hand now grazing her nape, breathing his hot carnal breath down her neck. "Will ye, Kylee? Will ye be my wife?"

Kylee's pulse quickened, her knees buckled. Not just because of his proposal, but for his proximity. His signature male scent scattered her brain. This was what she'd dreamed of her whole life. His was a proper proposal, from a man whom she adored, not an *arrangement* made by her mother. Jack had done it just right.

"Aye, Jack. I will. I'll be yours forever," she replied breathlessly.

Jack smiled, kissing her gloved hands one at a time. "Please don't be so eager to say yes, m'love. We have much to talk about before I can let ye marry the likes of me. And once ye've learned all there is to know, ye might want to change yer mind. Do ye understand?" he asked, looking deep into her eyes, as if he was gauging her reaction. He seemed to swallow a thickness growing in his throat, but then added, "And I'll understand if ye do change yer mind, Kylee, ye have to know, I'll understand."

Kylee felt the colour drain from her rosy cheeks. "What are ye talkin' about?" she snapped, her perfect moment tragically ruined by the diversion.

"Now, please don't go gettin' upset. 'Tis a fact that we know very little about one another. I want ye to have no regrets when ye walk down the aisle," Jack said as he kissed her again, making her toes curl and forget she was annoyed, salvaging her precious moment. "Tonight, we'll have a nice talk over supper. I want to know everything about ye. And wouldn't ye like to know who yer gettin' tangled up with?" he chuckled, beaming with that charming smile of his.

"Alright. Tonight," she yielded with a sideways grin. There was something special about Jack Manning. It made her so pliable. Whatever this enigma was, also made her want him so much. He could make her forget to breathe if he wanted to.

Late into the evening, a cottage came into view with a bright amber glow bursting through the darkness. They had gotten behind schedule, and were freezing cold, hungry and weary from riding throughout the day.

Kylee was anxious to dismount and get into the cottage, but more because of the conversation she anticipated than for her exhaustion.

She sensed that Jack was hiding something, yet it was something he wanted to get off his chest before they became man and wife.

'*Why would I change my mind, Jack? I've been waiting for ye my whole life,*' she thought with complete adoration as her gaze never shifted from him.

A young woman working the counter of the inn greeted them with a smile and walked the pair to their room.

"Here ye go, Jack. Let me know if ye need anything. The fire's been put in about an hour ago just in case someone found themselves needin' a warm place to get out of the cold. Enjoy," she said and then left, swinging her voluptuous hips all the way down the hall. Kylee wanted to scratch the brazen wench's eyes out.

"Ye know her, I assume?" Kylee hissed.

"Aye, I do," Jack smiled, refusing to elaborate. He should know by now, even in the short time they'd known one another, Kylee wasn't one to let things slide. Especially when it came to other women in Jack's world.

"How exactly, *do* ye know her?" Kylee asked as Jack opened the door, ushering her inside.

"Are we gonna have to go over this every time ye find I've befriended another woman?" Jack sighed.

"I just don't understand how a man like ye can have so many *lady friends*. I've never heard of such a thing," Kylee snapped back.

Jack grabbed Kylee's shoulders, causing her to flinch. She knew how this usually went. She'd lose her temper, and then feel his wrath. Gar had done it so many times before. She braced herself.

Closing her eyes, steadying herself for the onslaught of abuses and profanities to begin, she hadn't been prepared for what came instead.

"Shh, my wicked Kylee," Jack whispered, trailing kisses from her temple to her chin, cradling her in his arms. "No matter who any woman is, or ever was, there will never be, any as lovely as ye. Ye've captivated my heart and soul. Now and forever."

She opened her eyes to meet his devoted gaze. He'd vowed to never hurt her and she almost trusted that he'd keep his promise…almost. Gar had left so many scars.

"Now then," he smiled, dismissing her inquisition, "let us get settled in and we'll go to the kitchen and see what the cook has prepared for supper."

"A…Aye," she stuttered shakily.

Kylee couldn't catch her breath. What an unusual sensation, fear and lust all at once. Moving to the wash basin, she washed her face, and then fixed her hair in the mirror. She liked the way his affection looked all over her face. For the first time in her life, she felt like a woman.

When they'd been seated at the kitchen table, the woman from earlier, lit a fancy lamp between them, and then served hot bread with fresh butter. She curt-sied at the doorway and took her leave. Kylee still didn't want the wretched beauty even looking at her man, but she held her tongue.

"Now, love, where do we begin? There's so much I want to know about ye," he started. "Did ye always live in Ennis?"

Kylee bit back her jealousy and returned to the moment, with Jack watching her through the soft glow of the lamp, his bright eyes dancing with the reflection of the low flame.

"Aye, I was born there. I lived between there and Ardnacrusha with the Ryan's, until ye came and swept me away," she replied sassily, making Jack chuckle. "My father was originally from Dublin, but he remained in Ennis after he fell in love with Ma."

"And where is yer father now?" Jack asked, care-fully. It dawned on her that she had never mentioned her father before. Perhaps Jack thought it might be a sore subject, and his cautious demeanour was the re-sult of that.

Kylee nibbled on a piece of bread. "No one knows. Some say he ran off with another woman, while others say my mother nagged him to death," she laughed uncomfortably. "Where ever he is, I just hope he still thinks of me."

"I'm sure he does. I mean, *I* can't think of anything else," Jack praised. "The picture you carry with ye, 'tis of him?" he asked. Kylee nodded, renewed despair surfacing.

"If I could vanquish that pain in yer eyes, I would," he said, his gaze flickering from eye to eye, his concern genuine.

"He was a linens manufacturer, and a successful one. We didn't always live like we do. We once had a nice home and lovely things, but when he disappeared, so did the money. After that, Ma worked as a chamber maid for any inn that needed her, and she was fortunate to have gotten on regularly at one of them." Kylee took a long gulp of red wine, and then asked, "What about you, Jack? Where are yer people from?"

"We're all from Galway. My Ma was a wonderful, lovin' mother to my sisters and I. Father was a military man who was always off on some assignment. We just call him *The Major* now, but in truth, I don't call him anythin'. He and I haven't spoken in years."

"Oh, Jack! That's awful. Doesn't it hurt ye? I know if my Da were around, I'd be as close with him as I could."

"Aye, it used to hurt, but the constant reminder of his disappointment in me hurt much worse," he painfully replied and then oddly, changed the subject. "How was your childhood then, any happy memories? What are the things that makes ye most happy and at peace?" A grin pulled at her mouth. If Jack could read her mind, he would see that it was him who made her happy now.

"When I was too little to go to work, I helped Ma take care of our little house. After all my chores were done, I always found a corner to cuddle into with a book. Because I wasn't able to go to school, I asked

Ma to teach me to read. In the early days, after Da disappeared, she'd come home from a hard day at the inn and still find time to go over the letters with me. Those were my best days," Kylee sighed, "but then she grew tired of comin' home from work to teach me, or even spend time with me. No matter though, I'd learned enough to teach myself the rest."

"And so, ye spent yer days alone, takin' care of the house, and gettin' lost in books," Jack acknowledged, and Kylee nodded, daring to gaze into his eyes. Instead of the pity she thought she might find there, his loving gaze beamed with pride.

"My time daydreamin' promptly ended however, when I turned an age where I could work. I was only eleven or twelve when the Ryan's hired me. Even though I was merely a babe, that saint of a woman saved me from the workhouse. That was Ma's favorite threat – she'd send me to the workhouse. I was so grateful when Lady Ryan took me on. I moved in with them right away and I didn't have to watch Ma drown herself in wine and self-loathing."

"That's when yer mother gave up workin'?"

"Nay, not 'til a few years later, when Garvan O'Shea came into our lives, and ye know all about that." Kylee replied, her shoulders sagging, a frown replacing her jovial expression. The shame of putting up with Garvan's abuses for so long would haunt her to be sure.

~

His meal finished, one hunger sated for the time being, Jack kicked his legs beneath the table and sat back. The sad defeated change in her countenance made him uneasy. *Would there ever be a time when Garvan O'Shea ceased to plague this pretty lass?*

He raised a glass of ale to his lips and took a long draught. "Well. We don't have to talk about that part, but we can talk about the future," Jack said, his nerves boiling over. *Do I tell her? Do I keep it from her? She'll have nothin' to do with me, if she doesn't understand?* And so, again, Jack lost the courage to talk about his primal inclinations, his odious past and his connection to Heathen's Haven. "What do ye see in *our* future?"

Kylee straightened her shoulders but sighed wistfully. "I just want a simple life, where the man I'm married to loves and cherishes me. I want to feel trust and adoration in him. I want a man who makes me feel complete," she quietly whispered with an un-focussed, yearning stare.

Jack took her hand, stroking her palm with his thumb. "I promise to make ye feel all those things and more. What about children?" he asked. Kylee's eyes shot up and stared into his for a moment. Was she wondering which was the right answer? There were no correct answers when it came to her future, for whatever made her happy, Jack would make a re-ality.

"I want children." she said, trying to pull her hand away from his grasp. The fact that Jack was a guardsman for the Kelly's, and one who seemed to travel quite a bit, perhaps she didn't think he would want to be tied down with a large family. Even as she attempted to pull her hand free from his unyielding grip, he held on tight. If the sudden panic glistening in her eyes was any indication, she thought exactly that.

Jack cast her a cheeky grin and asked, "How 'bout a dozen? Will that suit ye?" When her lips curled upward, Jack rose from the table, and planted a kiss on the top of her golden head. "As many as ye want, Kylee. I told ye, whatever it takes for me to live the rest of my days with ye, I'll do it, and love every minute," he added.

NINE

Jack and Kylee strolled back to their room arm in arm. Their conversation over supper hadn't ended at the table, but expanded into the night as they made plans for their future together.

Kylee was overjoyed with the prospect of becoming Mrs. Jack Manning, picturing their modest little home, filled with the cacophony of little feet scampering about. It seemed, the future was boundless with promises of a fulfilling and happy life.

While Jack promised her no great wealth of all things material, he had promised her a life filled with joy and contentment. She would never again feel the wrath of evil or the humiliation of being used and abused. All she could ever want in life, was strolling alongside her, holding her slight hand in his rough calloused one. She was ready to put her life in Ennis behind her, including her mother, and sadly, Lady Ryan. Those were sacrifices she'd gladly make in to be with Jack.

Garvan O'Shea would become just a dreadful memory, one she would never have to think about again.

~

Jack on the other hand, was in absolute torment. On three or four occasions, he'd tried to broach the subject of love making and how his version of it differed from most men's. But he'd been unable to find the words. Kylee was an innocent who still possessed her maidenhead, and for that reason, he'd decided to let the subject rest until they were wed.

I could let that part of myself go. Then I'd never have to tell 'er.

The anguish of keeping his secret was eating him alive, but if it meant he'd lose her, he'd bury that part of himself as deep into his soul as he could, lock it away and swallow the key.

'Perhaps hidin' her at Emma's isn't the best idea,' he thought, conflicted, but he knew it was his only choice.

"Are ye ready for bed?" Jack asked as he caught her trying to stifle a yawn.

"Aye, I am. 'Tis been a long day, and I'm eager to look fresh and renewed when we arrive in Galway tomorrow," she sighed.

Capturing her hand in his again, he led her to their little room and closed the door behind them. The fire was blazing and the bed covers had been turned down. Jack poured himself a glass of whiskey while Kylee disappeared behind the curtain to change into her nightshift, leaving him alone and tortured by his chaotic insecurities.

Kylee's melodic voice sang from behind the curtain, "Ye have to turn around. I'm only wearin' my nightgown." *Dammit all to hell!* In an instant, Jack was behind there with her, holding her tight, gazing down into her soft turquoise eyes.

"I've seen ye in yer night gown," he rumbled through a devilish smile. "And besides, ye haven't the need to hide from me, Kylee. We'll be married as soon as we can, and I want to see ye. All of ye," Jack whispered, struggling for a breath of air.

She murmured something low and inaudible, wrapping her slender arms around his thick shoulders, accepting his kiss. The fact that she hadn't refused him, quickened his pulse and kicked his blood up a notch.

Taking her hand, he walked her to the edge of the bed and then he sat down, with her standing between his thighs. His hands slid from her arms, down to her navel, where they lingered there, palming her hips and tummy. He couldn't take his eyes off her. His fingertips grazed the outside of her thighs and then mimicked the path back up against the satiny flesh inside.

The tiny sound that escaped her lips stopped him momentarily, for these were forbidden places. Her eyes were filled with uncertainty, an inner conflict, yet she still didn't resist.

Jack stroked his fingers along the cleft between her legs, wishing away the fabric barrier between his gentle touch and her soft needy skin.

When Kylee's hands flew into Jack's hair, her fingers painfully twisted and grasped, forcing a low and indulgent moan from his throat.

'*She likes to play rough,*' Jack thought with amused approval and then reached for the hem of her nightgown and began hitching it upward.

Every inch closer to baring her, was one step closer to having her. In every sense of the word.

Leaning in, he kissed the silky flesh of her inner thigh. Kylee's lithe body arched back, giving him more access, while pulling and grabbing at his blonde locks.

"Ohhh! Jack," she cried as his hands found her bare buttocks. Round and full, yet firm. Jack knew he should stop, but he couldn't bring himself to break the connection just yet. Sliding his hand beneath the cotton shift, he ran his calloused thumb across her taut nipple, making her squirm and pant with need.

When he slid the nuisance nightshift up past her navel, nearly baring her lush breasts, he hesitated.

Perfect little submissive. The notion hit him in waves of both exhalation and disappointment. Upon his honour he could not drive her to madness – could not allow her to relinquish her innocence. Not until they were properly wed. Having her there before him and so willing, tore at the very fabric of his entire being.

Suddenly, something shifted in her gaze, reminding him how innocent she really was. Her eyes glistened with unshed tears, her torrent of emotion causing him to pull away.

"We can't do this!" Kylee breathlessly cried, and then quickly retreated behind the curtain. Her sobs cut through the heat between them, his heart pounding furiously. '*I pushed her too far, too soon,*' he realized, his head falling to his chest with regret.

His wretched guilt for having sullied her perfect flesh with his advances had him up off the bed, seeking her out to offer any consolation he could muster. Peeking behind the curtain, he found her crouched like a little girl in hiding, covering her face with trembling hands. Lifting her head, meeting his gaze, he found embarrassment and shame firing her bright irises. Jack drew in a deep, steadying breath.

Fetching her from the floor, Jack carried her to the bed, whispering words of comfort and regret against her honeyed-scented skin. He rested her upon the bed, covering her body with the thick patchwork quilt. Her chin yet quivered, but her eyes never left his.

"Why do ye cry, Kylee?" he smiled tenderly, as he withdrew his kerchief and dried her tears. Kylee rolled away from him, onto her side.

"Ye do not think me a lewd, promiscuous wonton? Ye have to know, I've never been touched,

Jack. Not by Garvan…not by anyone." Kylee took his kerchief and stuffed it against her nose, her shoulders quaking with despair. Jack turned her back toward him, and then leaned in and gently kissed her lips.

"Do not weep. Ye have nothin' to be ashamed of. Yer beautiful. And some day soon, I'll be able to show ye how much I love ye."

"Then, not 'til we're married," she hiccupped, her tears still drawing wet tracks down her cheeks. Jack could understand her reservations. After all, her reputation would be ruined were folks to find out she and Jack were staying in the same room. But he had a sinking feeling her fears stemmed from something more sinister. Her next words substantiated his fears. "So many times, I've had to fight Gar off for the same reason. Yet, my denials were met with much harsher consequences."

Now he understood. Jack was acting no differently than the bastard she was running from. Only,

Jack loved her; couldn't she see the difference? The mention of Gar's name infuriated him beyond words.

'*Am I gonna forever pay for that bastard's sins?*' he thought, but held his tongue. She'd been through so much, more than she might ever divulge. He vowed to try to be as understanding and patient as he could.

He had started this without thinking about the consequences. Kylee wasn't just another bar wench looking for a roll in the hay, and she wasn't one of Emma's girls who had little shame and fewer limits. He'd do well to always keep that in mind. He loved Kylee. For the first time, he loved someone other than himself. It was a powerful realization.

Jack let her turn away, but when she formed herself into a tight little ball in the middle of the bed, his heart broke for the distress he'd caused. Jack kicked off his boots and laid down next to her, stroking her hair until she fell asleep.

The next morning, he was startled awake by the cawing of a nearby rooster voicing its command to the world that it was time to rise.

'*Dammit!*' Jack cursed. He'd fallen asleep when he should have left before dawn to scout the two remaining camps of ex-comrades before they reached Galway. '*How will I know if we've been followed? I have to move her – now.*'

Despite his mounting panic, Jack tenderly shook Kylee's shoulder to rouse her without alarm.

"Kylee? 'Tis time to get goin'," he sweetly breathed.

When Kylee rolled over, stretching her slender arms above her head, she looked up with such sweet, happiness his heart nearly burst within its cage.

Then, she smiled. "Aye, I'll be ready in a little while. Will we have breakfast before we go?" she asked through a yawn.

Relief swept through him that she hadn't woken with thoughts of the night before, re-living her sorrow and shame. "Nay, Emma will be expectin' us in a little while, and she'll have the fanciest and tastiest pastries ye've ever eaten," he replied. He couldn't tell her he was in a mad rush to get going. Sleeping through the entire night had been a grave mistake. Jack Manning didn't make mistakes – especially when the stakes were so high. He was losing his edge. But he hadn't the time for regrets; his only concern was getting to Emma's place safely.

Jack stoked the still glowing embers back to life, giving Kylee the privacy that she needed to dress. As he watched the coals burn and spark, he said a little prayer to his gods that O'Shea would poison himself with the drink and die a miserable death.

When they were ready, Jack saddled Conan, and lifted her atop his steed, bracing himself for another day trapped too close to her, struggling to not combust.

Jack scratched at his day-old stubble. "We won't have a long trek this mornin', so I think I'll walk alongside for a while," he said and then kissed her hand. In truth, he couldn't bear to be so close, the remnants of the night before still smouldering within.

"Alright," Kylee replied with silent sadness.

"'Twill just be for a little while." Was her body craving his, as his longed for hers?

"I am sorry for my behaviour last night, my love. I acted like a child," she quietly said, watching his every movement as if his reply might cut her in two.

Jack thought for a moment on how to make her understand that she had nothing to apologize for. It was tough. She'd been an abused woman, a neglected child. She had to know that was no longer the case.

Smoothing Conan's mane, his loving gaze met her bright expectant eyes. "I am the one who is ever in your debt, my wicked. Nothin' is expected of ye, that yer not willin' to give, with yer whole heart." His words brought forth a small smile, the dimples in her cheeks becoming visible for the first time since yesterday.

Reaching down, Kylee touched his scruffy jaw. "Ye have my whole heart. Ye'll have to wait for my body." Kylee winked devilishly.

There's my saucy minx!

When they reached the outskirts of town, Jack brought Conan to a full halt and lifted Kylee off the beasts back.

"Why are we stoppin' here? Aren't we close?" she asked, scanning the horizon.

"Aye, we are. I just have to reassure ye that I'm puttin' ye into a safe place, Kylee. I would do nothin' to put ye in danger. Ye know that, right?" he asked holding her cheek in his hand.

"I know," she replied a little uneasy, no doubt wondering where his sudden change in demeanour came from.

"And Emma. She is to be treated with the same respect ye treat Lady Ryan. Is that understood?" Jack warned.

"I understand. I promise, I'll not bring ye any shame."

"Oh, Kylee, ye could never shame me. But yer temper does worry me a little," he laughed, and then kissed her cheek.

"I'll keep it in check. Miss Emma is yer friend, nothing more," Kylee said carefully, watching his expression, perhaps waiting for him to reveal that her paranoid suspicions were true.

Noticing how she held her breath, he took her gloved hand in his, and said, "'Tis time ye start trustin' someone. Ye'll have to trust me."

They walked hand-in-hand the rest of the way, Jack pointing out this and that along the road. This was to be Kylee's new home, lesson's in how to get around could never start too early.

As Emma's grand mansion came into view, Jack started to relax a little. He'd been looking behind them since they left the cottage earlier, and he sensed that it was beginning to make Kylee nervous.

"There. That's where ye'll stay for a while," Jack pointed. Kylee's jaw dropped at the sheer size of the place.

"Elegant. What does Emma do, exactly? How does she afford a place like this?" Kylee asked with wide eyes and mouth open in amazement.

Jack went over the story in his mind once more, careful not to muddle any details. He decided not to complicate it and answer her in quick responses. If Kylee wanted to know more, she'd have to ask Emma. Emma would know exactly how to conceal her business and protect Kylee from the debauchery that went on inside its walls.

"Emma is from a wealthy family. She inherited a small fortune and this hotel when her parents passed on," he replied. It was so far from the truth, saying it nearly made him sick. There were no parents, no inherited manor and certainly no money. Emma had earned her own way, fair and square, yet most unwholesomely.

"Oh," was the only word Kylee could muster up to say, apparently still awe-struck. Jack chuckled under his breath. *This is gonna be interestin'.*

Just as Jack and Kylee ascended the stone steps, the front door swung open.

"Jack! I have been worried sick about you and your lady! What kept you?" Emma threw her arms around Jacks neck, making him a little uncomfortable. Sensing his abnormal reaction, she removed herself quickly. If anyone understood Jack's body language, it was Emma.

Her petite features lit up with delight as her attention turned to Kylee.

"You must be Lady Kylee. I am Emma," she smiled.

"I…I'm just Kylee, Miss Emma. I'm no lady," Kylee replied, returning the smile.

Jack blew out a sigh of relief, for the last thing he needed was his ill-tempered little vixen to blow up at her hostess.

"And I am not *Miss* Emma, darling. You will just call me Emma. I do think we will be great friends," Emma grinned at Jack, and took Kylee's arm, linking it with her own, and led her inside the manor.

~

Kylee was amazed with this woman, but more than that, jealously slithered within her, fluidly and lethal. Emma it seemed, was everything Kylee was not.

Emma walked with prominence, as if royal blood coursed through her veins. She spoke with a perfect English accent, unlike the rough Irish brogue which came spewing from her own mouth. She wondered if this flawless woman had ever in her life spat a curse word…she doubted it very much.

Emma wore her raven hair long and straight, the front fringe slanting, covering much of her left eye. Kylee had never seen eye color as vivid jade as Emma's, and the outer shape of them puzzled her; the slight incline was incredible. This Emma was mysterious, stunning and alluring. Why Jack and she weren't married already both perplexed and outraged Kylee. *There's a secret between 'em, I know it!* The nagging feeling in the pit of her stomach would not cease its unyielding irritation. Something felt…off.

Because this divine creature seemed to set Jack at ease, Kylee pushed her jealousy down into the depths of her gut. She *had* after-all, promised him she would regard her host kindly. Biting her tongue, Kylee fought to keep her insecurities to herself.

Soon after they entered the massive hall, Emma showed Kylee up to her room, which incidentally was located far, far from the rest of the house. Kylee was glad though, for the distance between she and Emma afforded her privacy, and the absence of in-cessant reminders of her own flaws.

Jack, having never left her peripheral, opened the chamber door. Kylee had only ever dreamed of sleeping in a bed like this – four posters, canopy, ped-estal and all. Scanning the room, she began to forget her earlier envy, replacing the green emotion with appreciation that she was permitted such luxury. She had only cleaned rooms like this one at Lady Ryan's. Now, for a short time, this one was all hers.

"So, do ye think ye can survive up here in this shack for a while, wicked Kylee?" Jack asked, when Emma finished showing her guests around and took her leave, his tone laced with playful sarcasm.

"Jack, 'tis lovely. How will I ever repay Miss Em…Emma?" Kylee beamed.

"Ye'll learn that ye'll never be asked for repayment. Emma is most charitable, 'tis her best quality," Jack said proudly. Kylee nibbled her bottom lip. Could Jack recognize she was keeping her serpent-like tongue in check? If he had, he'd not shown it. "Now, my love, come here, so I can kiss ye proper. I've been dyin' to ever since we left this mornin'," he said, grabbing her waist, causing a giggle to escape her lips. He stifled it with his soft lips. His kiss was like tasting for the first time.

Suddenly, Kylee broke away, her cheeks flushed, her breaths quick and heavy. "Thank ye, Jack. Thank ye for savin' me from…from my life," she sweetly said when she was finally able to reclaim her senses.

"Ye can thank me by puttin' together a weddin'. Waste no time, my sweet. I want us to be wedded," Jack winked, eyes dark and seductive, "and bedded…before I leave."

"Leave? What do ye mean, before ye leave?" Her eyes went wide and she stepped back, putting distance between them.

Jack strode toward her, reassuring her with his embrace. "Aye, I have to leave as soon as I can. I thought ye knew I would. I have obligations at the Kelly's, and when I'm done there, I'll be makin' sure no one has heard from, or seen O'Shea," Jack explained, trying to plant tiny kisses on her cheek, but she refused them, turning her head.

"But ye can't just leave me here with that…that…"

"That what, Kylee? And I'll remind ye to be careful. Emma is very dear to me," Jack warned, a fire burning in his eyes.

This wasn't the first time Kylee had witnessed Jack's annoyance or anger since they met at the

Ryan's. She had pushed him to it then. She'd push him now.

If she were to drive him to madness, perhaps he'd stay. Perhaps he might take her away from there. In any case, the thought of him leaving her there with some stranger, sent her into a brand-new whirlwind of dread. And then, as if it were against her own will, her forked tongue spewed accusations she might never be able to take back.

"Of course, she's dear to ye!" Kylee spat, rolling her eyes. "But what I'd like to know, is how dear *is* she, Jack? How do ye know a woman *like that*?" Kylee sneered at him through squinted eyes and then grinned. Jack's jaw ticked – a sign that he was infuriated. "I bet ye're not the only man tastin' the sweet nectar of her fruit!"

"I know what yer tryin' to do and it won't work." His fists clenched at his sides – the only indication remaining of his annoyance. He turned away from her and drew in a deep breath. "Ye know nothin',

Kylee. Ye'd be better off keeping your crude and crooked ideas to yourself."

Kylee paced the floor, trying to think up her next cruel stab. She flinched when Jack's arms caught her unexpectedly. Her hands flew up in defence, but lowered them just as quickly when she realized the wounded expression in his eyes. He held her tight, his fingers weaved through the hair at the nape of her neck. His touch, so strong yet gentle, sang to her.

"Emma and I are friends, Kylee," he began quietly. "She has been a good friend to me, nothin' more. Think of her as ye would Brady Kelly. I assure ye, 'tis all she will ever be," he assured, holding her closely. Her blood remained frozen, until he kissed her neck, her cheek, and then her lips. His kisses had a thawing effect on her – it was a perfect gift of his. She secretly cursed him for it.

"Alright," she blew out, feeling conquered once again, "so when are ye going to leave me here with… Emma?" Kylee gave in.

"How soon can ye get a weddin' planned? I can call on Father O'Malley in the mornin'. Too soon?" Jack laughed as Kylee broke their connection. Regaining control over her thumping heart, she began unpacking the little she'd been able to bring along. Jack laid his hand upon her shoulder, prompting her to look up at him. "I just want us to spend a little time together as husband and wife before I go. We need this…to rewrite our story, love," he said, watching her closely.

"I don't even have a dress. I want to be beautiful. And what of the…" she hesitated. "I'm still officially betrothed to…ye know who." She dared not say his name.

"Oh, love, ye needn't worry 'bout that. There's no disgrace in breakin' the contract, especially when he's broken it time and time again," he replied, "and ye could wear a burlap sack on our weddin' day, ye'd still be radiant." His flattery caused heat to creep up from her toes. *Christ, this man.*

~

Jack left her in peace, letting it all unravel in her mind. He needed her to realize that she was in fact stuck there with Emma until he returned, and whether she liked it or not, she was to accept it and behave. He needed his words to echo within her. He loved only her. No matter how wicked she was at times. Yet, he couldn't deny the urge to spank her arse red, until she cried out his name.

As Jack closed her door behind him, he stopped and rested his back against the cold hard wood, wondering if she were on the other side, grasping it for dear life too.

Kylee had proved to be quite the opposite of what he'd first encountered. Instead of being malicious and short-tempered, she was quite vulnerable and needed protection. *'She's only malicious when provoked'*, he chuckled. Jack loved the fact that someone needed him and for the first time in his life, someone depended on him. He loved her for it.

He loved most of all, that no one would ever experience Kylee the way he soon would. She was his, all his. If only the nagging in his head would go away, he'd feel more at ease with leaving her at Emma's.

She's gonna find out about my other life, and when she does, she'll run from me as well. As if he could silence his own self-doubt, his hands covered his ears, then he immediately straightened himself again, ignoring the ceaseless disparagement. *How ridiculous!* Here he was, a strong soldier – warrior even – covering his ears against the rage ricocheting between them. His momentary weakness shamed him to the core.

When Jack reached the parlour, as expected, Emma lazily waited in a pillowed chaise.

"You have the little one safely tucked away?" Emma asked, rising from her relaxation. Jack plunked down into a chair and Emma moved behind him, rubbing the tension from his tense shoulders with expert fingers.

"Aye. But, ye have to understand, she is confused about our relationship; mine and yers," he said, raking his fingers through his dirty hair. "She can never know what goes on here. Ye have to promise me that."

"I can sense her severe jealousy, Jack, but I have to carry on with business as usual. You knew I would… before you brought her here. I have clients who depend on me. I cannot disregard them simply because there is an innocent maiden within."

"Well, can't ye try your best to keep it hidden? All she knows is that this is a hotel. Ye think ye can keep up that charade for just a little while? I don't think it'll be tough to find this O'Shea rake, so I won't be away for long," Jack pleaded.

"All right," Emma sighed, "I will try. But I am curious, however. Are you going to hide this side of yourself from her forever? You mean to wed the girl, am I correct? Have ye taken her to bed yet?" Emma asked, leading him to her own personal chambers. Ushering him into her feminine powder room, she poured hot pails of water into a large claw-footed tub, and gestured for him to get in.

The war between right and wrong wracked his brain. A stair case was all that separated him from his pretty colleen. The woman he was going to marry. He knew this was the last place on God's green Earth he should be, but where Emma was concerned, he was weak. A pitiful lecher in need of consoling. Jack sighed and locked the door, and then stripped off his malodourous garb and sank into the hot tub, grateful for its clean rose scent.

"Aye, I want to wed as soon as we can. Emma, I need her like I've never needed anythin' before. She's the source of the air I breathe.

"But nay, I won't take her to bed 'til it's proper, and I won't take her in the manner I'm used to. She doesn't deserve it," Jack said, putting his head in his hands, as if he could crush his desperation into submission. Emma poured the hot soapy water over his head.

"And here I thought I had finally convinced you that you are not as beastly as you once thought. If she makes you think poorly of yourself, perhaps, she is not the lady for you," Emma said, frankly, lathering an amber bar of soap in her hands.

The woman made perfect sense. She'd taught him long ago, that while some people had primal and basic inclinations, most were denied the ability to act on them. Instead of restraint and denial, she'd taught him to bolster his predisposition without the burden of shame and guilt. And now here he was, back where he'd started, sick with agony, the haunting awareness of his deficiencies just about gutting him. If Kylee knew the truth about his past and his relationship with Emma, he had no doubt she'd recant her affections. He'd lose her forever.

Emma massaged the soap into his scalp, delightfully scrubbing away some of his pain. "Would time in the dungeon help? It hadn't the last time you were here," Emma pointed out, her fingers working like barbs to his skull. He wished she would break the skin and rip his brain from its cavity.

When he began to quietly sob, she merely finished washing the couple days' worth of grime from her friend in silence. Tonight, Jack needed his friend Emma, not a willing submissive or even his master.

~

Kylee waited all night for Jack to return, but alas, he did not. The longer she waited however, the more resentful and uncertain she'd become.

'*Where does he sleep tonight?*' she wondered, her mind delving into the darkest recesses of what could be going on, worried he might be bestowing his sweet love upon Emma somewhere else within these walls. She dared not think it out loud. Disrespectful insinuations toward his dear, sweet Emma would not be tolerated, she was sure.

Kylee had never experienced love like the kind between her and Jack, before. She'd merely experienced someone else's version of it, degraded, beaten down and used by everyone she held close. Jack was, and would be, forever her saviour. She'd do well to remember that fact.

Resting in the massive cold and lonely bed, she could almost feel his lingering presence. She envisioned his hands skittering over her hot flesh, caressing her in forbidden places, making her feel like a woman.

'*Mrs. Jack Manning*,' she sighed and forced herself to sleep.

TEN

The next morning Kylee awoke to find she was still alone. A pang of deprivation and despair swept over her, her thoughts consumed by regret for the things she'd thrown in Jack's face the night before.

'*I may never understand his and Emma's friendship, but I will not lose him over it either,*' she vowed silently, holding her head high, proving her resilience. Was it his intention to punish her like this? Had their spat, a few prejudicial words exchanged between them been the reason he'd failed to return to her?

Kylee was in complete torment, confused and bewildered. Dragging her fingers through her sleep-knotted locks, she eyed the bed with a desire to crawl back beneath the covers, seek refuge beneath the heavy quilt and remain that way for the rest of the day. Before she'd had a chance to succumb to the urge, a knock upon the door startled her as it echoed throughout the room.

"Come in," she answered softly, as a harsh thumping in her chest nearly knocked the wind from her.

When Jack entered, Kylee sprinted toward him, falling into his arms, whimpering and snivelling, knocking Jack back a few steps.

"What's this about, love?" he asked, holding her face in his hands, gazing into her tear-reddened eyes with so much love it nearly shredded her heart. Kylee couldn't speak, couldn't find the words to explain what had come over her in her hours of loneliness and gloom. It was all she could do, just to breathe. "Shh, now. Ye have to stop this and tell me what's gotten ye in such a frenzy," he soothed, pulling her body into his.

"I...I didn't mean to anger ye last night. I...I promise, no more ill feelin's toward Miss Emma," she frantically yelped, "not if it means ye'll punish me like this."

"Punish ye? What are ye talkin' about, lass? Has somethin' happened?" Jack's face contorted with unasked questions, as if his head was spinning just trying to figure out the cause of her emotional downpour.

"Well that's what ye done, aye? Punished me? When ye didn't return last night, I knew ye were angry. I provoked ye, pushed too far. Ye pushed back," she cried, dropping to her knees. Head cast down, Kylee placed her trembling hands upon Jack's boots, holding on to them with desperation. "Can ye forgive me, Jack? I need to know I'm forgiven," she wept, with tears that tracked little streams onto his polished footwear.

~

Jack hadn't realized that not returning to her, might leave her feeling as though she was being chastised and perhaps, cast aside.

The truth was, after Emma had helped him bathe, he'd been left so emotionally drained that he had fallen asleep wrapped in a soft blanket on the chaise in the parlour.

The last he remembered was Emma going to the kitchen to fetch him a cup of honey-lemon tea. She'd said it would help calm his torrent of frazzled emotions. He supposed when Emma returned and found him to be slumbering peacefully, she'd left him alone. He couldn't tell Kylee all that, she'd never understand. She'd lose her mind knowing Emma had helped him wash away the tension and disquiet from his body.

Jack reached for Kylee's quaking shoulders, hauling her up in one swift movement, and began to shake her until she ceased her hysteria. Her body went slack and she gazed up at him from beneath tear-soaked lashes with fear and uncertainty. With a crushing pain inside, he pulled her close and held her, rocking her from side to side.

"I didn't mean..." he began, stumbling on each syllable. "I didn't return last night 'cause I took a bath and fell asleep quickly after," Jack whispered sympathetically. He knew her wounds ran deep, but he hadn't been quite prepared for how cavernous they actually were.

From here on in, every single decision he made and every word he spoke, he must consider her broken soul first. "I wasn't angry with ye. Not when I left. And I'd never punish ye like that. I'd never leave ye wonderin' where we stood. Never," he breathed against her neck. The rapid throb of her pulse against his cheek brought tears to his own eyes. His selfishness had brought all this about. "Come on now, m'love. I told ye to trust me, didn't I?"

Kylee nodded, wiped her tears, and fell into his arms. Jack carried her limp languid body to the bed, and laid her there to rest.

"Jack?" she whispered.

"Aye, my wicked Kylee?" he replied.

"Will it always be this hard?"

"Will what, love?" Jack asked, sitting down beside her, brushing her hair from her face. He could spend his lifetime gazing upon this woman.

"Lovin' ye. Will lovin' ye always tear me apart? Is this what it feels like to love someone?"

Jack felt wretched for her innocence but understood her question. Since they'd left County Clare, he'd confused her, tested her virtue, pushed her to seduction, and now here he was, leaving her with another woman, who he clearly had a unique chemistry with. Kylee's morals and integrity had been shaken, and she couldn't possibly know what to do or what to expect next.

The war raging within him sometimes clouded his better sense and judgement. It was taking a toll on them both.

"Kylee, love is terribly complicated at times," he began, trying to find a way to answer her question without making her feel patronized or infantile. "Ye have to remember that I am ten years yer senior, and I've had experiences that ye've not yet had. I've taken lovers, where ye have not," he softly explained, as the colour drained from her face.

"Stop! Forget I said anythin'! I don't want to hear anymore," she shouted, waving him away and turned her face into the pillow.

"But ye have to. Ye see, I've never loved any woman, as I love ye. Our love is the kind that lasts, for all eternity; not just a little while," he tenderly said, lifting her to meet the sincerity in his gaze. "When I am sure ye are safe from O'Shea, we will leave here, leavin' behind all the bad memories. We will then go to my home, and ye will make it *our* home. We will raise our children there, and ye'll never again question my devotion to ye.

"So, nay, to answer yer question, sweetheart, lovin' me will not lead to heartbreak. It will lead us to a life of happiness and contentment. This, I can promise ye. But, don't ever forget, Kylee, I'm *not* Garvan O'Shea. There's never a need to fear me."

Her gaze never wavered from his. Somewhere deep down, he knew she believed him, but the anguish in her soft stare tore his heart to pieces. He'd have a lifetime to make right, what so many close to her had wronged. Jack leaned in, sliding his hand up the side of her melancholy mask, into her soft golden locks, fisting a handful with lusty reverence. Her tongue darted out, wetting the tender flesh expectantly, and then accepted his kiss fervently, reciprocating every movement he made until they were both breathless. If there was one skill Jack boasted about, it was his ability to make a tormented lass forget all her troubles.

"I believe ye, Jack," Kylee breathed, tearing herself away, but then, her hands fisted his shirt collar and a serious mien washed over her tear-glistened face. "Send for Father O'Malley. Ye'll have no reason not to return to me tonight," she added, her voice low and husky. She amazed him. Such innocence, yet such power. She was oblivious to her own appeal and magnetism. With promise of what was yet to come, Jack rose, moving quickly about the room, tossing his things into his leather satchel.

Turning back toward her to find her still leaning against the headboard, a scrap of quilt worrying between her fingers, Jack let out a playful shout. He was the happiest man alive at that moment, and not even her reluctance to get dressed could dampen his mood. "Well, love, get yer arse out of that bed!" he smiled, keenly. "There's much to be done. I have to meet with my team and then I'll head over to see the priest. I'll want to have the service at Kelly's keep, if it's all right with ye. The security is best there, and they're the only family I have in the world," Jack said, beaming with excitement. "I'll have Father O'Malley meet us there at five o'clock."

When he finally noticed her still sitting there, jaw agape, a stupefied expression across her face, Jack picked her up in a flurry of excitement and swung her around. Her arms instinctively wrapped around his neck, her cheek pressed into his. "Aye, husband. Five O'clock," she whispered.

On the way toward Kelly's keep, Jack stopped at the church to make arrangements with Father O'Malley, who appeared both pleased and relieved that Jack had finally found a woman to settle down with.

The old priest knew of Jack's history with women, though only through gossip. Jack's secret was one he hadn't even shared with God, and it would stay that way now that Jack was determined to put that part of himself on a shelf for good.

Arriving at the stronghold, Brady met his old friend in the foyer. He wrapped his bulging muscled arms around him, picking him up off the floor and shook him in the most awful bear hug Jack had ever suffered. It was clear to see his friend had recovered from the shooting and was at full strength. As he struggled to fill his lungs with air once more, Jack couldn't decide if he was glad of it or not.

"Jesus, Jack! I was wonderin' what was keepin' ye. I expected ye back long before now. I figured you'd find the girl and then take the girl," Brady chuckled, leading them into the study, where the two settled into chairs in front of the hearth, each with a abundant glass of brandy.

"I couldn't just take the girl! My name's not Brady Kelly. That's the kinda thing *ye* do, remember?" Jack laughed, resulting in Brady's face turning red. '*Well, ye still lack a sense of humor,*' Jack mused inwardly. He slapped Brady's knee, and they both began to laugh.

"Where is she then, this fire-tongued imp that's gotten ye into a snarl?" Brady asked.

"I've hidden 'er at The Haven. It seemed the most logical place, for no one, save ye, knows about Emma. It made so much sense to bring her there, 'til we actually got there. What a feckin' mess!" Jack chuckled, raking his hand through his hair. "But, I think it's all behind us now. We're gonna marry this afternoon. Here, at the keep, if ye don't mind." Jack grinned from ear to ear, waiting for Brady's reaction.

It seemed, Brady had swallowed his tongue for a moment, and blinked quickly a few times before he found his words. "That's quick, Jack. Are ye sure about this?"

Brady seemed to hold on to every detail, as Jack explained all that had happened since he'd set out to find Kylee, and all the reasons he just couldn't live without her. Having found love just so recently, Jack knew Brady would understand and give them his blessing. After all Jack had done to keep he and Violet together, how could he not? "Alright then, so five O'clock. We'll be ready here. I'll have Mary take care of everythin'," Brady beamed.

"Fine. But, we have to keep it as quiet as we can. If O'Shea's been trailin' us, and he hears of it, it could put her in danger. Put us all in danger," Jack replied, gravely.

"Aye, I'll make sure Mary keeps it simple, quiet, and quaint. Violet will be thrilled to see ye married, as will I. I do think Vy would've married *you* if I hadn't been shot and she hadn't felt so sorry for me," Brady snickered, lightening the mood again.

"How *is* Violet? Where is she?" Jack goaded, staring down into his glass of whiskey with a dirty grin. The implication of impure thoughts would drive Brady to madness. Where Violet was concerned, Brady was humourless, and tolerated no man to even look her way, especially Jack. This time, Brady couldn't be provoked.

"She is still in bed, if ye must know. And wipe that smirk off yer face. I know what ye're doin'. Not even *ye* can make me lose my temper, these days." Brady grinned winningly. "I've ordered her to take it easy for now. She carries my child and I think it takes a great deal of her energy to function here for an entire day. So, as per my instruction, she sleeps in late, and turns in early," Brady stated, quite proud of himself for putting her in the situation to start with.

"Well done! Congratulations! How will she feel about ye leavin' for a while to help me with my O'Shea problem?" Jack carefully asked.

"She'll be fine. She understands that as brothers, we stick together. Sometimes we may do things that aren't of sane mind, but we stick together just the same. She'll be fine here with Mary," Brady reassured his friend. "And besides Mary, Liam is here. Every day while I'm down at the shipyard managin' the new crew with Morgan, Liam is here handlin' the books. But he spends more time with Vy than workin', tendin' to her every need. Ye should see him, Jack. 'Tis some sight.

"Unfortunately, she's ill most every mornin', but Liam's right there in his impeccable starched suit to hold her hair, and wipe her forehead with a cool cloth," Brady said. It was the first time Jack had ever seen pride in his eyes regarding his brother, Liam. Aye, they'd been raised completely different – Liam spending most his boyhood away at school, and Brady running bare-footed in the wilderness under his mother's watchful eye – there was no rivalry between them. Brady gushed about how grateful he was for his brother's support, but Jack detected a little envy lingering just below his stony exterior. Even if Brady wanted to be more attentive, to be the one taking such good care of his Vy, it wasn't a possibility. Two shipbuilding conglomerates had just merged. Brady had no choice but to be down at the dry dock at the crack of dawn each day to ensure Murtagh was running things the *Kelly way*.

Since the merge, part of the arrangement was for Morgan Murtagh, the Ryan's notorious hard-arse crew chief, to remain in Galway to take the wheel, giving Brady the freedom to return to the cottage come spring, taking his wife and their babe with him. If Brady was still spending every waking moment down at the yard, instead of home with Violet, Jack suspected Murtagh was not yet ready.

The man would be tested in a few days however, when Brady set out with Jack to put an end to Garvan O'Shea. The entire crew at the shipyard would be at the mercy of Madman Morgan Murtagh. Jack couldn't help but pity them some.

"And the weddin'? How did it come off?" Jack asked regretfully.

"Ye would know, had ye stayed here to bear witness to it," Brady blandly stated, "but I understand. I know ye had to go. If it had been Vy in danger, there would've been nothin' on this green earth to stop me either," Brady added, easing Jack's guilt.

"I have one more favor to ask of ye before I return to Emma's to fetch m'bride. It's more for Violet, really," Jack said as he rose from the chair and swallowed the remainder of his highball.

"Anythin'," Brady replied, slapping his friend on the back as they strolled out of the study.

~

Kylee waited with electrified butterflies swirling all around in her belly, then, a quiet knock came upon the bedroom door. She hadn't answered it, nor had she called out, but it slowly opened anyway, and a coal-black head popped in.

Emma waited for Kylee to wave her in and beamed an elegant smile when she did.

"Do you mind if I come in and help you get ready?" Emma sweetly asked, sincerely. "This is going to be a grand day, for you both. I am certain it will be the best day of your life."

"Aye, ye can help me get ready, but I really don't know what to do first. I don't have a weddin' gown. I've gone through all my dresses, and can find none to suit such an occasion," Kylee replied miserably.

"I am quite sure I have something that will do just fine. For now, we need to get you freshly bathed, and have one of the girls – one of the chamber maids –" Emma corrected, "come and fix your hair into a lovely style that will make Jack weak in the knees," she added, offering her graceful hand for Kylee to take. Kylee's gaze met Emma's as she slid her fingers into the enigmatic woman's palm.

Emma pushed the door to her own chamber wide. "This is my personal suite. Everything in here is at your disposal." She helped Kylee into a piping hot tub of lavender and vanilla scented bubbles.

Desperately embarrassed with her own nudity, Kylee kept her bare body hidden as much as she could. "You have no reason to try to conceal yourself, Kylee. You are beautiful. I can see what has driven Jack to madness!"

Kylee sighed as relaxation consumed her, each moment lingering in the last. "Bah! My hips are too wide. My arse, too big!" Kylee replied, without even thinking.

Emma dragged a soapy sponge along the pearls of Kylee's spine. "Alas! And perfect, perky breasts, flawless ivory skin and hair of spun gold. I'd say Jack Manning conjured you from his dreams, sweet girl." While Emma's words sounded sincere, Kylee couldn't help but doubt them. She had never been told she was beautiful. It would be insanity to believe it, especially coming from a stranger.

"Ye know I can do this myself. I've been bathin' myself since I was a youngster."

"Yes, yes, I know, dear. I'm going to wash your hair for you. Then we will get you ready for, well, the wedding night," Emma said, a subtle smile tugging at her lips. Heat rushed to Kylee's cheeks at the mere mention of the wedding night.

While she was no lack-wit concerning the consummation of wedding vows for purposes of procreation, the intimacies leading up to that point were somewhat a mystery. Garvan had asked for things – unfamiliar things – on several occasions. Her incessant denial never ceased to throw him into a fit of terror, but thanking the heavens, he'd not forced them upon her…not until the night she fell. Those intimate acts remained elusive, and now Kylee wasn't sure she wanted to know.

Despite her discomfort, Emma spent the rest of the morning explaining things to Kylee in great detail, leaving her breathless and eager, yet scared to death with the thought of being alone with her soon-to-be husband. The realization of her inexperience weighed heavily on her.

She'd had no idea that men and women alike, pleasured one another in the ways which Emma had described. And now her only fear was that she wouldn't measure up to the string of lovers she imagined Jack had taken in the past.

"So, he'll want me to kiss him where…down there?" Kylee blushed into the mirror as Emma stood behind her brushing the tangled wet locks into a smooth shimmering veil.

"Never mind that right now. Jack will tell you what he wants, I have no doubt," Emma stated frankly, then noting the sour look on Kylee's face in the mirror, she quickly added, "Not that I know from experience, Kylee. Don't fret. I just know Jack. He's an eager teacher *and* student in all things. Let the moment guide you and do not be afraid. He will not judge you."

Kylee's anxiety was boiling over within her. This woman standing behind her seemed to hold so much power over Jack. She knew things about him that Kylee may never know. To say it unsettled her would be an understatement.

'I can't worry 'bout this now. I'm marryin' the most sensitive, carin' and gentle man I've ever known. I promised I'd not try to compete with Emma,' Kylee repeated over and over in her mind, in hopes that she would listen to her own good sense and relax.

After what seemed like hours had passed, finally Kylee was ready. Emma and her flock of *chamber maids* had done a splendid job. The girl was absolutely stunning, and all the girls who'd helped, congratulated themselves despite Kylee's own reservations.

Just as the finishing touches were being completed – a dab of perfume here and there, a stray tendril of hair put back into place – Jack busted in shouting his hellos with pure cheer and merriment.

He stopped dead in his tracks when he caught sight of her, while the ladies all about fussed over every pint-sized detail. Their gazes met, a pregnant silence falling between them. His expression was soft, full of love and joy, but then, a small crease worried his brow.

"Ladies, please leave us," he commanded in a quiet, yet raspy tone. To Kylee's wonder, they all dropped what they were doing, curtsied and quickly ushered out the door. "Kylee, ye look beautiful. I have never seen yer hair swept off yer face like this. I love it, for now I can truly see how beautiful ye really are."

"Thank ye. The ladies here have been very kind to me," Kylee replied, blushing and stared at a speck on the floor.

Jack took her hand in his, placing a kiss in her palm. "Tell me what's wrong then," he urged. The fluttering of her own damn heart filled her ears, the slight contact nearly making her swoon. It was best to just tell him what was bothering her, else he might never cease scalding her hand with his fiery touch.

Kylee blew out a desperate breath. "I've still no gown. When I meet Lord Brady, I want to look my best. I don't want him thinkin' I'm just a lowly peasant."

"Is that all? Well, Kylee, I'm sorry to tell ye, he knows all about ye. And he doesn't care what station ye were born into, he knows I love ye," Jack chuckled. "Violet even sent ye a gift for yer weddin' day." Jack passed her a large box and watched with delight as she opened it.

Kylee's frown disappeared instantly when she revealed a cream and white wedding gown with sequenced appliqué and a powder-pink bow. Gently pulling it from the satin-lined box, she rushed to the mirror and held the elegant garment to her body. Her own image caused her to smile; for the first time in her life, she marvelled at her own reflection.

"Oh, Jack, 'tis wonderful!" she beamed. "Now get out! I have to get dressed."

Jack laughed, held her chin and kissed her lips. "I must admit, I am quite proud of m'self for thinkin' to ask Lady Violet if ye could borrow it. Of course, she was more than happy to oblige." Kylee couldn't wait to thank her new benefactor, and it would seem, all the people in Jack's world were cut from the same mold. Their generosity held no bounds.

Kylee and Emma made their short journey in Emma's private and grand carriage, the interior made of plush magenta silk cushions, thanking the heavens Jack hadn't suggested they go on horseback. What an awful impression she would have made on the Lord and Lady of Kelly's keep, were she to arrive stinking of manure and beast sweat.

Gazing through the window as they neared, a flock of staff materialized, waiting on the large stone steps for their guests. Oddly, Jack dismounted, handed the reins to a stable hand, and then rushed inside. A tall burly fellow with steely-blue eyes and coal-black hair, helped Kylee and Emma from the carriage and led them into the foyer.

"Lovely Kylee, my name is Brady. Ye already know my beautiful wife, Violet. Ye'll have to excuse Jack. I suppose he's so enthusiastic he forgot to make introductions," he said, a kind smile tugging at his stubbly jawline. "Emma, nice to see ye again," he added curtly. Emma politely nodded her reply.

"Delighted to see ye again, Violet," Kylee said and then turned in the direction of where Jack had disappeared, gazing wistfully. "Aye, I suppose he is excited," Kylee happily replied.

Once she was inside, Kylee was awestruck with the magnificence of the place. It was brilliant. But she couldn't help thinking about how daunting the task of cleaning the many rooms must be.

The study, which was decked in streamers, ribbons and paper flowers hanging from every book shelf, served as a most beautiful setting. Kylee sighed happily. Where the desk would have been, Jack stood, hands clasped in front of him, talking with a priest.

Violet removed the long matching over-coat, revealing the gown Kylee wore beneath. Jack pinned her right to the spot with his smouldering gaze. *He's speechless!* Stepping slowly from the doorway, she met him where he eagerly waited and placed her hand in his.

"Beautiful, wicked Kylee. I'll treasure this day always," he whispered, making her proudly shine.

Although the service had been kept a secret, small family affair, it seemed Father O'Malley would go on forever. Kylee and Jack waited impatiently, staring into one another's eyes with vibrant love and adoration. Just when she thought the old priest might never shut up, he finally said the words she'd been longing to hear.

"Ye may now kiss yer bride, Jack," proclaimed the jovial old vicar, breaking their spell.

Jack sucked in a deep breath, exhaled with a slight exuberant growl, and then grabbed his wife with fervour and severity, kissing her until she felt it all the way down to her toes.

Whatever concern she'd had for the night which lay ahead was diminished in that moment, for now she envisioned their bodies entangled. As one, at last. It mattered naught that all eyes in the small make-shift chapel were upon them, nor did their state of lust cause heat of embarrassment to rise in her cheeks. She was Mrs. Jack Manning now, and as this man's wife, she'd kiss him how ever she liked! The small crowd consisting of the family and a few treas-ured house-staff applauded, breaking their fevered embrace.

Violet reached out, pulling Kylee into her arms. "Kylee, I've never seen Jack so happy. I wish ye both all the happiness in the world," Violet said sweetly, kissing Kylee's hot cheek. "Mary has prepared a feast fit for a king to mark the occasion. I do hope ye can stay a while."

"Thank ye," Kylee leaned in and whispered in Violet's ear. "And fer lendin' me yer gown, Violet. 'Tis beautiful," Kylee added with an appreciative flush.

"'Tis magnificent on ye, my dear!"

Leave it to a man to interrupt women's fascination and appreciation of fine clothing. Jack interjected by saying, "We'll stay for supper, but I have to get Kylee safely back to Emma's. Ye know, I *do* have work to do, as I hope to have her in the same condition as you, as soon as I can," Jack winked at Kylee, turning her flame red. At the mere suggestion, Violet's hands splayed across her yet slim belly, but it seemed faeries had begun to dance inside her own.

Despite Jack's promise to leave right after supper, their wedding celebration went on, well into the night, as they laughed, drank wine, and danced while Morgan played his fiddle.

Just before dawn, Jack and Kylee thanked and bid them all farewell, as they stepped aboard the carriage. Emma offered to ride Conan, giving the newlyweds some time alone before they returned to the manor.

Once inside its confines, Jack's dashing smile was replaced by hooded eyes – all lust and adoration.

"Ye were wonderful today, love," he said as the carriage began to move. "Violet and Brady are quite smitten with ye."

"They are a lovely family, Jack. I can see why ye love them so," she replied, stifling a yawn with the back of her gloved hand.

"Oh no ye don't! Ye don't get to be tired this night, my little imp. I want to show ye *how much* I love ye once I get ye back to The Haven," Jack grinned, electricity burning in his gaze. Kylee felt the weight of his desire down into the pit of her stomach. Somehow, she wasn't tired anymore. Now, she was eager to get back to the manor and show her husband how much he meant to her, as well.

ELEVEN

J ack carried his pretty bride from the comfort of the carriage, up the manor steps, kicking the door open with one solid boot.

Although he was eager to get her home, he also realized Emma's place was not, in fact their home. He longed for the day when he could take her away from the tawdry atmosphere of Heathen's Haven and carry her across the threshold of the tiny home his mother had left him.

Kylee's body seemed to hold no weight as Jack all but sprinted up the stairs to the room – their room, even if, for just this night.

He gently set her upon the huge four-poster bed and stood for a moment, merely admiring her, drinking her in, as she returned his smile with tenderness and the eyes of a woman. He sensed her readiness.

"Sit up, love," he said, pushing the need to bark orders and control the scene down into the depths of him. Emma had always gushed over Jack's ability to take a timid girl such as Kylee and force her to overcome her burden of modesty. She'd said he'd been special in that regard, and that his real gift was the fact that he'd only demand obedience and trust from his women in return. The difference in then and now was, this was his life, and his heart. Kylee would never be treated the same as his past string of lovers.

Emma's words rang in his ears, *'For better or for worse, Jack. You cannot hide your true nature from her. It is unfair to you both,'* she'd said. *'She will find out. You'd best tell her before all is revealed at a most inconvenient time.'*

Shaking Emma's voice of reason out of his mind, Jack helped his bride with her overcoat.

'*I need to take extra care. I am not her Master,*' he reminded himself.

Pulling Kylee to her feet, Jack marvelled in the way she remained silent, waiting, watching his every move. Taking her face in his hands, he placed a whisper of a kiss upon her lips, her hot sweet breath nearly burning him alive. He needed to feel her flesh, his own skin craved the heat of her body.

Taking her gently by the shoulders, he turned her around, his fingers skilfully working the buttons on her dress. With each inch exposed, the skin on skin contact caused her to tremble. She drew in a deep breath and he wondered if she'd remember to exhale. Making quick work of the laces on her bodice with rapacious speed, Jack fully exposed her milky shoulders.

His hands ceased their mission, but for a moment. "Are ye all right, my wicked Kylee?" he whispered on her neck, placing kisses between each word. When she nodded and leaned into his cheek, he continued. Before he could get her gown free, she turned and reached up, seeking his lips. She kissed him feverishly and urgently, with her hands in his hair, pulling him deeper and deeper into her own needy world.

Enchantment engulfed him right where he stood; his beautiful bride, warm and welcoming beneath his touch. Any reservations that she might be reluctant and shy, or that she might need extra tenderness and coaxing vanished. She wanted him. For the first time in so long, he was truly wanted. Not the master, nor the slave, but the man. The realization caused his heart to race and his mouth to become dry.

Sliding the gown from her upper body exposed perfect breasts, the same flesh he'd been longing to bury himself in. He recognized her desperation as her chest heaved with fervent ardour and her skin flushed effortlessly.

She brought his head to her neck, where he began trailing his kisses. First, on her clavicle, then her shoulders, making his way to one taut nipple, where he tasted, licked and teased. Her head fell back, giving him complete access to her partial nudity, as she moaned her appreciation.

~

As if possessed by the devil, Kylee's fingers fidgeted with the buttons of his shirt, working their way down until his blonde curly chest was freed. The mere sight of her handsome solid husband would be forever seared into her brain, like a hot branding iron, Jack's mark.

She traced the lines of his muscles with her fingertips, and then tasted his salty skin with tiny feather-like kisses, leaving him breathless. His chest rose and fell as if he was holding onto one last thread of sanity, his fist clenching and unclenching at his sides. It wasn't lost to her that her husband was showing some great measure of restraint for fear of ripping away her innocence, but she'd gladly be rid of it. Give it all to him. She'd give anything for sense of propriety to leave him, freeing him to devour her whole, if that's what his heart so desired.

Kylee receded toward the bed until the backs of her knees made contact. Jack's body leaned in, burying her beneath his heavy weight with a kiss that left her lips swollen and throbbing. Suddenly, he stood, a passionate air permeating the very air around him. He stripped away her crinoline, petticoat and her under things with loving care. With each layer removed, he kissed her lips, gazing deep into her eyes with wild lust and abandon.

Right then, she was the wicked Kylee he'd accused and teased her of being. The heat from the hearth fire grazed her skin, but it was the smouldering fire in his eyes which caused her to burn. Now standing at the foot of the bed, she eagerly waited while he seemed to grapple with indecision. Even the reflection of firelight on his flesh appeared strained.

Laying before him, exposed for the very first time, Kylee helped her husband settle the raging conflict he seemed to be having. "Ye won't break me," she panted. A glimmer of happiness crossed his face, the demons inside him, becoming vanishing intruders.

He shrugged out of boots and trousers, and then crawled up the bed to lie beside her, his gaze trailing over every inch of her impatient heated flesh. How much more could she endure? This man now laying beside her would drive her to madness if he didn't soon touch her. The hunger to have his hands upon her turned her mouth to desert. Her head swam with all sorts of reasons for his reluctance.

"I love how ye look in lantern light, Kylee. Ye glisten," he breathed, his hand finding her lush breasts again. He sighed then against her cheek, "Perfection."

"Oh, Jack," she murmured with breathless anticipation.

Kylee could see all of Jack's nude body. The mere sight and musky scent of him stirred sensations in places she'd only recently discovered. His chiselled and sinewy muscles contracted and expanded with every singular movement he made. She was in awe of him.

His thick solid manhood rested against her hip, drawing an unfamiliar instinct to reach out and touch that part of him. She couldn't help thinking about her and Emma's earlier conversation. How men liked to be touched and kissed there, and Kylee wondered if she would ever get up the courage to bring Jack to pleasure like that.

Then, Jack's warm breath and wet lips found her flesh, tracing a path from her breast to her hipbone, ripping her from the torment of inexperience.

"So soft and needy,' he breathed, euphoria raking her insides.

Taking one rosy nipple into his mouth, his hand slid from her knee to the warm apex between her thighs. Kylee sucked a breath into her lungs between her teeth and held it there. Warmth engulfed her insides, her head danced with passion and her heart filled with love. She could've been molten steel, her husband the blacksmith of her body, molding her, shaping her into whatever he desired.

With a tender touch, Jack moved her leg to the side, opening her up to his touch. His fingertips grazed the throbbing swollen nub inside, and Kylee's eyes flew open, an uncontrolled gasp escaping her. She pulled at his hair, thrashed about, never having felt anything like it in her life. Laying on his side, cradling her in one strong arm, while his other dished out torturous ministrations upon her greedy body, Jack paused, their gazes connecting in such a profound manner, it was if their souls had finally given up the long search for the other.

"Don't stop, Jack," she insisted breathlessly.

Jack continued to stroke her faster and faster while flicking his tongue over each nipple, one after the other until Kylee was writhing and quivering.

Her insides felt as if they were about to explode like molten lava. The unknown sensation being so foreign to her, she was almost afraid. But instead of pulling away in fear, she rode the waves of rapture until she was spent and lifeless on the bed beside him, her hands clinging to the muscles in his arm.

"Ye're ready for me now, my love," he whispered, the heat of his words dragging out her pleasure in the most delicious way. Moving over her, covering her soft body with his, her legs spread wide between them. As if it was second nature, her arms found their way around his neck as she pulled him into a deep, passionate kiss. Even the mere taste of him had her begging for more.

His hardness against her inner thigh caused her to push her hips off the mattress with a covetous need to join.

Then, she felt him there. Just a little further and she'd get what she craved. But suddenly, Jack extended his arms, putting distance between their bodies and spoke with reassuring eyes. "I'm gonna hurt ye, Kylee. I don't mean to, love. 'Tis always that way the first time," Jack said apologetically, his gaze never leaving hers as he entered her.

~

Her body was like a vice around him, squeezing, refusing to let him fully enter. Bracing himself on shaky elbows, his hands tangled in her hair, his lips crashing down upon hers as he pushed past the barrier. He hushed her cry of pain with the tenderness of his mouth, and then moved further, and deeper. His first instinct had been to command her, to teach her how to trust him unconditionally. But how could he explain that he needed her in ways most men refused to admit they even dreamed about. Instead, he held fast, grasping at the last of his self-control.

'*This must be what heaven is like,*' he thought as her body finally accepted all of him, relaxing around his thickness. He slowed the pace again to let her adjust.

"Are ye alright, love?" he whispered.

"Aye. Please, don't stop. Love me like you've never loved another," she pleaded, but the truth was, Jack already *had* loved her like no other. He'd never felt this kind of tenderness and devotion before now. The sensations she brought about left him wanting so much more of this.

Unable to hang on to what was left of his sanity, those simple words, transformed him. Passion and fury consumed him all at once. He was devoured by exhilaration and need, pumping his hips against her furiously.

Her hot breath on his neck, her small body beneath him, nearly sent him into oblivion.

The scorching passion within them erupted simultaneously, making Kylee wail and Jack grunt like the beast he truly was.

Both of them spent, they lay motionless, in a state of amorous affection until they drifted into a dream-filled slumber.

Through the morning, they remained intertwined, thoroughly and perfectly consumed with heavenly lust for one another. Jack had woken her up twice with warm hands and sweet kisses all over her aching body, each time, bringing her to madness.

Jack and Kylee lingered in bed for the entire day, holding on to the moment for dear life, both silently fearing if they parted, they could never re-live the tender moments again.

Jack's head was resting on her bare belly when he heard the call of her hungry body, howling for food.

"Kylee, love, we must get ye somethin' to quiet that bear in there," he laughed.

"Aye," she yawned blithely. If she felt even close to how he was feeling, she'd be perfectly content to starve, just to remain there in that moment. "I loathe leaving this room, my husband," she smiled, stretching her arms above her head. *My husband.* Jack's heart soared. *He* was her husband.

"Come on. Must be supper time soon. I'm sure Emma's had somethin' special prepared for us," he said as he stood. Taking her hand, he pulled her up with him, "It wouldn't be polite if we didn't at least make an appearance."

After he'd helped her bathe, washing every square inch of her still-sensitive body, Jack helped her into a simple pink day dress belonging to one of Emma's girls. Until Jack was assured her safety, Kylee would have to rely on the charity of others, borrowing dresses, an overcoat and shoes. 'Twas a good thing all Jack's friends were female, for she had a wealth of fabrics and styles to choose from. He ushered Kylee into the chair at the vanity and brushed her golden hair until it was dry. Her obsessive, yet quizzical gaze never left his, while words seemed lost to her. He could almost read her mind. No doubt, this little vixen was not used to being fussed over or taken care of. Jack vowed to change that. He would forever be her caregiver and relish in every moment. As the brush cut through her smooth locks, Jack's mind wandered.

When Emma had first taken him under her wing, she'd taught him that after-care and affection would enhance a woman's experience, resulting in trust like no other. Jack had pig-headedly disputed this in the beginning.

"How can I spank, tease and chastise these women, makin' them my slaves, only to become theirs once it's all over?" he had argued.

"Darling, you will find these women are coming to you to live out their fantasies. If they go away feeling used and despondent, do you really think they would have had the ultimate experience? We do this to bring out the best in them, not to beat their spirits down," Emma had expressed with patience and kindness.

And now, here he was, taking care of the woman he would spend the rest of his life with, and hiding from her, everything Emma had ever taught him.

When the two emerged from their room, they both felt a gut-wrenching pang of loss. It was almost like the dream had come to an end.

Sensing her sadness, he halted their descent down the staircase. "We won't stay down there for long, love. I've much more to give ye this night," he promised, his gaze zeroing in on her body. The smile she gave in reply told him Kylee's body had awakened, and she was loving every minute of it.

Ever the coy little imp, she blushed and swatted him away, and then made her way down the steps.

When they entered the dining hall, Emma was nowhere to be found. The long table was set for only two, and a card was left between the place settings. Kylee gasped delightfully at the effort Emma had clearly gone to in arranging this romantic meal.

Kylee ran her finger along the fine white china plates resting on shimmering gold chargers. "Even after the terrible way I've treated 'er, she's gone to all this trouble."

"Aye. Emma understands how ye must be feelin'. And she wouldn't want ye to be feelin' guilty about it, either." Jack winked, hopefully easing her troubled conscience.

Jack seated Kylee to his left and filled the crystal wine glass with bubbling champagne, which he knew Emma only broke out on very special occasions.

Through the candle light, he watched as Kylee beamed with enchantment.

"Ye know, when I take ye away from here, when we leave the manor, I can't offer ye riches and luxuries such as these? Ye understand that, don't ye?" Jack looked away from her, pained with regret that he couldn't give her everything she deserved, only a small home with a creaky floor and a wood stove.

Kylee took his hand, kissing it with genuine adoration. "I'll only ever need you, love. I'm not accustomed to all these *things*, but I have to admit, it feels like a holiday or a dream," she giggled, and then became serious once more, "I've no need for a wealth of material things, just an abundance of love. Yer love," she said. If she could sense his shame for not earning a significant income, she'd never let on. *Oh, the gift of this woman!*

"That, Kylee, ye'll never do without," Jack said as he softly stroked her hand.

"Now, read the card!" she exclaimed, instantaneously bettering his mood.

Jack picked it up, unfolded the crisp paper and held it up to the light and read aloud.

Dearest Newlyweds,

The cook has prepared a lovely dinner for you both to enjoy, alone.

I do hope you find it satisfies your pallet and is a means to regain your strength after your first night together.

Jack, take care of your angel, for she is beautiful and extraordinary and deserves your whole heart. Hold nothing back.

Kylee, be patient with him, and love him unconditionally.

Love,

Emma

Kylee's face reddened at Emma's knowledge of their actions. Jack picked up on her discomfort right away, smiling at her innocence.

"Emma is a woman who knows the ways of the world," he laughed. "Now, ring that little bell and see what happens."

Kylee smiled sweetly, picked up the ceramic bell, and dangled it between her fingers. As soon as it tinkled, an attractive young woman emerged from the kitchen, placed a large silver tray between them and lifted the cover. The aroma of pheasant and vegetables filled the room, making their mouths water.

Jack served his wife first, making sure she would be satiated and at full strength when he whisked her away, back to their little nest upstairs.

Neither of them spoke for a long while, as they ate slowly, enjoying every morsel of food that crossed their lips.

When they had finally finished, Jack stood, reaching his hand out for her to accept, and then led her upstairs again.

"This has been the best day of my life," Kylee softly said as they nestled in again, consumed with lust and fever for one another.

"Aye, my wicked imp, for me as well," he sighed, "but tomorrow I must go. Ye know that, don't ye?"

"I do," she quietly replied, "And I understand…I really do. But do ye really think Gar has caught up with us? Do ye really think he'll even try?" she asked with teary eyes, propping herself up onto her elbow, looking into his uncertain stare.

"When it comes to you, I'll take no chances," he said as he rose from the bed, baring his naked body. Jack turned and faced her with anger welling up inside him, his hands forming fists at his sides. "I don't want to talk about that bastard, not here, not with ye. Can't we just have this time for ourselves?" he barked.

"I'm sorry. I just don't…" she began.

"I know ye don't want me to go, Kylee. And I know ye don't understand why I'm goin', although ye say ye do. I have to make sure he never lays eyes upon ye again. He can't be given the opportunity to hurt ye," he growled, cutting her off. The fact was, Jack feared that if there was money, arrogance and reputation at stake, then O'Shea was capable of doing unfathomable evils to serve his own ego.

"Alright, love," she whispered, mollifyingly. He had never let Kylee see him angry, and he struggled to rein it in now. Her soft voice washed over his hardened flesh when she added, "Come, get back into bed then, we have to make the best of the time we have."

Jack crawled back in beside her, shaking off his uncertainties and fears about Garvan O'Shea ever catching up to them.

'*I have to find him first*,' he thought, his annoyance subsiding a little but making room for passion and fury. Tiny kisses turned fevered. Light, tender touches became brutal. A familiar sensation clawed its way inside him, slithering from the depths of his soul, and instinctively, he welcomed it.

Before he could blink, he was inside her. Her soft yielding flesh welcomed him home. Jack let out a low growl, raised her arms above her head and pinned them with one massive hand. Unable to move or touch her husband, Kylee let out a helpless little whimper as she struggled to tear her arms free.

~

"Let me touch ye, Jack," she pleaded. The severity in which he held her didn't inflict injury, but her pulse kicked up a notch or two.

"Quiet or I'll redden yer arse, wicked imp," he panted, as he pumped into her again and again. A giggle escaped her lips, for this was a completely different side of Jack. Overpowering. Commanding. He stopped dead and asked, "Ye don't think I will?" His gaze was different. Dark. Foreign. She didn't laugh again, for both the fear and excitement welling up inside her prevented it.

He took her with severity, not letting her move an inch. She couldn't tell if he was angry or in the throes of passion. Either way, this side of him quenched a thirst she'd not known existed. Images of Jack spanking her bottom overheated and spiked in her bloodstream. She couldn't help herself. She just *had* to test him.

"Let go," she protested. "I want to touch ye." Nervousness and anticipation grew inside her like a vine, wrapping around every needy part of her.

Jack rose from the bed in haste and retrieved a long piece of rope from his leather bag. She watched him with equal amounts of eagerness and unease.

He wrapped the length of rope around her wrists, winding it until he knew she wouldn't twist her way out, and then attached the other end to the bedpost in the same fashion.

Kylee watched in utter shock as her kind, sensitive and gentle husband contorted into something quite opposite.

His expression had a dark sinister undertone that sent chills up her spine. This side of him, to her surprise, was exhilarating and caused excitement to bubble beyond her wildest dreams.

"If ye insist on speakin' without permission, I'll make ye *beg* for me to release ye from yer own need," he growled.

Jack Manning – her doting and caring husband – was gone, lost within the beast lingering inside him. Despite her unforeseen excitement, she refused to smile. This Jack wanted her tears.

Kylee closed her eyes. The man who lay next to her, with his hands, and mouth moving about her body was a perplexing mystery. She was safe in his arms, no matter what. In that regard, she had no doubt. But what did he require from her in return? Still plagued by the mysteries of the art of lovemaking, Kylee gave in to her body's desire, closed the door on her over-active mind and took all he had to give.

Hands tethered, without the distraction of touching him, she was forced to feel everything. Jack kissed a path between each breast and then travelled to her needy mound, lapping at her with his tongue.

So intimate. So unbearably sensitive. This was the most pleasure she had ever felt in her life.

He'd taste and then stop, leaving her wanting more, struggling against her restraints, struggling to grab him, to hold him, to steady her quivering body.

Just as the explosion overtook her, he'd retreat. Again, and again he did this, until her whimpers became intense and sombre. "I can't take any more, Jack. Please." With a low growl, Jack finished what he'd started, pulling a satisfied wail from her throat, that even she didn't recognize.

As Kylee's damp body went limp, and the world around her had gone black, Jack reached up and untied her bonds, with a familiar and gentle touch.

Kylee was confused, yet strangely contented. This was not the man whom she married just the day before. Yesterday's Jack was her husband, the warrior. The man in her bed moments ago, was her lover. Questions and uncertainty claimed her mind. Questions begged for answers.

'What else is he hidin' from me?' she thought, emotions washing over her in waves. Sobs wracked her body, for both the pleasure and the chaos.

Jack took her into his arms and rocked her back and forth, rubbing away the redness the rope had left behind. "Shh, Kylee. Ye have to know I love ye. I didn't mean to…" he trailed off, obviously struggling to find the right words. "I don't know what I meant to do. I lost my head. If I hurt ye, I'm so sorry." Kylee looked into his eyes, finding that *her* Jack had returned, only now, he appeared wretched and submerged in guilt. Tears bubbled beneath his eyelids.

She reached up and touched his face. "Ye didn't hurt me, I'm just…" she trembled, for she didn't know how to put into words that she'd enjoyed the bonds, that her body had become hyper-sensitive. "I love ye, I'll always love ye," she added, unable to understand her own emotions, or the excitement that his actions had just brought about. She could only speak the truth that she understood; she loved both the man, and the lover.

Jack buried his face in her hair and then lifted her from the bed. Sitting her on the side of the tub, he rubbed salve over the chafe marks. "I've ripped away yer innocence. I don't deserve ye," Jack said, his Adam's apple bobbing furiously, as if each word threatened to cut off his air.

Kylee brought his lips to hers. "My love is unconditional. We'll figure all this out together," she replied and claimed his mouth with her own.

The next morning, when Kylee awoke, the bed beside her was cold and empty, save a note on Jack's pillow. With teary eyes and fearing the worst, she picked it up and began to read.

My wicked Kylee,

I hate myself for what happened last night. I know ye have questions, but I do not have the answers ye deserve, just yet.

I've gone to Brady's. From there we will make our way back toward Ennis, in search of O'Shea. Ye'll not fear him again. I hope when I return, ye'll not fear me either.

I regret ever bringin' ye here, as this place brings out the monster within me.

When all this is behind us, we'll go home, and start our future together – the way we should have.

All My Love,

Jack

Dread and despair swallowed her instantly. Kylee covered her head with the quilt and cried until there were no more tears left to shed.

TWELVE

Hot steam blasted from the nostrils of Gar-van's prized steed as he wasted no time reaching his destination. Nothing would come between he and his destiny.

Fury built within him with every mile he put between himself and his father.

'Cut me off will he? When I bring that little bitch back, he'll have no choice in handin' over what's mine. Kylee O'Roarke will be sorry for the rest of her pathetic life,' Gar thought, holding the reins with a deadly white-knuckled grip.

He didn't know where to begin looking for this Jack Manning fellow, for he'd never heard of the man. But when he made his presence known in Galway he was sure someone would give Jack up… for the right price. However, getting there would prove to be a challenge. He wasn't exactly a woodsman and the road was a desolate wasteland with the surrounding forests harbouring who knows what kind of creatures.

The first night tested his nerves as he made a small camp fire to stay warm by. Stuck out in the elements, the snow came pummelling down. He had nothing but a horse blanket, a pack of matches and of course, his trusty amber friend to keep him warm. He took another quaff, letting the liquid burn his throat all the way down.

The nearby howling of wolves had him second guessing his decision to forgo the inn he'd passed a while back. What he wouldn't give right now for that refuge and comfort.

He sank himself next to his warm steed underneath the thick blanket and prayed for daylight to arrive. With every icy shiver, he hated Kylee even more for escaping his wrath.

Gar had led a life of luxury and security, his father having given his only two children everything they'd ever thought to ask for. Fiona was always the favourite, as she was the precious gem of a daughter who'd done as she was told. Even now, as a grown woman, she dutifully obeyed the old man.

Gar hadn't always been a volatile scoundrel, either. While he was a young boy of eleven or twelve, his father had been priming him to take the reins when he'd reached an age to do so. He'd been an eager student back then, always following his father's direction and quick to catch on to the paperwork side of things as well.

He and his father would stay up late in the evenings going over the ledgers for the day. And Paddy seemed to beam with pride that Garvan had taken such a keen interest in the brewery, tavern and hotel. He'd proved to be a quick learner.

Things seemed to change when Gar turned sixteen. That's when he'd discovered women. One girl in particular had caught his attention and no one could've predicted the dreadful outcome. *The only woman I'll truly ever love.* She'd haunt him until his dying day.

Rachel Keane, a proper young lady, bred from a wealthy noble family, had turned his head. She hailed from generations and generations of well-to-do's. It seemed like the perfect match for everyone, as her family owned a shipping company. Having the two youngsters marry would solidify unlimited connections for the O'Shea's.

Paddy O'Shea and Brigg Keane, the girl's father, had set up business with plans to export the O'Shea's fine ale across the Atlantic Ocean to Newfoundland and Boston, where many of Ireland's people were immigrating since the famine.

This new island promised a fresh start for many, and if O'Shea and Keane could sell them a little piece of the motherland, it was a beneficial arrangement for both families.

When Rachel and Gar were first introduced, he was smitten with her upon first glance. She was angelic, with fine features and a petite frame. Her hair was as smooth and sleek as fine chocolate. Gar longed to bury his nose within the long soft locks to see if they smelled as sweet.

At first, she seemed put off by him. Like he was a nuisance she'd been forced to endure. Not having had his growth spurt yet, he stood nearly a foot shorter than she. The fact that she literally looked down on him, hadn't caused his spirit or his hopes of marrying her to wane. Quite the contrary in fact. Her dismissal and conjecture drove him onward.

Despite being a lad with a pudgy middle, dirty-looking red hair and bulging pimples peppering his face, Garvan waited patiently with flowers every Sunday morning after mass. Even though the likelihood of Rachel tossing said flowers to the ground was great, Garvan was eager to receive any kind of attention – good or bad – she'd bestow upon him. He'd been content to follow Rachel around, carrying her parcels, serving as a perfect doormat for her to walk all over, as she stuck her high-bred nose in the air.

A few months after they'd met, Rachel was sent to England for her last year of proper schooling, leaving Garvan to patiently wait for her return in the spring.

When the time came, he paced in front of her father's estate, waiting for the carriage to pull up to her door. When Rachel emerged, Garvan was no longer the awkward, pest of a lad he'd been. Now he was a man. And gauging from her expression, he'd done well that year apart, growing out of his boyish frame, pocked face and unruly feral-looking hair.

He now stood over six feet tall, his complexion had cleared, and he'd lost his baby weight. He oozed with masculine virility and charm – or so the young lassies who'd been vying for his attention had said. When their gazes connected, it seemed Rachel had been holding her breath. Perhaps she'd been dreading her return, dreading the constant attention from Garvan and his too-forward displays of affection. All grown up now, Garvan understood how to show his fondness, without making an arse of himself.

He held out his hand and escorted her from her carriage, and then complimented her on the dress she wore. "Beautiful, Rachel, stunning. Blue is definitely yer color," he adoringly praised.

"Thank you, Gar, you look so… different," Rachel smiled, a full blush tinting the apples of her cheeks.

"Been workin' hard this past year and it's done me good. But, m'lady, ye're as pretty as ever!" he replied, and then kissed her gloved hand.

"I…I don't know what to say, Gar. You flatter me," she said waving her hand to fan her reddened face.

That summer the two were inseparable. Rachel would surprise him with picnics in her garden, and

Gar would show up at her home holding a bouquet of Daisies, which he knew were her favourite.

On warm days, Gar took her fishing, although he knew nothing about the sport – being more of an indoor fellow. But they'd laughed and held hands by the riverbed, and patiently waited until her escort wasn't looking, so he could steal a kiss.

Garvan took her shopping in chic boutiques, buying her whatever her heart desired, and sometimes Rachel could even persuade him to buy something for himself.

He was certain he would never find a woman like this if he searched the world over. He loved her, and he knew she loved him.

"Will ye marry me, Rachel?" he asked one evening as they strolled hand in hand through her garden.

"We're too young yet," she giggled, looking around to see if anyone was watching, and then rose up on her toes to kiss his cheek.

"I know, I know. But we won't always be. And 'tis not like our families don't expect it. Hell, they set it up in the first place!" he laughed.

Gar laughed so often in those days, when life was simple and she was by his side. "I just want to know ye'll forever be mine, is all. I fear that one day someone better will come along and steal ye away from me," he replied seriously.

Rachel looked into his deep, worried brown eyes and smiled tenderly. "Never! No one could ever compare to ye Garvan O'Shea…no one!" She took his hand, brought it to her lips, and kissed his knuckles. "But yes, I will marry ye. We can announce what will be a long engagement tomorrow night at father's party," she exclaimed.

Gar wanted to shout hoorays from the top of his lungs and kiss her deeply, but being on her land, with her escort in pursuit of them, that was out of the question.

They announced their official engagement the very next evening, just as everyone sat down to supper. The entire hall was bursting with words of well-wishes, the young couple becoming the focus of the party.

Gar remembered his father leading him into Brigg's study, where the three of them could discuss the matter in private.

"Sit down, my boy!" Paddy had said, as Gar took a seat on the business side of the desk. His father cocked his head to the side and said, "Ye look like a natural behind that desk. Feels good to sit in a place of power and control doesn't it?"

Gar swept his hands over the cold marble desktop and smiled.

"Aye, it sure does," he replied.

"Well, then I think it's time to give ye what ye've been workin' for all this time," his father said reaching into his tunic pocket and pulled forth an envelope. He carefully opened it and began to read, "In the event of my death, I, Patrick O'Shea of Ennis, County Clare do hereby leave all my assets and holdings to my eldest child, Garvan O'Shea, with the exception of the family home, which is to be bestowed upon my daughter, Fiona O'Shea."

Garvan gaped at his father with wide eyes but said nothing.

"There's more to tell ye, Gar. Close your mouth b'y!" Paddy laughed and continued, "However, the day of Garvan's wedding, regardless of my circumstances, he shall acquire the rights and control of all the family businesses, to run and operate as he sees fit."

"Da! I don't know what to say. I mean, 'tis unbelievable!" Gar exclaimed.

"Well, son, I think it's about time I retire. Ye know the business. I've no worries of ye runnin' things while I peacefully live out my days, sippin' ale on the front porch. I'm gettin' too old for all this," Paddy said light heartedly.

A smile ignited Gar's features and a sense of pride took hold. "I can't wait to tell Rachel. She'll be so excited!" he shouted, nearly soaring from his seat.

"'Tis why I set it all up for after ye marry. I believe every successful man needs a good woman to keep him grounded," Paddy replied, a frown etching his face, no doubt remembering what it was like having a woman by his side. Fiona had taken their mother's life when she came screaming into the world, and while Gar had only been four when she passed, sometimes he found himself missing her. "She'll treat ye good, Gar. She'll help ye grow into a good businessman, husband, and father." Garvan embraced his father, and thanked him over and over again and then ran back to the great hall to give the news to his bride-to-be.

Gar and Rachel were well on their way to living the life they were destined to live, until a harmless riding excursion changed everything.

Rachel's competitive nature kicked in at full force, as she prompted her mare to take the first jump.

"Heeeawww! Up ye go!" she giggled as her mare cleared the first row of brush.

"Rachel, be careful, love!" Garvan had called after her. She stood in her stirrups, turned around, and blew a kiss back at her betrothed, and then smiled. It was the last time Gar would see the enchanting ray of sunshine beaming in his direction.

While trying to keep up with her rapid pace, he watched in horror as she urged her mare over a neighbouring fence. The mare flinched, losing its nerve, sending Rachel soaring over the beasts shaking head. She landed with a lifeless thud onto the hot rocky ground. The spooked animal was nowhere in sight by the time Gar reached her.

"Rachel! Rachel, open yer eyes, love. Rachel!" Garvan shook the motionless girl with urgency and panic. Lifting her into his arms, a pool of thick blood dripped heavily as he carried her to his horse, laying her across its thick back.

When finally he'd arrived at her house, he carried her up the steps, hollering for help as he kicked the door until someone opened it.

"Oh, dear Jesus! What's happened?" Rachel's mother shrieked.

"I…she fell…the horse knocked 'er…" Garvan couldn't even spit the words out of his dry, hoarse mouth.

"Brigg! Brigg! Come, hurry!" her mother screeched. When Brigg Keane appeared, the color and life drained from his face.

"Give her to me, Gar," he'd said, dislodging his daughter's limp body from Gar's embrace. "Go and fetch the doctor, boy!"

Gar sprinted to his horse, which now had her blood streaming down its flank. He rode with severity, despite the anguish threatening to knock him from his own mount.

Upon his return with the doctor, he waited for what seemed an eternity outside her bedchamber door, each treacherous tick of the clock on the wall mocking him, forcing his guilt and despair to the surface.

Then he heard the unfathomable. Rachel's mother let out a high-pitched cry from within, her sorrow echoing throughout the manor.

Gar couldn't think. He didn't know what to do. He knew the worst had happened, and his assumption was confirmed when the doctor emerged, wiping his bloody hands in a rag. The haggard man shook his head at the now trembling Garvan. He bolted from the house.

When he reached the courtyard outside, he watched as her mare lazily trotted up the driveway, reins dragging along the dirt beneath its feet.

"Imprudent, bloody animal," he growled, boiling vengeance causing the blood in his veins to surge. *'Tis all yer fault.*

In three long strides, he was reaching into his saddle bag. He withdrew his pistol, walked up to the horse, and pressed the gun to its head. He pulled back the hammer and squeezed the trigger, heartlessly and mercilessly extinguishing the beasts life.

He could muster no emotion as the huge animal wobbled to the ground with an awful groan, it's nostrils flaring as it struggled to suck in each breath. That sound still haunted him sometimes as he slept.

Garvan was never the same after that day. Living without Rachel meant a life of misery. What disturbed him mostly now, were the visions of her. The remembrance of their happiness, followed by the certainty that he would never find joy again.

As Gar rested upon his steed's belly seeking its warmth, but still shivering uncontrollably, the ancient memories and agony flooded back. He tried his best to make them go away; liquor usually done the trick, but not this night. Rachel's memory was relentless.

Here, chasing after Kylee in the wilderness, he felt as forlorn and abandoned as he'd felt in those first days, months, and years that followed Rachel's death.

He'd been torn apart. The kind and carefree boy who had once existed was no more.

Taking another swig and pulling the blanket to his chin, he cursed under his breath again, reflecting on the years that followed. It seemed, when Rachel died, he'd lost all control, as reality was always just out of reach. He drowned his misery with ale, wine and whiskey – whiskey being his favourite anaesthetic.

Paddy, on more than one occasion, had found his once intelligent and immaculately kept son, in a pool of his own drunken mess. Gar recalled none too fondly, getting a kick in the arse.

"Gar! Get yer dirty arse up off the floor and get to bed! A bath wouldn't kill ye either," his father had shouted, but Gar refused to budge. Like so many times before and after, he'd just groan and go back to sleep. That's the way things became. Paddy and Fiona tried their best to take care of Gar, help him get over the loss, but nothing seemed to work.

In the early stages of his grief they had been sympathetic, but enough time had passed for him to move on, yet he hadn't.

Garvan sank deeper and deeper into a realm all his own, where most days and nights seemed to blur into one. It wouldn't be long before Paddy reached his breaking point and gave him the ultimatum, and while Gar had been powerless to stop his reckless behaviour, he knew it had been coming.

"Gar, come into my office!" Paddy had shouted. Garvan's head popped up after just having downed another tankard of ale, and was wiping his dirty bearded face with the sleeve of his torn and tattered shirt.

Grunting and staggering, Garvan lazily made his way toward his father who rolled his eyes as he held open the office door. "Gar, for Christ's sake!" Paddy sighed, closing the door, blocking out the noisy patrons on the other side. "I used to have such bright hopes for ye. What's happened to ye, b'y?"

Gar glanced in his father's direction, the concern and worry evidently aging the man beyond his fifty-odd years. Instead of guilt and shame, Garvan could only find hate and blame in his sodden blackened heart.

"Wha' ya talkin' about ol' man? I grew up…issss all," Gar slurred.

Paddy wiped his face in his hands and shook his head. "I'm talkin' about this need of yers to self-destruct, Gar. The drinkin', the gamblin', the treatment of the ladies. Don't think I ain't heard what ye been doin' to 'em. It all has to stop, lad. Ye should be ashamed of yerself!"

Garvan pointed his finger, narrowed his gaze. "Nay! They should all be ashamed! The way they use me, grovellin' at my feet for just a copper! And after I've given 'em the best screwin' they ever got!" he spat with a crooked grin.

Paddy cocked his head to the side, a serious crease now between his brows. "And what do ye think Rachel would say if she could see ye now with nothin' to call yer own and no hopes for the future? Do ye think she'd still love a filthy drunk like you?"

"What do ye mean, nothin'? Why! I've still got all of this. Isn't it wonderful?" Gar spread his arms wide, shooting his father a yellow-toothed smirk.

"Aye, ye have no idea what ye *could've* had. It *could* have been wonderful. I know I promised ye that ye'd run it all, but ye have to remember, that was upon the day ye wed," Paddy replied, his face blotching, blood-red with anger. "Ye have no idea how close ye came to havin' it all. I would 'ave still granted it to ye, but I can't now, after ye've seen fit to ruin yerself." Paddy placed his hands upon the desk in front of him. Garvan knew it was to keep himself reined in. Then, tears bubbled in Paddy's brown-eyes. "Watchin' how ye let it all slip away nearly tore the guts outta me.

"From here on in, I don't care what ye do to yerself, but I won't have ye bringin' Fiona and the business down with ye. Ye've left me no choice, Gar. If ye want the business, ye must marry. Let some pretty little colleen help ye set things right. Until that day comes, the arrangement stands."

"The arrangement stands?" Gar sobered instantly. "Ye won't retire 'til I marry?" he laughed, disbelief behind every thick chuckle.

"Aye. 'Tis what I'm sayin', lad," Paddy quietly replied. "I can't let ye destroy all I've built, Gar. Find a nice girl, settle down and raise a family. I'll trust ye with the rest when ye've grown into an honourable man."

Garvan had never given Paddy a reason to fear him until that night, but as swift and horrendous as a Spring Atlantic storm, Garvan had unleashed a tailspin of devastation.

With two fists of pure fury, he'd destroyed everything in his sight. The entire office had been reduced to rubbish and poor Paddy O'Shea had been reduced to a quivering milksop, huddled in the corner.

With each tirade, Garvan became more and more volatile, leaving behind as much devastation and destruction as he could. Fiona and Paddy had always picked up the pieces. Until now.

Now, the consequences of every misdeed he'd committed were upon him. He'd run out of options. All he could do was reflect upon the circumstances which brought him to this lonely place, somewhere between Galway and Clare. It was purgatory with no end in sight.

The cold piercing wind nipped at Gar's appendages, causing him to wake suddenly, fumbling around in the dawn to see if his ten fingers and ten toes were still attached.

'I'll not be made a fool of any longer,' he thought as he lifted his flask to his chattering mouth and let the whiskey warm him from the inside out.

The night of reflection, loneliness and despair had left him filled with a maddening rage. He was more determined than ever to return to Ennis *with* Kylee, whether she liked it or not.

He'd do whatever was necessary to prove to his father that he hadn't hurt the wench, and that she'd left on her own accord. And when he finally found her, by Jesus, he'd force her to the alter one way or another and claim what was rightfully his.

'*That Manning bastard will pay for takin' her too*,' he thought repugnantly.

His malevolent mind was in overdrive as he mounted his steed and headed out in search of her.

When I find 'er, she'll be beggin' me to bring her back to her Ma. And I will, with pleasure.

As his journey dragged on, he began to notice small lodgings along the way. Some were nicely kept cottages, while others were mere shanties, providing protection from the harsh pre-winter blizzard.

Coming to a halt just outside one such meagre place, more concealed than the rest, he thought it might be nice to warm his weary bones by a stove.

Hoping for some signs of life at the early hour, Garvan shouted, "G'mornin'. Can ye see it in yer heart to let a wayward fella warm his shiverin' skin by yer fire?"

The man who answered the door eyed Gar suspiciously, but granted him entry to his home, urging him to sit in a rocker by his warm crackling stove.

"Many thanks to ye." Garvan kicked his feet out in front of him and rubbed his hands together over the stove top.

"Who might ye be? What brings ye out here in the middle of the forest this time of mornin'?"

"I…ah…the name's Manning. Call me Jack," Gar lied. His gaze scanned the perimeter of the room looking for something to eat…or something to steal, his focus lingering upon the butcher knife hanging from a nail in a beam. "Say, have ye anything to satisfy an empty stomach? I have money. I could pay ye."

"I can certainly rustle somethin' up for breakfast, if ye don't mind stickin' around for a bit," the man replied, his expression and movements faltering just a little.

Did he know Jack Manning? Had he detected the deceit? Gar hadn't considered this until now, as the haggard old chap's kind smile had been replaced with a scowl.

"Thank ye, sir. Say, what do I call ye?" Gar asked, narrowing his gaze, scrutinizing each gesture, while still viciously massaging his hands over the hot stove top.

"Ye can call me Peter," the grizzly man replied, never taking his eyes off his guest for a moment. "Where are ye from, Gar?"

And there it was. The answer to Garvan's questions. He hadn't been paranoid; the man knew exactly who he was and why he was here. The only thing remained was how long Garvan would go on pretending he hadn't noticed Peter's slip-up.

Peter cracked four eggs into a frying pan, finally taking his eyes off the enemy. Perhaps he really hadn't realized his blunder. Or perhaps he was daft enough to believe Garvan hadn't noticed. Either way, there was a serious and deadly game at play, one where Garvan knew he'd eventually win.

"Ye're welcome to stay for a while if ye like. I've an extra cot if ye need to sleep a spell," Peter offered.

"I'll not be stayin' old man. I've business to attend to in Galway," Gar replied, as he stood and withdrew his knife from its scabbard. Peter's hands came up defensively, his gaze landing on the blade hanging just to his right. "Ye know who I am, aye?" Garvan pushed.

"I know, ye filthy bastard, and I'll not let ye leave here alive." Before Peter's head had a chance to tell his hand to reach out and grab the dangling weapon, it was too late; Garvan's dagger had landed square in his chest. The sound of cracking bone was music to Garvan's ears. A melody he longed to replay again and again.

He pulled the blade from Peter's chest, this time plunging it into the side of the old crow's neck. Moving in so close he could nearly taste the bitter tang of iron, he studied the wound as he twisted and gouged until blood came spewing out in spray. He watched in awe as the withered man's eyes bulged from their sockets in disbelief. It was the first time Garvan O'Shea had taken a human life, and he marvelled in it. Peter Dooley hadn't had a fighting chance against Garvan's self-righteous fury.

Pulling the gory blade from torn flesh, he wiped the blade clean using Peter's own shirt and let him fall to the floor grasping at his wound, sputtering blood and bile.

Garvan laid perfectly fried eggs in front of him and took a seat at the table, while the writhing man lay helplessly on the floor at his feet. With each leisured savoury bite he took, it was like he tasted food for the first time.

"The sight of ye will be warnin' enough that I mean to get 'er back. When Manning finds ye, he'll know this means war," Garvan snarled as he rose from the table, imposing one final swift kick to Peter's stomach, finishing him off altogether. As if he still hadn't had enough, Gar cruelly spat on the dying warrior.

More determined than ever, Garvan set out again to find Kylee and teach Jack Manning a lesson in minding his own business.

THIRTEEN

Kylee awoke on the second morning as a married woman, but memories of Jack's letter came flooding back, filling her with the deepest sadness and longing she'd ever experienced in her life. She stretched her arm across the cold void in the bed while her other hand still held his written words. They were an explanation of sorts, one she still didn't understand. The soft down mattress beneath her body cradled her, stripping her of any willingness to move. She re-read his words again and again, forcing her dry throat to swallow against the swelling mass of emotion.

'*I hope you'll not fear me either*,' he'd written.

Her focus flickered to her reddened wrists, her mind agonizing over how lost she'd been in a whirl-wind of sensuality and eroticism the night before.

His letter and quick departure proved he'd jumped to the conclusion that he'd frightened her. And now, he'd fled in shame and wretchedness. If only he'd known her truth – that she'd never felt so alive, so cherished, so worshipped and loved.

He'd ignited fires within her that she hadn't even known were lying dormant, and unfortunately, he'd departed before she'd had the chance to explain all of that to him. If only she could tell him now.

'What would I say? That I'm a wanton? That I'm no better than a common whore? That I long to be within his embrace and his bondage again?' she thought, anxiety consuming her, exhausting her back into a state of slumber.

"Kylee? Are you awake, darling?" came a soft and calming, far-off voice. Kylee uncovered her head from her feathery prison and squinted to locate the source. Her eyes narrowed when Emma sashayed across her floor, bearing the weight of an elaborate tray of food. "You must be absolutely starving."

In actuality, the sight and smell of the food as it hit her nose, almost made her gag, and so she curtly replied, "Nay, I'm not in the mood to eat, Emma. I'd thank ye to leave now."

Emma gasped, as if Kylee's dismissal surprised her, but the reaction only caused Kylee to sink further beneath the covers. She cared not that this was Emma's house; she cared even less that the woman meant well. Jack – her husband – shared a bond with this woman that wouldn't be shaken by Kylee's brand of malice.

The shattering icy tone in which Kylee banished Emma from the room was met with a sympathetic smile.

"Oh, Kylee. Please don't be cross with him for leaving. You knew he would, am I correct?" Emma asked. Even though her eyes reflected worry, Kylee bit her cheek to stop herself from saying what was on her mind. *Of course, she knows he's gone! The venomous wench probably knows every move he makes!*

Kylee turned away from the unwelcomed guest. "I'm not angry that he left. Ye know nothin'! Get out! Get out and just leave me be!" Kylee shouted, tears spilling down her cheeks.

After a sigh and then a dreadful silence, Emma spoke again. "What happened to your arms, Kylee? We must get that looked at and bandaged. We don't want you to fall ill with infection," Emma urged, now sitting beside Kylee on the bed, stroking her hair.

Kylee rubbed the bumpy flesh at her wrists, refusing to admit that it did sting…a little.

"This? This is nothin'," she quietly replied.

"Then why are you so angry, sweet girl?" Emma asked. "Tell me, you can trust me."

Kylee's head was spinning. She didn't quite grasp the weight of her own heart and emotions. She'd known Jack was leaving in the morning, and she'd understood that it was to protect her. But the pain in his words ripped through her like a serrated blade. She needed to confide in someone before it devoured her.

Kylee hung her head and sighed. "Emma, the…the things we did last night, here in this room, I can't speak of. They're…intimate things," Kylee fidgeted with a corner of the blanket, as tears streamed down her pink cheeks. "But, I let him leave here thinkin' that he'd hurt me, thinkin' that he'd done something wrong, when the truth is, I have never in my life, felt as close to another person, or as loved as I did last night."

The corner of Emma's mouth lifted with Kylee's confession, and suddenly her warm soft hands were steadying Kylee's franticly fidgeting ones.

"Kylee? Do you want me to help you?" Emma asked carefully, as Kylee's glossy eyes flickered to meet her gaze.

"What do ye mean? How could ye possibly help me? I've made a mess of things, and now he's gone and I can't tell him how he made me feel."

"Then tell *me*, Kylee. I know you consider last night's activities to be private and intimate, but I have known Jack for a very long time. I may be able to shed some light on the situation."

Kylee thought for a moment, leaving a great silence between them. Emma reached for Kylee's chin, turning her gaze back, and then smiled.

The genuine concern in Emma's gaze fought against Kylee's inner hostility, and won. "Please don't think me immoral, strange or a wanton. I've never lain with a man before Jack," she began and then paused with fiery cheeks.

"Continue, Kylee. Tell me how you feel," Emma insisted.

"Well, that first mornin' when we arrived back here from our weddin' at the Kelly's, he'd been so tender. I knew then, I would never love anyone like this, even if I lived to be two-hundred," Kylee rose from the bed wrapped in her thick blanket, and walked to the window, refusing to meet Emma's scrutiny. "Then last night, he…he was different."

"Different how, love?" Emma probed.

"At first, he'd been gentle, but then it was like somethin' took hold of 'im, and he was angry…but *not* angry. We'd been talkin' about him havin' to leave in search of Gar, and I don't know…he just snapped. Pure fury, that's what it was like."

"Oh, Kylee. Did he frighten you?"

"No…I mean, aye." *Sigh*. "I wasn't afraid. He threatened, and I taunted. Ye see these marks on my wrists?" Kylee turned and held out her arms. "These are from the rope he'd used to bind me. He refused to let me touch him. I was forbidden to speak. I was at his mercy."

"And *then*, were you frightened?" Emma softly asked. Kylee blinked a few times, gathering her thoughts. Emma seemed to ask these questions as if she'd already known the answers. Perhaps, Jack had already regaled her with the entire sordid ordeal.

"Nay. I was not afraid. After the initial shock of it, I never once felt anything but an intense need to give all of myself to him. He made me feel like I was alive. His, only his. I felt helpless…but I took more delight in that than I ever imagined," Kylee blew out. Emma nodded, patting Kylee's shoulder affectionately. The woman seemed to understand. *How could she understand?* "I know I'm just awful to have thoughts like these. What woman in 'er right mind would allow her husband to abuse her so, and take pleasure in it?" Kylee shouted. Gnawing at her bottom lip, she turned back toward the window to shield herself from further persecution.

Emma went to Kylee, steadying her but for a moment, their gazes connecting for a ripple in time. Lifting the blanket from Kylee's shoulders, Emma ushered her to the closet. "Let's get you dressed. There is much to talk about and so much for you to learn," she said. Emma just smiled in that special way only she could, and for a moment, Kylee felt a little better. A flutter in her belly ignited. *Emma might prove to be a great asset if I'm to ever understand that husband of mine.*

~

The time to break her alliance with Jack had come. There was no way Emma could bear witness to the girl's wretchedness for one more moment. She had to come clean – make Kylee understand what made her husband tick. The poor girl was in pieces, assuming she'd hurt him and drove him away. Kylee couldn't have been more wrong. It was time to rectify the situation.

Jack had come to Emma in the early hours of morning before his brutal departure. He'd described the horrendous and unforgivable way in which he'd treated his inexperienced and only recently deflow- ered wife. The picture he had painted of himself had been of a riotous, carnal beast finally released from its cage.

"I threatened to redden her arse, Emma," he'd quietly said, refusing to meet her gaze, "and I wanted nothin' more in this world than to follow through.

"As soon as I uttered those words, she provoked me, and I reacted in the only way I know how. The need to control and conquer 'er was bigger than my concern for her welfare. I tied 'er hands above 'er head and to the headboard.

"Her senses were heightened. I could feel 'er yearnin'. But lettin' her touch me would have distracted her. I couldn't have her distracted. I wanted her to feel untainted relentless pleasure. But she didn't submit. She fought against the ropes, instead." Jack buried his head in his trembling hands. Emma hadn't seen him so beside himself in years. "I hurt her, I know that now. Ye should have seen how she sobbed in my arms, it was heartbreaking."

"Shh, listen to me, love," Emma said as she lifted his head, forcing him to meet her kind eyes. "Now will you admit that you cannot hide or neglect this part of yourself? You should have explained what was happening *as* it was happening. It is a basic rule, Jack. She has to know that this runs thick in your blood."

Jack seemed to watch her closely as if his own reflection in her deep pools might reveal the mysteries within himself. Emma sighed and continued, "You are a good man, and I am sure you will be a better husband, but you have to let her into your world. Your whole world," she urged.

Jack stood, raking his fingers through his short dirty-blonde hair in frustration. "Nay! I'll not do it, Emma. She's too fragile, too pure. I'll not taint her by bringin' her into this fuck'ry," Jack roared.

That had been the last straw. Where good sense usually persevered, Emma knew that his wisdom had been drowning in a sea of guilt. But this time, he'd gone too far. Emma had taken this man who couldn't comprehend his inner urges under her wing, in his youth. She'd made him see that he was just a man – not some monster he'd come to believe he'd been. And now, here he was, in shambles again. Everything she'd taught him had been for nothing.

She searched his face for the Jack Manning whom she'd come to admire, respect and adore. He wasn't there. All that remained was the shell of who he used to be, only weeks before…before Kylee. The pain of it cut through her like daggers, straight to her core.

"If you feel this way about our lifestyle, Jack, then perhaps it is best if you take her from here…tonight," she said, turning her back to him so he couldn't see the hurt that lay beneath her solemn expression. She felt the warm heat of his presence behind her in an instant.

"I'm just so…" he whispered desperately, "please don't make me take 'er away from here. I'd fear for her safety anywhere else," Jack pleaded, rubbing her icy shoulders, and then turned her to face him again. "Ye're all I have – all I've ever had. I need ye now more than ever."

Emma was losing her patience. She wanted to slap some logic back into the lout, but being a lady prevented it.

"All right, Jack," she sighed. "All I ask while you're away is that you think about what you want in this life.

"Will you be content living a lie merely because you *assume* she will not understand or approve? Or can you help her embrace your inner beast? Help her learn to love not only you, but the side of you that you try so terribly to hide?" Emma walked to the serving table and poured him a cup of piping hot coffee and urged him to drink.

"Thank ye," he said, retrieving the cup with shaky hands. "I understand that her being here will prove to be a challenge for ye. And I'm not sure what I'm gonna tell her when she asks about what happened tonight. But I can promise ye, I'll think about it. I doubt I'll think of much else."

"Good." Emma replied curtly. "If I let her stay, and she opens up to me about what went on between you two, I am not going to lie to her, nor will I hide anything that goes on here. Those are my terms. Can you live with them?" These terms were harsh but Emma meant every word.

She'd left him with little choice in the matter, knowing Kylee's safety was of the greatest importance. It was the only card Emma had to play and she'd played it well. The coming days would bring a wealth of knowledge and awareness to her young charge, but Emma was eager to give Kylee a glimpse into Jack's life, waging on the girl's openness and acceptance.

Then Jack narrowed his gaze on his dearest friend, as if she was now the enemy. Emma's heart sank when Jack's pointed finger jabbed into the satin robe she wore. "If I lose 'er because of what she learns about me, I'll never forgive ye. Remember what she means to me, Emma," his voice thick with warning. The flame in Jack's eyes reminded her of the first days when she'd invited him to the manor.

So full of self-disgust and disquiet. He was a mirror image of the boy she'd rescued, even now.

"If you show her who you truly are, and she still leaves you, then, Jack I'm sorry, but it was never meant to be," Emma said, carefully, stilling a quiver threatening her bottom lip. "I think you will do more harm by leaving her here this way, without really talking to her about it. You really need to tell her yourself."

Jack shook his head, a pained and tormented expression pulling at the lines in his face. "I can't go to 'er. I can't even look at 'er without seein' the pain I caused. If I could, what would I say? I have no words to explain what came over me. I need to get away from here. She'll understand in time. She knew my intentions to leave her here in search of that bastard she'd been tangled up with," Jack replied, totally exhausted. "I still have to make sure he's not out there somewhere, lookin' for 'er."

Emma simply nodded despite the fact that she disagreed with his methods. But she'd be damned if Jack thought Kylee would stay there under her roof and remain oblivious to what really went on within the walls of The Haven.

The time has come to school Mrs. Manning on the ways of her husband's world.

FOURTEEN

Jack and Brady set out for Ennis as soon as they had broken their fast. It had been an awkward and silent meal – quite ridiculous really, considering the two had so very much to discuss. Jack brooded over the leftover gruel, wishing he hadn't arrived so early. Had he waited even another hour, Mary would've had a fresh batch prepared for the rest of the household, and most likely warm oatcakes and pork-side too. But he couldn't have waited. There was no way in God's name he could live with himself waking up next to his shattered fragile wife. Not after all he'd done to cause it.

"Are ye gonna' tell me what's gotten yer arse all hot this mornin'?" Brady asked as the two saddled their respective beasts. "Don't tell me the wee little she-devil's causin' ye trouble again," Brady laughed.

Jack's temper was at an all-time high and he would have loved nothing more than to pummel his friend to a pulp, but he didn't need another reason to hate himself today.

Instead, he quietly replied, "Nay, just worried about 'er there with Emma, is all."

"Ye got no worries 'bout that, ol' boy! I'm sure Emma will take good care of 'er," Brady winked. Jack knew if he didn't start talking soon, Brady would ceaselessly provoke him until he did. "What room over there do ye think Kylee will like best? Hmm, I'm thinkin' the red room. She seems like a girl who needs flowers, romance and the like."

Rousing anger always did the trick. "Enough, Brady! For all things holy, enough," Jack shouted, startling Thunder, thus requiring Brady to calm his steed and quiet his distressed whickers. "She'll never know what goes on over there. I should have never told ye about that place. Drop it before I beat the piss out of ye!"

"Not 'til ye tell me what happened. All I know, is that ye both left here the other mornin', newly wed and happy. Today, here ye are, contrary, full of shame and not fit to talk to. The last time I seen ye this way was…"

"I know when it was, now shut the hell up! I don't wanna talk about the past, present or the future. Let it go!" Jack started out of the stable, but Brady caught hold of his arm, his silvery sapphires on full alert, pinning Jack beneath his unwavering scrutiny yet again.

"What have ye done? Why do ye hate yerself so?" Brady suddenly, yet softly asked, searching Jack's gaze. If remorse and shame was edible, Jack could've fed it to the horses. They could have fed on his flesh for weeks.

Jack shook his head. "I let the beast out last night." Brady took a deep breath. "And now she has finally witnessed that horrific side of me I vowed to hide from her forever," Jack said, slumping against a bale of hay. "I don't know how she feels about me today. I can only assume she fears me now. I can't even think about it. I have to keep 'er safe from O' Shea."

"Jack, ye need to tell 'er about The Haven. Ye need to tell her the truth. I bet ye'd be surprised. The way that girl looks at ye, hell, she'd love ye if ye were the Devil himself."

"Nay. She can't ignore this, Brady. She's so innocent. How could I expect her to understand a different flavour of what she's used to? She's known abuse. How will she see my tactics as anything else?" Jack went on to tell Brady all of the intimate details about how he'd violently taken Kylee, how he'd tied her, refused to let her find release. It had been a form of amorous torture – body worship at its finest. He'd taken complete control of her every need, and until he permitted her a reprieve, she'd have been under his care…his spell even. The subject of Garvan

O'Shea had entered their bedchamber and now, even explaining it to Brady, Jack had no innocent notions that it hadn't fucked with his mind some. Knowing the bastard had lain his dirty mitts upon his sweet innocent wife made his blood curdle in his veins. Those thoughts alone had sparked Jack's cruelty and severity. "Her tremblin' body told the tale of the traumas she's suffered, both then and now. Her wide, questioning eyes haunt me. Her unreadable expression and silence gutted me."

"Well, we'll deal with it when we return. Ye know she's safe and sound with Emma for now, and will remain there 'til we return," Brady said as he mounted. "Right now, we have to find that Gar fucker and put an end to 'im ever findin' her. Make sure he never enters yer marriage bed again. Have ye thought about that yet? How you're gonna ensure her safety in the future?"

"Nay, not yet. But we need to find out what his intentions are. Or, if he even has a notion of comin' after her. She may hate me by now, but I'll protect her for the rest of my pathetic life," Jack vowed, pulling himself atop his steed. "I say, we head back from which we came, follow the old road, and check in with my friends. If there has been any sign of strangers, they'll know."

Just as both men emerged from the stable, Violet came rushing their way with a soft smile, bearing a package wrapped in a checked table cloth.

"Wait! Brady, wait!" she sang. "I've packed ye some lunch. I won't have my two best fella's gettin' hungry later on," she smiled prettily. Brady returned it with a broad grin. He jumped down from Thunder's back and wrapped his muscled arms around his wife and then laid his hand across her small belly bump.

"Please don't worry yerself over us. We'll be fine. And take care of the little bun, don't over-exert yerself while I'm away. Liam and Mary will see to yer every need," he said and then kissed her lips passionately, breathlessly.

"I'll take it easy, I promise," she sweetly replied.

"We both know Liam won't so much as let ye lift a finger," Brady laughed and kissed her again, this time on the tip of her nose, making her wrinkle it up in that way that caused Brady to beam. "I love ye, fair colleen."

Before Violet could reply and gush, Jack interrupted the lovers' lament. "Thank ye, Violet, for the lunch," he cut in. "I'll take care of him, I swear to ye," he said, smiling for the first time today.

"Aye, take care of each other," she replied, blowing them both a kiss, and bid them farewell.

Riding side by side for what seemed like days, so lost in his own head that he almost hadn't noticed they were approaching the first of his comrade's camps, Jack looked up at the rickety thatched-roof shack.

"Marin Dooley lives there now. Do ye remember his brother Peter?" Jack pointed, as they cautiously advanced on the paltry site.

"Aye, he was the commander of the guard when we were still in short pants," Brady replied.

"That's right. I dropped in on Peter when Kylee and I were travellin' from Ennis. He said he'd send word to Marin if Gar was spotted. Let's see what he has to say."

Before Jack could even dismount, Marin Dooley was standing in the doorway, pistol aimed straight at them.

"Who goes there?" the old man screeched, as his trembling hands fought with his weapon.

"'Tis me Jack. Jack Manning. Lower yer weapon b'y!"

When Marin focussed on him, a toothless grin found his face.

"Jack! My boy! Come in, come in. Who's yer friend?" Marin coughed, staggered and then caught himself on the edge of the porch rail.

"This is Brady Kelly. Yer brother, Peter, used to work at the Kelly's, do ye remember?" Jack asked.

"Aye, I remember. The poor bastard would be still commandin' the guard there if ye hadn't stolen his job from 'im, eh Jack!" Marin laughed. "What brings ye here to see the likes of me?"

"I meant to see ye last week, but I had a pretty little package with me and needed to get 'er tucked safely away," Jack replied with a tight lump in his throat as visions of Kylee haunted him. "Have ye heard from Peter in the last few days? He said if there were any strange happenin's on the road, then he'd get word to ye."

"Nay, haven't heard a peep, not out of any of them. I likes it that way though. Keepin' to myself and all. What kind of strange stuff brings ye worry?"

"Lookin' to see if me and the wife have been fol-lowed from County Clare. There's a man who might not like to see she's moved on."

"Yer wife? Well, congratulations, my boy!" Marin swatted Jack on the back so hard he nearly lost his balance, landing him right on his arse. "But nay, nothin'. No news is good news, right?"

"Aye, I guess it is, or at least I hope so. We're gonna go on to yer brother's place just the same.

Probably make camp there tomorrow evenin'. If he's waitin' on provisions, we'll gladly take them up to him. Save ye a trip," Jack said. "In the meantime, if ye see anythin' or *anyone* out of the ordinary, make sure to take caution."

"What does the lout look like? What's the bastard's name?" Marin asked as he packed sugar, tea and coffee into a burlap sack and handed it to Brady.

"Garvan O'Shea. Ye'll know 'im when ye see him. He's a dirty drunk, with red over-grown hair. Don't let him in. I don't know how dangerous he is. Take care of yerself, old man. We'll be seein' ye on our way back."

Jack and Brady set out again. Jack was relieved that Marin hadn't received word from his brother. So much, he considered not continuing onward. Instead, he fought the urge to return to The Haven and fall into Kylee's arms. Reveal all his inner demons, with a glimmer of hope that she might love him anyway.

The following evening, as the two men approached Peter Dooley's shack, the air turned glacial.

The trees whispered their ominous tales, despite the lack of wind. With gooseflesh prickling his skin, Jack waited for Peter to emerge as he always had when company arrived, but no one came out to greet them.

Brady began to dismount, but Jack stopped him with an outstretched hand. "Wait. Somethin's not right. Peter always comes out to greet company or scare off trespassers," Jack gravely said, his eyes flickering from the lifeless camp to the surrounding forest.

"Perhaps he's out on a hunt," Brady replied.

"Perhaps," Jack said, slowly dismounting, and cautiously made his way to the door. "Hello? Peter?" He knocked and then pushed it open. About half way, the wood barrier became impassable. Something on the other side prevented entry. Jack sucked in a breath and squeezed his body between the door and the jamb, only to find a gruesome sight.

Peter Dooley lay dead in a pool of his own blood.

"Brady! Come quick!" Jack hollered, frantically searching all directions for a killer still lurking.

When Brady caught the ghastly sight of Peter, he gagged and then turned away, holding a kerchief to his nose. "I think it's safe to assume Garvan O'Shea is hot on yer tail, Jack. And he's out for blood."

FIFTEEN

Garvan watched silently within the shadows of Peter Dooley's meagre shack. When he'd first spotted the travellers, he hadn't been alarmed. In fact, he'd barely paid any attention at all. He merely continued to eat what the old man had left in his pantry – as skimpy as it might've been.

Gar had considered ridding himself of the stiff lying next to the door, but that task was the last thing on his mind. With Kylee still out there, and the promise of his father's fortune still to come, his only thoughts were, '*Get my gut stuffed and then find Kylee.*'

Nevertheless, he couldn't deny that taking a man's life for the first time had both exhilarated and astounded him. Leaving the corpse where the poor bastard lay, served a dual purpose: to satisfy his lazy streak, and gave him the ability to admire his own handiwork whenever he wished.

He'd been relaxing at the kitchen table, a flask of brandy close to his lips when he heard one deep voice break through the morning stillness. Forced to make a move, Garvan dashed through an open window at the back of the camp and then waited, listening closely. Who were they? What did they want with the departed recluse?

Garvan stuck closely to the outer wall, clinging to the weather-beaten wood. He hung on to each and every word exchanged between the men; no detail was too small. Then, he peered out from the corner and watched them, the flask still clutched tightly at his side. The taller man was still looking down at the body while the stockier fellow had taken a seat on the wooden porch steps, his fingers raking through his cropped light hair. Did they know this man? Had Garvan actually taken someone's loved-one? A person of importance? He searched his heart for guilt but instead found satisfaction.

"We need to give 'im a proper burial," the fair-skinned man solemnly said.

"Aye, Jack. But, it will have to wait. The ground is frozen and we'll not be able to get the job done in a timely manner. I think we need to get him to Marin. His brother will know what to do with his body," the other offered.

"If O'Shea's followed us here and is responsible for killin' Peter, then we have to get to The Haven and make sure the women are all right," the first added grimly. *Jack?* Could this young, stocky fellow with the short, blonde hair actually be Jack Manning? Hearing his own name was confirmation enough. *Such a lucky turn of events!* Gar's first glimpse of Jack told him he could best him, either with weapon or hand to hand. Sheer size and motivation was on his side, indeed.

He considered taking the lives of these two Galway brutes, but decided against it for fear of never finding the key to his family fortune, Kylee – his greatest motivator.

"Aye, I agree. No tellin' what that bastard's got up his sleeve," the black-haired brute agreed.

'What in bloody hell does Kylee see in 'im? The Haven, eh?' Gar seethed, bubbling with jealousy and damaged pride.

Jack and his friend quickly cleaned Peter's wounds and dressed him in a fresh shirt.

"Brady, you'll go back to town. Go to Emma's, and check on Kylee. I've hidden so much from her, I can't hide the fact that she's in danger," Jack said as he helped load Peter's body onto the cart. After Thunder's harness was set, Jack added, "When ye get to Marin's, tell 'im how sorry I am that I could not deliver the body myself. But, I have to make my way back to check on the others. He'll understand."

"Aye, and I'll stay close to Emma and Kylee 'til ye return. Hopefully, Gar's not found them yet,"

Brady said wrapping his thick arms around Jack, bidding him farewell.

"Take care of them. And watch yerself," Jack replied, slapping the man on the back.

Garvan seized the perfect opportunity to have the dark-haired ruffian lead him straight to his misplaced bride-to-be. Excitement rumbled in his stomach for he was so close to finding her now.

All these nights he'd spent out in the elements had toughened him and all he could think of was retribution. He didn't care that the wind was bitter, biting his every limb, nor did he concern himself with the notion of starving. He was close to Galway, close to *her*.

'Now, let's see where this Brady fellow leads me,' he thought, quite pleased with himself.

Gar kept his gait at a slow and easy pace, careful not to be detected by the man he'd been following for hours. He scratched at his itchy red beard, and wriggled in his saddle to ease his discomfort.

"Jesus! Ain't this fella gonna stop for the night?" he swore under his breath. He just wanted to get to Galway, find Kylee and be on his way.

With the fresh taste of blood and death on him, there was no doubt that Gar would definitely kill Jack Manning's friend. He spent the countless hours following Brady now, conjuring up hideous ways to do it.

I'll know when the time comes, after he's led me to her.

~

Despite the early hour, Brady was forced to startle Marin awake. But this was something that had to be done.

He hated being the old man's bearer of disastrous news, but Peter Dooley deserved a better death than he'd been given. The least Brady could do was to afford him a peaceful funeral.

He'd have to get this done quickly however, for each hour that stretched between himself and home, he prayed O'Shea hadn't found the girls. If he'd been able to kill a defenceless old man there was no telling what the low life might do to the ladies of The Haven – especially if he learned it was a pleasure house under the guise of an inn. Brady took a deep breath and banged on Marin's door.

"Marin! 'Tis Brady Kelly, Jack's friend. Open up, I need to speak to ye," Brady hollered, and waited as he listened for the rustle of someone moving about on the other side.

Although he'd undoubtedly been shaken from his sleep, the silver-haired man answered the door amicably and smiled up at the tower standing on his porch.

"Brady? What brings ye by this early?" Marin asked, poking his head out around the wall of flesh. "Where's Manning?"

"Can I come in? I have distressin' news." Brady's tone was grave, yet earnest.

"Aye, come in. Sit," he said as he thumped into a chair and waited for Brady to be seated as well. But Brady stood as rigid as stone.

"Jack's gone back toward Ennis, warning the ex-brothers-at-arms of the lurking danger. I am sad to tell ye that yer bother's death served as the first alarm," Brady replied, watching the colour drain from Marin's face. This was the worst kind of news to deliver, causing a surge of sympathy to roil within him. He thought of his own brother Liam, and how receiving the same type of news would be devastating beyond repair.

"Peter? My brother's…dead?" Marin repeated, knowing already from Brady's grievous expression the fate that had befallen his only living kin.

"Come with me," Brady replied as he ambled back outside, leading Marin to his brother's cold corpse. "We couldn't bury him. I am sorry. We thought ye would want to send him off in a way befittin' the soldier he was."

"Thank ye, Lord Kelly. I thank ye for that. How did this happen?" Marin asked as he examined Peter's remains for the cause of death. He stopped short when he moved Peter's shirt away, revealing the long black gash in the side of his brother's neck. "Oh! dear Jesus! Who's done this to him? Who'd have cause to do such a thing?" Marin wept.

"We're certain now that Jack was followed by the fiend Garvan O'Shea. And we think he tried to force information of Jack's whereabouts from Peter," Brady quietly replied, unhitching the cart from Thunder's bridle. "Jack and I are very sorry for yer loss, and I assure ye we will bring the bastard to justice, one way or another."

"Aye," Marin absently replied. "Before ye go, help me bring him inside. I'll not have the wolves tearin' at him in the night. Give 'im a proper send-off, I will," he sniffed sadly.

Brady carried Peter's stiff carcass inside and laid him on a small cot on the far wall, while Marin poured himself a tankard of whiskey. When he held a drink out for Brady to take, Brady smiled, but shook his head.

"Thank ye, but I have to get into town. I have matters to attend to. Again, Marin, I am deeply wounded by yer sufferin'. If there's anythin' ye need from the Kelly's, let us know. Take care."

Brady mounted Thunder and kicked his heels into the beast's haunches with such force it made the steed rear back onto its hind legs and then take off into a full gallop into the forest.

Brady held his breath as he stopped in front of Heathen's Haven. If he went inside and found that harm had come to the women, he'd never forgive himself.

"Emma? Kylee? Jesus! Is anyone here?" he called, his long strides through the foyer leading him up the stairs. His thick fist thumped upon each door, and with each silence that followed, his heart caught in his throat. *Am I too late?*

When finally, a sweet voice came from beyond a door, he burst through to find Kylee quietly sitting in the window seat with a book in her hand. A heavy sigh of relief fell from his heaving chest. She did not seem at all relieved however, for most likely he'd startled her. His presence caused her to drop her book, and fear washed over her pretty face.

"Lord Kelly!" she trembled. "Ye frightened me half to death. Where's Jack?" Kylee's eyes filled with tears, no doubt assuming the worst. "Is he…is he dead?" Her tiny delicate hand flew to her mouth, covering the quiver in her bottom lip. The sun shone bright behind her, causing a warm aura to envelop her golden hair.

Brady gently took her shoulders, moving her toward an upholstered chair. "Jack's fine. He's gone back toward County Clare," he replied, falling into the wing-back next to the hearth, warming his weary body. "I don't want to cause ye alarm, dear Kylee, but I fear ye have been followed." Brady told Kylee everything that had happened, about Peter Dooley's death, explaining that Jack had gone back to check on the rest of his brothers and mentors. That Jack lived by a code and he'd be loyal to it to his grave. If the lass was ever going to understand her new husband, she must first understand the base fundamentals upon which his brain operated. Jack Manning was a soldier first and foremost.

Kylee began to shiver. "Gar's found me? Oh, Brady! What about Jack? What if Gar kills him? Jack should have come back here with ye."

"Oh, lass, don't ye be worryin' about him. He can take care of the likes of Gar O'Shea. And we're not sure if he's followed ye all the way here to Emma's yet. It seems he's only gotten as far as Peter's, then the trail is stone cold."

"I miss him," she whispered, wringing her fingers nervously.

"He'll return as soon as he assesses the situation along the road. He has to make sure that if Garvan is out there, that he can't get to ye. 'Tis better this way," Brady assured, sensing her uncertainty. Now, if he could only convince himself it had been a good idea, it might calm the nervous blood pumping in his veins. Jack had seen Gar, Brady had not. For all he knew, Garvan could've been following him! Swallowing back that particular terror, Brady changed the subject. "Jack's quite vexed by ye, ye know," he said, shooting her a sideways glance and smiled a charming grin. "So, what's been keepin' ye busy while yer husband and I have been away these past few nights?" Brady casually asked. He knew having Kylee stay with Emma was a touchy situation, but a necessary one. And, he also agreed with Jack that the innocent lass shouldn't be exposed to Emma's eccentric lifestyle without the supervision of her husband. "Have ye been spendin' much time with Emma?" He watched as her cheeks flushed crimson and she shifted uncomfortably.

"Aye, a little," Kylee replied.

"A little, aye?" said Brady with a sideways scowl, sensing her embarrassment. He knew by the flame in her cheeks and the spark in her eye that more was going on here than she would reveal. He decided to bite his tongue about the sprawled copy of '*Venus in Furs'* lying at her feet, title page staring him straight in the face. "I'll speak with Emma before I go. Now that I know ye're safe, I have to go home to check in with my own lovely wife." Kylee nodded quickly, no doubt anxious to see him go. "Where is Emma? No one answered when I called out." Brady narrowed his gaze upon the withering girl, now flustered, fidgety, revealing that she indeed knew exactly what went on within these walls.

"Umm…I would think she's takin' care of her guest. A gentleman arrived last evenin'. He's rented a room for only two nights," Kylee replied, attempting to casually pick up the naughty book and set it title down on the window seat. Then she went about fixing the curtains, straightening out the bed-spread, doing just about anything to distract her tell-tale emotions from any topic concerning Emma. If there was one thing Brady understood, it was the ways of women and how they kept their secrets. "He seems very regal and important, indeed," she added in a huff, a small amount of innocence still sparkling in her soft eyes.

"And I s'pose there were no other hotels in all of Galway for the man to stay?" Brady snorted his annoyance. Kylee lowered her gaze, almost shamefully. That one reaction proved she'd learned the whole truth about The Haven.

'*Jack's gonna lose 'is mind,*' Brady's thoughts groaned.

Just as Kylee opened her mouth to speak, Brady held up his hand. "'Tis lovely to see that yer well, Kylee. Jack will return before ye know it." And then he shut the door with a loud crack.

The urgency to speak with Emma caused his heart to pound a thunderous rhythm inside his chest. How could she be so careless as to let strangers in when there was a threat upon their lives? 'Twas negligent and ridiculous! He prowled through the manor, his brooding temper clawing its way up to the surface. He tried his best to remind himself that Emma was a lady – an irresponsible one, but a lady just the same.

Unable to locate her within the usual rooms of the house, there was only one place she might be. Brady had never been down there before, but he knew the entrance to a dungeon when he spied one. The staircase was encased in cold gray stone, but a soft, amber glow burned from below. Just as his foot hit the top step, Emma appeared at the bottom. Thankful he'd not have to go down there in search of her, he cleared his throat to make his presence known. Emma's bright expression turned upward. The insufferable woman had the gall to smile, no doubt noticing that Brady's face was red-hot with anger.

"Brady, you've returned sooner than I had expected. Where's Jack? I assume the hunt for the beastly Garvan O'Shea has concluded?" Emma casually asked, ascending the staircase, nonchalantly brushing past Brady's breathless wall of muscle.

"Jack's still on the road. He sent me back to check on ye, and not soon enough by the looks of things! And, to the contrary, the hunt has just begun. Kylee tells me ye've just had a guest register for a few days," he said. Emma grinned and nodded. Could the woman not see how dangerous her actions were?

"Yes, a judge, from Carlow I think. This is his first visit," she explained, elegantly perching herself onto the chaise in the sitting room, completely ignoring his foul mood. The urge to shake the woman had never been stronger.

"How can ye be so careless? How do ye know ye can trust he is who he says he is? There is danger lurking, or have ye forgotten?" Brady snarled.

"I know his brother…intimately. He is, let's just say, fond of playing house, playing the part of the wife," Emma smirked, knowing full-well that he hated all conversations pertaining to the happenings at Heathen's Haven.

"Ye know ye weren't s'posed to take on any new clients! There's too much at risk," Brady exclaimed.

"How could ye be so foolish, so senseless? Jack is not gonna be happy 'bout it."

Emma pinned him with a serious gaze. "Jack is well aware of my plans to carry on as usual. Do not mistake me for some stupid, impetuous child, Mr. Kelly. I do take precautions," she bit back, defensively.

"Well, fine then," Brady blew out. "When that man leaves, accept no more guests 'til Jack and I both return! Got it? Right now I have to get back to the keep and check on Vy. I can't worry that ye're gonna be foolish enough to open yer doors to strangers again."

"All right, *Lord Kelly*. As you wish, *Lord Kelly*," Emma replied in a sugary sweet, yet condescending manner, pushing all the wrong buttons.

Brady swallowed the urge to hit something and pointed his finger, adding, "And one more thing. Do not, and I mean *do not* teach Kylee anythin' that Jack doesn't want to teach her himself." Brady barked. Usually when he used this tone with anyone, they cowered in fear, quick to agree with anything he commanded. But Emma wasn't just anybody. She lacked fear. *Infuriating female!*

"Run along, Lord Kelly. You have a wife at home waiting for your return. Leave Kylee in my capable hands. I'll not expose her to anything which might upset Jack, I promise," Emma smiled. Her high and mighty attitude was exasperating but he hadn't the time to argue with the woman now. His own woman was waiting.

~

Kylee lingered in the hallway as Emma showed Brady to the door, grateful for his departure. If he knew the truth, he probably would've dragged her from The Haven himself. And that wouldn't do well for Emma's and Kylee's devious little plan.

When Emma turned and their gazes fixed on one another, a small chuckle bubbled in Kylee's throat thinking of the day before, when she'd first been shown the lower level of Heathen's Haven.

Since then, she and the mistress had become fast friends, as close as sisters.

It seemed Kylee's suspicions and jealous inclinations about the mysterious woman were groundless. Emma was indeed like family to Jack, and she'd have to rely on that kinship in order to better understand her warrior husband.

That fateful first day, Emma had led her down the staircase to the lower level, which Kylee had come to learn was dubbed "the dungeon". Confused, she took in her surroundings, curiosity blooming within her.

The dungeon didn't look like any other she'd ever seen or even read about in her books. Beyond the stone there were no bars, no way to see who dwelled inside each room, and no stench of rotting evil. This hallway was well lit with doors on either side, every one a different colour. This place was truly inviting.

"Ye call this a dungeon? This is the furthest thing from it, I'm sure," Kylee quietly observed, her heart beating faster with each foot step further into the unknown.

"Come, dear girl." Emma simply smiled, leading the innocent, naïve girl to a red door and opened it slowly. "Splendid, there's no one here. Come inside, we'll sit and chat a while."

Kylee followed her into the dimly lit chamber, eyeing her surroundings with apprehension and awe.

This place was oozing with lust and everything related to love and devotion. The huge brass bed in the middle of the room was covered with pink and red shimmery cushions. Multi-coloured flowers painted the walls. The scent of lavender and something a little sweeter lingered; vanilla perhaps. It was a feminine sanctuary, an amorous room to…share with a lover. Kylee shivered, a thrill chasing the blood in her veins.

Emma urged her to sit at the white woven table that looked as though it had already been set for a romantic meal for two. Kylee blushed as her gaze met Emma's, both of them holding on to the silence.

It was as though Emma could see straight into her mind and see her visions of sharing this room with Jack.

Then a realization hit her like a blow to the heart, sharp, unrelenting.

'Oh, God! He's shared this place with others. Perhaps with you,' Kylee thought, her hand covering her lips to stifle her gasp, her eyes flickering between Emma's understanding gaze and her surroundings. Emma nodded, substantiating Kylee's assumptions, yet remained stoic and compassionate.

"Why did ye bring me here?" Kylee whimpered through shaky fingers.

"It is not what you think. I just want you to know what we really do here," Emma smiled tenderly.

"I…I don't understand," Kylee replied, her own tiny voice somehow foreign. She stood and walked to the bed-side table where her fingers drifted across long strands of peacock feathers, and then rubbed the silky texture between her fingers. She turned again to

Emma with questions hidden beneath her tear-stung stare. "This is not an inn," she finally burst out.

"No, it is not. Why would I call an inn 'Heathen's Haven'?" Emma asked, her head tilting slightly. Kylee yearned to have all the answers, but it seemed Emma preferred to wrench each one from her like pulling a tooth. Slowly and painfully. Each realization fractured her heart a little more than the last.

"I don't know, Emma. I thought it was just *The Haven*," Kylee said dropping her gaze, and then shot her head up, eyes narrowing on her new friend. "This is a brothel!" Kylee cried and then rushed for the door. She wanted to be out of that room, out of that damned house, and away from all the depravity and vulgarity it encompassed.

Having the good sense to act fast, Emma caught a hold of Kylee's arm, swinging her into a sisterly embrace.

"Shh, do not be upset. You are wrong," Emma said, taking Kylee's face in her hands, forcing their gazes to meet. "Please, sit. I have so much to tell you."

Kylee huffed, hiccupped a sob and uncomfortably returned to the chair, studying Emma as she paced back and forth the room. This was the first time Kylee had witnessed anything other than the cool, confident and elegant Emma, and so she'd at least let the woman explain.

"If this is not a brothel, Emma, then what is it?" Kylee snapped, tired of the confusion, exhausted over her own feelings concerning Emma and Jack. It was time for the truth to emerge no matter how much it shattered what she thought she had with him.

Emma seemed to watch her closely, a silence hanging between them as if she'd been mulling over how to explain herself. Then, she opened the proverbial Pandora's Box with just one question.

"Kylee, do you have fantasies? I mean, does your mind wander sometimes, taking you to places you've only ever imagined?" Emma asked, seating herself across from Kylee. She picked up a bell from the middle of the table and dangled it between her fin-gers. As soon as the delicate cling-clang sounded, a young woman appeared, wearing little more than a pathetic scrap of satiny red and pink fabric. If she stood against the wall, the waif would certainly blend into the backdrop and disappear.

The girl entered with urgency, then dropped to her knees in front of Emma, auburn hair curtaining her face as her head bowed.

"Yes, Emma. How may I be of service?" the girl asked without even looking up.

"Tea please, Rory. Kylee and I would like to take tea and talk a while. See to it that we are not dis-turbed."

"Your desires are my desires," Rory replied and left the room again, leaving Kylee dumbfounded.

"Is that girl yer slave?" Kylee asked, mouth agape.

"No, Kylee. She earns a living in service to Hea-then's Haven. She is here upon her own free-will, as is everyone within these walls," Emma laughed breathily. "Do you have secret thoughts about things you would never admit to, for fear of damnation?"

Kylee thought for a moment. Since the first time she'd met Jack, she'd only fantasized about him. Those images had grown into a hunger since he'd left in search of Gar. He'd stirred something within her that she didn't fully understand, something she wished she could ignore for the shame it caused.

But the way he'd commanded her, the way he'd made her all *his*, she craved it. Craved the closeness, the passion, the way he'd branded her with his touch.

"Aye," she sighed, "when I met Jack there was something in the way he looked at me that sent my head reelin'. I knew from the start that I wanted to belong to him; only him. I'd do anythin' to please him, Emma," Kylee admitted with crimson cheeks.

Just as Kylee thought she would die with embarrassment, the girl named Rory entered again balancing an elegant silver tea service. She laid the tray on the table, and then bowed to Emma.

"Thank you, Rory. Please stay close, as I may call upon you again." Emma kindly said.

"Your desires are my desires, Mistress," the girl smiled, without making eye contact with either Emma or Kylee. When Rory left the room, Emma poured the tea, and handed Kylee the piping hot cup.

"There is no question, Kylee, that you love him dearly. What I am asking is, if you learned that Jack was as much a part of this place as me, Rory and the other girls, would you feel any differently about him?" Emma asked, and then continued without giving Kylee time to absorb the question, "Sometimes we feel things we know are unconventional. We've been taught that certain desires are wrong, when in truth, the only time they are wrong, is when you choose to ignore them, or use them to hurt others. Jack doesn't ignore his primal needs, nor should you.

"So tell me, dear girl, are you burdened with such primal fantasies?" Emma asked frankly, her mystical gaze burning through Kylee's psyche.

She watched the way Emma's lips moved, as if honey had been created upon them. She struggled to articulate the correct answer. Her head was a swirling storm of sensual memories linked to a shameful aching in her heart. Emma's scrutiny was forcing her to reach down into the depths of her own soul, and she knew she was in a fight for her life if she was going to try to deny anything.

"Only since mine and Jack's last night together," Kylee nervously admitted and shifted in her chair. *Why is this so hard to admit?*

"Don't be nervous. There is a wonderful explanation as to why you're having these fantasies all of a sudden," Emma replied with encouragement, and placed her hand on Kylee's knee. "It is because Jack made a part of you come alive. He has been waiting for a woman like you his entire life. And now, if you are willing to learn, I can teach you all you need to know about what makes your husband the man he is."

Kylee didn't even have to think about it. There was something different about Jack. He wasn't a cruel man. He was a protector – her salvation. The glimpse into his world a few nights past, told her he'd been holding something back. She wanted to be a part of that side of him, she yearned to know everything. "I will do anything ye say. I want to be everything he needs," Kylee confessed desperately, squeezing Emma's hand. She knew she was inexperienced, weak and ignorant, but the gleam in Emma's gaze strengthened her resolve.

"Very good, Kylee. When you have finished your tea, I'll let you see the rest of The Haven. But you have to keep an open mind and cast no judgement," Emma scolded. "Submitting to another person's will takes discipline, but can be quite liberating if executed correctly."

"Aye, I understand," Kylee whispered into her cup. The contents of her stomach threatened to come spewing up with frayed nerves and the fear bubbling within her. *Deep breaths.*

That first day had been nerve wracking with uncertainties. How she was supposed to feel about The Haven being just as it was, a safe haven for heathens with bizarre and unusual appetites? It was no surprise that Jack was at his best here, for he commanded obedience without even speaking at times.

She reflected on their last night together and regretted not knowing how to please him. She regretted her reaction. Despite his threat of a spanking, she should have voiced her approval, her delight, the addictive passion she'd felt. If she could do it all over, she would have behaved so differently. But she refused to dwell on it now. Instead, she vowed to take instruction from Emma, to be a good student while Jack was away, and a perfect submissive when he returned.

SIXTEEN

"*N*ow Kylee, let yourself go. Remember, you have to keep an open mind," Emma reassured her student once again. Could she not appreciate the fact that standing nude, in front of the other ladies at The Haven, was absolutely terrifying?

Kylee blew out a harsh huff. "Couldn't we have done this in private? How will havin' me stand here, naked as the day I screeched m'way into this world, help me better understand *Jack's* needs?" she protested, feeling as if she were undergoing an intense inspection, being judged and scored by Jack's *supposed* former lovers.

Emma smiled kindly. "I'll not push your insecurities too far just yet, but you have to realize your own beauty and gifts. Find comfort in your own skin. To do that, you must free yourself of the burden of modesty," Emma replied, dragging her delicate fingers along the back of Kylee's shoulders, causing gooseflesh to form from head to toe. "Now, the basic principal for surrendering your body, mind and soul to your beloved, is respect."

Kylee watched with wide eyes as Emma and her ladies formed a circle and walked all around, probing her with their hungry eyes. Kylee wanted to burst from the room – the room made for lovers – where she'd first sat and sipped tea with Emma. But longing to grasp the inner workings of Jack prevented her from moving.

"I already do respect him. Is there any doubt?" Kylee asked worriedly.

"I do not speak of respect between a husband and wife, Kylee, but the respect between you and your master. Jack's needs are primal, ferocious and even severe at times. In order to achieve this deeper bond with him, you will have to respect that in the bedchamber or his dungeon, he is Master, and you are his dutiful submissive. You must always trust that your pleasure and safety are his greatest rewards," Emma explained.

Kylee relaxed a little, distracted by the conversation, and then bit her lip. "That seems quite one sided, doesn't it?" she said, focusing solely on Emma, forgetting all about the other four women still circling her.

"Quite the opposite. When you relinquish your will to him, only then, will *you* gain all the power. And you have no need to worry about whether or not Jack will respect you, he already does. He will never intentionally harm you, and so the game-play he seeks will benefit you both, I assure you," Emma replied, and then smiled. Kylee was now standing with her arms relaxed at her sides, almost unaware of her nakedness. Emma placed a hand on Kylee's shoulder as she rounded to face her once again. "Lesson one, complete. Thank you, ladies. You may return to your rooms. That will be all for now."

All at once, the group bowed to their mistress and quickly exited the room.

Emma handed Kylee a black silk robe and helped her into it. "Come, let us discuss what you've learned this morning," Emma said, leading Kylee back up the stairs to the kitchen where they ate lunch and began talking about things Kylee never dreamed she'd discuss.

Emma asked, "How did you feel about baring yourself to the ladies of The Haven?"

"It was strange at first, but then I was able to ignore the embarrassment while ye were talkin'." Kylee quietly replied, losing herself in the scone she was nibbling.

"That's how it will be when you are with Jack. You'll see. When he is in control, you will clear your mind and trust him to instruct, play and push your limits. If you let him, he'll reroute all those apprehensive thoughts too. Your shame and modesty will become a thing of the past."

Kylee reflected on that notion, but for a moment. Then she sighed. "This is all so new to me. I don't know what my limits are, Emma. I'm havin' a hard time wrappin' my head around it," she replied, her voice laced with anxiety, a knot forming in her throat.

"I admit, this can be hard at first. But it's because we grow up believing it is wrong to behave in such a hedonistic manner.

"Our clients aren't chained by practical conventions or idealisms of the church. I opened Heathen's Haven so that people, no matter who they are, could come here, and have all their dreams and fantasies come true, without judgement. As you learn to trust him, your limits will fall away, and be replaced with open-minded, mutual respect, love and trust." Emma sipped from a dainty cup, holding a saucer just below her chin.

Kylee's eyes shot up, sincerity and conviction coursing through her veins. "I want to learn. I want to trust him. I know he would never hurt me, but this all feels so foreign," Kylee paused and then asked, "If this is not a brothel nor is it an inn, then how do the ladies here make a living?"

Emma brushed crumbs from the countertop into her palm, tossing them into the washtub. "My clients – both male and female – are most appreciative to have a place like this to come to. A safe place. And so they are very generous with monthly donations. That is why anonymity is so important. No one uses real names here," Emma explained. Kylee hung on to every word. "Essentially, they're also paying for discretion."

"I see. Then, Jack helps fund The Haven? He helps with the lady clients?" Kylee softly asked, a sickening ached burning in her stomach.

"No, he doesn't. Jack is a special friend to Heathen's Haven. He is a special friend to me. Can you understand that?" Emma asked, a soft sympathetic glint shimmering in her jade orbs.

"I…I guess I can try. But this whole place is so strange, I don't know what to think," Kylee admitted with a huff.

"Yes, I know it is. Everyone feels the same way in the beginning." Emma rested her cup and saucer upon the table and folded her hands over Kylee's. "I have an idea. Why don't you watch Rory with Mr. C this evening? He's booked in the green room."

"Ye mean he likes to make love in the wilderness?" Kylee asked with wide eyes, her mind drifting to the first tour of the labyrinth below. She'd learned so much in such a short period of time.

"Well, not exactly. Mr. C isn't here to make love, as he is devoted to his wife. But he does romanticise about being tied to a tree in the forest and flogged with a stiff twig," Emma chuckled. The fact that Emma was able to make light of her client's predispositions lightened the burden in Kylee's mind.

"I…I guess it would be all right. Do ye think he would mind?" Kylee asked, desperate to learn as much as she could, as fast as she could. When Jack returned, her knowledge of his world would both astound and delight him. She hoped.

"Not at all. While we play out their fantasies, *we* still set the stage here – not the client. Even if they are naturally dominating, the final say is ours," Emma replied with a light smile. She seemed comfortable explaining all of this to her eager student. "I must say, you are an enthusiastic student. Much more so than Jack had been when he first came to me."

Kylee's cheeks reddened, a jealous pit forming in her heart, where blood constricted, threatening to end her. Instead of giving in to it, she asked, "Tell me about that, Emma. I need to know."

Emma nodded slowly and began the tale of how she'd found Jack, and the friendship that had grown between them in the years since. When she was finished, Kylee was no longer resentful or envious of their bond. Now she was equipped with a deeper understanding and even a little sorrow for what he'd endured – how far he'd come to be the man he was now. *Mine*.

That evening after supper, Emma led Kylee down the steps to the dungeon. The sconces lining the walls burned bright, offering a warm and welcoming atmosphere, but Kylee's stomach was twisted with knots of apprehension. She would be forever changed from this point on. What kind of depravity would she witness?

When the green door opened, Rory bowed to Emma, and smiled at Kylee with an earnest grin.

"Please, take your seats," Rory commanded, gesturing toward the cushioned wingbacks against the far wall.

The lighting was soft and dim with only two candles burning in the entire room. The scene was difficult for Kylee to see, but she could faintly make out a large figure standing against a knotty wooden beam in the middle of the room.

When Emma and Kylee were settled and waiting with wide eyes, Rory then ignited the sconces all along the walls. Kylee gasped. Emma patted Kylee's knee, offering comfort. *Breathe.*

The area was lined with greenery, beautifully and intricately designed. If Kylee didn't know better, she would have thought she was in the middle of the forest, with foliage scattered about. The high ceiling glowed with elaborate painted clouds and blue skies. Even the floor was covered in shaggy tapestry resembling meadowland.

Kylee could fully make out the client now. His chest was bared as was his legs, but his modesty remained intact, covered by a wide scrap of leafy-looking fabric. His hands were bound behind the beam, his eyes blindfolded and his mouth gagged. Rory picked up a wide twiggy bough and whipped it through the air, causing Mr. C to flinch. Kylee flinched with him.

"Nod your head if you need to be punished Mr. C," Rory ordered. The hefty lump fixed to the beam nodded vigorously. Rory raised her arm. The vast breadth of the branches howled within the room and then connected with the man's shins. He whimpered, but then began to nod his approval with urgency.

With each and every whack, Rory's weapon connected further up his body, narrowly missing his manhood, but each time, he moaned for more.

Rory removed the blindfold so he could experience his façade of the wilderness with sight as well as touch. With her palms, she rubbed the small red marks that her whip had left in its wake, easing his discomfort. Kylee's heart skipped a beat when she noticed the man crying. Her eyes shot to Emma's and then back to Mr. C. His eyes did not reflect sadness, but reprieve.

Mr. C never seemed to notice that Kylee and Emma were watching in the shadows, he was enthralled with the scene, and with Rory. It was the most intimate act Kylee had ever witnessed.

"Would you like me to untie you, Mr. C?" Rory purred. He nodded. "Would you like the gag removed?" He shook his head that he did not. Rory untied him and he slumped to his knees.

She bent to him, falling to his side on her knees, rubbing his chafed wrists, soothing him while humming a sweet tune.

Emma quietly stood, gently pulling Kylee up to her side and moved unobtrusively toward the door, leaving Rory and Mr. C to fulfil his fantasy. Kylee would have so many questions for Emma once they were alone in her bedchamber.

"Why would Mr. C want to be punished like that, Emma?" Kylee asked while Emma combed out her golden mane before bed.

"The most important part of what I do is to understand the clientele. That man down there is a high profile figure with many responsibilities. His wife is dutiful and loving, as are his children. He loves them dearly.

"His occupation as a court judge forces him to punish lawbreakers for the crimes they commit," Emma began. "but, sometimes the burden of it exhausts him. He believes that for every man he's sent to hang, he must too be punished. This is a side of him that he cannot share with even his wife. And so here he is.

"It is not for me to question, but to help him meet his need, in a protected manner."

Kylee was beginning to understand now, but needed to know so much more. "Can ye tell me what Jack likes? What *his* secret fantasy is? Why didn't he trust my love for him enough to let me in on this part of his life?" Kylee's eyes stung from unshed tears.

"Kylee," Emma said, narrowing her gaze, "you *do* know Jack is going to be furious when he finds out what we are doing. He didn't want you exposed to any of this. He's been trying his hardest to keep this side of himself from you, for he fears you'll not understand," Emma huffed as impatience took hold, an uncommon occurrence for her.

"He won't be angry, Emma, not when he returns to a wife who can meet his needs. *All* of them," Kylee whispered, feeling desperate and a little over-whelmed.

"He loves you dearly. I wish you could see that. No matter what, he loves you. You do not have to do this," Emma replied, sympathetically.

"Perhaps. But he'll always run to this place, into yer arms when he's lookin' for something more. I need to be that something," Kylee stared into Emma's kind and mysterious eyes, revealing her inner most fears. "I *will* be everything he needs."

Emma nodded, an uncertain scowl painting her face. A long spell of silence fractured the air around them until Emma finally spoke again, giving Kylee hope for a united front against her husband's whims. "All right. I'll continue to teach you, but make sure Jack knows it was you who yearned for instruction," Emma replied, exasperatedly. "Brady expects him to return by weeks end. That only gives you five days to prepare."

"Aye. Train and groom me for when he returns. I'll be ready. I want no surprises when he finds me waiting for him in his favourite room…" she paused, "Which room would that be, by the way?" Kylee asked with eager, hungry eyes.

"Let's take it slow, darling, for you have much to learn. Patience will be the first item on that list," Emma smiled as she helped Kylee into bed, and as a mother would, tucked her safely in. "In the morning, we will start demonstrations. I will instruct Rory and Shelagh to take you through all of the rooms and then we can begin breaking you."

Kylee shivered beneath heaps of warm blankets. It all sounded so exciting and erotic, yet she was fearful of not being able to bend and do what was asked of her.

"Breakin' me?" she trembled.

"Yes, love. You'll understand when it happens. And it won't hurt, if that's what worries you. Now go to sleep," Emma blew out the candle and left Kylee to her thoughts in the pitch black.

She lay sleeplessly for hours. The promise of sleep was the farthest thing from a reality, for the anticipation of Jack's return prevented it.

With only yet witnessing a man being flogged, her mind's eye pictured Jack tying *her* to a beam and flogging her. It was a horrific thought, but one she couldn't shake from her head. *Could he possibly hurt me? Would he enjoy hurting me?* She refused to believe such a notion!

As she drifted somewhere between torment and curiosity, she chanted her own new-found mantra until it exhausted her and she finally succumbed to sleep.

His will is my will. His desires are my desires.

The next morning, Emma's bustling about in the room startled Kylee awake.

"Time to begin. I hope you had a good rest, for we have only four days at best, before Jack returns. We cannot waste time sleeping it away," Emma sang, ignoring the sleepy girl.

When Kylee forced her eyes open, the room was still bathed in black. Emma had stoked the fire in the hearth and lit the candle beside her bed. Even with the curtains wide open waiting for the daylight to creep in, there was none.

"Emma! Jesus! 'Tis still dark. I don't think I've even fallen asleep yet," Kylee moaned in a lethargic, sleep-deprived whine.

Emma merely laughed sweetly. "Think of Jack, Kylee. Put the lack of sleep out of your mind and focus on why we are doing this.

"But, of course, if you are not serious about it, I can return to my chambers, return to my own comfortable bed and let you do the same," Emma cheerfully scolded. The realization washed over Kylee, causing instantaneous compliance. She leapt from the bed and all but ran to get washed and dressed.

"What will we do today?" Kylee called from the adjoined dressing room.

"Mr. C has one more day here with us. He has asked for privacy, and me specifically, so I will trust

Rory and Shelagh to take care of you today," Emma began. "Your only task will be to observe."

"What could I possibly observe with two women? Ain't I s'posed to be learnin' how to please Jack?" Kylee snapped.

"Trust me. Trust *them*. Today you will get the shock of your life. But tomorrow the real lessons begin. Tomorrow you will be cast in your own fantasy."

Kylee held her tongue. Trusting in others was an all-new idea for her, but she would have to place her trust in Emma and her girls. The end result would bring her closer to the mystery of Jack's hedonistic preferences, closer to the man.

After she'd broken her fast with queasy unease, Rory appeared in the dining room, accompanied by a tall girl with elegant features and hair the color of freshly harvested strawberries.

"Kylee, I'd like you to meet Shelagh. She will aid in your instruction today," Rory introduced with a gleam of pride. "When you have finished here, we will take you below and initiate you into a world unlike anything you have ever imagined."

"Aye, I imagine ye will," Kylee nervously chuckled. "Nice to meet ye, Shelagh."

"And you," the girl replied so very sweetly. Kylee couldn't help but wonder if the two angelic creatures standing before her had ever tasted Jack the way she'd been longing to. Her heart began to thump furiously with jealous severity.

Kylee rose from the table on shaky legs and quietly followed them down the steps to the labyrinth beneath the manor.

'*Keep an open mind…please keep me from* losing *my mind,*' she silently prayed.

"You have already seen the *Lover's Lair,* and witnessed game play in the *Forest of Dreams*, so we will bring you into a different world today," Rory asserted with such confidence and certainty, that Kylee couldn't help but feel envious for lacking in such qualities.

"Can I see what's behind the black door?" Kylee quietly asked. The two girls looked to each other for the right answer.

Sensing Kylee's nervous anticipation, Shelagh quickly, yet gently took hold of Kylee's trembling hand. "The first lesson we will teach you today will be to only speak when it is asked of you," Shelagh kindly stated, and Rory nodded in agreement. "Follow me into the *Sapphire Sanctuary*. You will take a seat on the far wall; a sofa has been placed there for your comfort."

Kylee bit her tongue for the remainder of the day. No matter what she witnessed in the *Sapphire Sanctuary*, the *Rose Room* or the *Angel's Palace*, she would have to wait until Emma was finished entertaining Mr. C to ask the questions that plagued her.

When the evening meal was set upon the table, Kylee took her place across from Emma. She wished that Rory and Shelagh had been permitted to take their supper with them. They might better articulate how she'd felt about her day of observation.

It seemed, Emma knew better however, and ensured Kylee had privacy to tell Emma about her day of instruction – in her own way. Kylee sipped her soup from a shiny polished spoon and waited for the mistress to broach the subject. Each minute that passed was torture. Finally, Emma gently laid her spoon down on the napkin beside her, and folded her elegant hands in front of her chin. Their eyes met for the briefest of moments, Kylee's gaze dashing away quickly as her cheeks turned bright red with awareness.

"Kylee, if you're going to do this, you have to be willing to communicate," Emma began, breaking the silence.

"I'm trying. I am," she replied weakly.

"If you cannot even speak about what you learned today, how will you ever be able to tell Jack what *your* likes and dislikes are?" Emma reasoned.

Kylee looked up from her bowl, making contact with Emma's kind gaze and stubbornly held it.

"I can tell ye I have no interest in bein' with another woman the way Rory and Shelagh were today," Kylee huffed, dropping her spoon onto the china with an impolite ding.

"Yes, I know that it was a bit much for you to understand, but you were supposed to take more from the experience than that." Emma smiled.

"I did, or at least I think I did," Kylee shifted in her chair, trying to find the words. She knew that after today she would never again look at Rory and Shelagh the same. Suffering back her insecurities, she swallowed hard, "Jack has kissed me…down there, the way Rory kissed Shelagh."

"And did you like when Jack did that?"

"Aye. It was unlike anything I have ever felt before. How did he know to do that?" Kylee was beginning to warm up, letting her mouth form words and questions she never thought possible. Emma smiled as if she alone possessed the answers to the mysteries of the universe.

"He knows what you need, Kylee. Always re-member that when you are with him. He will *always* know what you need, and fulfill your wants as well," Emma explained gently, watching Kylee with keen interest. Kylee stared into her soup again. The reflec-tion peering back at her was that of a woman. She felt empowered. Reborn.

"Tomorrow, ye will teach me what his specific needs and wants are?" Kylee asked with hopeful eyes.

"Yes, but in the most basic form. I will teach you a foundation to build upon. But each scene will change from day to day, fantasy to fantasy," Emma sipped her wine. "Do you have any other questions about your experience today with Rory and Shelagh? Did it stir any feelings or emotions?"

How could she possibly put her feelings into words? Tempering the discomfiture, Kylee began, her gaze lost to the glistening glass of wine in her hand, "It was difficult to focus at times. I kept won-dering if Rory or Shelagh had been intimate with

Jack, in the way they'd been intimate with one another today. Perhaps 'tis because I miss him terribly," Kylee frowned and then her eyes darted up quickly and met Emma's. "Despair. That's how I feel here without him."

"You haven't really known him for very long. You still do not know what makes Jack the man he is. I find it difficult to believe that you miss a man you barely know," Emma stated, a little too frankly.

Kylee's hackles rose just a little but she was able to keep her cool. "What I *do* know, is that before I met Jack Manning, I was doomed to a life of servitude and misery. 'Tis *all* I ever knew. I was forced to be the obedient and dutiful daughter, put everyone's needs before my own. He's saved me from that life," Kylee replied, raising her voice, but when Emma smiled back at her, she understood why Emma pushed her to vocalize it.

"And here you are, learning how to submit and be the obedient and dutiful *wife*. Running from one horrid existence into the welcoming embrace of another," Emma paused for a moment. "Can you leave your old life behind? Can you forget all that Garvan has done to shame and scar you? Before we continue tomorrow, you need to be sure. Jack needs all of you in order to give you all of himself."

"Submitting to Jack will help us grow closer, I know that now. I accept him…all of him." Kylee declared and then threw her napkin on top of her plate and sighed.

"Be sure, Kylee, because when he returns to his submissive little vixen, he will show you no mercy," Emma explained with a slight grin. "But, you will be ever so satisfied."

Kylee thought about Emma's statement for a moment, and then met Emma's gaze again. It was the first time Kylee's fears of the unknown fully subsided, for now she was completely open-minded to anything Emma could throw at her.

'*I will be everything to him. Now and forever, his will is my will,*' Kylee thought with more determination than she'd ever felt in her life.

The next morning Emma showed Mr. C to the front door and bid him farewell. There was no doubt that he would become a regular at Heathen's Haven, for he kissed Emma's hand, and then with a warm and grateful smile, he handed her the thick envelope containing his *donation*.

Kylee watched the exchange and marvelled in the appreciation written all over this man's face.

'*A safe haven for heathen's, indeed*' she silently chuckled.

Emma closed the door, turned to Kylee and with a broad grin, took her by the hand and led her down the steps to the wonders below.

"Today we will play beyond the black door, for this is Jack's favourite place, and you will need to know what is expected in here more than any other. What lies inside will prepare you for anything," Emma assured with a honeyed smile. Kylee's nervous anticipation caused a mischievous grin to form, and she nodded for Emma to lead the way. She was more than ready.

When they entered the room behind the black door, she could clearly understand why this would be Jack's favourite room in the manor. This place radiated with feral masculinity.

As Emma lit the sconces along the walls, the equipment hanging on hooks around the perimeter became illuminated, giving Kylee a better sense to who her husband really was. Knowing this was his favourite playroom was having a heady and thrilling effect on her. The excitement of things to come awakened deep burning desires within.

"Take a walk around. Pick up the tools, hold them in your hands. Feel their power," Emma encouraged.

Kylee floated around the room, looking at everything all at once. It was almost too much to take in.

On bright metal hooks, iron cuffs dangled and belts lay flat, waiting to thwack something. Some were small and insignificant, while others were thick, heavy-looking and intimidating. She instantly noticed the wall mounted rings and the long lengths of chain hanging freely from them. A scorching heat inside her began to simmer.

On a table along the far wall, there were all sorts of curiosities lain about just waiting for her inquisitive touch. She picked up a smooth silver bar. She blushed furiously, for she instantly assumed what this was used for.

"It doesn't hurt. And I am certain Jack will not use this until you are ready," Emma said as if she could read Kylee's mind. "Here," Emma took her hand, led her toward a closet and opened it to reveal less intimidating gadgets. "Pick up the feathered whip. Crack it through the air as hard as you can. The sound that resonates will raise your awareness, heightening the experience."

Kylee smiled and relaxed once again, letting the long whip flow from left to right in one fluid motion.

"Are you ready to submit to me, Kylee? This first test will prove your dedication to the process."

"I am. Your desires are my desires, Mistress," Kylee chanted as she'd heard Rory do many times before.

"Close your eyes then, and listen to my voice. Focus on me alone. Only speak when I permit you to, and only move when instructed," Emma's voice was as soft and sweet as liquid sugar. Kylee pressed her ambiguity down far into the depths of herself until she could hear nothing but Emma's words; they became loud, clear, and grave.

Emma led her to a standing plank on the left side of the room, shaped like a massive wooden X. She carefully removed Kylee's robe, letting the silky fabric fall to the floor. "Slide your hands into the straps, and I'll secure you down here," Emma explained, her fingers dancing across the delicate flesh of Kylee's ankles. When finally she was bared and fastened, the soothing hum of Emma's voice suddenly caused her to shiver. "There, are you comfortable?"

"Aye," Kylee whispered, gooseflesh pebbling her skin.

Without warning, Emma thrashed the first of many different textured whips across her body. Unable to move, Kylee thought her skin would split apart on contact, but when Emma rubbed and soothed the afflicted area, the sensation left her longing for another crack.

"Are you afraid?" Emma hummed.

"Nay, I am not," Kylee replied breathlessly. "Again."

"This is the part you have not learned yet, love. You must not give commands. Do you trust me?"

"Aye."

"Then trust that I will give you what you desire and need. But you must never ask," Emma replied, cracking the suede whip down upon Kylee's inner thigh, nearly causing the restrained girl to faint. After the initial sting subsided, a warm flush filled her. She couldn't explain it, but she wanted more. What she *craved* was Jack.

'*I will be ready when he returns,*' she chanted, and in her mind's eye, at that moment, Emma *became* Jack.

With every thrash her focus became sharp. Jack's voice suddenly replaced Emma's. Her brain could no longer distinguish between fantasy and reality as the cruel sting of the whip caused warmth to flood her insides. Pain and fear fled, leaving behind a need so great it swallowed her into a vast abyss of ethereal pleasure and lust.

Jack, can ye feel me? I'm waiting. I'm ready. Come back to me.

SEVENTEEN

For three days, Garvan watched through inebriated eyes as the black-haired brute, Brady, paid his visits to the manor across the street.

Each day was the same as the last. Sometime close after midday, Brady's steed meandered through the street, always from the same direction. Minutes later the brainless lout disappeared inside the luxurious old manor, unaware that his every move was being meticulously monitored.

Despite his disappointment of having to follow Jack's friend to Kylee's hideaway – with no sign of Jack or the girl – Garvan knew he wouldn't have much time to make his deadly move. Waiting for her rescuer only incensed him beyond all logic, a fury growing deep, and burning hot within him.

However, between the free-flowing whiskey and the hangovers which plagued him each morning, he hadn't the discipline or the energy to make his way across the street and burst inside to claim his prize, yet. Instead he chose to stalk her like prey until his first opportunity arose to get inside without warning. It gave him a small measure of satisfaction to watch her every move, monitoring the shadows of her pro-file through lacy curtains. Kylee hadn't the faintest idea how near he truly was. *Hide from me, will ye?*

He might've even been contented to continue his surveillance, but the staff and patrons of the *Ornery Pheasant* began asking too many questions about the unkempt stranger, leaving Gar with no other choice but to set a plan into motion.

'*Today's the day,*' he thought, evil brewing, coursing through his icy veins. His only option was to remove Brady from the equation. Sure, he could walk over there, haul the girl from the clutches of her keeper and attempt an escape. But when Jack's friend discovered her missing, a search party would ensue and he'd be lynched if he was caught. No one could bear witness to her disappearance. Considering all his options, a plan took shape in his foggy brain.

With the stealth of a sloth Garvan made his way across the gravel street and took his hiding place beneath the front door staircase. Catching Brady unawares and off-guard as he entered the manor seemed to be the most rewarding strategy. *If* he was able to execute it correctly.

'*Stay focussed, Gar,*' he thought, the urge to revert back inside the pub and drown his anger gnawing at his insides. He steadied his shaky legs, withdrew into the shadows and waited for Brady to appear for his daily check on Kylee.

Adrenalin surged through his bloodstream when the Galway rogue came into view atop his intrepid steed. Despite the frosty air biting his bones, beads of sweat broke out on Gar's brow and his heart began to race. He took his blade in hand, peering out between the planks, ready to put an end to this.

When a heavy boot thumped upon the third step, Garvan thrust his weapon forward, slashing into Brady's shin, taking the thick man by surprise. What happened next was pure dumb luck.

Instead of triggering a brawl, the shattering blow to the leg caused Brady to stagger. Unable to catch himself, his bulky skull hit the ground with a solid thump. There was no struggle. No noise of agony or alarm. Just a heap of meat lying on the cobblestone sidewalk, blood pooling beneath wild raven hair.

Garvan emerged from his hiding place and made quick work of dragging the unconscious beast into the neighbouring alley.

Once concealed, Gar kicked Brady's immobile body until his guts seemed to turn to mash and his face too, had been bloodied. Garvan smiled. But his rein of terror had only just begun.

As if leaving him there to bleed out from his injuries wasn't enough, he straddled the lifeless man's torso and drove his blade into Brady's chest until his fist brought up solid. Blood spread quickly against a cream linen shirt, like a red plague of disease and destruction. '*Life number two,*' he thought, waiting for an outpouring of guilt to commence. But as with the first life he'd claimed, he could find no such emotion.

"Meddlin' bastard," Gar mumbled, getting to his feet and peered out from the corner of the alley to ensure his crime hadn't been witnessed. When he was certain no one had seen, he stalked toward the entry of Heathen's Haven.

Garvan tested the knob, but it brought up solid. Already having surveyed the property for alternate points of entry, he knew his only way inside was for someone to grant it.

Casually wrapping his knuckles upon the door, he waited, hands now in fists deposited into deep pockets and shuffled from foot to foot. The mistress would be expecting the black-haired brute this time of day. Garvan would use that knowledge to his advantage.

~

Right on time, Emma hurried to answer the door. Brady Kelly did not like to be kept waiting, she'd learned. The day before, she'd been busy with Kylee's instruction deep below the manor. Just by happenchance Rory had been in the kitchen baking bread and heard the rumble. The girl had been able to fetch Emma in a timely manner, but the two or three minutes Brady had been forced to wait hadn't helped his repulsive and condescending demeanour. She hoped he was in better spirits today.

As her hand landed on the knob, she thought briefly to just make the arse wait, then blew out a sigh and swung the door wide.

The pair of eyes that peered down upon her sent shivers up her spine. Her thoughts flittered quickly toward Kylee's description of the grubby-looking, red-headed menace. Her heart lurched. Her skin went cold. Garvan O'Shea had found Kylee.

'*What would Jack do? What would Jack want me to do? Where are you, Brady? You should have been here by now,*' her mind raced, but she tightly gripped onto her remaining composure in spite of the panic wracking her nerves.

"Yes, may I help you?" she kindly asked, battling with her instincts to take flight. *Run!*

"Kylee O'Roarke. Where is she?" Gar barked, pushing his way past the petite woman, nearly sending her to the floor.

"I do not know who you are looking for, sir, but I would be pleased if you left the same way you came in," Emma snapped, calming her nerves, her chin jutting forward with her signature air of authority.

As quickly as the words escaped her lips, his thick fingers wound tightly around her slender delicate neck.

Each digit branded her flesh with its own cruel grip, but despite her pain, she fought him with everything she had. Her eyes began to water. She grabbed and smacked at his muscled arm, her legs coming out from beneath her, but unfazed, he squeezed a little more, making it nearly impossible to breathe. Air wouldn't come no matter how she struggled to inhale. It was all over now. Her mind drifted to the ladies in her care. *What will become of them? I've failed them all.*

Of its own volition, Emma's body relaxed in his hold, acceptance replacing dread and fear. Then, suddenly he released her, letting her fall to the floor in a gasping heap, clutching her windpipe, desperate for air.

"Now, tell me where the little whore is. Or I'll tear this place down brick by brick 'til I find her," he growled, bending at the waist, meeting her defiant glare.

"Never!" she spat. "The only thing getting torn apart here will be you, when Lord Kelly arrives."

Gar latched his fist onto the sleeve of her dress and pulled her back to her feet with such force that the wind was narrowly knocked from her lungs again.

"Ye will bring me to her, now," he snarled through stale breath, causing her to gag on the sour stench. "And ye can stop waitin' for that sorry bastard. He'll not be comin' to yer rescue any time soon." Gar pulled the sticky blood-covered knife from its leather sheath and held the blade close to her neck. She could feel her pulse throbbing against it.

Completely silent, Emma made her movement toward the stairs to the basement.

She moved as slowly as she could, trying to stall without angering the sweaty monster holding the knife to her throat. But each time she slowed her pace, the edge of the blade cut into her delicate flesh a little more.

"Move." he snarled.

As they made their descent, Emma decided that when Kylee opened the door they would attempt to over-take him, locking him in one of the rooms until Lord Kelly arrived.

In the corridor, flaming sconces heated her flesh as they passed each coloured door. She prayed Kylee was finished her instruction with Shelagh. The outcome would be dastardly were Kylee caught in a compromising and vulnerable position. Yet, if Shelagh still lingered, their chances of taking him down increased greatly.

Gar leaned in close to Emma's ear, ripping her optimism away with each puff of breath. The spray of his spittle on her cheek made her sick to her stomach.

"Call out to her. Tell 'er that her beloved has returned. And sound happy about it, I'm warnin' ye," he whispered. She shook her head furiously in refusal. He pressed the blade to her vein, causing her to tremble.

"Kylee," she began, ever so quietly.

"Louder," he growled, the urgency in his tone increasing.

"Kylee, open the door. There is someone here to see you," Emma called, trying her best to sound cheerful, but her undertone was filled with terror. Unfortunately, Kylee didn't notice.

~

Inside the room with the black door, Kylee's heart thumped with excitement. She hadn't seen Jack since that dreaded night – the night in which she'd acted like a child, resulting in him leaving her there, lonely and confused. But she'd learned so much since then, and she was ready to be his everything. She forgave his abrupt departure, and she prayed that he forgave her inexperience.

'Oh, he's early! I didn't have time to get things ready the way I'd planned,' she thought fretfully, yet bursting with excitement.

"One moment. I'm not ready," she sang through the door, bustling about the room, rushing to get in the perfect position for Jack to find her.

Kylee and Shelagh had been using the dungeon for most of the morning. She'd learned the purpose of every single item in the closet and how to use them safely. Her instructor had left Kylee to her own devices some hours ago, letting her get acquainted with each tool and gadget all on her own. Now, Jack was on the other side of the door, hopefully with as much excitement, love and longing as she possessed.

"Hurry, Kylee. He's…He's very anxious to see you," Emma called. With a shaky hand, Kylee reached for the deadbolt, granting entry for her husband.

When the door pushed open, Kylee was kneeling at the entrance, her blonde head downcast, her robe open, baring only her silky naked shoulders.

A small whimper escaped Emma, grabbing Kylee's attention. Horror engulfed every facet of her being as her nemesis and tormentor pulled the length of his sharp blade from one side of Emma's ear and connected it to the other. Kylee was again powerless as she watched Emma's blood rush down over his violent hands, bathing her white floral kimono in deep crimson.

Her gaze connected with evil, the blackness of his eyes ever the more sinister than she'd ever seen them. She hadn't the will to scream. Her heart fractured. And while pieces of it belonged to Emma, more belonged to Jack. *His Emma is gone*. A silent tear wetted a path down her cheek, her gaze never leaving Garvan's. It was only a matter of time before she met the same fate as Emma. Why else was he here? How stupid she'd been to think she could escape him.

"I guess ye weren't expectin' me, were ye?" Gar growled, tearing at her indecent frame, pulling her up against him.

Kylee's gaze flickered between his and her friend now lying on the floor, void of all life. She trembled inside, her mind sprinting between realization and disbelief.

Run, Kylee. Run!

But before her senses caught up to her limbs, Gar was shaking her furiously, forcing her to look into his cold, heartless face.

Every instinct within her told her feet to move, her mouth to speak and her body to fight. But as both shock and dread claimed her, she was left at the mercy of this madman.

"Time to get ye back where ye belong. Get dressed, ye filthy whore," he simply said with eerie satisfaction.

EIGHTEEN

Panic struck Brady like a dagger to the gut when he finally forced his eyes to open. It was black, pitch black, all around him, the time of night unknown. *How long have I been here?*

He quickly scuffled to his feet, but when the pain surged through his body, his movements slowed again. Struggling to make his way from the alley to the front entrance of the manor, fear of what he might possibly find within plagued him with each searing footstep.

He'd been stabbed.

Peering down at his shirt, his hands fisted the blood-soaked crusted material until he found the wound on his right lower torso. *How am I still alive?* Brady inhaled a deep breath. *My lungs work.* His palm flattened over his heart. *Still beating.* He staggered forward. *Kylee!*

Holding his slashed rib cage, he held fast to the railing, pulling himself every inch closer to the impending doom that awaited him.

"Emma! Kylee?" Brady searched the main level, shouting the girls' names as he dragged himself along. "Jesus! Will someone fekkin' answer me?"

Just as he was about to battle the staircase to the bedrooms above, his ear cocked to the faint sounds of whimpering. Cries from below.

The urge to rush down the stone steps overwhelmed, yet his beaten and battered body prevented it. His slowed pace seemed to stop time altogether, for the tiny cries became blood curdling shrieks with every step he took. His heart began to knock in his chest, his breathing became loud, laboured and severe.

"Emma? Can anyone hear me?" he bellowed. Just as he reached the bottom of the steps, Rory cautiously poked her head out from behind the black door at the end of the hall. Brady could see that the girl was kneeling on the floor and in a hysterical condition.

"What's happened, Rory?" he hissed through clenched teeth. As he neared, Rory's rocking form cast shadows upon the walls, a woman's tiny frame clutched tightly in her embrace. Brady stood over them, unable to think, fighting for each breath.

Rory's wide glistening gaze met his. "It's Emma. A stranger…" she began with an unsteady small voice. "A strange man took Kylee, Lord Kelly. I crept down here after he left. Look what he's done!" she sobbed, smoothing Emma's limp hand in hers.

Searing pain in his chest, the bite of a knife wound in his leg, Brady slid down the wall just outside the door, but refused to look at Emma. He couldn't afford the wave of guilt and responsibility just yet. He'd have to survive first.

Jack will never forgive me for lettin' this happen. How was he going to explain it all to his life-long friend? '*I got me arse kicked by a half-witted drunkard,*' he reminded himself, disgracefully.

"Did he harm Kylee, too?" Brady asked in a whisper, tearing Rory's gaze from her deceased mistress.

"I…I don't know. When I heard the ruckus, I was too afraid to come down here to see what was goin' on. I was hidin' in the kitchen when he pulled her from the manor," Rory trembled, stuttering over each word.

"And ye didn't see what way they went?" Brady asked, forcing himself to remain calm. Even if he wanted to go after them, he was in no shape to attempt it, and since the day had come and gone, he knew they would be all but vanished by now.

Brady's injuries forced him to remain in the corridor bearing witness to Rory's insurmountable grief, while they waited for help to arrive. Despite the fact that his bleeding had slowed, he was in desperate need of medical attention; he prayed for Jack's arrival.

"I didn't follow them out, Lord Kelly. I was scared of him and worried for Emma, so I ran right down here as soon as they left," Rory snapped, and then wiped her sniffling nose with the sleeve of her dress.

He needed to get word to Violet. She would be frantic with worry by now, having expected Brady to return home before sundown. Had he told Violet where he'd been going these past few days, perhaps she might've sent someone by now. But since he'd hadn't wanted his bride to know he was affiliated with Heathen's Haven, he'd kept it a secret. *Foolish oaf!*

"Rory, do ye think ye can ride? Or are ye too shaken up to make yer way to my place? You'll be safe there with my wife, I assure ye," Brady kindly guaranteed.

"I can't leave her like this, Lord Kelly. And I haven't seen Shelagh since all this happened. What if she's hurt too?" Rory cried.

"Jack is due back any time now," he assured, or at least he hoped. "When he returns, we will find Shelagh and have her sent to the keep as well.

"As for stayin' here with Emma, ye know there's nothin' ye can do for her now. And I don't want ye to be here when Jack finds 'er. For yer safety's sake," Brady explained, lifting his arm, pulling his sticky bloody shirt from the torn flesh and assessed his wound through gritted teeth.

"Aye," Rory quietly replied, her eyes wild with horror at the sight of Brady's lesion. "Jack will be devastated and I don't need to bear witness to it. I'll ride to your home and inform your kin of the situation," she said and then bent in, and kissed Emma's forehead. "Good-bye, my lady."

"Go, Rory. My mount is outside tied up to the rail on the side of the house. When you get to the keep, ask for Liam. Do not speak one word of this to anyone else," Brady growled that last part, and hoped that she feared him enough to listen. The last thing he needed was for Violet to become hysterical in her fragile state. "Do ye understand, Rory? Not to any-one…just ask to speak to Liam."

"Aye, Lord Kelly. I understand," she replied. Rory rose from the floor and held her hand out to the crumbling man. He took her offering with rickety ap-prehension and she squeezed it gently. "God keep ye, Brady."

"And ye, Rory," he whispered.

Brady drifted in and out of exhausted sleep for a period of time he couldn't determine. Dreams and vi-sions seemed to mesh into one huge nightmare, each scene more frightening than the last.

He dreamed that Jack had returned and found Emma's dead body lying next to him. He could faintly hear the sobs resonating from his friend's throat as he tried to explain how Garvan O'Shea had found Heathen's Haven and managed to escape with Kylee.

His unconscious eye watched in horror as Jack pulled a knife from its sheath and drove it into his best friend. He could almost feel the tearing of his flesh when Jack pulled the blade upward, gutting Brady until his entrails spewed out onto the floor all around the once fair and beautiful – now dead – Emma.

His gruesome delusion was mercifully interrupted when he heard faint footsteps descending the staircase.

"Liam. In here," Brady groaned, unable to open his eyes, as if the gory visions were ingrained into his brain preventing him from looking away.

~

When Jack rounded the landing and caught sight of Brady slumped over in a mess of blood and sweat at the other end of the corridor, his heart hitched in his throat. A deep rumble in his gut nearly sent him to his knees.

"Brady! Jesus! Brady, 'tis me," Jack called, as he rushed to Brady's side. As he closed in on his friend, the sight of Emma lying in the doorway ahead stopped him dead in his tracks. He looked to Brady with anguish and horror.

"I wasn't here, Jack. I wasn't here," Brady coughed, "O'Shea..."

Stepping over Brady's extended legs, Jack slowly closed the distance between himself and the heart-rending sight of Emma. A crime it was, that she'd met her end in the same room where she'd shown him his own beginnings.

"Kylee? Where is she, Brady?" Jack moaned, kneeling next to Emma, fixing her disheveled clothing, smoothing her hair from her face. With two gentle fingers, he pulled her eyes shut with a delicate touch.

'*Yer desires are my desires, my mistress. He will pay for what he's done. I swear to avenge ye,*' Jack silently vowed.

He'd given himself all of ten seconds to grieve for Emma. There were pressing matters still at hand, an evil pawn still at play. His pain quickly transformed into fierce unbound rage.

Brady spoke again, breaking through the turmoil. "He's got 'er. Caught me off guard just as I got here to check on 'em," Brady scowled, as if every syllable he'd dragged from his lips inflicted unimaginable pain.

"How bad did he hurt ye? Can ye walk?" Jack asked, concern welling up inside.

"Aye, I think I'll be fine, just tired now," Brady replied, lifting his arm from the wound he'd been shielding, revealing the gash. Jack bent briefly to assess the wound, quickly removed his kerchief from his pocket and firmly pressed down in attempt to slow the streaming blood.

"I have to go after them!" Jack shouted, the enormity of the situation hitting him all at once. Garvan O'Shea had extinguished the lives of two people Jack cared for, and had disappeared into the wind with his wife – the love of his life. And, clearly Garvan's intention was to put an end to Brady as well. All this because Jack couldn't bring himself to face the woman he loved after he'd brutalized her. *Should've kept watch over them m'self!* After all, he was the captain of the guard at the keep. He knew what it meant to protect the people he loved, and this time he'd failed.

"Ye can't go after them now, Jack. Come on! Think straight. Calm yerself and consider what ye're doin'. If he took the time to abduct her, then odds are she serves some purpose," Brady sputtered. Jack might do well to listen to his advice; Brady was familiar with the purposes of abducting a beautiful woman. O'Shea had to have plans for her. "If he seeks revenge because she left him, then puttin' a blade to her throat would have done the trick. But, he didn't," Brady counseled. *He does have a point.* "I think he's bringin' her back to Ennis."

Jack paused for a moment, his fingers digging through his short-cropped hair. "Aye, I think ye may be right. He needs her if he's to inherit his father's fortune," Jack added, remembering the argument he'd overheard at O'Shea's brewery between Gar and his father. "For that reason, I don't think her life is at stake, yet, but God dammit, Brady, she's my wife! I can't sit idly by, waiting for ye to be well enough to help me. God only knows what that bastard has put her through already." He pictured his pretty goddess at the mercy of the filthy O'Shea. He shuddered at the thought.

Jack lifted Brady's arm up, wrapping it around his shoulder, helping him to his feet.

"Ye have to let me mend a little before we go after her. I won't let ye go alone," Brady winced even with the small movement.

Just then, Liam and Rory appeared, lending their arms to Jack's cause of getting Brady up and out of the basement.

When they reached the parlour, the doctor was pacing back and forth, eagerly waiting to help the Kelly lord.

"Lie down on the settee, Brady. Let the doctor fix you up before you return to the keep. Violet will be frantic if she sees you like this," Liam scolded, cringing at the sight of the bloody mess his brother was in. He then turned and laid a sympathetic hand upon Jack's shoulder. "Rory told me what has happened.

"My condolences for the loss of your friend. I have dispatched half of the guard and they're all waiting for you outside. Kylee will be safely returned to you. I just know it."

"Aye, thank ye, Liam. But ye can send them all back to their posts with Brady. I'll need no help tearing Garvan O'Shea apart to get her back myself," Jack replied angrily.

"Well then, if that's how you feel, I'm coming with you," Liam stated, his chin jutting out with uncharacteristic confidence.

All attention turned to Brady's howling as the doctor shoved the first of many stitching needles into his tender throbbing flesh, pulling the slashed skin tightly together. But even in pain, Liam and Jack's conversation didn't go unnoticed or ignored.

"Augh! What do ye mean the guard will remain at the keep with me? I'm not stayin' home in bed like an infant while ye two go on to Ennis half cocked," Brady yelled. "And what in bloody hell do ye know about huntin' down a killer?" he asked, glaring at Liam with a pointed, accusatory finger.

"You're right. I know nothing with regards to deviants and killers. But when we arrive in Ennis, don't you think O'Shea might be spooked if he sees Jack Manning traipsing through town on the hunt?" Liam had a point.

No one knew who Liam was. He didn't look anything like his brother, and he wouldn't be mistaken for someone of authority, being just a simple business man in a fine suit. "I'm going to the brewery to pitch a business deal is all. Perhaps I'll find Kylee, perhaps we can set up an ambush and steal her away again. You, my dear brother, need to stay at home and take care of your very pregnant wife," Liam replied smartly, seemingly undaunted by his brother's derision.

Brady opened his mouth to argue, but the doctor quieted him with yet another jab to the ribcage. Brady held fast to the cushion, squeezing and tearing at it to overcome the pain, but if looks could kill, Liam Kelly would've spontaneously combusted where he stood.

~

"Let's go, Liam," Jack murmured, squeezing the muscles at the nape of his neck for some sign of relief. Then, he turned to Rory and took her sullen face into his strong hands. "The Kelly's will see to it that Emma's laid to rest properly. I want ye to go to the keep with Lord Brady. His lady wife will need some help in the comin' months. It's a good place for ye. Now, be a good girl, and go get yer things packed."

"What about Shelagh? Jack, I haven't seen her since before the attack," Rory sniffed.

"I'll leave two of my men here, so if she returns, they can send her to ye. That sound alright?" he asked, finding strength where there was none. The anguish and loss he tramped down inside would destroy him if it were allowed to bubble to the surface.

"Aye," Rory solemnly, yet obediently said as she turned and disappeared upstairs. A flicker of sorrow for the girl escaped through a fine line in Jack's defenses. She'd lost everything. Her home, her employment, and her family. After what she'd witnessed, her world would never be the same. Jack's thoughts were invaded again by Liam's and Brady's presence.

"Let's get ye home, Brady. Doc, is he all right to ride?" Liam asked, as he helped Brady off the settee and onto his outstretched arm for support.

Brady didn't seem to like this new side of Liam. His little brother was taking charge, executing orders, and in complete control. Brady, as the eldest was accustomed to it, he'd even perfected it, but here was Liam – *the new little lord of Kelly's keep* – taking over. The weight of it might've left a sour taste on Brady's tongue, but he kept silent about it. However, the brooding scowl which had now etched itself into his facial features, mingled with the slight twinge of pain – neither of which, had gone unnoticed by Jack.

Before the doctor could give his consent, Brady hurled himself atop his steed, looking down upon the lot of them with a staunch air of superiority. *His last attempt to repair his pride.* Jack chuckled under his breath, for that small feat may have just about killed him, but he'd never show it. *Stubborn bastard!*

"Careful, brother!" Liam chastised.

Just as Brady pointed a finger again at his brother and opened his mouth to issue a tongue lashing, all eyes fixed on the pretty, strawberry-haired girl leisurely approaching, seemingly oblivious to the terror that had occurred within Heathen's Haven.

"Shelagh! Shelagh, where have ye been?" Rory shouted through tears of gratitude.

"I was visiting with an old friend who's been ill. What's everyone doing standing out here in the street?" Shelagh asked light-heartedly. Jack went to her side immediately.

He wrapped his strong arms around her tightly and began to explain, "Kylee's been taken, Shelagh. I know ye thought Kylee was just here as a guest of the house – my guest – but that wasn't entirely true," he stated. "I was hidin' her here from her fiancé."

Rory and Shelagh gaped at one another, and then back to Jack.

"What are ye talking about, Jack? I know all about Kylee! I've been train…" Shelagh started, but then quickly shut her mouth, likely catching her blunder when his empathetic expression turned cold, dispassionate and angry.

"Continue, Shelagh," Jack growled.

"She just wanted to please you. That's all. We've all had a hand in it. Myself, Rory and even Emma," the girl trembled like and errant child.

Jack nearly spewed up the bile gathering in his throat when the realization hit him, picturing what the ladies of Heathen's Haven had really been up to.

Kylee now knew what his secrets were. And in an attempt to please him, she'd been learning to give herself to the monster within him.

"She was never supposed to know what goes on here! It was irresponsible of ye! She's just an innocent girl!" Jack shouted, wearing his temper across reddened cheeks.

"Emma just couldn't lie to her. The girl had so many questions. I'm sorry, Jack, she wanted to learn," Shelagh looked at all those in attendance, and finally noticed who was missing. "Is Emma gone to bed yet?" she asked, stepping to retreat inside.

Jack viciously caught her arm. "No. Ye can't go in there. As I said, Kylee has been taken by O'Shea. I regret to tell ye, Emma didn't survive the intrusion," Jack replied, gravely, his voice something of an intruder in his own ears.

'There, I've said it! I can't ever take it back or make it right. She's gone,' Jack thought with more misery than he'd ever felt in his life. Admitting his Emma was gone made his stomach churn, but the

impending doom of his beloved Kylee caught his heart on fire.

Shelagh crumbled in front of him and Rory rushed to comfort her. Emma had always taught him compassion and empathy, but right now, he was not their master. His own emotions teetered between anger and despair, and he hadn't the strength to offer anything resembling kindness or comfort. *Kylee must be found.*

"She's dead," Rory softly added, holding her friend close. "We have to go to Lord Kelly's home. He says he will give us work and a place to live. Everything will be okay. Shh, don't cry."

Jacks head was spinning. Everyone was at a standstill. No one made an attempt to leave. Brady remained stoically upon his mount, the doctor was patiently waiting for Shelagh and Rory to get aboard his carriage, and Liam, who didn't understand any of this, was watching the exchange, trying to piece it all together. Liam had no idea that Heathen's Haven was not, in fact, a hotel, and Jack wasn't about to explain it to the lad.

As if Brady could read his mind, he nodded toward the ladies, pain still burning in his gaze and said, "I'll explain it all to ye when ye grow up." Brady smirked smugly at his little brother but to Jack's surprise, Liam was utterly unaffected by his brother's snide remark. Brady sniffed, head stubbornly high. "Let's go, Doc. I have to get back to Vy."

Rory and Shelagh wearily climbed aboard the doctor's carriage, wedging themselves closely together as if they were the one and only comfort for the other now. Jack shut the carriage door, bidding them farewell, with zero emotion, zero empathy, only a deep seeded blood-lust for vengeance and revenge.

When finally Jack and Liam were alone, the urgency to get after Garvan and Kylee was the only thing keeping Jack from falling apart.

He'd been travelling for over a week, and looking back on it now, he'd been stalling his return to her. Shame for his behaviour on the first days of their marriage, kept him longer than planned with every visit to his ex-comrades' shanties along the back road.

He wished and prayed now, that if he could go back and do it all over, he never would have left her in the first place. No, he'd have gently brought her into his world, in a way she could understand.

"Do we take the old road or the new?" Liam asked. He was quite the inexperienced little idiot, but the fact that he was here to lend Jack a hand, said something about how much his character had grown.

"I would've passed him if he'd been on the old," Jack replied.

'The nerve of that bastard. Not even tryin' to conceal himself on the old road,' Jack thought with teeming hatred.

"All right then. Shall we get your bride back?" Liam kindly smiled.

Jack left instructions with the two guardsmen to stand watch over the manor until Mary and her maids arrived from the keep to take special care of Emma, still lying in the dungeon.

"Ye do understand, Liam, Emma must be afforded the most respectable service," Jack choked out. "Ye may think she was a common whore, that this house was just another brothel, but ye have it all wrong. We have to make sure she's taken care of. Discretely."

"Of course, Jack," Liam reassured, despite his obvious surprise in learning the truth. "You know Mary, she'll take care of everything."

"Right then. Let's go," Jack finally blew out.

Adrenalin coursed through his veins. He had to let go of Emma now, but he swore that once he found his precious Kylee, he'd never let go of her again.

NINETEEN

Kylee quickly became reacquainted with that feisty side lurking within her. The last time she'd swallowed her nerves and found her bravery was when she'd first met Jack.

She'd tried so hard back then to ensure he'd hated her. She'd called him out, spat malicious words from a forked tongue, cursing him to the devil. She thought she might save Jack from having any involvement with Garvan, but Jack Manning wasn't a man to just walk away. And of course, her efforts to break their unmistakable attraction had been futile. He was her husband now; that fact alone made her captivity even more devastating. Would he know she'd been taken? Had he learned of Emma's death yet?

So many questions plagued her as she found herself travelling back toward her homely hell with the monster from her past, praying for the courage to put an axe through his skull.

Since they'd fled Galway, Garvan had been drinking heavily. At first, she ignored his slurred speech, his clumsy staggering and even his spiteful snide remarks. But when the sky above blanketed them with stars, they'd been forced to make camp, where his advances within the dark of night were almost too much to suffer. Kylee had once again been required to fight.

He'd waged war upon her and she matched him blow for blow, biting, punching and kicking until finally he grew tired, passing out in a comatose lump beside her.

Her torn clothing and achy body displayed the proof of his savagery, but she chanted her new mantra. She believed in herself and her husband. He would find her.

I am strong. I am unafraid. I can do this. They were words she'd learned at Heathen's Haven – intended to help her overcome her anxiety when she and Jack were reunited. She needed this mantra now more than ever if she was going to survive whatever Gar had planned for her.

The mere notion of returning to Ennis before now had made Kylee ill, but this morning, as her village came into view through the black thick of fog, her hungry belly and exhausted body needed to be tended to. She hoped and prayed Fiona was willing to help.

Perched atop his steed in front of him, she noticed Gar scanning the empty street, his grip on her tightening as if he expected trouble. She'd never seen him so hesitant or wary. Where was his usual arrogant self? Hopefully drowning in his own guilt.

Once outside the brewery – home free without detection – Gar dismounted, standing tall and proud, Kylee's previous assumptions of his culpability vanishing. Of course he'd be proud! Of course he'd gloat! He'd been able to recapture his unwilling bride. But with no one out and about at the early hour, his jovial manner faded quickly, evil once again surging through his veins, causing a sour taste to rise in Kylee's mouth.

"Get inside, ye filthy bitch!" he fumed.

Kylee dismounted, repulsion spreading like wildfire within. Seeing that he was eager to exhibit his great accomplishment, Kylee couldn't help but knock him down a notch. She spat the little moisture that remained in her mouth onto the toe of his boot.

As expected, he countered with a backhanded whack to her already bruised cheek. Despite the sting, her small victory remained intact. She had become impervious to his violence throughout the years and now had better sense to brace herself for the blow.

How could he not know that with every cruel punishment he dealt, her inner strength would double? Couldn't he see the defiance and resolve in her icy stare? With every new barbaric brand, she smiled inwardly with the knowledge that when Jack found her, he'd end Garvan O'Shea's very existence.

"Go to hell!" Kylee proudly snarled, straightening her disheveled dress. She flicked golden locks back from her face and sauntered smugly past him, into the brewery, holding her breath with each step. Garvan's simple grin sent terror through her, flowing like a flooded river of angst. She tried desperately to hide her fear. He may have let her away with her snide remark, but he certainly wouldn't forget.

Once inside, Garvan went straight behind the bar, poured himself a large tankard of ale and swallowed it in one sloppy gulp. Wiping his wet beard with the back of his hand, he stood and stared for a moment at the statue still frozen by the door.

"Well, get in here, wench. Ye can get yer arse up them stairs and wake Fiona too," he slurred.

"What did ye think ye were gonna achieve by bringin' me here, Gar? Ye know I'll never stay. Ye know *he'll* come for me. Ye know *he'll* take me away from ye and this God-forsaken place. So, why even try?" Kylee's tone was mocking, visibly angering the slipshod sleuth.

"Because when ye dishonoured yer kin by leavin' yer betrothed here to wonder what in bloody-hell happened to ye, some folks pointed a finger at me!" Gar shouted and then downed another tankard. "I can't have the whole village thinkin' I made away with ye! I brought ye back as proof that I didn't kill ye…yet!"

Yet. That one small word heightened her awareness, making the little hairs on the back of her neck prickle against the fabric of her blouse. He hadn't emphasized the tiny syllable, but it was ear-splitting just the same. She knew it was just a matter of time before he tried to end her. If she disappeared now, folks would believe she'd fled again and Garvan would go forever unpunished. *I have to stay and fight!*

"Oh! So ye didn't bring me back here to marry ye in order to get yer hands on yer Da's fortune? I've known for a very long time what my purpose was, Gar, and I'd die before I see ye inherit what ye don't deserve!" Kylee spat, her hands on her hips, looking him up and down with as much disgust as she'd ever felt. His eyes never even flicked up to look in her direction. "It'll never happen! I said I'd never marry ye and I meant it!" And then his gaze shot up, a rotten grin spreading across his cheeks. There was the sinister demon she'd remembered.

Kylee took the first step up the staircase with caution, grasping the railing tightly, bracing for an impending blow. Instead of pursuing her, Gar yelled at the top of his lungs, "Fiona! Da! Get down here! I've returned with me bride! Get up, hear me? Get up!"

Kylee continued her ascent up the steps, ignoring the creature still greedily guzzling his father's profits. She was met at the top by a very cranky Paddy O'Shea, still in his sleeping gown.

"Jesus, Mary and Joseph! What are ye doin' makin' all the racket at this hour of the mornin'?" Paddy grumbled, raking his fingers through his wiry gray hair. When he noticed Kylee, he stopped fast where he stood. His colouring blanched as if he'd come face to face with a ghost. "Kylee? Is that really you, child?"

"Aye, Mr. O'Shea, 'tis I. Good morn'," she whispered with a small grin. "I fear he's in a very foul mood. Perhaps ye should go back to bed b'fore he notices ye."

"Never mind him right now. Come, let's get ye settled in with Fiona," he said, leading her through the sunlight filtering into the hallway from his open bedchamber door, illuminating the cuts and bruises that his own son had inflicted upon her.

Ignoring the shouting from below, Paddy looked Kylee over, wincing at the mere sight of her. The sadness on the old man's face was unmistakable, as a tear escaped the corner of his wrinkled eye.

"It doesn't hurt. It will be okay. My husband will find me soon and take me away from here," she stated, forcing a smile.

"Oh? Yer husband?" Paddy quietly stammered. "Does Garvan know ye've married another?" he asked, ushering her inside Fiona's door with his finger to his lips, signalling to the awakening Fiona to remain quiet.

"Nay, I've not told him that yet for fear I would not make it here alive," she replied in a whisper. Kylee put her head down, shame and sadness taking residence in her mind. These were Gar's kin. She shouldn't expect sanctuary. They would have to remain loyal to him, wouldn't they?

Fiona quickly yet quietly, jumped from her bed, wrapping her arms around Kylee. Relief swept through the room; Kylee had returned and was abundantly welcome.

"I was so afraid he'd done somethin' awful to ye," the tiny fire-haired girl whispered, and then frowned when she noted the abused state Kylee had been left in. "Come, I'll get ye washed up and some fresh clothing to wear. Da, just look at what he's done!" Fiona whispered, shamefully shaking her head.

Paddy swept his hands through his grey hair again, frustration and tension etched into every movement. "This is all my fault. I should 'ave never let the boy away with so much after Rachel passed. I'm just sick about it.

"If he doesn't pass out soon, he'll be up here lookin' fer ye," Paddy sighed. "I don't know how I can protect ye, girl. We best pray that he drinks himself into oblivion."

"I could go back to my uncle's place and wait for Jack. That's where I was hidin' before Jack found me," Kylee said as she followed Fiona into the small dressing room and changed into one of Fiona's night gowns.

"Nay, Kylee. Ye can't go back there. Garvan went there after ye, and beat your uncle almost to death to find out who took ye away," Fiona explained regretfully. "He is alright now though, don't worry. When you didn't return here with Gar, we thought he'd found ye and killed ye. I'm just so glad that you're alright."

Just then, a notable silence fell upon the tavern below. Paddy stealthily opened the door and poked his head out for a better listen. Nothing. Peace.

"I don't hear anythin'. Ye think he's down for the count?" Paddy wondered aloud. He crept down a few of the stairs, to find Garvan was in fact sprawled out on top of the bar, snoring like a hibernating bear. "Ye'll have a little peace this mornin', Kylee. Now, climb into Fiona's bed and get some sleep," he said with a compassionate smile.

"Thank ye, both. Fiona, can I trouble ye for somethin' to eat first? I haven't eaten much since I left Galway and I'm ravenous," Kylee asked humbly.

"Of course. Gar's good for at least a few hours, so ye'll have time to eat and rest. Then hopefully, we can get ye sent home to your mother before he awakens," Fiona said, retrieving Kylee's dirty torn clothing from the floor and balled them up in her arms. There was so much mending to do. "I am so sorry, love. The shame of what he's done to ye makes me dizzy. Do get some rest."

As much as she detested to think about it, going back to her mother was Kylee's only option. When Jack's search came up empty at the brewery, Kylee knew he'd have the foresight to search for her at the house where she was raised. Besides, once Siobhan realized the cruelty Gar had inflicted, then surely, she'd finally protect her girl from the beast – at least until Jack arrived to protect them himself.

After Kylee devoured a small plate of food, soothing her rumbling belly, she lay in Fiona's bed, forcing her eyes closed. Persuading her body and mind to rest was as useless as trying to sleep. It was no use. The plaguing need to get far away from Garvan O'Shea had settled in, refusing to give her peace. Paddy and Fiona may have faith that Garvan's drunken slumber would last, but she did not. And she refused to wait for them to put a plan into motion to help her escape. She had to go – it was now or never.

Despite knowing Garvan would look for her there first, she was hell-bent and determined to get home to her mother. Jack would know to look for her there.

Fighting off her fatigue, she dressed in the heavy wool gown Fiona had laid out. She had to somehow slip past all of them unnoticed. If Gar thought for one moment Fiona or Paddy aided her in any capacity, his wrath would know no bounds. Kylee vowed not to have that on her conscience.

Peeking out the door into the bright hallway, she squinted, adjusting her eyes to the sunshine seeping in through the large window at the far end of the hall. Tip-toeing like a mischievous child all the way to the top of the stairs, she stepped down the first few to look around the tavern.

Her heart thumped heavily in her chest, weighed down with two choices. She could slip out through the front entrance, or she could find her way to the back, making a run for it from there.

From where she crouched, Garvan no longer slept atop the sturdy bar. She wondered if he'd been put to bed by the timid little creature, Fiona, who'd dragged his drunken arse up to bed so many times before. *Where is he?*

Paddy was bustling about behind the bar, tidying up the mess that Garvan had left. With a thick knot forming in her throat, Kylee waited patiently for Paddy to disappear out back.

When Paddy vanished through the swinging doors, Kylee took her chance. Light on her feet, air filling the space between her footsteps and the floor, she darted out the front door and into the cool morning air. She ran until her lungs were heavy and full of icy breaths, all the while, praying her mother would welcome her with open arms until Jack arrived to take her away.

The tiny home stood as it always had, appearing neglected and abandoned. But as she inched the door open, the smell of her mother's pungent perfume fiercely burned her sinuses.

Kylee had always hated that smell; it reminded her of the whores who frequented the O'Shea's brewery in hopes of scoring a hefty purse for the night.

Suddenly, her thoughts took her back to the night Siobhan had given her to the devil himself with no consideration for Kylee's fear of the man.

'*I'll not hold a grudge. She is my mother, and I, her only child*,' Kylee reminded herself.

She had so much to share with her mother. Siobhan had always sacrificed her own happiness to provide for Kylee, now it was Kylee's turn to take care of her ma. Excitement bubbled in her belly as she imagined her mother's reaction when Kylee explained how everything would be all right from now on – that Jack would take care of them both.

With shaky fingers, she gently knocked on her mother's bedroom door and turned the knob softly. It was after all, an ungodly ripe hour, so bursting in unannounced wasn't the way Kylee wanted to rekindle their relationship.

When she entered, the shades were drawn shut, enveloping the room in pitch black. Kylee felt around with her fingertips until she found a lamp and matches on the bedside table. It filled the room with a soft warm glow.

Through the smoky glass shade, a distorted figure illuminated in the background, rising up from the darkness, causing her to drop the flame, returning her to darkness, once more.

"Mama?" Kylee trembled. Something was wrong. Very wrong. "Are ye awake?"

Kylee's instincts were on high alert as her gut screamed with panic. *Get out as fast as ye can!* "Mama?" No reply came, only the sound of rapid breaths. *Am I gasping? No. I'm not.* Kylee turned quickly, reaching for the door. A wall of sinewy flesh and stale breath blowing down upon her halted her escape.

"Ma!" Kylee cried as she moved to find her way in the darkness to the other side of the room.

"Kylee, love. Come, sit on the bed. We have much to talk about," her mother drawled.

Kylee's breathing kicked up a notch, becoming erratic and urgent. *Not enough air!* Her body trembled involuntarily. The rattle of her bones echoed in her ears.

And then there was light.

Siobhan lay on her side, facing the door with nothing but a sheet covering her. It took a moment for Kylee to see it, but a grin depicting so much evil had taken residence upon her mother's sweet face. She'd seen that look before, but this was the first time Kylee had seen it for what it truly was. Merciless. Hard-hearted

Kylee's gaze turned immediately from her mother's, then toward the door, where Garvan stood in his under-things, lamp in hand, mirroring Siobhan's expression. Kylee's skin crawled with chaotic revulsion.

"I…I don't understand," Kylee cried. "What is…what are ye doin'…Mama?"

"Oh, Kylee! Grow up!" Siobhan snapped, rising from the bed, donning her satin robe. "This is what happens between lovers, isn't that right, Gar?"

Ignoring Siobhan altogether, Garvan set down the lamp. His thick fingers wrapped around Kylee's throat, pinning her to the door. Their gazes locked.

"What are ye doin' here, Kylee? Ye know ye were s'posed to stay in yer room," Garvan growled.

Kylee's fingernail dug trenches into his flesh, fighting against the vice-like grip.

As if she'd been cast from the wetness of honey, Siobhan reached out calmly and gently, removing his hands from her daughter's neck. Still that wicked unsettling expression remained. Kylee sank to the floor with a thud, holding her throat and gasping for air with tears spewing from her eyes. So much about the entire situation was disconcerting. *They're lovers?* Another onslaught of disgust and bile threatened her very existence.

"Lover, if ye kill the little wench, ye'll not inherit anythin'. Remember that," Siobhan smiled sweetly.

"Tie 'er up. We can't have her runnin' away again. I'll make some tea."

Kylee couldn't believe what she was hearing. The fact that her own mother was consorting with her worst nightmare was enough to make her gag on the fresh air she was gulping into her lungs.

Siobhan left the room without a care in the world for what an angry Garvan O'Shea would do to her daughter. She closed the door with a smirk and blew a kiss in Gar's direction. Kylee's stomach churned.

"Gar, please don't do this. I…I can't marry ye. Why can't ye find some other girl to help ye inherit the fortune?" Kylee began, pleading with him, begging for her life. She tried to remember the empowering words that she'd learned at Heathen's Haven, and how Emma had taught her to be in control of every situation. But this scene, two against one, was no fantasy, and Kylee didn't know what she should do.

"I don't want another! I want ye! I'll not live with the shame of givin' ye up…I'd be the laughin' stock!" he shouted, his face reddening with fury.

"Ye don't love me, Gar! I can't see why it has to be me," she cried.

"I might've agreed with ye, 'til ye ran. But now, 'tis gotta be this way….even if it's for pure satisfaction of ruining yer pathetic life after ye humiliated me. And, let's not forget how long I've been waitin' to sink myself inside that warm body of yers." Garvan poured a shaky tankard of wine and threw it back. "I've had yer mother for years now, all the while picturing the younger, virginal, and virtuous daughter. 'Tis ye, 'cause I say it is!" Gar shouted and then grabbed her around her waist and threw her down upon the bed. Kylee was frozen in fear as she watched him take a pair of her mother's stockings from the drawer and then straddled her waist, trying to get a hold of her wrists.

Her mind raced. She remembered when Jack had tied her to the bed. Although she didn't realize it then, she had enjoyed it, and the feelings of helpless-ness that went with it. But this beast on top of her was not Jack, and there was no kind of love accompany-ing his manhandling. *Danger, Kylee, danger.* Panic rose within her.

"Get off me!" Kylee fought with every inch of her petite frame. A new sense of courage, built from memories of her beloved Jack, rose to the surface. "I am married to another! Ye can't have me, not now, not ever! And he *will* come for me!" she roared, the sound coming from some foreign place, a dark, deep place. Jack would want her to fight him with every-thing she had, and never give up.

'*Your desires are my desires*,' she thought with the heart of a lion. She drew her knee up, and arched her back, trying to shake the beast off her.

Her knee connected with his groin, sending him to the floor in a pile beside the bed. She quickly leapt off, and made a dart for the door.

He reached out and held her ankle tightly, keep-ing her from reaching the knob. Kylee staggered and quickly took inventory of the room, looking for any-thing to aid in her escape.

Her hand found the handle of the fire poker next to the mantle, and without even thinking about it, she thrust the heavy pointed iron down into his arm, breaking his grip on her leg.

"Augh! Jesus Christ! When I get my hands on ye I'll bloody-well murder ye!" Gar howled in agony. Kylee stood back with the weapon in her trembling hand as if she were wielding a great long sword, awaiting his next attack.

'*He'll never let me go. He'll always hunt me,*' Kylee thought for a moment about her future. If she managed to escape, could she really go on for the rest of her life, watching over her shoulder for Garvan O'Shea to rip her from happiness again? He'd al-ready killed Emma. He was capable of killing her too.

"I belong to another, Gar. Let me out, please," she pleaded one last time.

"Married to another? Who in bloody hell, would marry the likes of ye?" Gar growled through clenched teeth, struggling to get to his feet.

Even though his cruel words didn't affect her, she wasted no time. Kylee struck him down again with a blow to his back. He went down with a thump.

Instead of waiting for him to regain his position, all sense completely left her and she knew what she had to do.

With Gar struggling to get onto all fours, Kylee drove the point straight into the back of his skull with a steady hand, sending fragments of bone and splatters of blood to pepper the wall next to him.

He rolled to his back, and then he didn't move. Kylee held her breath. She waited and listened for any sign that he may still be alive. His body twitched, just a little, sending panic through her that he would rise again.

She thwacked a hole in his forehead through streaming tears until there was no strength left inside of her to raise the iron bar. She dropped the gory mess at her feet, exhausted.

The bedroom door crashed open, and Siobhan stood there in awe at Kylee now covered in blood, Gar's blood. The blood of her lover.

Siobhan lunged at Kylee, taking the girl by surprise.

"You filthy little whore! What have ye done?" Siobhan roared as she went straight for Kylee's hair, tearing and pulling out clumps. "You silly girl! He could have given me a better life! He was everything to me!"

"Stop! Please, Mama! Stop," Kylee begged, as she didn't have the strength to fight back. This was her mother. The woman who had given her life was now trying to rip it from her.

"This is the end of ye, Kylee! Ye hear me? The end!" Siobhan slapped Kylee's face again and again, trying to provoke her to fight back. But she wouldn't. The aching in her heart drained her of everything she had.

When the beating finally ceased, Siobhan slumped down next to Garvan's lifeless corpse, her body retching with silent tears.

"This is not the end for me, Mama," Kylee began softly. "This is just the beginnin', for both of us. Ye'll see."

She knelt at her mother's side. The shock of killing Gar, and the fact that she'd been able to inflict such harm on another human being, hit her hard. Remorse threatened to consume her.

What would happen to her when the authorities came to arrest her for murder? How would she be able to live without Jack, locked away in a cell for the rest of her life? Would she be sentenced to death?

'No! Kylee! Don't think like that. Jack will know what to do,' she reminded herself. *'I have to think of the future…our future.'*

"I have married Jack Manning while I was away, Mama. And ye'll see, everythin' will turn out alright. He's a good man and I love him dearly," Kylee cried as she smoothed her mother's soft auburn hair, soothing her as best as she could.

Siobhan gazed up at the hopeful blue eyes looking down at her. Her face twisted, jealousy surrounding her like flames to fuel.

"Ye'll take mine from me? And ye expect me to watch ye live out your life with the man you love by yer side?" Siobhan whispered in a low growling tone, sending shivers down Kylee's spine. Kylee got to her feet, and carefully backed out the door. "Who do ye think ye are? Ye don't get to live a fairy tale! Ye're Kylee O'Roarke. Yer father was a no-good-for-nuthin' and that's exactly what ye are! I shouldda' put an end to ye the same day I ended his wretched existence!"

TWENTY

The ache in Jack's heart for the loss of his friend was unrivalled by the urgency to find Kylee. *I will find her, dammit!* The fact that Garvan had had a head start – an advantage – meant nothing! Jack sensed her. Soon, he'd hold her again.

Jack and Liam approached the outskirts of Ennis, coming to a halt for a quick breather. He was exhausted, his mind wracked in suffering, but there was no time to rest or lament now.

"What's the plan?" Liam asked, no doubt grateful for the opportunity to play a part. It was no secret that Brady had always regarded him as weak and incompetent. This was the younger Kelly's chance to prove himself.

With any hope, Liam would grasp a newfound sense of self, become a strong man who was unfettered by the shackles of book keeping and ledgers. Jack understood the lad's need to have so much more than that.

"Well," Jack started, "I can see nowhere else O'Shea would take her, only back to his father's place, the family's brewery. He holds no land or property of his own but he needs to bring 'er home to force 'er hand in marriage. 'Tis the only way he can inherit the business."

"I think you beat him to the altar," Liam said with a sideways glance. "I guess he's not taking it well."

"Nay, we don't know yet, if he's even aware of that little detail," Jack replied with immeasurable worry of the unknown. "And ye have to remember, O'Shea is one sick bastard. 'Tis all about vengeance now and proving somethin' to his poor ol' father," Jack explained, his heart hammering heavily in his chest. "Liam, ye'll go and meet with Paddy O'Shea. Pitch him a fake business deal. Make it a lengthy one. I'll need time to search the grounds for her."

'I'll tear that brewery down piece by piece if I have to,' Jack thought with his own vengeance mounting.

"Aye. I can keep the old man busy for hours if I need to," Liam smiled. The lad seemed energized. If there was one thing Liam knew and knew well, it was business. For the first time, Jack preferred the company of the younger, more civilized Kelly.

~

Liam strolled into the brewery through the front tavern doors with his leather satchel draped across his shoulder. His eyes roamed the expansive yet elegant room, noting the large crowd gathered in the corner playing some kind of card game and making a racket.

As he walked up to the bar, his nerves were beginning to fray at the sight of the greyish-red haired man standing behind it. Just then, to his right, a young woman, with the same fiery locks appeared from the staircase.

Pushing his apprehension all the way down to where it couldn't trip him up, Liam cleared his throat and opened his mouth.

"Hello, sir. I am looking for Paddy O'Shea," Liam stated, regaining his composure.

"'Tis I, lad. What can I do fer ye?"

"My name is Liam Kelly. I've travelled a great distance to chance a meeting with you. I have a business proposition you may be interested in," Liam lied. "Is there somewhere private we could talk?"

Paddy looked around the tavern and rubbed the back of his neck.

"Fiona! Come 'ere girl," he called, pleasantly.

When the small girl joined them, her expression was equally as pleasant, yet curious about the stranger.

"Aye, Da?" she hummed.

"Where's yer brother? I have to meet with Mr. Kelly in the study. Go find Gar and have him watch the place 'til I return."

"I haven't seen him since he arrived back here the morning b'fore last," she frowned. "I can take over, Da. Go and meet with Mr. Kelly, I'll be fine. I've been slingin' ale at this lot for years." A courageous smile showed perfect teeth and a dimple in her cheek.

Paddy huffed out a long sigh and cursed under his breath. "Alright then, but if any of these louts get outta hand, ye come and fetch me right away," he said.

"Aye, Da. I will," she winked at her father and shot an inquisitive glance in Liam's direction.

'Oh, Lord almighty. Gar's not here. For Jack's sake, I hope Kylee is," Liam thought, panic raging within him. Time was of the essence. They *had* to find Kylee before the unthinkable happened.

~

Jack crouched beneath the back window where he could see the humongous vats of fermenting ale lining the walls of the brewery as he peered inside.

He watched as Liam and Paddy O'Shea walked through the double swinging door and disappeared through a small hallway.

The time had come – it was now or never. If Kylee was being held inside this place, Jack would face the devil himself in order to get her back. The shame for having left her at Heathen's Haven in the first place would haunt him 'til the end of days.

'I'll spend the rest of my life makin' it up to 'er,' he silently vowed, pushing the guilt back down. He didn't have time to let the fires of hell consume him just yet.

Slowly opening the rear service door, Jack carefully poked his head inside. He could hear the grunts and cheers coming from inside the tavern and knew he'd have to stay on his guard in case Garvan was the source of some of the disorder.

He looked down the hallway where Liam and Paddy O'Shea had disappeared, and was relieved to find it empty.

'Liam must have Paddy enthralled with notions of makin' a substantial amount of money by now,' Jack thought with a little pang of remorse that it was all a rouse. Paddy, after-all had little to do with any of this, but he'd become a victim of circumstance.

Opposite the hallway, a brightly lit stairwell caught Jack's attention. Adrenalin surged as he moved toward it. Might his bride be just a few steps away?

Just as he reached the top step, a small voice interrupted him – his fist raised – before he'd had the chance to beat on every door.

"Can I help you, sir?" asked the carroty-topped waif, clearly frightened, nervously twisting a kerchief in her hands.

Jack turned and faced the girl with the wild inferno hair. Her face paled, but her expression flashed with recognition. She remembered him.

"Ye were in here a while back," she said, accusatorily. "Yer…yer not a guest of the hotel, sir. What is yer business here?" she trembled, yet stood her ground. After-all, this place was her home, hers to defend if need be and she'd just caught this man as he was rearing back to put his foot through a guest's room door. Jack couldn't blame her for being confrontational.

He recalled Paddy calling her Fiona and that this meek and shivering girl was Gar's little sister. He would have to tread lightly.

Jack shifted uncomfortably. This was going all wrong.

Then, like a flicker of light, the little mouse smiled.

"Yer Jack Manning, aren't ye?" she whispered.

Jack almost swallowed his tongue. How did this girl know who he was? Had she been told to keep a watch for him? Was Garvan lurking about, ready to attack?

"Aye, I…I am," Jack said, his head snapping suspiciously in all directions. "I'm lookin' for…"

"I know who yer lookin' for. Kylee's not here, Mr. Manning," Fiona said, taking Jack's hand in hers and led him into her bedchamber at the end of the hall.

Jack carefully and silently followed her.

Entering the room, his gaze immediately fell upon Kylee's favourite blue dress which had been washed and pressed, despite the ragged holes it now displayed.

"She was wearing it when she arrived a few days ago. I had her change out of it so I could wash it for her. I hadn't had the chance to mend the torn spots yet," Fiona explained, despair causing water to form in the corner of her eyes.

"Where is she now, Fiona?" Jack asked, his fingers inspecting the wear and tear of Kylee's abandoned garments.

"We – that is – Da and I, were gonna help her get to her mother's place after she woke up from her nap.

But I fear she slipped out while we were downstairs," the girl sorrowfully replied.

"And Gar? Where is he?"

"I don't know. I only pray he hasn't found 'er," she replied sadly. "He was awfully angry when he left."

Jack sat down on the bed and exhaled loudly.

"Please, Fiona, start from when he brought 'er here and tell me everything," Jack urged, heart shattered, feeling completely lost.

This girl knew nothing about the stranger falling to pieces in front of her, but the softness in her gaze told him her heart bled for his suffering.

Fiona turned the chair placed at her writing desk to face him, and sat with a straight back and crossed ankles. "They arrived the other mornin' before dawn, I believe. Da woke me up, ushering Kylee into this very room where I could clean her up and tend to her wounds."

His expression must've shocked her, for she paused for a moment. "Continue, Fiona," he softly urged, sensing her apprehension. He had to keep his emotions in check. This poor girl was already afraid of the soldier perched on the side of her bed; he needn't give her cause to run. He had to keep Fiona talking. Jack tugged at his collar, nodded and then forced a small smile.

"I assure ye, she will be fine," Fiona said and then cleared her nervous throat. "After she ate, Da and I agreed to keep watch o'er her so she could rest. By the time we'd settled her in, Garvan had gotten thoroughly drunk and passed out. We thought she'd be safe from him, for a while at least.

"When he woke up however, he went lookin' for a fight. We found him up here, poundin' on the door, tryin' to wake her, for what reason, I don't know. Probably to torture the poor girl some more. But Da and I held him off. Gar was furious.

"He kept shoutin' that he was finally gonna get what he was entitled to, that Kylee had returned with him to become his wife and at long last, he'd take over the business. Da and I knew though, she'd already married ye, but we couldn't tell him that. He would've retaliated. I doubt any of us would've survived it. He's not the man he used to be."

"Aye. He's a killer now." Ignoring the loud gasp that filled the room, Jack strode to the window, peering down onto the street where vendors were beginning to set up for the day. "What happened after that? How can ye not know where she is?" Jack asked, frustration and impatience making him want to smash something.

"Because, Mr. Manning, it is unclear *when* she left. Garvan left here in a ball of fury after Da renounced him as heir. So with him gone, we didn't see the need to stand guard over her.

"Business went on as usual for the day, until I came up here to bring her supper. Da and I were in a frenzy when I found the room empty. She must've crept out while our backs were turned, or perhaps she'd left even before Garvan had gone up there in search for her," Fiona explained, her hands upturned in question.

Jack picked up on the blame she'd placed on herself and felt the urge to console her. "'Tis alright, Fiona. I'll find 'er. You say ye were gonna help her get to her mother's?"

"Aye. I think she went alone to spare Da and I the trouble it would've caused if Garvan found out we helped her," Fiona said, wiping her watery eyes with the back of her hand despite still crushing the kerchief within a tightly wound fist.

Jack turned, facing her once again, pinning her with an intense gaze. "I must get to her! From what I hear, her mother's cold embrace won't save her from that evil bastard. That woman will stop at nothin' to attain financial comfort. Why a mother would betroth her young daughter to such a ruffian is beyond me."

Fiona hung her head shamefully. Jack wished he could take back what he'd said. "Pardon me, Fiona. He is still yer brother, I shouldn't say such things. I am sorry," he said, apologetically.

"So am I, Mr. Manning," Fiona replied. "When he brought Kylee home in such a battered state, I swore I no longer had a brother." Fiona paced the few steps between each wall of her room, and then raised a brow at him. "Da and I have been suspicious for a while now that Garvan and Siobhan O'Roarke were involved somehow. He's known to visit her often, even while Kylee is safely tucked away at the Ryan's. But if ye knew what kinda mean-tempered fella Gar is, you'd know why we kept our mouths shut about it."

"Ye don't have to tell me what he's capable of, Fiona. I know all too well, and I intend to make him pay for his crimes," Jack said, his worry and despair once again replaced by rage and the need for retribution. "How do I get to the O'Roarke place?" he asked bluntly.

"Ye'll have no trouble findin' it. 'Tis an old, run down thatched-roof cottage just on the outskirts of town. 'Tis different from the other homes in the area as it isn't flanked by a barn or other outbuildings. 'Twas never a farm. It hasn't been kept up since Mr. O'Roarke was alive, and so 'tis the only cottage in the area like it," Fiona explained, blessing herself, paying respect to the dead. "If ye take the old road toward the River Shannon, I'm certain ye'll find Kylee."

Jack thanked Fiona with a tight smile, and then stormed down the stairs and out through the front tavern door. If Garvan had returned unbeknownst to him, he cared not. He'd slay the man on sight. He'd move heaven and earth to find his bride.

Jack considered fetching Liam from his falsity in the study, but thought better of it. Liam was safer left where he was – discussing business with Mr. O'Shea.

'Brady would never forgive me if somethin' hap-pened to the little lord,' he thought, urging his mount onward at a break-neck pace.

Jack could smell the fresh dampness lingering in the air, wafting from the river. The scent of manure and barn animals mingled with the pleasant odour of wild flowers. He slowed his steed.

All around him were pretty, yet modest homes, surrounded by hay barns, hen houses and cattle sheds. All of them were attractively flanked by flower beds and neatly trimmed hedges. He knew right away that this was clearly not the place in which he sought.

He continued onward until his eyes fell upon a home reflecting almost exactly what Fiona had described – a thatched roof, greying and weathered stone. The place stood all alone against the world, almost in defiance of the other homes which proved its inferiority and poverty.

Jack slinked around to the back of the pitiful house to a small half-door and gently squeezed, releasing the latch.

It was so eerily quiet. Until a blood-chilling wail sounded from another room. With every step he took, Kylee's muffled cries caused his heart to thump louder and harder, to the point where her howls were nearly inaudible over his own panic.

He stopped in his tracks as he inched his head inside the parlour door. Dread rose within him when he found his pretty bride sitting in a chair, wrists and ankles bound, and blindfolded.

Across from her, the bloody corpse of Garvan O'Shea was propped up as large as he'd ever been, wearing a fine, pressed suit with a red rose perfectly tucked into the lapel.

An ancient wing-back chair served as the perfect support for the dead man. And despite the black hollowed cavity in his head, his skull remained upright, staring straight ahead – with the help of a leather strap across his forehead, of course.

He recognised the stench of death and stifled a reflex gag as he cautiously neared the body. The familiar and unforgettable reek filled his nostrils, instantly and unconsciously bringing his kerchief to his nose. He crept past the macabre sight, careful not to startle Kylee. He was so proud of her in that moment. She'd managed to stay alive in the midst of the apparent chaos.

TWENTY-ONE

S omeone was near. Kylee could feel the fine hairs on the back of her neck prickling in warning,

'*I can't endure any more torture, mother. Please God, let it end,*' Kylee prayed as silent droplets fell from the corner of the blind fold. Terror crushed her, her mind raced, wondering what else her mother had in store.

Siobhan had shown her only child no mercy in the days since Kylee had become imprisoned and brutalized as a consequence of killing Garvan.

'*I should've fought back. Jack would've wanted me to fight back, even against her,*' Kylee lamented regretfully, recalling the events which led to her captivity.

Following Siobhan's discovery of her dead lover, fear for her life and of her mother's instability prompted Kylee to run from the house. Where would she go? Back to the brewery wasn't an option, for she'd just murdered Paddy O'Shea's son and Fiona's brother. She'd be ill equipped out in the elements to travel to the Ryan's. A neighbour, perhaps? At least until daybreak.

Kylee made it all the way to the end of the lane, almost to a neighbouring farm house before her mother caught up with her, pulling her back with a fist full of golden hair.

"Awh! Mama, please!" The only reply that could be heard were the ramblings of a mad woman.

Once back inside the dismal house, Siobhan had tied Kylee to the chair, forcing the girl to observe, as she readied her corpse for the *blessed event*. Her mother's devotion to Garvan, after everything he'd done to terrorize her, even after death, was bewildering. But Kylee dared not speak of it. Unleashing her tongue might just unleash the unholy evil lurking inside her mother.

Once Siobhan was satisfied with Gar's appearance, her attention turned back to Kylee with colossal hate and a need to punish. Kylee's breath hitched in her throat as Siobhan moved toward her with a thick scrap of cloth and then covered her eyes.

When the world had gone black, Siobhan had begun inflicting her tortures with detached emotion and malevolent intents. The fact that Kylee was of her own flesh and blood, mattered not when the first bead of hot wax to fall and sear Kylee's fair skin caused a satisfied ring of laughter to escape her mother's lips. Kylee's upper chest was on fire.

"What shall I do with ye next, ye little bitch? Ye must be taught a lesson," Siobhan seethed, cracking a thick strip of leather together, while Kylee remained utterly mute. "I'll take me time killin' ye, no fear about that. Not like when I put an end to yer father. He went swiftly, as one would with a knife through the heart," Siobhan casually stated, and then delivered the first of many leather-kissed wallops to Kylee's restrained and helpless body.

That initial blow stung something awful, but Kylee never made a sound. She forced her mind to drift to Heathen's Haven and she forced herself to implement the inner control she'd been taught there.

I will not call out. I will not give her the satisfaction.

Her mother's impatience seemed to kick up a notch with Kylee's silence, and so, with every lick of leather, her strikes became merciless and inhuman, splitting gashes into Kylee's fair skin. She knew they were open wounds, the air seemed to freeze the blood which spilled from them.

Arms, legs, face, it didn't matter. Siobhan showed no preference to where she landed her torturous whip.

Finally, Kylee could take no more and finally surrendered. "Please, Mama. Stop! I'm all ye have left in this world, and ye're gonna end my life too?"

Kylee shouted through shaky breaths. "Just stop. I can't take anymore!" she howled.

"Oh! Ye'll take more, I guarantee it. And ye'll beg for yer life until I see fit to end it!" Siobhan growled, her hot breath invading Kylee's senses. "I know what'll make ye wish ye were dead. Stay right there, my lovely, I have a treat for ye."

Siobhan's footfalls faded and although Kylee couldn't see, the creaking of the cellar steps announced her mother's exit. She was safe, if only for a minute. Powerlessness and exhaustion overtook her, and Kylee finally let her head fall. She drew in greedy breaths until the pain caused her body to give in to sleep.

Suddenly, a soft touch made her flinch and return to her own personal hell. Kylee wriggled and opened her mouth to scream, but a calloused hand covered her lips as the bulky cloth covering her eyes was gently removed.

"Shh. I'm here, Kylee," Jack whispered, as she struggled to focus on his handsome face. *Are ye real?*

Am I dead. Seein' things? When a soft kiss fell upon her forehead, she cried silently, fierce sobs wracking her to the core. Relief swallowed her whole as she let out a long, liberating groan.

"I knew ye'd come. We have to get out of here!" she said in a trembling whisper.

"Aye, love," Jack replied softly, his hands fussing at the restraints at her feet.

"Hurry, Jack," she breathed. "Ma will be back any time now."

Just then, a shadow descended upon them and Jack froze, gazing up into Kylee's blanched face. They stared deep into one another's desperate pools as the sound of a woman's humming came closer and closer. Jack pulled a dagger from his belt and frantically struggled with the tightly knotted ropes at her wrists, as Kylee tried wriggling free.

"Another guest for the weddin'?" Siobhan hummed. "I hadn't been expectin' anyone else. 'Tis not polite to show up without an invitation, ye know," she casually said, holding a tattered, cream coloured dress up to her body, and twirled around as if she were dancing.

Jack was speechless.

Then, as he looked around the small space, the scene began to make sense.

Candles placed on every surface were burning an amber glow, wilted flowers were bursting from vases upon the mantle, and the dead man was dressed in his finest.

"Ye must be the husband, the saviour, her salvation?" Siobhan mocked. "Kylee, tell yer husband how improper it is to barge in, uninvited."

Kylee gaped at Jack with uncertainty and desperation.

He'd most likely placed all the pieces together now and would soon realize that Siobhan had completely lost her mind. She was going to marry the corpse of Garvan O'Shea and force Kylee to watch the macabre affair. Afterward, there was no telling what Siobhan might have done to her had Jack not arrived. She couldn't think about that right now.

If she and Jack didn't get themselves out of there soon, they would all perish.

Jack and Kylee dared not speak and made no sudden movements. He seemed to fall into soldier mode, feeling it out, watching for any chance to bring her mother down. Then the mad woman did something preposterous.

"Fine, fine. Stay if ye must…and ye must!" Siobhan huffed, disappearing again. She called back from the other room, "I must get dressed!"

Alone again, Jack frantically whispered, "Jesus, Kylee!" He made quick work of her restraints. Hands freed, Kylee rubbed them for a quick minute to let the colour return and then wrapped them around Jack's neck, planting kisses all over his stubbly face.

"Come on, love. Let's get ye home," he gently smiled. "Can ye walk?"

"Aye, I think so. We have to move fast. Something's not right. She'd never just let me escape. She might've lost her bloody mind, but she still very much wants me dead," Kylee said, struggling to rise from the chair. As she wobbly stood, she looked into Jack's eyes, thanking the heavens that he'd come for her. But then her attention shifted to the ominous figure standing behind them, holding a gun to Jack's back.

As if she were choking on a piece of dry meat, Kylee fought to find the words to warn him of the danger. Only when her expression turned alarming and the distinctive click of the hammer sounded throughout the room, did he swing around, shielding Kylee's body with his own.

"I told ye I had a treat for ye. Stay…" Siobhan sang with amusement, "'tis a beautiful day for a weddin'. Isn't that right, my love?" she said to the corpse, and then licked her lips and pressed them feverishly to Garvan's cold ones, not taking her eyes or the gun off Jack for a second. Then, she stood and closed the distance between them, placing the barrel flush against Jack's heaving chest.

Siobhan narrowed her eyes at the newcomer. "It'll go straight through ye both, ye know. Ye can't save 'er."

"Ma, a weddin' is no place for a revolver," Kylee chuckled nervously, pushing all her fears down into the pit of her stomach. She'd have to bury them in a deep chasm in order to overcome this scrape. "Ye can't hold a bouquet if ye're holdin' that gun. Gar? Isn't that right?" Kylee shakily asked the dead man as she maintained a tight grip on Jack's back waist-band.

Her mother's eyes flickered, almost like there was some sense returning behind them.

Kylee stepped out from behind her husband, and slowly ambled toward her mother. Jack held her arm, begging her with his eyes not to do what she was about to do. She could not play the martyr and still come out unscathed, but she knew that fact. She'd accepted it. But if there was one chance that Kylee could help sanity return to her mother, then Kylee was willing to put her life on the line to do it. With

Jack by her side, Kylee knew he'd step in if he had to. Jack was capable of making tough decisions.

She moved toward her mother with an outstretched hand, begging her mother to give up the gun with not as much as a word spoken between them.

Just then as if Siobhan could see right through Kylee's intentions, she snapped her hand back, and fired the gun above their heads.

"Who do ye think ye are?" Siobhan growled. "Yer just a filthy little peasant bitch. Did ye think I'd let ye kill my beloved and then run off into the arms of yers? I think not!" Siobhan brought the pistol forward, holding the barrel tight against Kylee's temple, forcing her backward, and once again into the chair.

Kylee looked up at Jack with ferocious panic, noting the pained and powerless expression distorting his features. Her eyes were saying good bye and she could make out the words *I love you* forming on his lips. When Siobhan's weapon trained again on

Jack, Kylee's heart stopped beating. She ceased to breathe.

"Let's see how ye like watchin' yer beloved wither and die," Siobhan snarled, pulling back the hammer.

'No fuckin' way! I'll not give her up, not today, not even in death!' Jack thought, his anger as hot and thick as the flames of hell. With nothing to lose, Jack lunged at Siobhan, taking her by surprise and knocking the gun from her grasp. His attack sent her straight into her dead lover's cold embrace, and Jack scrambling for the gun on the floor beside them.

The pistol bounced in Kylee's direction and she scurried to seize it before Siobhan could regain her footing.

Holding the cold steel in her fist was liberating. "Don't move, Mother! Not. One. Inch." Kylee stood strong, pointing the gun straight at her mother, despite the heartache it caused. "Let's go, Jack. We'll leave her to her *beloved.*"

Siobhan moved toward them with radiating evil as if she would burst into flames at any moment. She stopped dead when Kylee pulled the trigger, purposely sending a misguided shot into the mirror over the mantle, shattering it instantly. Siobhan fell to her knees and covered her ears.

"I said don't move," Kylee repeated, frigidly. "I am leavin' and I shall never return. If ye try to stop us then make no mistake, I *will* put a bullet in ye. Ye'll be alone in this life and the next, but it matters not, for ye're dead to me already," Kylee boldly added. All of a sudden, there was no more fear, no more pain and no more hiding.

Siobhan watched as the daughter who'd been taught to fear, respect and obey, all but disappeared. Kylee was replaced by a strong and confident woman.

As if sanity had reclaimed her, Siobhan shouted, "Kylee! Don't go. I'm sorry. Ye have to understand. The fault lies with yer father! If he hadn't hidden his fortune and denied me the things I deserved, I would've never been forced to kill him. I just wanted what I was entitled to!" Siobhan cried. Kylee pitied her mother at that moment, for she truly was disturbed.

"Aye, Ma. And when ye found the fortune, ye realized that it would never be enough. I was never enough. Would Garvan O'Shea have satisfied yer hunger for mere *things*?"

Siobhan looked at Gar's ghastly corpse, and tears sprang from her eyes. "He loved me, ye know," she replied quietly.

"Well, ye can have each other now," Kylee spat, lifting her chin proudly.

As if a bolt of lightning flashed in Siobhan's eyes, she smiled a wide grin. A second later, she fished a long stem of broken glass out of the broken mirror rubble and drove the pointed edge into her milky wrist.

Mother and daughter, their gazes locked, as one dared her to do it, and the other dared her not to. Siobhan didn't hesitate as she pulled the length of it up through her forearm, letting her blood spill all around her, as she fell to her side on the floor.

Kylee rushed to stop her, but Jack held her back. "She's still capable of hurtin' ye, love. There's nothin' ye can do for 'er now," he whispered. He turned her head into his shoulder, shielding her from watching the life drain from her mother.

"It's over, love. She's gone," he muttered tenderly. "Let's go home."

TWENTY-TWO

Before she could leave that God-forsaken place behind her, Kylee trudged wearily back to the doorway of her tiny family home, while Jack patiently waited atop his steed.

She picked up a bottle of old whiskey from the porch floor, pondering for a moment with some irony, that the stale fluid most likely belonged to Gar at some point. She sombrely tore a strip off her already ragged dress sleeve and stuffed it inside the bottle neck.

As if Jack could sense her intentions, he joined her and struck a match, igniting the tatters.

"This hell-on-earth will cease to exist," Kylee quietly said. Jack nodded and reached his strong arm around the small of her back.

"Don't look back, Kylee. Just throw it, and walk away," he replied softly.

Without hesitation, Kylee flung the flaming bottle inside the door, splashing flaming liquid all over the terror that lay within.

Kylee could feel the heat from the swelling inferno but dared not look back.

Her only regret was not learning where her mother had buried her father's body. She would have loved to visit his final resting place and say a proper good-bye to the man who'd only lived for her, in a photograph. The sadness and crime of it nearly brought Kylee's tears back to the surface, but she tried to remind herself that the future would hold so many beautiful things – things her father would delight from, if even, from heaven.

Jack helped her mount, and then climbed up behind her.

"We need to see the O'Shea's before we leave. Paddy and Fiona deserve to know what's happened. And I'm certain they'll help mend and tend ye," Jack said, breaking the silence.

"Aye, I know," Kylee regretfully replied, letting her head fall back against Jack's warm chest. The soft beating of his heart offered so much comfort and she loved him for it.

"No matter what's happened, I just know they will take care of ye there. Then, when ye've recovered, we'll go home," Jack added, smoothing her wayward strands of gold from her face.

Completely spent, Kylee drifted off to sleep. Too weak and too drained to even keep her body upright, she still felt his strong arms encasing her, holding on for dear life.

They drew to a stop outside the brewery. Kylee squinted against the lamp light shining through the large front window and then she was drifting toward it, cradled in Jack's arms.

As the force of his heavy boot crashed the door aside, she flinched and looked around. All eyes in the tavern turned to the frightful looking pair, the place went completely silent. Everyone who were only moments ago drinking, playing cards or with a hand up a skirt, were fully enthralled by the stranger holding Kylee tightly in his arms.

Fiona frantically rushed from behind the bar.

"Mr. Manning! Ye've found her! Oh dear, baby Jesus, is she alright?" Fiona asked, her eyes falling upon the fresh bruises and lesions that Kylee hadn't possessed the last time she'd seen the girl. Kylee wanted to cover herself, hide them away from view.

"She's exhausted. She needs to be tended to and needs plenty of rest. Ye think ye can help me?" Jack wearily asked.

Fiona didn't flinch. "Take 'er up to my room. I'll run and fetch me Da," she replied and then disappeared through the swinging door. And then, Kylee drifted into unconsciousness once again.

~

Jack disregarded his own exhaustion, and with heavy feet, ascended the stairs and placed his wife onto Fiona's bed. He pulled a chair from the hearth side and sat nervously beside her, holding her lifeless hand in his.

What an arse I've been! I'm so sorry for all of this. Jack's head fell onto the bed beside her. His remorse and self-loathing would cripple even the sturdiest of warriors. This woman could have given him the love and understanding he'd been longing for. But instead, he'd chose to leave her at the mercy of pure evil. *And my dear, sweet, Emma. What have I done to ye?*

Without the strength to restrain them, fresh silent tears of anguish burst from his eyes.

Then, Paddy appeared in the doorway. "Oh, Christ, for all things holy! What's he done?" Paddy trembled. "Is she…is she…"

"Dead? Nay, she should be though," Jack quietly replied wiping his face with the back of his hand. "And if it puts yer mind at ease any, most of this was *not* inflicted by yer son. Her Ma was some piece of work."

"Was?" Fiona asked as she scrambled to the wash basin and wrung out a fresh cloth to wipe the crusts of blood from Kylee's brow.

Jack nodded sadly and turned his gaze to Paddy who nervously wrung his hands in his apron tail.

Jack drew his eyes away from Kylee and pinned Paddy with an icy glare. "There are things we need to discuss, alone. Your study, Mr. O'Shea?" Paddy nodded at Jack's request and moved toward the door. "Fiona, I can trust that ye will take extra care with her?" Jack asked, placing a feathery kiss in Kylee's palm. There was so much to explain. And explain he would – in private, with the head of the household and a strong glass of whiskey.

"Of course, Mr. Manning. What if Garvan returns? If someone doesn't stand watch, he might come back enraged and hurt us both!" Fiona exclaimed. Sensing her terror, Jack couldn't help but feel sorry for the girl. One should never fear their own sibling. Older brothers were supposed to protect their little sisters, weren't they? Jack couldn't tell her that her worries were in vain. Not until he'd discussed it with Paddy first.

"That won't happen. I guarantee it," Jack coolly replied, leaving the speechless Fiona to tend his wife's wounds.

Jack followed Paddy down the steps, through the back and into the study where Liam was pacing the floor. He must've been confused and weary by now, having been left in the study with no information on Jack's whereabouts.

"I got her, Liam," Jack said in a small, drained voice.

"Thank God!" Liam blew. "How is she?"

"She'll live. But she's pretty broken," Jack stated, shooting Paddy an unforgiving glare.

Paddy hung his head, shame burning in his weathered old cheeks. "'Tis all my fault. I'd let the boy run me for years. I never thought he'd get this out of hand. Wait! Ye two know one another?" he asked, a bushy brow shooting up.

"Aye. I work for Liam's family," Jack replied. "I asked him to come. I didn't know if ye could be trusted and I needed to find Kylee."

"There would've been no need. I'd have handed the lass over to ye m'self just to get her away from Garvan," Paddy replied. "I would've never stopped ye from findin' her. She's yer wife! She told me so!"

"Well, hell! What was I s'posed to think? Ye were his Da. I'd protect my own kin, if I had any. I could only expect ye to do the same," Jack said, downing the first of many fingers of amber fire.

"What do ye mean, I *was* his Da?" Paddy asked, his face going pale with the hidden meaning behind Jack's words. It didn't take but a minute for him to put it all together. Kylee was alive. Garvan had not returned to be dealt with by authorities. Paddy had to be wondering why. Jack yearned for the old man to just ask the question so he might be done with it.

"Her mother is dead. At her own hand," Jack began. "I don't know the circumstances behind it, but yer boy was deceased before I arrived.

"Kylee is weak and needs to rest, so I'll not have anyone barrage her with questions until she's fully recovered. 'Til then, if ye want to see what became of yer vile son, ye can find him beneath the ashes of the O'Roarke place." Jack stated and then downed another hot whiskey.

Liam noticeably winced at Jack's display of cold-heartedness, but Paddy never gave the insult any thought. Instead, he looked utterly destroyed.

"He was a good boy once, ye know," Paddy cried, his head cradled in his hands. "I don't want to know what happened. He was gone long before now. I'm just grateful Kylee made it out alive."

"As am I," Jack said.

Paddy wiped his face in his kerchief and straightened himself up. Jack admired his strength. "Ye're all welcome to stay here as long as ye need. Fiona and I will assist in Kylee's recovery in any way we can. Right now, I must go check on my dear child and explain to her what's become of her brother," he sniffled and removed himself from the study to go find Fiona.

Paddy wouldn't have to worry about Fiona. She would prove to be a savvy business woman when it came her time to inherit, and that alone was the bitter-sweetness of Garvan's demise – the boy he loved. The man he never understood.

TWENTY-THREE

Weeks later, after a tedious recovery, Kylee was being carried over the threshold of her new home. A stranger's home which she'd now call her own.

Being in Galway, so far from her childhood ties and the pain and memories they'd inflicted was a welcomed change.

Jack set her upon her feet. "Welcome home," he smiled. "What do ye think?" he asked, hope dancing in his blue eyes. When his gaze scanned the perimeter, a sly grin tugged at his lips. "This is not the same place I'd abandoned some years ago. When I went to work for the Kelly's it'd had been a mere shack with a pot-bellied stove and few furnishings. This place has been mysteriously touched by a woman's hands, my love."

"This is the work of the Lady Violet," Kylee mischievously replied. "Isn't it delightful?" Taking in her new surroundings, she decided it was certainly a place for her to call home.

Kylee slowly walked through the tiny house, taking note of the small works of art hanging on the walls, canvasses of Ireland's breath-taking landscape, orchards and fields. She stopped suddenly, inspecting two photographs sitting on a shelf in the hallway.

"Are these yer kin?" she asked.

"Aye," Jack replied and then pointed to each one. "Ma, she's been gone from this world for some years now. And The Major. We haven't spoken in some time. I'd like to keep it that way."

Kylee nodded but her heart ached for him. Something awful must've happened between them to cut ties like that.

Just as her hand swept across the face in the raised glass, Jack pulled her hand back and kissed it. "Hold on, love, I'll be right back," he exclaimed.

He hurried to Kylee's carpet bag and dug inside, retrieving the sketch of her father. When he returned, her eyes brightened with delight. Despite being ill for the past while, she'd never skipped her nightly routine and she wouldn't start now.

She placed a kiss onto her fingertips, then onto her father's face. Finally, Kylee had the closure she deserved, knowing he hadn't abandoned her. Her heart erupted with love when Jack set the picture on the shelf beside his own folks.

"Now, this home belongs to us," he said and leaned in, kissing her cheek. A smile blossomed while a fire ignited in her belly. After the many nights she'd spent healing, each passing day were spent fantasizing about this moment.

"Can I see the bedroom?" Kylee asked, brazenly batting her long lashes. All the time between them had left her yearning for his touch, eager for a taste of him.

She hadn't held him as a woman would since the days surrounding their wedding, and she'd been so naïve and inexperienced then. Now, because of her time at Heathen's Haven, Kylee understood what he longed for most. She was more than ready to give herself to him in all the ways he needed – or commanded.

Jack smiled and held her hand in his. With anticipation swirling in her belly, he led her to the door at the end of the hall and opened it. When he glanced inside he shot her a sideways grin and chuckled. "I suppose Lady Violet has been in here as well?"

The room was large, taking up the entire far end of the house. Inside, this was a bedchamber befit a princess, with white lace curtains, plush white bedding and a floral canopy. A white wicker breakfast table and two matching chairs were placed in front of a large set of double doors. Jack opened them, letting in the clean scent of freshly fallen snow.

A gasp escaped her, her gaze landing on the two matching book shelves filled with stories begging to be read. She hadn't asked Violet or Shelagh for them. She shot her husband a crooked grin.

"Yer not the only one with friends 'round these parts," he cheekily said.

Kylee shivered, rubbing her arms. Jack closed the French doors and rushed to her side, crushing her to his body to warm her. He couldn't have known her shiver was built upon the eagerness to crawl into that big bed together.

"I'll never leave ye alone in the cold again. Ye know that, don't ye?" he asked, assuredly, holding her face in his strong hands.

"Aye. I know, my love." Kylee reached up onto her tip-toes and placed a lingering kiss on his lips, holding his stubbly face in a warm caress. Unable to contain her excitement any longer, she pulled away, and smiled. "I have a little surprise for ye, Mr. Manning. Or perhaps I should just call ye Master J?"

Jack's expression became unreadable. Was he astounded? Or would he be displeased with her knowledge? Kylee swallowed her insecurities all the way back down. She'd been so apprehensive and worried about this for weeks and the time had finally come to prove to herself and her dashing husband that she did in fact possess a female prowess like no other.

During her recovery, she lay in bed meticulously planning the unveiling of her skills and acceptance. She'd learned so much in a short period of time during her stay with Emma, Rory and Shelagh at The Haven.

I'll take care of him now, Emma.

She'd had nothing better to do than plan and write letters. One to Lady Ryan, explaining that she'd married Mr. Manning and would be staying in Galway to be with him.

And another to her uncle Joe, asking if he might come to visit her before she left Ennis for good. And he had. Kylee was ever-so grateful to see that he was in good health and that Garvan's assault hadn't left any permanent damages.

The most important correspondence was between Kylee and Shelagh. With her new-found friend and tutor working for the Kelly's now, Kylee had the girl help her finish what she'd started at Heathen's Haven, and put to good use all that she'd learned in her short time there.

'*I'm sure Shelagh has done a superb job equipping this place with my requested necessities,*' Kylee hoped optimistically, remembering Shelagh's reply stating, "*Everything is ready. Remember to breathe.*"

"Open the closet door, Master J. I'll return shortly." She graced him with a shy smile and disappeared into the adjoining dressing room.

Kylee was sure, even without looking inside, that the closet was supplied with every instrument and play-thing that the newly reunited couple would need to become completely and intimately reacquainted.

"Lord T'underin' Christ!" he cursed loudly.

"Is everything alright, husband?" Kylee giggled.

Silence.

When Kylee emerged from the dressing room, Jack was sitting on the corner of the bed, resting his forearms on his knees. Pausing in the doorway, giving him a moment to process, she waited for his reaction. He didn't even look up. The war within was eating him alive. She could see it as plain as day.

'Emma said he would be this way. I must make him see that I need to be a part of this,' she thought, and without hesitation, Kylee stepped forward and stood in front of her self-loathing husband.

She thought of all of the advice Emma had privately given her concerning Jack's likes and dislikes, and made sure that her every move was just-so.

In a brand new, sheer satin gown, Kylee knelt in front of him, her golden hair tied and draping down her back. She lifted the material off her slender shoulders and let the fabric cascade down her arms, yet held the garment between her breasts.

With her head and eyes down-turned, she said the words that would be her undoing, "Yer desires are my desires, Master J," and then she waited.

It felt as if an eternity had passed, the silence in the room thickening the blood pumping through her body. Kylee waited nervously, yet patiently for his battle with the demons inside him to end.

And then, like a ray of sunshine bursting through the atmosphere, she felt his delicate touch at the top of her head. His hand was warm as it moved down to her cheek, stroking her flesh with the pad of his thumb. Then lastly, his finger lifted her chin to pull her gaze to his.

"There will be no goin' back if ye do this. Ye'll be dammed for all eternity," he said gravely, jaw clenched, searching for a response in her loving gaze.

"I'll never be damned, my love. 'Tis deliverance. I know what ye want, let me learn what ye need. Let me be all ye'll ever crave. Lovin' ye in every way, from now until forever is all I'll ever desire.

"Teach me, guide me, spank and chastise me, but love me in a tender and patient manner, for yer desires *are* truly mine," Kylee spoke every word with pride and determination. The feverish look smouldering behind Jack's blue eyes told her he'd heard her, loud and clear.

This was it, he could not hide that part of himself any longer. Now he had to trust in her devotion and understanding. She held on to the hope that he would. Kylee knew in her heart she would still love him after the beast was unleashed – even after she'd been thoroughly devoured by it.

She was still kneeling in front of the bed when Jack moved away. Without as much as a glance in his direction, she kept her eyes fixed on the floor, and waited. Over the sound of her own heart thumping, she could hear the faint ruffling sound as he removed his over-coat, his shirt and then his boots. She dared not look, despite her need to see him in his primal form.

Jack moved about the room with brooding intensity. She could feel every uncertain strain moving through him.

"If yer choosin' to suffer my wrath then I'll see to it that ye think twice before askin' me for this again,' he growled. "No more hidin'. Yer my wife, for better or for worse. Tonight, ye get the best of both worlds," he warned. Kylee trembled with a mix of fear and excitement.

He pulled a length of soft cord from a hook in the closet and fastened one end to the top of the corner post, letting the other end hang freely.

"Rise," he commanded with such authority it made her knees weak. Jack stepped all around her, reminding her of her first days of training at The Haven. If he was trying to intimidate her she would certainly meet his challenge. She wanted to show no sign of modesty, for fear that he would assume she was not ready. And she was, so very ready.

~

Jack's tender touch turned cold, ice coursing through his veins as he yanked the delicate nightgown from her body, leaving her standing as naked as the day she came into the world. Kylee didn't flinch. His loins ached, his heart pounded furiously, not for the beautiful woman bared before him, but for the perfect submissive, now meeting his gaze with love and compliance.

'Jesus! What'd they teach 'er?'

"Stand o'er there, by the bed. Raise yer arms above yer head," he commanded. Kylee moved on steadfast legs to the bedpost, stretched her arms high, grasped the dangling end of the rope, and wound it around her wrist without instruction to do so. "And no matter what, do not look away from me. I want ye to witness everythin' this monster has to inflict upon ye." Jack's tone was dark and full of self-doubt. The pleading gaze staring back at him begged, *'Take me into yer world, Jack.'*

Kylee stood perfectly against the cold wood, oblivious to the perfect storm of pleasure-pain soon to be inflicted by Jack's hand. He skilfully fastened the cord in a noose-knot around her wrists. "Now, ye can't get away. Do ye need to change yer mind?" he asked, his steely gaze searching her face for regret.

She jutted her chin in defiance but never broke contact with his intense scrutiny.

With bindings completely fastened, her tongue darted out quickly to moisten her dry lips. He placed a feather-light lingering kiss upon them. Her breath was hot, her breathing shallow and needy.

Jack's emotions nearly ripped him apart. The possibility that she would leave him if he hurt her, almost halted the scene. Not to mention if she hated him come daybreak. He couldn't endure such a thing. Then Kylee broke the most basic rule. She spoke.

"What are ye waitin' for?" she taunted. Emma had to have told her he wouldn't put up with a brazen submissive – that he would thoroughly punish if he needed to. Why did she need his brutality? She didn't understand how taxing this might be. "Do it, Jack. Let it out," she whispered and then smiled.

Jack paced the room furiously, reminding himself that she'd wanted this. She'd even trained for it. With a quick glance back, her calm grin threatened to burn him alive but urged him onward.

He found an unforgiving flogger in the closet and brought it close to his nose, inhaling its musky scent of cured leather. He'd missed that. His every move was watched with wide eager eyes. He cracked the whip with intent to frighten and intimidate, but her reaction – a delightful, breathy gasp – merely kicked the beast inside him into action.

With Kylee completely helpless and subdued, Jack was equipped with the skill to turn her body to magma with total control of her very essence.

He slid his hands from her wrists, down to her chest where severe, ridged buds had formed, where he played, teasing and warming her to his touch. Naturally, this level of debauchery caused her natural first instinct to rear its unwanted head, involuntarily casting her eyes downward with embarrassment. Jack held her face in his strong hands.

"Look at me. Watch, as I drive ye to utter madness and leave ye powerless," he growled vehemently, consumed by lust and enthralled in the scene. His intensity must've prompted some hidden panic because her hands shook in their bindings.

When he raised his arm and drew the whip high in the air, she closed her eyes tight, waiting for the scorching hot beam to burn her flesh.

The first blow barely licked the delicate skin under her breasts, but he knew it would feel like a tiny flanker of fire on her flesh. When the sting subsided, it would be replaced by a sweltering heat, crawling deep within her, and reignite the very flames that Jack had first set ablaze the night they were married.

"More," she mewled, needing another and another.

Jack quieted her plea with dangerous lips crashing down upon hers and then drew back again, inflicting steady lashes of the whip across her helpless body. With each new stroke, her skin welted, leaving behind pink streaks and a building hunger until she appeared light-headed with heady intensity.

He soothed each and every mark with hot, passionate kisses, trailing his way from her breasts to her inner thighs. Her bound body arched toward his, greedy and needy.

As if he sensed it, he withdrew. "Not yet," he whispered in her ear, now completely mesmerized with the need to inflict ultimate fulfilment upon her.

Red-faced, with heaving chest, Kylee bit back her protest. He knew she might resort to begging. Her senses would be on high alert by now, and he had added to it, trailing soft, wet kisses from her foot, up her soft legs and lingered in the sweet cleft of her sex. Kylee fought with the restraints as soon as his tongue found her heat. He'd slowly drive her to madness before this night was over.

Jack could feel her muscles tighten and lapped at her with quickening rapid force, bringing her to complete rapture.

"Now, Kylee. Ye have permission, let go," he breathed against her hyper-aware skin. His mouth devoured her until her knees bent and her body went flaccid. He quickly untied her wrists and lifted her onto the bed.

She gaped at him with a satisfied smile and reached her arms out, inviting him to share in her pleasure.

"Ye amaze me," he sighed against her neck, as he rubbed the life back into her tingling limbs. Because he'd never get enough of this woman, he'd then worshipped her breasts with his tongue. He tasted every inch of flesh, aching to feel her come apart beneath him.

As if involuntary, her legs parted, and her hips bucked to meet him. Her shaky fingers found the button of his trousers but she paused and looked into his eyes with the silent question.

"The beast's been quieted, for now. You were perfectly submissive, my wicked Kylee. I'm all yers," he smiled tenderly and then helped her remove the fabric between them.

"Ye think I'm wicked now, wait 'til I let ye in on all *my* secrets," Kylee whispered breathlessly.

As Jack sank deep into the recesses of her heat, he was filled with a sense of joy and contentment which he'd never known existed. He'd been completely accepted, wanted and loved by this woman, and he vowed to make her every need and desire his reason for living.

The realization hit him hard with each thrust, with her hands in his hair, planting kisses over his stubbly face. His loving was ferocious, severe and without mercy.

Her body tightened around him, clenching like a vice until he was a spent, yet satisfied heap in her arms.

The fear that he would lose her was all but a memory now, for he knew that in finding herself, she'd found him too.

He'd never let her go again.

If you would like to leave a review for Heathen's Hurricane go to Amazon.ca/com or Goodreads.com. Thanks so much for reading and/or reviewing!

CAITLYN'S RAPTURE

Keep reading for an excerpt from the next book
in the

Stormy Encounters Series by Tanya Benoit

Caitlyn's Rapture

Spring-1859

Liam grasped the wooden wheel of the Caitlyn's Fancy with a white-knuckled grip, as both anticipation and unease shrouded him like the clouds looming overhead.

This was the first day of the rest of his life.

"So, little lord, are ye ready to make some serious money?" Morgan asked as he stepped onto the raised quarter deck. "I don't know what them O'Shea's were thinkin', gettin' tangled up with a ship captain, who's never skippered a ship b'fore," he laughed.

"Have a little faith, Morgan. I'm confident that you will teach me everything I need to know," Liam reassured his first mate. "Fiona O'Shea is as determined as I am to see this through. A few years ago, the O'Shea's planned to export to Newfoundland but the deal fell through, so here we are. Fiona needed our beautiful ship to move her fine product, and I needed to get out of Galway. You'll see. This will prove to be rewarding for everyone involved."

Morgan cocked a crooked brow at his captain. The mere mention of Fiona O'Shea always put him a little on edge. "Yeah? Well, I think the wee lass has lost her bloody mind!" he huffed, and then went about inspecting the sails and the rigging for the clipper's maiden voyage.

Enchanted with the ocean smells, the brush of the wind in his perfectly combed hair and the growing distance between him and Galway, Liam drew in a long breath of clean fresh air and exhaled slowly.

Leaving Brady, Violet and his precious nephew behind had almost killed him, well, Violet and the babe anyway.

Brady had become irate and impossible since Liam announced his plans to sail the ship across the Atlantic. Liam was grateful to just get clear of the unruly Kelly lord.

The last encounter he'd had with his brother was still fresh in his mind. "What do ye mean? You're not seriously considerin' sailin' 'er yerself?" Brady had laughed in Liam's face, leaving him reeling with that familiar twinge of incompetence only his big brother could impose upon him.

"Yes, Brady. That is exactly what I intend on doing," Liam replied calmly. "You have Violet and little Sean now. I'm not needed here as I was, and I long to see the world. You'll have to try to understand." Liam said, trying to sound convincing, but the truth was, the new sense of worth he'd found, the yearning to take charge of his own life instead of doing as Brady told him, was overwhelming.

It felt right to be out from under the steady piles of paperwork and ledgers – to be out from beneath his brother's arresting shadow.

"What in Jesus' name do ye know about sailin'? Ye don't sail 'em, Liam, ye only keep the books on buildin' 'em," Brady shouted, but Liam's mind was made up. He was going, with or without his brother's permission.

"I've a good crew hired. We will get through just fine."

"Aye! And takin' my crew boss!" The vein in Brady's temple began to throb. "What am I s'posed to do here without Morgan?"

Liam strode to the desk and filed away the remaining papers that had been strewn across the top, undaunted by Brady's agitation. "You've only just hired the man last Spring. I'm sure you can find someone who can get the job done. Seamus needs a promotion. I think it's time he received one," Liam countered with steady bravado and smiled.

When Liam left Kelly's keep that day, he vowed to return a different man, a man who took orders from no one.

Morgan broke his spell, shaking him back to the present. "Little lord, ye do know these waters are notorious for pirate activity? I hope our few guns can withstand an attack," Morgan gravely reminded him.

"Pirates, Morgan?" Liam cocked his brow in disbelief. "Perhaps in the past, but I doubt we'll have much to fear from them now. Unless you are worried about the ghosts of pirates long departed," Liam winked with a slight grin tugging at his lips.

He drew in another long fresh lungful, tasting the salty traces on the back of his tongue. Nothing could shake his unrelenting optimism.

"Do not fear, Morgan. We will take whatever the sea has to offer, whether it be storms or pirates. But, I know in my heart that we have good fortune on our side," Liam smiled. "Fair winds and following seas to us all."

Liam was ready to face anything. He'd wage war with the Devil himself if it meant uncovering the family secret and winning back Victoria's affections. With the swelling seas ahead, he gladly left Ireland behind.

ABOUT THE AUTHOR

Tanya Benoit, who currently resides in Newfoundland and Labrador, Canada is a laboratory analyst for a major mining company and has been putting pen to paper her entire life. Her enthusiasm for all things historical, prompts her to create characters with many layers and place them in the past. Her family is originally from the small town of Lawn on the Burin Peninsula, Newfoundland, but her ancestors hail from Ireland. The Stormy Encounters Series has truly become a labour of love…a means of exploration into her family's history.

You can visit Tanya's website and sign up for her newsletter at: www.tanyabenoitbooks.com

Or follow her on Facebook and Twitter.

<u>**OTHER TITLES BY TANYA BENOIT:**</u>

Stormy Encounters Series:

Violet's Storm (Book 1)

Caitlyn's Rapture (Book 3)

Still the Thunder (Book 4)